D1526263

MALFUNCTION

Book 1 in the Malfunction Trilogy

J. E. Purrazzi

Cover design, editing, and formatting by Poole Publishing Services LLC
Developmental editing through Sione Aeschliman

ISBN: 1976347882
ISBN-13: 978-1976347887

Table of Contents

Dedication

Firstly, to my lost boys. I love you with all my heart.

And to my amazing writing team: My Editors: Susie at
Poole Publishing Services and Sione, who treated this
book as their own but never took away my voice.
And to my Critique Partners: S.M. Holland, who always
makes me feel like a superhero. E.B. Dawson, who always
looks for the deeper meaning. And Janelle Garrett who
thinks just like me.
And for all my many beta readers, readers and the people
who have been waiting for this release. You make all the
hard parts of writing worth it.

Chapter One: Comeback

Menrva Penniweight leaned over the touchscreen on her work surface and tried to ignore the diminutive woman who hovered over her shoulder.

"We aren't on speaking terms," Menrva said.

"So who am I supposed to talk to about these samples?" Leslie Abella asked.

Menrva frowned and turned to her mother. Leslie wasn't an impressive looking woman, despite her reputation for scrambling into positions of power. Standing only a few inches taller than Menrva, her petite frame filled out her ironed lab coat in a perfect hourglass shape. She'd pulled her thick black hair into a tight bun over her honey-toned skin and dark eyes.

Menrva looked most like her mom. The only sign of her father left was her curly hair.

"You are welcome to give me any necessary samples, but I don't want to socialize," Menrva said, snatching the sample from her mother's manicured nails.

"I thought I taught you to be polite," Leslie said.

"You didn't teach me anything, Mother." Menrva twisted the vial in her hand and studied the contents. "Wrecker?"

"That is your area of study, isn't it? Of course, I might be wrong, since apparently I'm not allowed to have any real information about my only child's life."

Menrva sighed. "What am I looking for?"

"I need a count on the stem cells in the sample and a comparison to an average Wrecker." When Menrva raised an eyebrow, her mother added, "This isn't all Wrecker; it's something...different."

"Different how?" This wasn't the first time Menrva had gotten a request like this. In fact, the whole lab seemed to be less focused on Wrecker research lately. They had even pulled off a few of the scientists for other studies, though she hadn't heard anything about what those projects entailed.

It was strange. Wreckers had always been a priority.

Leslie smoothed her hands over her coat without answering and turned to walk through the enclosed lab. The workstations were now empty, leaving only blinking machinery and pale blue light filtering from multiple screens. In the center of the room, a glass cylinder held the corpse of the alien in question. Leslie paused by the display, picking her cuticles as was her habit.

The creature inside was intimidating, even torn open and floating in fluid. Easily ten feet in height, this one was on the small side. If the models they used in the Sims were accurate, it looked vaguely like a bear or even a gorilla, though a second set of arms made the comparison a weak one. The most jarring feature was probably its face. Though most of its body was covered in short, velvety black hair, the exoskeleton lay exposed in places. As a result, its head looked not unlike a fanged human skull.

"If you can't help me with the sample, just tell me," Leslie said. "There are other people who can do your job, you know."

Menrva rolled her eyes, hoping that her attitude was visible. "I'm the only geneticist specializing in Wreckers that we have in the Hub. If you had someone else, you would have given it to them. The fact that you are here means you've already exhausted your resources." It felt good to shove that back in her face. Menrva didn't like the fact that Leslie was here, even if Leslie was forced to humble herself a bit to ask. As much as Menrva wanted to leave her hanging, Leslie could always get what she wanted by using the City to apply some pressure. Her work was too important to them. "I'll add it to the list," Menrva said finally.

"I need it before the end of the day tomorrow. We have some potential breakthroughs on my formula and I can't stall my entire operation just for you."

"I'll add it to my list," she repeated, placing the vial in a protective case.

Leslie took a few steps toward the door, her simple shoes tapping loudly on the tile. She paused for a moment at the threshold and looked back at Menrva.

"You know, your father—"

Menrva raised her hand, cutting off the words before they came out. "Just because he's dead doesn't mean I've forgiven him. So don't bother trying to use him to manipulate me."

"You used to love him, you know," Leslie said, not even bothering to hide the accusation in her tone.

She still loved him. Just because she was angry didn't

mean she loved him any less. It also didn't mean that Leslie loved him any more.

After another moment of silence, Leslie took the hint and closed the door, leaving Menrva in the silence of the lab.

She stared at the screen in front of her, trying to focus on the trail of gene markers. It was pointless. Menrva knew herself well enough to know what it was like to do mental tasks when she was frustrated, and Leslie was nothing if not frustrating.

In another thirty minutes, she'd planned to head to the gym anyway. She could just leave early and get in some extra time to work off the emotions before bed. Half of her sandwich from lunch was waiting for her in the fridge to give her an extra boost after the workout, but she might have to cut her usual rotation short again. The cafeteria had been low on protein lately. Even beans and nuts were becoming harder and harder to get.

She saved her work with the flick of her fingers across the touchscreen—it would be there tomorrow, just as it had been for the past nine years—and turned out the lights.

Menrva was often the last person in the lab. Nobody wanted to be the one to switch the lights out and turn their back on the suspended alien body. It may have been dead for at least a century, but that didn't make it any less terrifying to be alone with it in a dark room.

Shuddering, she half-sprinted to the door like a child running back to bed after a midnight bathroom trip. It seemed justified. After all, this wasn't an invisible monster under the bed; it was one that had devoured over three-quarters of humankind and wanted more.

Double-checking the door to make sure it had locked behind her, she turned down the lonely hallway. A glance up at the screens plastering the ceilings in the wealthy city center showed a sunset playing across every pixel overhead, a typical sight. The color was a vivid contrast to the endless white corridors.

After ten minutes, she slipped into her pod and sighed deeply, breathing in the familiar smell of home. Menrva closed the door, shrugged out of her lab coat, and dropped it onto the counter. No need to worry about a mess; she would be putting it back on in eight hours or less.

"Whoa, I know you've missed me, but no need to jump the gun."

Menrva gasped and spun around. It was a voice she knew well, and one she hadn't expected to hear again. One she wasn't entirely sure she *wanted* to hear again.

A man around her age sat on her couch, a sly grin hanging on his youthful face. He was short and willowy with pale skin. A pair of mining goggles parted his wispy, baby-blond hair. His standard-issue track suit was torn and crusted with black dirt that stood out starkly against their surroundings.

"Cowl. Cowl Coven?" Menrva said. "What the hell are you doing in my pod? They will kill us both if they find you here!"

Chapter Two: Reacquaintance

Cowl stuffed down a rising tide of irritation, brushing aside the cloud of numbers and equations that tended to drift into his unoccupied mind. Menrva stood at the door, her dark, round eyes narrowed until they nearly blended into her tan skin. She probably was right to be surprised or even irritated with him showing up, but it wasn't fair to get offended so quickly.

It was strange how much a person could age in three years. Her curves were more pronounced now on her short stature, making her once-sporty build look more feminine, womanly. If it weren't for the shocking pale blue of her formerly dark hair, she would have looked gorgeous.

Cowl grinned, trying to ignore the odd feeling crawling into his stomach. "Nah. You don't have anything to worry about. They won't touch you. Made it big as a geneticist, I hear."

Did her eyes just narrow more?

"I like the place," he continued when she didn't say anything. "What happened to the guy you were with? What's his name?"

"You've been missing for three years," Menrva interrupted, her voice steely. "You'd better be able to sum up why you are here in about five seconds, because that's how long you have before I call the guard."

Cowl dropped his grin. No way she would actually call the guards. Not after all the two of them had gone through together. "Come on, Nerve, I thought you would be happier to see me." The two of them had been close friends since Basics. Or they had been before he migrated down to the Pit. Maybe he should have checked in on her during some of his runs back to the Hub. "Look, I didn't want to get you in trouble. I wouldn't have come unless I was desperate," Cowl said, softening his tone.

Menrva shifted her weight lower, her hands bent forward like she was waiting for an attack. "What do you want?" she asked.

Cowl stood, and a little waterfall of dust slid off his legs and onto the white couch and floor.

"You still trust me?" he asked.

Menrva backed toward the comm unit. Her body language looked pretty much like a loaded gun.

"I take that as a no. Please. Just let me explain." Cowl held up his hands, palms spread in a peace offering, trying his best to turn on the lost puppy look that used to work so well on her.

Menrva's face softened a bit. Apparently the look still had its charms.

"I'll give you two minutes," she said, her voice shaking as she spoke.

Focus. "I need help. I have this friend...a good guy. A really good guy. He's hurt pretty bad." He took a deep breath and shifted his weight. "He's been out for almost three days now, and I'm really worried."

The words brought the anxiety crashing back into his head. He had a pretty good idea what was wrong with Bas, at least from a technical side. If it was anything less serious, he would have found another option. Maybe do some research and try to take care of it himself. The human body was stupidly complicated, though, and with something this sensitive...No, he needed Menrva.

"I'm not a doctor. I'm a geneticist," she pointed out.

"You did a lot of training about the human body before you settled into your specialty."

"That doesn't mean I know anything. It was general training. I did mostly dissections and the most basic of basics."

"That's more than me," Cowl pointed out. She was a really smart girl--woman--Surely she could remember what she needed to remember and figure out the rest on her feet. She had to. If she didn't..."Remember when we were kids and we went with Starke to the Industrial Tier and met that family? The one with all the kids that were so sick?"

"I remember..." She eased back into a more relaxed position.

"You stepped right in and helped out, even if it was none of your business...shit...I mean that in a good way."

Menrva crossed her arms and sighed heavily. "Get to your point."

"My point is: you've always been someone who cared. My friend is in real danger, and I can't trust anyone else. As much as I'm wanted he's...They'll kill him. We don't have anyone else." He didn't want to manipulate her, but he couldn't be honest, either. Not if he wanted her to come.

"So this is dangerous?" she asked.

Shit. He'd really shot the gears now. "Not with me leading the way. Come on, you know I've got this."

"The City will track me." She pointed to the back of her neck where her chip was implanted.

Cowl did his best to avoid rolling his eyes, though it was a losing battle. The City's surveillance systems were probably intimidating to the average citizen, but they were no match for his programming skills. "I've got you covered. Remember, I'm a certifiable genius...well, certifiable *something*. Point is, they will be none the wiser."

She paused, rubbing her neck absently and staring into the distance. Thinking. Judging. Deciding. Why did this have to be so complicated?

"Nerve, I'm not gonna lie, I'm a bit desperate, or I wouldn't be here. I think he might be dying."

After some time, Menrva nodded stiffly. "Ok. If it's that serious." She scanned the room, carefully avoiding Cowl's eyes. "If I can't do anything for you, just remember that I warned you."

He relaxed. "Thank you. You're an angel."

"Do I need to bring anything, or do you have all the supplies you need? I have a med kit here, just the standard." She pointed at a simple white box adorned with the familiar red cross, attached to the nearest wall.

"It can't hurt."

Menrva pulled the box from its place and pulled the simple strap off the side before Velcroing it around her waist and heading for the door. He reached back, pulling a gun from the holster under his shirt. Cameras and scanners were easy enough to get rid of, but if a guard showed up, he'd want the advantage of having his weapon in hand.

"What the hell, Cowl!" Menrva stumbled back. It wasn't that Cowl with a gun was an alien sight for her. He'd always bent the rules around firearms, repercussions be damned. She seemed threatened, though. "Just a precaution," he grinned. "It's not for you; don't worry." No one was getting between Bas and the help he needed.

"I *am* worried. Guns are worrying."

He shrugged. "It's just a baby gun; I've got to be ready for trouble."

Menrva crossed her arms, her chin lifting subtly in that distinct way that meant she was not happy. She didn't have to be, as long as she was helping. If Bas survived, she could forgive him later.

Cowl punched the manual override on the door to avoid the scanners and ushered Menrva out into the hall.

"You should at least put the gun down," Menrva whispered loudly as she fell in step behind Cowl. "It's not exactly subtle."

The only thing less subtle than the gun was the dirt covering every inch of him. The gun he could hide; the dirt he couldn't. So, probably better to keep the gun close by. Besides, it made him feel better.

An old woman shambled toward them, leaning heavily on her cane. Quickly, avoiding Menrva's suddenly accusing glare, Cowl tucked his gun behind his back.

The lady took far too much notice of the two of them. Her bulging eyes flitted back and forth between them, rolling around over her hollow cheeks like loose marbles.

Her head swiveled on her thin neck as they passed her.

"Slut," she hissed.

Cowl almost dropped his gun and definitely dropped his chin.

"Good evening to you, too," Menrva said, firmly, not bothering to look back at the woman.

There were probably a lot of really bad words that could accurately be attached to Menrva. They were the same ones that stuck to him, which is why they were such good friends. Well, *had* been such good friends...

Still, "slut" was *not* one of those words.

"Been busy, have we?" he asked.

The look on her face almost made him feel bad.

Doing his best to seal his lips together, Cowl waved Menrva forward and paused at a hatch on the wall.

Cowl pulled open the hatch and ducked into the space between the inner and outer walls of Bunker. It was dark, dank and smelled of iron and mold. Slim, grated walkways hung between the two sides, looking much more precarious than they were.

He hesitated as he passed one airlock, but kept going. The Hub was swarming with workers right now. More than usual. It was strange, especially for this time of night. Usually they shut off the outside lights and pulled the workers in at the end of a workday, but they had been going strong over the last week. There must have been a major project of some sort. Back when Starke was alive and had worked on the outer walls of Bunker, he'd been home every night at the same time.

It was going to make getting out a bit trickier, but thanks

to Starke's tutelage, Cowl knew exactly where to go to take advantage of the quiet spots he'd seen from the ground.

"Where are we going?" Menrva asked.

"I thought you were going to trust me." Cowl smiled, hoping it came across as encouraging, not creepy. "I won't hurt you. I need you. Besides, I would never hurt something so beautiful. What kind of philistine do you take me for?"

She didn't speak as they carefully negotiated the walkways in the dim lighting to the airlock.

The doors whined as they slid shut, wear from years of occasional use and disrepair making the mechanisms arthritic. The glint of the chrome was long gone, replaced by rows of scratches and dents. A voice warbled through the speakers, warning them of long-dissipated radiation as it sealed the inner walls off from all perception of harm.

The cylindrical chamber stank of mold and rust. The outside door opened, scraping along its tired track as the hazy light of the maintenance floodlights leaked in.

Cowl carefully maneuvered on to the makeshift elevator, doing his best to help Menrva without actually touching her. It was not much of an elevator, just an old contraption for maintenance.

This was the point of no return. If she were going to snap and turn him in, this was her last chance. The pale cast of the outer floodlights revealed Menrva's distrustful glares, but she settled into place and looked over the edge to the darkness of the Pit below.

"Hold on," Cowl warned as the contraption lurched into motion.

Chapter Three: Blood and Metal

The elevator descended too quickly for Menrva's comfort into a darkness so complete that she might as well have had her eyes shut.

Above them, Bunker seemed to be floating in a pool of white light.

The Hub itself was shaped like a thick doughnut. Spindly passages extended along the ceiling of the massive cavern to connect it to its various Tiers. The closest ones were larger: the Farming Tier, the Industrial Tier, Food Processing Tier. Housing units, simple rectangular structures that were dwarfed by the tiers all around them, held all that was left of humanity after the scourge of the Wreckers had wiped the earth clean.

The cart jerked to a halt in a cloud of powdered dust that filled Menrva's nose and mouth, choking her. Cowl shoved a handkerchief into her hand. He had one wrapped around his nose and mouth, under the goggles he'd fixed in place. She did the same, though the handkerchief only proved a slight improvement.

Cowl turned on a flashlight, and the light reflected off the drifting particles in the air and the residue that encrusted the Hub's struts. The spider legs extended upward, keeping Bunker suspended and giving it some added stability, scant as that was.

"Well, they won't find my body down here," Menrva said lightly.

Cowl chuckled. "Would it help if I let you carry the gun?"

"No, I'd probably shoot myself." Menrva had never held a real gun. It would probably be no different from the first person shooter games she had played in VR, but she wasn't going to take any chances. Nothing about this situation was virtual.

"Now, that would be impressive; you're a small target," Cowl said.

He began trekking through the dust. The haze he kicked up made it hard to see him after only a few feet, and Menrva had to hurry to keep up with his stride.

Fallen rocks lay in disarray around the rent earth, making each step dangerous. Cowl seemed to know his way around it, though, and carefully picked a path through the chaotic landscape. Menrva stumbled often, but he was quick to give her light whenever she did.

They had left the elevator far behind by the time Cowl slowed. His light shone on a jumble of broken earth that marked the beginning of the cavern wall. It was dangerous being this close. Menrva hunched down, trying to make herself smaller, as she looked up. Some of the debris around them was big enough to crush her if it fell from above. Of all the possible ways to die, that was not one she had ever feared before. Despite the stabilizers, the compromised ground was constantly shifting and settling. Boulders regularly dislodged and became deadly projectiles. It didn't take a genius or a geologist to see the lethal hazard. They shouldn't be anywhere near here.

"Why are we here?" Menrva craned her neck to look up at the wall.

"This is where I live." Cowl pointed to a cave made from fallen rocks.

How had she missed it? Light clawed its way past a ragged blanket serving as a door and pooled on a path winding around the rocks.

Menrva squinted through the dust in the air as she followed him into the cave. The interior looked more like a bachelor's pod than the hole in the ground it was. Cowl had used a collection of foraged materials to build a floor and some semblance of walls. A table, broken in half, was balanced against a wall. On it, a few scratched and dusty computer monitors connected to a machine, maybe a generator, filling the room with pulsing blue light. The warm glow of a few hand-crafted oil lamps added an orange hue. In every corner, cans of food and overflowing supplies poked out.

A separate room sat away from the light, filled with blankets which were presumably meant to serve as beds. A large man lay on one of them. At least, it could have been a man. Menrva had never seen anyone quite that large.

She narrowed her eyes in an effort to see better. "Is that him?"

"His name is Bastille," Cowl answered. "Bas."

Menrva lifted one of the lamps from its place and inched forward. The golden light spilled into the room, revealing the unconscious man. His thick black curls framed a long, serious face and sharp cheekbones. He was handsome, though not in a classical sense. Understated freckles mottled his olive-toned skin. Just from a glance, Menrva could see the Native American and Japanese influences in the bone structure around his eyes and cheeks, indicating they were probably his dominant genetic roots. That was odd. There was a good amount of Asian genes in Bunker, but the Native American bloodlines were all but extinct.

If Cowl was right, Bastille had been unconscious for a while, and she didn't have to be a medical professional to know that was a bad sign.

"What happened?" Menrva asked, reaching a shaking hand to touch Bastille's skin. "No fever."

"His brain is swelling," Cowl answered as he kneeled down beside her. "At least, that's what I'm guessing is the problem."

"Edema? Seriously? That is some real shit. You can't expect me to know what to do here. If you want your friend to live, you need to take him to the medics right now."

"Trust me, Menrva, if I take him in he *will* die."

"What, is he a murderer?" Menrva asked.

"He's dying," Cowl repeated. "Do you really need to know more than that?"

Menrva glared at him. If he'd told her all this before she came down, she wouldn't have come. That's probably why he hadn't. "I don't know why you brought me. How am I supposed to help him?"

"I got you because of this." Cowl turned his friend over with some effort and shone the light on a black half-sphere protruding from the base of his skull. A mechanical device was fused into his spine, exposing red, pulsing blood veins under clear portals. Through the little windows, the spine was clearly visible. Thin tendrils of what could only be Live Metal attached the device to the bone.

"What the *hell!*" Menrva pulled away. "What did you do to this guy?"

What had she just walked into?

"Seriously, Nerve, even if I would do something like this, I don't have the expertise to get it done. I'll explain, I promise. For now, just do what you have to do to save him. I'll get whatever you need."

Menrva bit her lip, struggling to tear her eyes away from the horrific contraption as Cowl rolled Bastille onto his back again. He really didn't look like he was in good shape. If the choices were execution at the hands of the City or a small chance that she could actually help him, it seemed obvious. She didn't want to be in this position, but it was better than nothing.

At least she had some idea what she was doing. She just needed to get this over with and get out of here as quickly as possible.

She took a shaky breath. Most of her life had been spent tearing things apart: bodies, chromosomes, genetic code. Putting things back together was a good bit more difficult. Odds were stacked against his survival, but could she walk away now and not even try?

"If it's gotten to this point, he probably needs surgery."

Cowl nodded in agreement. "Then let's do surgery."

"I'm not a surgeon, Cowl. I don't know what I'm doing."

"We are both geniuses. Between the two of us, we can manage this, right?" he said.

Intracranial pressure was no laughing matter. There wasn't a lot of room for the brain to swell, so, at the very least, brain damage was a factor. The pressure had to be released. The best option that she could think of was the oldest: trephination. All she would have to do was drill a hole in his skull and drain the fluid to open up some room for the brain to expand. From there, it was a matter of reducing the swelling. Cooling the brain could help. Drugs were a risk. She didn't know enough to be able to choose which one he needed.

Her training was far too narrow for specific diagnoses. She knew the basics of how the body worked from her apprenticeship classes, the same broad studies med students started out with.

"Okay, fine," she said. "I need clean water, a razor, a scalpel, and a drill."

As Cowl rushed about the small, dark space gathering items, Menrva pulled open the medical kit and ripped into a bag with a pre-filled syringe of morphine. The drugs in the case were valuable, and she wouldn't be able to get replacements without filling out a report. The only reason they were included was because of the frequency and intensity of headaches with the VR. She wouldn't be filling out a report, though. What would the City say about her performing surgery in the Pit on a clearly dangerous man?

She pulled out a bottle of antibiotics and laid out the materials she could find on a few layers of anti-bacterial wipes.

"Can you use a razor for your scalpel?" Cowl asked as he dropped an armful of supplies on the floor.

"If you sanitize it." Menrva pulled on a pair of sterile latex gloves from the kit, frowning as her hands trembled. Shaking hands and surgery did not go well together.

"One step ahead of you." Cowl lit a candle and slowly ran the tip of the razor through it. This wasn't exactly a clean room. Trying to keep contaminants out was going to be a nightmare.

"Light?" Menrva asked.

Cowl flicked on his flashlight and leveled the beam onto her workspace.

Working quickly, Menrva shaved a portion of Bastille's hair away, struggling to keep her heartbeat subdued. Cowl heated a small drill bit over the candle, removing the soot with a disinfectant wipe. The drill wasn't a pleasant thing to look at, considering what she was about to do with it.

The bottle of antiseptic seemed too small for the job of cleaning the dirt off the friend's scalp. Menrva scrubbed it the best she could before scooping up the syringe.

"Are you *sure* about this?" she asked.

"Yes. There isn't any other option," Cowl answered.

She pressed the needle into Bastille's scalp. The skin swelled slightly as the fluid slid under the skin, ballooning outward before it was absorbed.

Menrva sucked in a deep breath, holding it until it burned her chest and throat. Slowly, she released it and grabbed the razor. Before she could second-guess herself, she pressed it into the skin. When it hit the bone, she drew it over the cleaned flesh in a wide curve. She braced herself for Bastille to scream, jerk awake, or even twitch – but he didn't. She could just imagine he was dead. That would make it easier.

There was too much blood for her to entirely convince herself of that.

Wiping the flow, she scraped the skin back until it hung down in a long flap. What she needed was some sort of clamp; it could be a cleaner cut. The skull, pink and gunky with clotted flesh, stared back at her. It was not the first skull she'd seen. A variety of scientists worked in her lab, and there had been a fair share of Wrecker dissections in the room while she worked. She'd stood in on a few, too, if they were short-handed. She shouldn't feel this sick at the sight.

"Shit," Cowl said. "Okay. Drill?"

Menrva carefully took the machine from him and stared at it. Motorized. It would be much harder to control. She could easily break right through the skull and into the actual brain. The proper tool for this procedure would be diamond-edged and controlled by a computer to ensure it stopped in time.

"If we are looking at the average width of a human skull wall, no more than a half of a second at this speed," Cowl said, leaning over her shoulder. "My math is solid, but my facts might be off."

"Do you want to do it!?" Menrva snapped. It was probably good information, but she didn't want to hear anything out of his mouth at the moment. "If you want to help, go find something we can use to reattach the bone fragment when I'm done."

"Ah... staples?"

Menrva pressed the drill bit against Bastille's skull. How

stupid was she to not have prepared a way to close up after the surgery? It was probably because the likelihood of him surviving such an amateur surgery was pretty extreme.

Ignoring the part of her brain screaming for her to stop, Menrva squeezed the trigger on the drill. The machine wailed for a half a second, punching quickly through the thick bone. Had she gone too deep? She didn't dare look up at Cowl. If she killed his friend, maybe he'd go ahead and use that gun on her.

Carefully, wincing as the metal ground against the edge of the bone, she pulled the bit free. No fluid followed the bit out. If she'd hit the brain, there would probably have been some sort of residue.

Menrva carefully freed the chunk of bone from the bit.

By the dim yellow light of the flashlight, Menrva could just see the red tissue inside the hole. Using the corner of the razor, she cut a hole in the membrane and carefully tilted Bastille's head until a pinkish fluid trickled out.

"Do you have a brighter light?" she asked, struggling to keep her tone even and comfortable. The man was still breathing, so hopefully she hadn't done anything irreversible yet.

As Cowl searched, Menrva let the fluid drain out of the skull, careful to catch it on a disinfectant wipe. She used some saline in a syringe to flush what she couldn't get to, continuing until the liquid ran clear. Somehow, it was easier than she expected it to be. Maybe she was in shock, but it felt almost like she was watching herself work from above. Everything she knew about the human body just clicked. There was one thing she was sure of: This man wasn't a normal human being. From what she understood, there was no way he should have survived this long with this kind of injury and still be alive. The brain was a very sensitive organ.

Of course, just one glance was enough to show he was unique.

Before she could think about it another second, Menrva scooped up a spare syringe, pushed it sharply through the sealed package it was in and screwed the needle on. It took her only a second to find a vein. Taking a quick, precautionary look at Cowl's back, she drew the plunger back until it was filled with blood and, snapping the needle off, jammed it into her pocket. Whatever was going on here, his blood would have answers. She might not end up using it, but she would regret if she didn't get a sample. Something was suspicious.

"There's nothing," Cowl said, coming to sit by her.

"It's okay. I think I can close up here." Menrva didn't even look at him as she rinsed the skull fragment in antiseptic and carefully lowered it back into place. An infection here, this close to the brain, would be bad news.

The staple gun was almost more terrifying than the drill. Menrva had a hard time holding the skull fragment in place for the first few staples. It was such a small piece: fitting enough staples in so it wouldn't come loose was a challenge. If Cowl's friend lived through this, he would have those bits of metal in his skull for the rest of his life.

After wiping the site clean one last time, Menrva sutured the skin back over the exposed bone and sighed heavily.

Chapter Four: Skin

Cowl stared at Menrva, sitting across from him and looking for all the world like his mother used to when he found himself in trouble. She had changed so much. When he'd hung around her before, she was just as wild as he was, if not more. Eager for trouble and always curious, she never stopped moving for a second. Now, she was all serious and grumpy, like an old woman's personality had been superimposed over hers.

That was part of the reason why he didn't want to tell her much. Sure, she wasn't going to go rat them out, but the fewer people involved the better. He knew Menrva, though. If he didn't tell, she would go looking and get messed up in a whole lot of hell. No, it was better he control the flow of information. Give her the right spin, try to keep her away from the edge of the cliff, so to speak.

"So, you remember where I used to work, right?" he began.

"Of course. You were in programing."

"More or less, yeah," Cowl said, leaning forward to check on Bastille again. He hadn't moved. It was probably too much to hope for anything yet.

"Anyway," he continued with a heavy sigh, "I was working late in the office one night, catching up from a run the night before. These City employees came in with a Borg, though I didn't know what he was at the time. They were in there for some of the equipment, and they had him get up on a table. One of them, a doctor, started cutting into him. The big guy acted like he didn't even feel it. They were talking about some sort of malfunction and how they need to fix him before the next Tournament. After a couple minutes of digging around in there, pulling out cords and shit, the Borg started screaming and throwing himself around. The doctors yelled about how he'd lost Connection before some soldier types came in and just blew the Borg away. They cleaned it up and left, and no one noticed me hiding in my office."

Cowl paused, waiting to see how Menrva would react. She hadn't freaked out yet. One thin brow arched over her eye dubiously, but she hadn't tried to stop him. Whatever. If she didn't believe him, maybe she'd just think he'd gone nuts and not look any further into things.

"They mentioned he was hurt in a Tournament Sim, so I went back a couple nights later and hacked in."

"That sounds like a stupid idea," Menrva said, her eyes drooping until her whole face spelled out her exasperation. "I know you are good with computers, but it was arrogant thinking you could run that program without being caught."

Why was she being so melodramatic? She used to love those dumb ideas.

"Well, you know me: the stupid one." He shrugged. There was a lot of work to do. Bas was alive for now, but he wasn't out of the woods and he wouldn't be until Cowl got the issue with his Live Metal under control.

"So yeah. I tried to hack into the game. Little did I know that the 'game' was actually a program to allow me to control Bas's body with my brain. When I went into the Tournament Sim, I actually connected to him. I ended up getting him out of the place he was in-- the Compound, he calls it-- bringing him down to the IT department where I was. I still can't quite say what I was thinking." Cowl squeezed his eyes shut, trying to remember the emotions that ran through him when he'd first met Bas. There was a bit of time there, back before he met Bas, where he'd just been numb. Now, the memory filled him with all sorts of anger.

Bas had been so inhuman back then. He'd been quick to take Cowl up on the chance to escape, but everything else was a struggle. Getting him to talk was torture, and he would barely even look at Cowl, much less interact. A lot had changed, and a lot more needed to change.

It had been months before Bas had been able to start behaving like a real person. Since then, there had been a lot of work: Panic attacks, sleepless nights, migraines, and a million little rituals they had formed to deal with the fallout.

"Anyway." Cowl blinked away the memories, laughing at the odd sense of nostalgia rushing over him. "I figured if the City wanted him, they probably shouldn't have him. I was already in deep shit anyway. Three years later, and here we are."

Menrva chewed the inside of her lip and played with the ends of her hair, twisting them around her fingers. She was uncomfortable. Well, he didn't like this much, either.

"So, you can control his body?"

"I don't," Cowl replied, maybe a bit too sharply. "But yeah, it's the tech that does it. Like a scientific version of a demon possession. Except his spine is waterproof, so those old Catholic rituals wouldn't work."

Rolling her eyes, Menrva tugged her fingers free of a braid and crossed her arms. "How does it work?"

Of course she wouldn't be happy with a basic explanation. He'd hoped she would take his little story as reason enough to steer clear. Most people didn't like getting involved with things that the City "discouraged."

"Well, you know how the VR works, right?" He tapped the chip in the back of his neck.

Menrva nodded. "Electric currents are traded between the brain and the machine. The currents from the brain tell the computer how to move. The currents from the computer convince the synapses they are interacting with something that isn't there." Menrva rambled off the statement without pausing to take a breath.

Menrva came from pure stock, and her parents were matched for intelligence. Cowl didn't need to dumb things down.

"Sort of." He reached up, pulling his tablet down from the shelf above him. "I pulled this out of the City Net a while back."

"You hacked into City Net?"

The wonder in her voice was probably the best compliment she'd ever given him; she wasn't free with nice words, even before he'd left. He briefly studied the image on the screen before handing it to her. It was a simple diagram of a human body, cut away to show the bones and nervous system. Superimposed over the image was a web of black threads, all leading back to a single line down the spine.

"This is an example of the augmentations in a typical Borg."

"Borg?" she asked, taking the tablet.

"Cyborg, Borg, Skin, Mod, Suit. There are a million terms. The City calls them Biobots, but hey, I'm a rebel." He shrugged. "I think it's a bit nicer than the others, don't you?"

"Like you are worried about being nice," she muttered, spreading her fingers over the interface to zoom in on the picture.

He shrugged in answer.

"So, what does all this mean?" she asked, not looking up.

"The bionic spine receives signals from a User who connects, just like you would to a VR. It then blocks the appropriate signals from the Borg's brain to his spine at the brainstem and instead uses the artificial nervous system to transmit the User's signals."

"And I imagine it interferes with the neurons in the brain to send the appropriate signals back to the User."

"See, you're getting it now. It's a very effective army built to fight the Wreckers and nothing else."

Menrva turned off the tablet, a look of disgust flickering across her face. "And are they awake during all this?"

A familiar pit opened in Cowl's stomach at the thought of what his friend once had to regularly suffer through.

"Yeah. It's not a full override of the body, it's more of an abusive relationship"

At that, Menrva winced and shifted uncomfortably. If only that was the worst of it.

"And how did this all get implanted? It's completely inundating his body. There is no way they could get that all in there with surgery alone, not without killing him," Menrva pressed.

Still with the questions! Maybe he shouldn't have asked her to come down. She had a bit more medical training than him, but genes and medicine were pretty different. It was mostly the Live Metal he was worried about. There didn't seem to be much she could do about that.

"They add the Live Metal when the baby is developing. It fuses to the nervous system and grows right along with it. The Spine isn't implanted until later."

Menrva shook her head. "Wow. How do they get the mothers to agree to that?"

Of course, most people connected that if there was a baby, there had to be a mother. It was still the accepted way these things happened. Chicken and egg and all that nonsense. But it was outdated when it came to the Borgs. "They aren't carried traditionally. They grow the kids in these mechanical egg type things. I've only seen the schematics." Cowl waved his hand to dismiss the information. "They are genetically modified so they can physically handle the strain. A bit of everything, but most of the foreign DNA is Wrecker, I think."

Menrva pressed her lips together and shook her head slowly. "And how do you know any of this? Do you have proof?"

"Proof? Come on, haven't you seen Bas?"

"So, because he's a big guy and has a hunk of metal on his back, I'm supposed to believe this crazy conspiracy? Really? Because you aren't exactly an unbiased source in this."

"Seriously, is it that much of a stretch? Think about the kind of shit they've already done."

Menrva crossed her arms. "Like what? Executing Starke? You might have loved him, but he was breaking the law."

Cowl's chest burned, and he couldn't force the words out. If she wasn't Menrva, he would have blown her to hell in an instant. He cleared his throat and shook off the anger. "Maybe it's time you go."

"Look, I'm sorry. I didn't...It's just that you are talking about my research here. I've never seen any sign that it was being used for anything but better understanding Wreckers." Her tone lightened. "I loved Starke, too. What happened to him was not right."

"No. It wasn't," Cowl hissed. "But this isn't about him. This is about Bas. This is about the City, and I know you've seen the shit they do. They are supposed to protect people, and they kill them and enslave them, all in the name of survival, while they blind anyone who could do something about it with 'important jobs' and VR." He motioned at Bas. "Is it really so insane to think they could keep something like this from us?"

Maybe it was hard for her to imagine that her hard work was going toward something like this, but it wasn't that outlandish. They had the motivation and the means. The science was centuries old, though Cowl didn't know that much about it. He didn't really care to think about it. Wreckers were terrifying and he didn't like to imagine Bas as anything but human.

Vague emotions marched over Menrva's face as she looked from Cowl, to Bas, to the floor under her shoes and back. After a long while, she finally broke the silence. "So, you are telling me that, not only is the City producing genetically modified cyborg babies, but they are controlling their minds, too?" The disbelief was obvious in her voice, but she didn't push it any further. She just nodded and pushed on.

"Okay, so what happened to give him the edema? Was it related to the stuff on his back?"

"Kind of." Cowl scrubbed his hands through his hair and checked on Bas again. How long until he woke up? "You see, the Live Metal veins in his body are constantly growing."

"The stem cells, right?"

"Yes, but, unlike the typical applications for Live Metal, you can't just program the nanotech in the artificial nerves and leave them. The human body is always changing, and each person is different. So the artificial nerve growth is governed by a computer program on City Net. Now that he's disconnected..."

"The Live Metal is growing wild," she finished for him. "The growth must have caused some tissue damage and the swelling."

"Who's telling this story?"

"I'm not a child; you don't have to explain the minor

details."

"In my defense, most people are stupider than you." Cowl made a face at her. "I'm working on rewriting the program, and the AI is still trying to hack the code. I'll get it before it's too late." Eventually the Live Metal veins would encroach into Bas's vital organs or start balling up to create synthetic tumors. Cowl had run simulations, but it was impossible to tell how long it would take without getting body scans to see where it already was.

This latest issue pushed up the clock. Something was happening in or around Bas's brain, and, if Cowl didn't act fast, something serious could go wrong soon. Brain damage, at the very least.

Cowl scooped his scarf from the table. The silence stretched as Menrva studied Bas.

Maybe Bas shouldn't be alone. He had just undergone surgery. There wasn't a ton Cowl could really do for him, but his chest tightened at the thought of what might happen while he was gone. Bas was all he had left.

Ignoring that slightly over-attached piece of him, he shoved his way out the door and waited for Menrva to catch up. Bas was a big boy, more capable than Cowl gave him credit for. There wasn't anything Cowl could do for him but wait.

"One thing I don't get," Menrva said as she pulled her borrowed handkerchief over her face.

"Shoot."

"If these super soldiers are so great, why the whole creepy puppet deal?"

Cowl paused and flicked on his light, exposing the

particles hanging in the air. "War's hell," he said, finding the tracks from their earlier passage preserved in the dust. "Wreckers are a whole different level. They are natural predators that can spit acid for defense. Their screams can burst your eardrums, and that is all before they even get those hands on you. Putting any normal human in battle like that is a recipe for disaster. Pain and fear can cripple any normal soldier, but if you can't feel it...if you think it's just a game...you take the kind of risks that win." He reached back to keep her from stumbling over a rock and guided her onto the path marked by their tracks.

"That makes sense. Our studies indicate that Wreckers can influence their prey to feel a heightened sense of fear, though we aren't sure how they do it," she said, brushing off his hand and focusing on her steps.

Apparently Menrva hadn't had normal conversation in a couple years. She sounded like she was giving a lecture.

"So, they don't feel pain?" she asked.

Cowl scowled. If only that were the case. "The Borgs feel everything, they just can't do anything about it," His voice was hushed by the emotion thickening his throat. "As long as the User thinks it's all in good fun, the soldier keeps fighting. I guess they learned that trick from the Wreckers."

"Wreckers only have the simplest technology. They are more animals than anything," Menrva said, obviously confused.

"Come on, you dissect the things. Don't tell me you haven't seen it."

"I don't dissect them, I study their DNA. That is totally different." She paused, her face pensive in the soft light of the flashlight. "Wait, the biological links? Is that where they got the idea?"

From what they could understand, Wreckers ran in packs led by one alpha female who seemed to have the ability to directly control the males through nearly telepathic signals. It was a biological 'radio' of sorts, a way for the entire pack to unify under one common goal.

The silence stretched on as Cowl focused on the journey. It was a long walk, and the quiet made it longer. All he wanted right now was to be back in the cave, working on the code to rein in Bas's tech. He was stuck, though, until he got her home. Even this close to the Hub, there were a lot of risks. When the lift finally came into view, it was all he could do to keep from breaking into a sprint. Instead, he forced himself to keep step with Menrva and wait until she climbed onboard. The light from his flashlight bounced across her face as he climbed on after her. She looked angry, stricken almost. Maybe she wasn't as big of a jerk as she seemed. Maybe she just sucked at expressing herself. She'd never been much of a talker.

"You good, Nerve?" Cowl asked as he pulled the door and opened the airlock.

She answered with a quick, stiff nod, her eyes focusing on him briefly. For a moment, she looked like she used to. Sure, that gorgeous, thick black hair was replaced with the blue mess she wore now, but she really hadn't changed that much. She looked as vulnerable and angry as she once had, back when she was a kid. Back when he had thought he was in love with her.

"It was good seeing you again," Cowl said, pulling his

scarf down.

"You haven't changed at all," She crossed her arms.

Sure, he hadn't. Let her think that. "You can't improve on perfection." He winked.

"That's too bad. Get out of here. I can't be seen with you." She stepped toward the airlock, a hint of the old banter coming back into her voice. Maybe it wasn't fair of him to expect her to act like herself when he had dumped her into something so crazy. He never was much good with people.

"Worried about getting arrested, or about your social status?" he jibed, hoping to keep up her good mood.

"I'm about to push you off this platform."

"I'll see you again, sometime." Probably not, but he could hope it was true.

She looked back briefly, her face serious again. Slowly, reluctantly, she nodded, and stepped into the airlock.

Well, that was that. She hadn't turned him over to the guard. Maybe it would be worth checking in with her, someday.

Chapter Five:
Enemy on the Homefront

Pictures of bullets blazing through a hostile environment stretched across the cafeteria walls, depicting the glorious moments of the last Tournament. Menrva rocked on her feet, her arms looped around her waist, watching the pictures with distaste. Lunch break was the worst part of her day. The crowded cafeteria was always full of accusatory eyes. Today, getting back to the lab was even more tempting than ever.

She was going to get answers. More than that, if this plan worked out, she would use those answers to gain some actual power in her life. If Cowl's story was true, her investigation into the cyborg's blood should bring some attention. If the blood revealed markers from Wreckers, it would at least be partial confirmation. If the City *did* react, that meant they were behind it.

She wouldn't know the City's motivation or the details until she got on the inside. If she proved she had something to offer, they were sure to accept her. Especially with Leslie in a position of power.

Why did the deli have to be so busy? She'd gone early, during the rush hour, that's why. Now the deli worker, who seemed to have a special hatred for Menrva, was making sure she prepared everyone else's orders first.

"That was a good one, wasn't it? Pretty epic," a teenage boy said, hovering at her elbow as he locked eyes on the screens. Only the occasional kid or pervert would risk having anything to do with her these days, a fact that got irritating quickly.

"I didn't watch," she said, turning deliberately away from the youth. "They aren't so interesting after you've won three of them. You're Sam Skutter's oldest, right? Let him know I said 'hi,' would you?" Menrva said.

The boy's face turned a few different colors as he contemplated the implications of the Hub's local 'dirty girl' passing on a friendly greeting to his father. A moment later, he scuttled away, leaving her both relieved and slightly disappointed that her solitude had been restored so easily.

She distracted herself by studying the soldier in the new screenshot flicking past her. His back was turned to her, a familiar mechanical spine exposed through the armor. If she hadn't known what it was, it would have looked like just another piece of the suit. The sight was like a gavel falling.

When she played Sims, she had qualified for multiple Tournaments. Being a bit of an outcast, she always had extra time to mess around in the first person games. In addition, the real world experiences she got while causing trouble with Cowl helped keep her in top gaming form. How was it that winning a few competitions qualified a teenage girl for controlling real human beings in actual life or death situations? Nausea curdled in her gut as she realized the implications.

That was assuming Cowl's story was true, though. She wasn't going to condemn herself until she had the proof in hand, even if it was plausible.

Right now, she was just eager to get back to the lab and see the results of the blood test. If Bastille wasn't actually genetically modified, as Cowl had asserted, he was still an interesting case. He had to have a strange form of gigantism or something.

She just had to get back to the sequencer before one of the other team members found it. Most of them didn't go near her work, so it was a low risk, but better safe than sorry.

"Hey, Drew," she called over the counter to the middle-aged woman who was cutting her deli sandwich. "Forget toasting it. I just remembered something at the lab that's actually pretty urgent."

Drew raised an eyebrow and shrugged, but didn't move any faster. She turned to the deli worker beside her.

"So anyway, Simson's getting less and less hours in water retrieval. The City's lowered our stipend to less than twenty credits a quarter," she said, picking up a conversation with one of the other workers. She rubbed the back of her wrist against her temple.

"Oh, honey. That's not enough for your family. Those boys are growing."

"I'm scared they are going to move us down to the Tiers. That would kill me, Mar. I just don't understand. It's not like people are using less water."

Menrva picked a hangnail on her thumb and tried to

ignore the conversation, which was getting in the way of her finished sandwich and freedom. It was concerning. There were a lot of people losing their positions lately, particularly those who worked in more menial jobs. Rations for food were getting tight, but not for water. Drew was right. There wasn't any obvious reason for them to cut hours. Not unless they were preparing for something. Maybe it was part of the terraforming efforts? But they wouldn't be working on that as long as the Wreckers were still on the surface and, as far as she knew, nothing had changed there.

"They can't move you down. They won't..." the other worker caught a glimpse of Menrva and shot an accusatory glare over Drew's shoulder, as if she was eavesdropping by choice.

"The Dorchesters moved down last month. Two more families the month before. I know at least five families who are having trouble making ends meet..." Drew shook her head, her back now fully turned on Menrva.

Menrva cleared her throat loudly. It was awkward, standing on the edge of an obviously personal conversation. That was part of the issue with being a social outcast.

Drew's lips turned down bitterly as she wrapped the sandwich with sharp movements, crushing the bread in her fingers and leaving ugly dimples over the surface.

"Could you have one of the runners drop my groceries off today? I don't have time to go back to the pod," Menrva asked.

The surprise on the woman's prematurely wrinkled face

was obvious. Menrva didn't like anyone in her apartment, so she was one of the few residents who always picked up their monthly rations. Drew's lip twisted as she looked Menrva up and down, as if trying to find evidence of some great sin hidden on her person.

It wasn't fair that they took so much offense at the rumors. After all, what she was accused of wasn't all that uncommon.

"Of course, anything we can do to help," Drew's disgust was only just hidden behind a thin veil of professionalism.

She handed Menrva the crumbled lunch order and held out her palm expectantly. Menrva considered her before pulling out an extra credit along with the smaller portion, and wrapping it in the thin paper. No matter how smashed her lunch was, Drew's kids deserved full bellies. Menrva couldn't use all the credits she was being given anyway.

Sighing, she stuffed the food in her lab coat's oversized pockets before jockeying through the lunch crowd to reach the door. Another glimpse of the Tournament highlight reel showed a Wrecker falling under a hail of bullets. Under his feet, the bloodied remnant of one of the soldiers laid out like a dissected science experiment. She didn't want Cowl to be right.

The walk back to her lab took longer than she remembered. She passed at least four guards scattered in the high traffic areas, and all seemed to be watching her. It was probably just paranoia. Over the past two years, there seemed to be a lot more guards on patrol.

Most of the staff were still on break, only a few stubborn scientists persisted in their studies, so the lab was quiet.

Menrva's uneaten sandwich jostled against her leg as she dropped into her chair and tapped her password in the interface. It took her three tries to get it right.

The data flashed across the screen, making her fingers go numb. There was no way the sandwich was getting eaten now.

Bas's blood was undeniable proof of at least part of Cowl's story, boasting an impressive degree of augmentation. Pieces of DNA matching a countless array of specimens, most notably Wrecker, had been expertly pieced together throughout his chromosomes. The level of skill it must have taken was profound. It was like a piece of music: not a single note was displaced. They worked together perfectly to support the final product. This would have taken teams of scientists lifetimes to perfect. Only a genetic engineer of the highest caliber could have pieced together this kind of elegance.

The program had found some anomalies as well, strands that couldn't be traced to any known species. Most likely they were mutations caused by Bas's body as it desperately tried to compensate for the damage done with the tampering. Wrecker stem-cells were renowned for their ability to adapt; no doubt they had done their fair share of the heavy lifting with the mutations.

All this proved was that someone was tampering with genetics. That was nothing new. CRISPR gene editing had been around since the 1990s. The real question was what role the City played in all this and to what end.

If the City was messing with genetics, there was one easy place to look. Leslie had high clearance, and she'd brought a blood sample earlier that she herself admitted wasn't all Wrecker. She described it as 'different.' If Cowl was right and there were others like Bastille, Leslie's samples could be a good cross-reference.

Menrva pulled up the result from Leslie's blood samples and ran a comparison. A few blocks ran up similar. Some were Wrecker or other genes, obviously taken from the same source. That wasn't too surprising.

There were matching human donors. Though you couldn't go as far as calling the two sample subjects 'siblings.' Not even 'half siblings,' but it was clear they shared a few DNA donors.

Leslie's subject, the female, had a much higher portion of non-human DNA. Wrecker, mostly. It was almost half of her modified genetic information. Enough that it would be hard to call her human. Bastille definitely skewed toward the 'human' side.

What could be proved by Leslie's sample was that the City was involved, at the very least. So now, how was Menrva going to use this information to catch their attention and do it in a positive way? They probably already knew she had the sample.

If she built a good report and handed it off to her mom, it might be worth something. Leslie was pretty high-ranking, and it seemed like her work with Live Metal was being used, as well. She at least knew this blood sample was modified, though how much she knew about everything else was questionable. Even if she did know more, she wouldn't tell Menrva. She cared too much about her work for that.

Another question nagged at Menrva: in what capacity was the City involved? Either they were running a program, as Cowl had suggested, or they were at least aware of whatever had produced Bastille. There was little doubt in Menrva's mind that her research here wasn't going to go unnoticed.

One thing the City always valued was information., After all, it was what kept Menrva in the Hub. If she had information no one else could provide, they couldn't do anything against her. They wouldn't want to. It was a fair exchange: information they wanted for information she wanted.

So now the challenge was to get something unique out of the research she had in front of her before the City lost their patience with her tinkering.

They were probably already watching, so why not impress them?

Chapter Six: Puppet

The stones under Bas's hands were hot, the warmth of the living earth. He ran his fingers over the rough floor and savored the feeling of the pebbles rolling under them. It was foolish, to keep checking, but he couldn't always stop the compulsion to ground himself. It had been years since the last time he was Connected, but he could never shake the feeling that he was about to lose control. He held his hand in front his face, blocking out the meager light from the lantern, and clenched his hand into a tight fist.

"How you feeling?"

Bas jumped and dropped his hand as Cowl ducked into the tiny space.

"Better." Pain shot through his head as he turned to look at Cowl, drawing a grimace that was still half-faked. Human expression was a foreign language to Bas; he had to practice.

"It's good to see you functional again."

The last few times Bas had been lucid were a blur. It was hard to put a finger on what had been happening during that time, or how long it had been since he'd passed out. Waking up had been jarring. Cowl didn't need to know that, though. He was worried enough as it was with the Live Metal advancing.

"How long?"

"Since you passed out? Almost a week, brother. But you've been in and out since Nerve came by to help four days ago."

Nerve? Bas shifted through the smudged memories but quickly gave up when the throbbing in his head increased.

Cowl dropped his pack on the table, spilling cans of fruit and bottles of water over the surface. "I've been having this insane craving for cinnamon rolls — like pregnant-lady insane. So..." He held up a frosting-smeared bag filled with squashed bread, "I stopped by for breakfast."

"Great," Bas said.

Cowl wasn't always smart when it came to his compulsions. If it had been Bas, Cowl would have given him an earful. It wasn't fair to nag, though. Cowl had given up more than Bas could ever understand. Cowl had left a comfortable, safe life in the Hub for his sake, even before they had been friends. Those first few months out of the Compound hadn't been easy, either. Cowl took risks, but that was just part of who he was. He was capable, so it evened out a bit. Besides, knowing him, he'd been obsessing about the Live Metal programing since Bas passed out and needed the break.

"Look, I can spy." Cowl leaned over the computer screen. A few minutes later a full video of a room in Bunker dropped onto it. He grinned and pointed at the figure on the screen. "See?"

"Who's that?" Bas leaned forward. He pushed Cowl's hand away so he could see the petite girl on screen. A riot of braids were woven into her pale blue curls. Her lab coat tugged against soft curves.

"You don't remember? I've probably told you about her five times, at least," Cowl said.

"Honestly, I don't remember a whole lot except a headache." Bas rubbed the scar on his head carefully. Staples pressed against his fingertips as he traced the cut. What was a little more metal?

"She's the one who put that hole in your head. Saved your life," Cowl explained. He nodded at the monitor. "Just checking she's all right. I wouldn't want to put her in any danger."

Hopefully Cowl had been keeping a close eye on her. She could have told anyone about what had happened. The City thought Bas was dead; he and Cowl had made sure of it. If she let anything slip, even by accident, they would not give up until he really was dead.

"You knew her?" Trying to imagine Cowl's life before they met filled him with an off-balanced blend of curiosity and fear. There was a whole world of human relationships and concepts that just made no sense. Cowl was the only example he had of a friend, and it was really strange to think of him having that kind of relationship with anyone else. That and family. Family was another strange idea.

Cowl laughed. "We went to school together. We used to be close, but I think she decided to hate me."

School was confusing. Like training, but without all the fears Bas associated with the word.

"Menrva's mom works with Live Metal, and she studies Wreckers. I figured she might come in useful, since I pretty much have the normal things handled." Cowl dug into the doughy mess of cinnamon and bread on his lap.

The mention of Wreckers was still enough to make Bas shudder. They were terrifying creatures. No unmodified human had hope of facing them, elite predators that they were.

There was something about the Wreckers, something in their very presence, that could send pure terror through him. During those times, it was hard to think, hard to be aware of anything but crushing fear. The Connection was never something he would be thankful for, but he had no doubt that, if he were in control of his own body during those moments, he wouldn't be able to move.

"Whatcha thinking about?" Cowl interrupted him. "I think I know that look. Robo-face."

"Wreckers." Bas reached over to pull a cinnamon roll from Cowl's hand. "Nothing important."

"That's a strange thing to be thinking about."

Bas shrugged. He chewed the bread slowly and then nodded at the screen. "You said she was an expert in Wreckers?"

"That's *not* why I asked for her help." Cowl sat up a bit straighter, wiping his fingers on his pants.

"I didn't mean...I'm just asking." Bas cleared his throat. Would he ever figure out this 'conversation' thing? It was strange, how he could say something and Cowl could hear and respond to something else entirely. Sometimes it was like he was reading Bas's mind. Sometimes it was as if he'd just been speaking to someone else.

"Should we be worried?" he asked. The woman Cowl had brought was a scientist. Scientists were...they didn't make him feel safe.

"We take care of each other. Nothing's gonna happen. We've made it three years, right? I'd say we're past the danger zone," he said, guessing at Bas's concern.

"We've never had to pull in outside help before," Bas said.

"What, Nerve? She's not gonna say anything. She's solid as the rock under our feet."

Cowl seemed pretty sure of his statement, but there was one thing Bas was pretty sure of: the stuff they were dealing with was heavy. It was a lot to ask someone to step into, especially if you expected them to just step away and never think about it again. He just shrugged. "She saved my life. I have nothing against her but, you know, stuff happens."

"Look, nothing is... shit, what's that?" Cowl frowned, pulling up a line of text running at the corner of the screen. "Someone else is watching." He leaned in. "The City is watching Menrva."

Chapter Seven: The Best Laid Plans

Menrva dropped her stylus and stared at the monitor in front of her. The words blurred and seemed to crawl in place, like larva. It was just exhaustion.

What had it been, three days? She'd stopped for a few hours here or there, mostly sleeping, bent over the desk when the other scientists were gone. The only problem was the Wrecker staring at her back the whole time, giving her nightmares. Ugly thing.

The notes had lost any semblance of order sometime in the middle of the first night, and now she was trying to link together her notes and sequences with scribbled lines and color coding. It wasn't working. Wrecker DNA was supposed to be highlighted blue, but somehow the code behind the human cardiac and circulatory system had ended up blue, too.

At least...that's what she thought had happened. The one string she'd just passed looked for all the world like a string of DNA code she'd thought was attached to Bas's neurological pathways. It was also blue. But the mutations in that strand was too pronounced. Had she confused Leslie's sample with Bas's again?

Too many Gs in this strand... That was in the wrong place.

If she hadn't spent her career detangling Wrecker DNA

already, this would have been much harder. It was quite a challenge even as it was. It took teams of scientists years to map out single strands of DNA. Isolating specific genomes could take a lifetime, and that was when you knew what you were looking for. Borg DNA was like looking into a box of mixed puzzle pieces and trying to get a full picture. Thankfully, she had an excess of information on both human and Wrecker DNA so it was just a matter of figuring out how they interacted and sorting out anything coming from a separate source. If only she could get a glance at the genetic engineer's notes.

The only definitive thing she'd nailed down so far was that Bas did indeed have strong Native American roots: pre-collapse genes. Any human father he had was dead over three hundred years ago, though the female donor seemed to be a Borg like him. That made it even more complex. Whatever genetic changes the mother had brought in would have their own set of entanglements.

So far she'd isolated twenty five donors, not all human or Wrecker, but with two dominant base genes and a healthy helping of alien.

What a mess.

When time ran out — and whoever was watching was going to lose patience eventually — she wasn't going to have anything worth the risk she was taking.

Sighing, Menrva pulled out the jailbroke tablet she had in her bag, a gift from Cowl in her teen years, and transferred the relevant notes by hand. She was doing as much work on the disconnected mobile device as she could, in order to keep the information out of the City's hands.

She could work on this more at home. She hadn't had more than a couple hours sleep since she'd come back from the trip down to the Pit. If she was going to make any significant progress on this, she needed to let her body and brain rest.

Stifling a yawn, Menrva dragged her hand over her eyes and stood up, stretching as she did. For now, the info could wait, but she couldn't get too comfortable. She stored the information in an encrypted file, careful to tuck it away where her coworkers wouldn't ask questions, and headed toward the door.

As she stepped close, the light above the door blinked an angry red. Menrva froze, staring at the obvious refusal. The scanner wasn't letting her through, and there could only be one good reason.

Panic bloomed in her chest and she turned to look around the room. Was there another door she could get through? A hiding place?

No, that was stupid. She'd set this in motion and now she had to have the courage to see it through to its inevitable end.

Menrva slipped back into the chair at her desk and looked over her notes again, her hand shaking as she swiped it over the screen. There was at least enough info here that maybe she could convince them that she would do more good working for them than she would dead, if it came to that.

Behind her the door hissed open and she struggled to shove the tablet into her bag. She turned to see a tall, broad-shouldered man standing at ease in the doorway. His hooded eyes regarded her contemplatively, though he didn't move a muscle. At either shoulder, a guard stood in their crisp, gray uniforms, hands already resting on their sidearms.

"Miss Penniweight," the man said. His immaculately manicured beard and hair was just barely touched with gray, which seemed to match his cold eyes.

Everything about him reeked of power and influence, of a man who didn't waste effort on looking intimidating or throwing his weight around. It wasn't Leslie, as Menrva had half been hoping it would be, but at least this man seemed to know who she was.

"Would you come with us?" he said without preamble.

"Might I ask who you are? Do you work for the government?" Menrva asked, trying to keep her voice from wavering. There was little doubt he was from the City. If she was going to reach her goal, though, she would have to make a good impression. It was easier to connect to someone once you had a name.

The man tilted his head slightly toward her, the first real movement he'd made since he'd appeared behind the door.

"My name is Jordan Launay. You might have heard your father speak of me. He and I were familiar."

"Am I under arrest, Mr. Launay?" Menrva asked, fingering the straps of her pack.

Launay raised a single, thick brow. "Will that be necessary?"

Despite her best efforts, Menrva shuddered. Launay

wasn't threatening, he was indifferent. That in and of itself was terrifying. Nature was indifferent. Wreckers were indifferent.

She had to put on a good front, though. If the City was going to believe she had any idea what she was doing, she would have to convey it through her confidence. It was basic human psychology. Confidence portrayed competence.

"Not at all." She squared her shoulders and flicked her hair behind her back before she stood, forcing herself not to rush. Control. This was all about control. "Lead on, Mr. Launay."

This was it: the litmus test. If Cowl was right, she would get her answer by the way the City reacted. Hopefully she'd get a chance to get dirty and study for herself. If Cowl was telling the truth, and they were doing what he suspected, she wasn't going to be able to do anything about it until she had some power.

Chapter Eight: Joy Ride

Cowl rubbed the beginnings of a dirty beard that clung to his cheeks and frowned at Bas's activity. He should be resting. How Cowl was supposed to enforce that was a mystery.

Bas pulled a handgun out of their stash and checked both the magazine and chamber before strapping on the holster.

"We need them to think you're dead. Let's just sit back and watch for a little while. I haven't seen anything that would make me worry."

Lips pressed tight, Bas paced in front of the door. He had to duck at regular intervals to avoid hitting his head. Despite all that, his face stayed blank, his body tight as if he were a marching soldier. He paused just long enough to drag a shirt over his torso.

"If we wait, we could be too late," he said.

"Too late for what? They could just need her to consult for them."

Bas shook his head. "That was Launay. He's too high-ranking to get involved in something so small."

"Launay?" Cowl's stomach twisted. Launay was one of those shadowy tormentors in Bas's past. Someone that Cowl hadn't had the opportunity to meet in person, though he had done his research. Bas was right. Launay was high ranking. He supervised the entire Compound, but he'd also been Bas's handler and kept the role after he'd been promoted. Bas knew him well, and had good reason to be nervous.

Here was the hard part, because everything in him wanted to trust Bas's judgement. But Bas was far from objective in this situation.

"Cowl, they won't hesitate to kill her." Bas leveled his dark gaze at Cowl. "And she's in this situation because she helped us...me."

"We don't know that," Cowl whispered, but he couldn't meet Bas's gaze. Dark memories danced behind Cowl's eyes. The guards, coming for Starke, dragging him out of their small apartment. He'd not been too worried. Starke got out of everything, but look how that turned out.

"Shit." Cowl jolted to his feet and jerked open the bin holding their arsenal. He strapped on a holster, glaring at Bas as he stuffed his sawn-off in place and switched the magazine on a handgun for one filled with hollow-point taser bullets. Taser bullets wouldn't damage the armored walls of the Hub but if they contacted skin they would send out an electrical current to maim or kill.

"I can't let you run around out there on your own, can I?"

Bas stared at him for a brief moment and tied his scarf around his nose and mouth. Going in half-cocked like this, with no plan and shit odds, wasn't their style. They got in some messes, sure, but usually they were dealing with scavengers and starving Pit inhabitants, not well-trained guards and Borgs. If Menrva was in danger, they had to be smart about how they pulled her out.

They ducked out of the cave and jogged toward the Hub. Bas moved fast, but slowed down occasionally so Cowl could keep pace. Even still, it took a good hour to reach the Hub.

It hung overhead like a ghost, the pool of light exposing a swarm of workers on the outer walls.

"We need a plan," Cowl said through labored breath. He tugged off the scarf from his face and immediately coughed.

Bas studied the Hub momentarily, his uplifted face catching the light drifting down.

"What did you have in mind?" he asked, drawing his hand over the lump the holstered gun made under his shirt.

"I'll go in, you watch the exit," Cowl suggested.

Bas raised an eyebrow. "I will do it." He motioned to a door in a large strut not far away. "What if you run into a Borg?"

"What if *you* run into a Borg? You've got the same chances in there as I do. Probably less because they want you dead more than me and I'm not going to..." Cowl trailed off. Bas didn't like to be reminded of his mental hiccups.

"You won't what?"

"I just don't think it's a good idea for you to go up," Cowl said.

Bas seemed to understand, and his features fell. He looked up at the Hub, his eyes searching the exterior.

"What if you hacked into a Borg like you did with me?"

Cowl's stomach turned sour at the thought, but it wasn't a bad one. Connections were no picnic for Borgs, and now that he knew what the Connection was, he never wanted to be on the "giving" end again. But, if he could Connect, he would already be in the Compound. It would cut out the possibility of any real danger to either of them, though he would have to get into the Hub to get to a VR chair. That could mean trouble. His old office would be occupied in the middle of the workday, and he had to find somewhere with access to City Net. Maybe he could get into the Tournament room and use the VR chairs there? They had access, he'd just have to turn it on. It was worth a shot.

Best case scenario, he could get another Borg out. It would at least give Bas someone to relate to. Worst case scenario, they killed some poor kid who had nothing to do with their little war on the City. That wasn't at all disturbing.

"Okay. That could be viable. It's at least better than all of us rushing to our deaths over what could easily be nothing."

"It's not nothing," Bas replied, though he seemed more distracted by the door. "If I remember right, there is an elevator here that goes up to the Compound. Some of the Gen Three used it back when we had the Wrecker breach."

"And you know this...?"

"We have our ways to slip in conversation. No one would have risked trying to escape, but a few of us played with the idea."

It was funny how Bas could be so isolated, and yet he

always seemed to talk about the other Borgs as if he were part of some giant entity.

"So, I was thinking we go up together. You can plug in and I will meet Menrva and the Borg at the exit."

"Bas, that's too close. I would—"

"If something happens I want to be ready," Bas interrupted. "Come on, we're wasting time."

Cowl shook his head and stepped around Bas. It seemed like a good idea, but things like this never worked out. If they made a clean getaway, it would be a miracle.

The door had no handle, but a screwed-on plate to the side provided some access to what was probably the internal wiring. Cowl pulled out his knife and carefully slid it under the plate. Waste of a good knife. Despite a lot of complaining from both hunks of metal, the plate eventually popped off, hitting Cowl hard in the chest. He held up his knife, frowning at the bent blade, before dropping it to the ground and peering into the dark space.

You'd think they would learn to hide their wiring more carefully. Wires were the lifeblood of everything in the Hub and they were far too easy to hack, or even just yank. He patched in his smartwatch, and after a second of fiddling, the door popped open. Inside, a low red light filled the cylindrical room and exposed a short flight of stairs that wound around the inside.

Cowl climbed upward and hit the switch, watching the cables dance around the shaft above him as the elevator lowered on moaning wheels. Bas kept his head tucked into his shoulders, as if he half expected something to strike it off. It was the small space. He was claustrophobic and had good reason to be.

The elevator looked like an oversized fruit basket. It had no real walls, just a chest-high gate encircling it, and a metal cage around it, which guided the cables. It didn't look stable but it would hold. They had for centuries, and there was some sort of upkeep schedule. At least, Starke had worked on a few before.

Bas stayed stiff and focused on the climb upward, passing layer upon layer of doorways. He was a soldier, and was probably scared out of his mind right now. But he'd never show it. It was Cowl's job to make sure he didn't have to face it head on.

"Here," Cowl said as the elevator approached one of a million landings. He flicked through a few screens on his smartwatch as Bas slowed down the elevator. According to the map, he wasn't far from the Tournament room.

"Keep going up. You're at the top."

"Okay," Bas said simply, still looking upward.

"Don't go past the airlock. I mean it."

Bas didn't answer, though his eyes narrowed just a bit, as if he were considering it. "They might be looking for you now, too. Be careful," he said as Cowl stepped through the gate and onto the metal grating.

"Hey. I've been wanted for the last three years. Nobody's touched me yet."

Bas only grunted in reply before the elevator started moving steadily upward again. Cowl swallowed his frustration and hacked his way into the airlock. As he waited for the air exchange, he double checked his AI. The program would clear the way for him to pass by the scanners without problems, and he always liked to get a look into the security feed before he planned his route. Today was a bit of a rush, though. He flicked through the feed quickly, eyeing the door ahead of him as he did.

The next step was finding Menrva. The AI was on that now.

Cowl kept his head low as he ducked through the halls. This was less than ideal. He passed more people than he really wanted to on the way, but at this point they were in so deep that backing out wasn't an option.

Cowl avoided the eyes of a strolling citizen and stood idly by the Tournament room door for a heartbeat while they moved on. Well, hopefully the guards would have too much on their hands in a minute to bother looking for him, even if someone did raise the alarm.

The lights flashed on automatically as Cowl slipped through the door and carefully closed it behind him. He wasted no time hacking into the City Net and sinking into the chair. The thought of Connecting to a Borg made him sick, but he wasn't going to leave Bas hanging in there for long.

Sucking in a heavy breath of clean Hub air, Cowl leaned back in the chair. The moment his head hit the rest everything around him warped. It had been a long time since he'd Simmed. It was easy to forget how strange it was. He opened his eyes to a blank wall in a small, cold room. He shuddered, remembering the day he'd first Connected to Bas and found him in a pod just like this.

Hesitantly, he held up a hand. It was slender, pale, with long fingers. A female Borg, probably Gen Five, which would be...twenty? Maybe younger? Hell, he was torturing a little girl.

If he could get her out, get that Live Metal snafu fixed, she could be glad for it. If she was Gen Six, she might not have even been topside yet. "Here's the deal," he said out loud. "I know you don't have a choice. Sorry, but you help me and I'll do my best to help you."

No answer. Of course.

Okay. He had to focus. Bas would be waiting...hopefully. If he didn't wait, Cowl would have to beat his ass while he was in a body that could match his strength.

He shoved out the door, still unlocked as they had been before, and paused as a passing guard turned to look at him in utter shock. A second later a siren started screaming through the hall. Unauthorized Connection. They would find a way to kick him out, but the AI would give them a bit of a distraction.

The guard reached for his sidearm but Cowl grabbed him by the elbow and threw him into the wall. He grunted cartoonishly and collapsed onto the floor. Cowl pulled the buzz cuffs from the man's utility belt and widened the thick rings at the end. He slapped them in place over the black box on the Borg's upper arm. It wouldn't block the more powerful Connection signal but the electrical components inside would mess with the remotes the guards carried, so they couldn't stop him in his tracks.

Footsteps rang out from down the hall — guards. Cowl took off at a full sprint, his senses whirling at the sudden speed. Shit, this kid was fast. All the better. If the guards got close, it wasn't just the programs he'd have to worry about but bullets, too. Taser or otherwise, that was not something he wanted to push them to.

"She went this way. Her tracker's malfunctioning," a voice said from behind. guard?

"This isn't a malfunction. Someone knows what they're doing."

They were right, he did. Cowl barely managed to skid to a halt in front of the first door. This looked familiar. Once upon a time, he'd done this same song and dance with Bas. Ah, nostalgia.

A red light, blinking on the scanner over the door, denied him access. Or exit, more specifically.

Gripping the top of the door frame, Cowl yanked downward, throwing some of the Borg's bodyweight into it. Bas had yanked this aside like paper, but she wasn't weak by any means. The metal screeched as it peeled away, revealing a nest of wires. Ah, more wires. Outdated piece of garbage. They should update to lasers and computer chips. This was so 2000s.

Cowl ripped the wires free and the door popped open with a hiss. For safety, electric locks always reverted back to 'open' when they lost connection.

A few bullets hit the wall overhead, bouncing off the armor with the distinct buzz of electricity. Cowl reached automatically for his gun. Not there. Shit. How could he get a gun?

He glanced back at the guards as the approached the door. He body slammed the half-open reinforced metal with all the speed he could work up in the short space. fleshy 'crack' resounded from the other side. Cowl shuddered as he pulled open the door. The guards slumped against the floor. It was better than the red stain on the wall he'd half expected.

Snatching a weapon from the guard's belt, Cowl turned down the hallway. It wasn't his sawed-off, but it would have to do.

There were surely more guards to come. They wouldn't get close, though. This Borg could move! Cowl hurdled down the hall, moving so fast he nearly missed his first turn.

The last time he saw Menrva, she was on the lower level in the Hub. Offices and shit. Serious people's workplaces. In other words, exactly the place where Menrva fit in best.

Cowl skidded on the polished tile floor as a group of guards appeared ahead. He bounced wildly off the wall, colliding with one of the guards. It was mostly clumsiness but it worked pretty well. He fired off a few shots, sending the second guard to the ground in convulsions. Another guard dived at Cowl, but he might as well have been a fly up against the Borg. Cowl flicked his elbow, shoving the guard back, and slammed the gun into his skull to finish the job.

Normally, he hated this close contact shit. Guns were faster, easier, and cleaner. It was fun when you were this strong, though. No wonder Bas got carried away.

Another wave of guards rounded the corner. Cowl raised his gun but hesitated when he saw a familiar face staring up through the mass of gray-clad soldier-types. Menrva.

"Stop!" a guard yelled, waving his gun in Cowl's direction.

He was so close Cowl barely needed to aim. He fired off a bullet and moved on to the next guard before bothering to check if the other had fallen or not.

Two men dropped in the space of one breath, convulsing as the Tazer bullets sank in. He swerved as a round sailed past him and bounced from the wall. Another guard approached, but Cowl threw him back against the far wall with a wild punch. As the guard began to slip down he threw himself forward, slamming his borrowed body into the guard's head with such force it should have imploded. He turned to see Menrva ramming her elbow into another guard's face. The guard's head snapped back, just far enough to catch the bullet Cowl shot.

Menrva turned to look at him. "Who are you, and what do you think you are doing?!"

"It's me, Cowl," he said, grabbing her hand and yanking her toward the exit.

She swore, stumbling after him and tugging her hand out of his. No way she could keep up with the Borg. "What is going on?" she yelled as Cowl slowed his pace to match hers. If she wanted to get caught again, she was making the right choices.

"Does this really seem like the time to stop for an explanation or can you maybe just pick up the pace?"

The hallway connected to another that swerved around in the typical, ring-like shape of a Hub hall. They must be close to the airlock. If only he had his smartwatch, he'd know for sure, but he wasn't bad at guesswork. It was mostly math.

A smattering of bullets flew overhead and Cowl ducked

as one ricocheted back at him. "Come on, move your ass. We're almost—"

Menrva screamed, cutting him off, and fell face down at his feet. Cowl slid to a stop, nearly landing on his butt as he struggled to slow his pace. As he turned toward her, Menrva rolled to her side, one hand clasped over her hip where a red stain spread through her lab coat.

Cowl reached for her but before he could get to her the floor rushed toward his face.

He was alone again in the emptiness of the Tournament room. They must have found a way to cut his Connection.

At least he had his gun again.

Now it was up to Bas. If Menrva was even still alive.

Chapter Nine: Down the Rabbit Hole

Menrva stared in wonder at the lanky teenage girl curled in a fetal position at her feet. She seemed to be barely awake, moaning with her hands wrapped over her head. A long, rigid bionic spine, just like Bas's, bit into her skin as she buried her head in her arms. The sight was sickening. She couldn't have been more than seventeen, maybe younger judging by how big Borgs were.

It was enough to distract Menrva from the pain in her hip. She looked under her hand where the blood wept through her pants. The walls of the narrow hallway seemed to press in on her. Where was she? This wasn't part of the Hub she'd been to before, and didn't even seem to fit in the simple, concentric loops of typical Hub halls. If only she could clear the soft buzz of adrenaline out of her mind so she could think. This hall seemed to be going outwards. If that was so, she would have to turn around to get back to the elevators in the center to reach the lower floors. She'd just run from there, though, and there were armed guards on her heels.

This had something to do with Cowl using a Borg to get to her. Who knows why? Maybe he thought he was helping, maybe he just didn't want his secret getting out. Whatever his reason, he had just effectively killed her. The

City would not trust her now. They would think she had a hand in this. Her only choice was to run, but where?

She looked behind her where guards approached, guns raised.

"Don't move!" one yelled. "I've got my gun on you. Don't move."

Should she try to help the Borg girl? She didn't look like she could do much on her own, and the guards would be on them both in an instant.

Shaking off the guilt rushing in, Menrva jogged down the hall, ignoring the yells behind her. Her hip hurt like hell, but it was supporting her weight. She just had to get out of range and find an elevator. Screw Cowl, starting this whole thing and then abandoning her to figure it out herself.

The ache in her hip slowed her down, but most of the guards paused to check on the Borg girl. It gave Menrva a couple extra feet of lead. There was no way she could have stopped to help her.

And now, with Cowl's stupid play, she couldn't offer *any* of them help. If she'd gotten into a position in the City, she could have at least started gathering some info, figuring out what was actually happening. Now she was abandoning a teenage girl to her tormentors just to survive.

Menrva turned the corner and nearly slammed into a massive man coming down the opposite way. She skidded to a halt, gasping. It was as if the bullet hole had ripped wide open and her guts were about to spill out onto the ground.

Trying to ignore the pain, she studied the man in front of

her. His face was familiar from Cowl's cave, but Bas seemed to have grown even bigger. Standing, he could have been almost seven feet tall, all muscle. His movements were smooth, catlike, and his eyes darted around the hallway, hardly resting on Menrva.

His hand shot to his hip and a drew a handgun, motioning for Menrva to get down. She dove forward, catching herself on his leg. Once glance behind her proved that the guards had caught up. Another gun nestled in a holster pressed against Bas's lower back. Without thinking, Menrva snatched it and checked for a safety. It was a model she was familiar with, one she'd handled in the VR.

She leaned back, aiming over her knees at the approaching guard. The VR hadn't translated the crazy kick from the discharge. The first bullet flew right over the guard's head, ricocheting off the ceiling. She shot again, catching the guard's shoulder. The nanocellulose-blend uniform seemed to protect him, but he spun around with the force of the impact.

The last guard fell, convulsing and choking on a spray of blood gushing from his throat.

Before Menrva could react, Bas grabbed her upper arm and scooped her against his chest. Her hip slammed into his rib cage, shooting pain through her entire body. The room seemed to blur as she struggled to drag in a breath. He cradled her like an infant in his arms.

"Watch my back," Bas said, turning down the hall. His voice was deep, vibrating through her. Did he want her to shoot the guards that came up behind them? She twisted her neck, trying to get a view around his arm.

Red spots danced in her vision as Bas clutched her close. His forearms were like metal bars, pressing into her injured body. She gritted her teeth as he ran forward, every step jostling her.

She couldn't handle much more of this.

A guard rounded the corner behind them and Menrva tried her best to aim, but the shocks of pain traveling through her body made it impossible to keep her hand from shaking. She couldn't tighten her grip on the gun and it dropped, slipping down Bas's shoulder and into her lap.

Bas leaned in, tucking his body around her until she couldn't see anything but his shirt inches from her face. She sucked in a deep breath and something solid connected with Bas's arms, ramming them back into her. It was all she could do not to scream. The obstruction gave way and a moment later everything went still.

The hum of rushing air filled the room, muffled by Bas's body. She risked a look around his shoulders. The lights above her flickered around a rounded room hemmed in with metal doors. An airlock.

Bas didn't move, focused ahead at the other door with a determined, silent stare. He didn't even seem to be breathing hard. Despite what his DNA said, it was hard not to think of him as a machine. Behind them, the guards banged on the door. They couldn't get through the door until the process was complete. Hopefully Bas could get a head start on them.

The thought of moving again made Menrva sick. She dragged in a deep breath as the other door opened with a sharp whine, releasing them out into a dimly lit stairwell.

Bas rushed down the stairs toward an open service elevator. Each step seemed to rip into Menrva's body. She pressed her hands against her face, trying to muffle the strained moans squeezing past her lips.

"Already? That was fast." Cowl's voice drifted down to her as if through a tunnel. "Good, I didn't feel like getting shot at today."

Bas lifted her higher, and Cowl's body pressed against her leg as he squeezed past.

"I got your ass. Go."

Metal rattled as Bas slid into the elevator, and Menrva dug her face into his chest, trying to keep out the waves of pain.

The pain crescendoed, and everything went numb. The world around turned into echoes and flashes of light, and then something collided with Bas's arms, forcing her head forward. She blacked out.

Chapter Ten: Change

A sharp pain in her hip jerked Menrva awake.

"What…" before she could say anything more something jabbed into her skin again, dragging a yelp from her lips.

"Hold on," a gentle, resonate voice said. "Just one more."

The pain ripped through her body, and she snapped open her eyes, searching for the source. The ceiling above her was a familiar hodge-podge of dirty old cloth and broken boards.

She pushed herself up on her elbows. Bas hunkered over her, a rather comical sight, being as large as he was. His fingers were red-tipped and trembled slightly as he pulled a suture shut over a blood smeared spot on her hip.

"Hey, you made it." Cowl smiled at her from across the room. "Bet you're glad you were out for all this."

"That depends." Menrva's voice was hoarse. "How crappy of a job did you do?" She looked down at the wound. Blood spread in marbled patches across her hip, staining the waist of her pants. It couldn't have been too serious. It looked as if it had only just caught her flesh. It sure hurt, though.

"Looked pretty straightforward. Bullet went right through, it's just the fatty part of your hip," Bas said as he caught her curious gaze. He clipped the needle from the knotted string before taping a square of gauze over the site.

"Fatty, huh?"

Bas stared blankly at her. So he wasn't good with sarcasm. How was that possible, living with Cowl?

"Thanks for the patch job. It looks good." Menrva pressed a finger against the stitches. If she were in the Med Unit right now they would have used artificially grown skin to seal the wound. It wouldn't have left as much of a scar. She could be proud of this one, maybe. It was a good deal more respectable than some of her other scars.

"So, you already know the good news," Cowl interrupted from his seat in front of his screens.

"That would be?"

"We are all alive."

Menrva pursed her lips and shook her head. "I didn't need your help with that."

"Sure. Whatever." He brushed it off. "The bad news is now that the City knows Bas is alive, they are gonna be hot on our asses."

"They didn't know he was alive?" Menrva asked. A blood sample couldn't have tipped the City off to that truth, but Bas showing up in the City would for sure.

Bas's brow furrowed. "I know this is my fault, Menrva. I'm sorry." He seemed sincere enough, but the emotions didn't quite translate to his face.

"No. It's not your fault," Menrva said, turning to look at Cowl. "You shouldn't have come in after me, though. I knew what I was doing."

Cowl chuckled. "Don't look at me. Bas was the one

getting all hot and bothered."

An odd look passed over Bas's face, as if he was trying to match Cowl's expression before giving up and letting his features fall back again. Finally he sat, his back rigid and his hands on his knees, and looked expectantly at Cowl.

Apparently he didn't want to be part of the conversation.

"So, what exactly were you doing?" Cowl asked.

Menrva frowned. "Well, I was getting some answers. I took a sample of Bas's blood -"

Cowl jolted to his feet. "What!?"

Bas wilted, his face an expression of pure disappointment. It was probably the first honest and pure human emotion she'd seen from him.

"You took a blood sample? I never took you for a moron," Cowl said, features twisted in anger.

"Did you expect you could give me some half-assed explanation and I would just...what...go home and forget about it? I could have done some real good. You were the ones who messed it up by crashing in there and pulling me out."

Cowl's face blazed red in the pale light. "You have no clue what you just did."

"I knew exactly what I was doing. Anyway, it's not the sample that gave Bas away."

"At least, you are safe," Bas said, interrupting the argument. It sounded rehearsed, awkward, but it seemed to distract Cowl.

Cowl scoffed. "Yeah, so glad you didn't get yourself killed, or us for that matter. At least not yet." He mumbled the words just under his breath and crossed his arms like a child throwing a fit.

"Cowl," Bas interrupted.

"What?"

Cowl took a long look at Bas before he sat down again, muttering something under his breath. Probably one of his swear-littered rants. Menrva had never seen him back off so easily. When he got angry it was hard to reason with him…well, harder than usual. Starke used to be able to get through to him, but no one else. Not even her. Obviously, whatever the two of them had been through had made them close. She really had been easy to replace.

Shoving the thought out of her mind, Menrva folded her hands over her knees, wishing she could just disappear. She could probably find her way home, but home wasn't safe anymore. It wouldn't be ever again.

She would have to be content to sit here with two angry men and hope they weren't going to change their minds about the value of her life. Maybe they wouldn't kill her. Cowl wasn't that capricious, was he? Bas, well, she couldn't say anything for sure about him.

She studied his face, looking for any sign of anger or violence. What had he looked like when he was killing those guards? Did he have that same blank, cold look on his face? It wasn't natural for a living person to look so dead.

Cowl seemed to notice the expression at the same time as her.

"Bas? What's wrong?" Worry tainted his voice. So it wasn't natural. Something was off.

Bas shook his head, as if breaking free from a dream and

refocused his dark, intense eyes. "What?"

"Where did you go? What's wrong?" Cowl leaned forward like he wanted to grab Bas and shake him.

Slowly, a look of pain began to grow on Bas's features. If anything, it looked less natural. "Just a headache," he said.

Cowl rubbed his hands over his head and frowned.

Maybe it was just the remnants of his injury. Bas had just gone through what almost amounted to brain surgery...unmedicated and in this dirty, festering hole. A headache could mean a lot of things, especially with the medical issues Cowl had talked about regarding the tech.

Cowl climbed out of his chair and reached for Bas's shoulder, but he pushed his hand away. "I'm okay. I just need to lay down for a while."

Pinching his lips together, Cowl glanced desperately at Menrva. What did he want from her? She didn't know anything.

"Okay. I guess just..." he rubbed his hand over his hair. "I'll be here."

Bas nodded stiffly and lay back on the free bed, carefully shifting his weight. The bionic spine seemed bulky. It must have been a nightmare to live with.

It didn't take long for an uncomfortable silence to spread over the small shelter. Cowl watched Bas with concerned eyes, casting an occasional glance in Menrva's direction until finally he let out a heavy sigh and turned back to his computer screens.

At least he didn't seem angry anymore. He wasn't happy with her, either. Each tortured minute held a new worry for Menrva. She couldn't go home, and that was Cowl's fault. She should be the one who was angry.

It was hard to mourn her life, though. Sure, work was fine, and training was a good way to blow off steam, but there wasn't anything else that was worth the wasted emotion. Supposedly even as a social outcast it was better to be part of civilization than to be out on your own. That hadn't been Menrva's experience, though. Sure, she didn't want to be in the Pit. It was dirty, dark and hot. Somehow, she felt like it would be better for her down here. Cowl might be pissed off at her, but at least he saw her.

Cowl typed something on the computer's interface before leaning back and giving up on whatever project had been keeping him busy. He spun the chair to focus his eyes on them. "I don't get what you were even thinking. The girl I knew never would have done this. You've changed."

Menrva froze, her stomach dropped so fast it left her with vertigo. "What do you mean?"

Cowl's face grew stern, an alien expression on him. "I'm not an idiot, Nerve, though I know you think I am." He didn't give her a chance to protest. "You were my best friend. I knew you better than I knew myself. You were my family. Not anymore, I guess."

That was a strong statement coming from him. He hated family; his own had done nothing but abandon him. His father took no interest in his two sons, leaving before Cowl was born. When Starke, his older brother, was caught and executed for his involvement in the black market, their mother committed suicide, leaving Cowl alone. He had functionally raised himself even before that. If not for the countless nights Menrva had spent with him, he wouldn't have had anyone at all. Cowl had a way of getting into trouble, something Menrva had enjoyed at that age. His intelligence had made his practical jokes epic, but it also had made it hard for him to relate to most people. Unfortunately, it also made him perceptive when he actually wanted to be. Though no one could accuse him of tact.

"I don't want to talk about it." Menrva shifted further away from Bas. He didn't even move. He could have been dead, if not for the soft movement of his chest and the occasional twitch around his eyes.

Cowl shrugged. "Okay." He focused back on the computer, his shoulders bunched. "The City is running sweeps. We can't stay here. The cave is obvious enough without adding our heat signature," he said. "It's been almost twenty-four hours since we got you down here. That's a lot of time, especially if they use Borgs. Which they probably will. Fine mess you got us into."

She walked over to stand by him, studying his furrowed brow in the pale light of the computer screen.

The Cave was quiet as death. Menrva was the first to break eye contact. It always unsettled her when he got angry. He was a dangerous man, but he wouldn't try anything. Would he?

A low groan emanated from the corner as Bas sat up, rubbing his head with one hand. Cowl grinned suddenly, the tension dissipating as he turned to look at him.

"Awww, you was sweepin wike a baby."

Before Bas could answer, the computer chirped, the sound almost deafening in the small space.

Bas climbed to his feet, wincing slightly. "What's up?"

"Company." Cowl scanned the room.

"What do you need me to do?" Menrva asked.

"You've done plenty." Cowl frowned at the door. "They will probably have infrared scanners."

"Determined," she said.

Bas unlocked a chest and began pulling out a variety of guns and other weapons. "We should leave." He held out a gun to Menrva.

The cold metal winked viciously in the light. She wheeled backward. "No, I don't shoot."

"You did last night." His hand didn't waver, steady and determined.

Scowling, she lifted the gun. Its weight was unfamiliar, sobering. This object could make a toddler dangerous. It was one thing shooting a few rounds in a Sim, it was another aiming for a human being, especially if they were like Bas and didn't have a choice in what they were doing.

"Hey." Bas's firm voice broke through her thoughts. He had knelt down, but with his height he was still practically eye to eye with her. "If you can't handle using it, I'll take it. A moment of hesitation is all it takes to die."

She squeezed the gun, the curve of the black handle pressing against her skin. "I've got this," she said. Maybe that was a lie, but she could make it true. Capability was mostly a matter of confidence. Bas and Cowl weren't going to have to pull her weight.

Bas stood, shifting a rifle to his back and twisting two handguns expertly into place. "If you need us, let me know. We've got your back." He handed an armful of weapons to

Cowl and clipped a machete onto his belt. He seemed more at ease with the weapons in hand.

"I got the backup." Cowl plugged a cord into the chip on the back of his head. It wasn't built for much, but it was still a computer, capable of holding a few gigabytes of memory. Menrva had used that trick a time or two.

After a moment he unplugged the cord and joined the preparations again. The men buzzed around the cramped cave. They must have practiced before — or at the very least planned it. Would this be how she lived her life now? As a fugitive with a gun and a portable life? At least she had the distrust down already.

Menrva tied a scarf around her face, twisting it over her hair while she waited at the entrance. Dirt had already collected in her braids, stealing the silk-smooth texture she was so used to. There didn't seem like much she could do to help. The two men were efficient.

Menrva pulled aside the curtain at the door and froze. A yellow haze filled the massive cavern outside. It was barely enough to call light, but compared to the pitch black before it was brilliant. "What happened?"

"They turned those on while you were out," Bas said, looking over her shoulder.

"They have floodlights out here? Why?"

"Wrecker breaches," Cowl said. "According to Starke, they haven't been used in fifteen years, since the last time the Wreckers got into the Pit."

"Does that mean there are Wreckers down here with us?" Menrva asked, struggling to keep her voice steady. A breach...that was more than they could handle right now.

"Could be for us," Bas said.

"I hope you are just being paranoid." Cowl stepped out the door twisted his neck to get a good look at the Hub. "But at least we can move faster now that we can see in front of us."

It was going to be harder to hide now, but nothing was going to sneak up on them, either.

Bas doused the oil lamps and nodded toward Menrva as if to encourage her forward.

"Try to keep up," Cowl said, his hand resting on the butt of his shotgun where it stuck out from his shoulder holster. "You could get us killed yet."

Chapter Eleven: Hunted

Cowl squinted through the dusty goggles into the glow from his smartwatch. Getting from the cave to the closest Dust Town had once been a nightmare without using a light. Now they had the opposite problem, but it was still too dark to risk going without tethering themselves together. The Pit was an amorphous mess of dirt and rock and holes into the center of the earth, and even in the weak light it was dangerous. You wouldn't have to wander far before you were just another shadow in the gloom.

Thanks to the overreach of the City, it was easy to 'ping' their position off the chip readers overhead. Of course, knowing where they were going didn't mean traveling over the shitty ground was any easier.

The rope binding the three of them together tugged on Cowl's waist as Menrva stumbled. They should have just left her behind. She wanted to be in the City's hands, why not give her what she wanted? Forget the fact that she'd all but betrayed them. Forget the fact that Bas went back to the one place on Earth he least wanted to be to pull her ass out. Now she was just plain slowing them down.

If he wasn't such a nice and forgiving type of guy he'd put a slug in her skull. She was lucky he was such a gem.

"How are you doing?" Cowl asked Bas. The headache

from earlier was still concerning him. Sure, it was partially the effects of getting his skull drilled open and then running around the Pit like a cat who'd just been force-fed moonshine. It was funnier than it sounded. Still, there was a reason why he had needed that hole cut in the first place. The sooner they could get to a safe place, the sooner Cowl could get back to work on a solution.

"I'm fine," Bas said. "Menrva is the one who's injured."

Of course he'd be concerned about her; he never thought about himself first.

"I'm not sure I'm talking to her right now," Cowl said stonily, hiking his pack up on his shoulder again. All this stuff they had to carry because she'd forced them out of hiding, and she couldn't even carry it because she'd been shot.

"Where are we going?" Menrva asked, slowing even more.

Cowl sighed and dragged his feet. "If I tell you, you gonna turn around and shout it to the City?"

"What I did had nothing to do with you. I wasn't betraying you!" Menrva retorted.

"Oh really. So, taking a blood sample from the guy you were supposed to be helping and, knowing—"

"I know what I did, idiot," Menrva snapped.

The rope attaching Cowl to Bas tugged as he got too far ahead before slackening abruptly as he overcompensated.

"In case you didn't notice," Menrva continued, "you can still have a blood sample from someone who is dead. We can preserve them indefinitely. Me working with it didn't give away the fact that Bas was alive or that you guys were down here."

Cowl sneered, stumbling over a rock. "They would have gotten it out of you. You couldn't just go back and do nothing?"

"Look. You can get angry. You can argue. But I didn't do anything wrong and I refuse to feel guilty or apologize."

"Arrogant as always," Cowl muttered.

"No, I just know what I'm doing. You are the one whose primary characteristic is ego."

Cowl turned to answer and slammed into Bas's back, just avoiding a pinwheel back into the dirt. "Shit. What's up?"

He rubbed his fingers over his lips, checking for blood where his lip had collided with Bas's tech.

"Check the enemy position," Bas said, leaning toward the Hub with his eyes narrowed.

The search had started from the base of the Hub, radiating out. Based on their last reading, the City should still be a good ways behind them. They'd slipped out to the east while the City closed in from the west.

Of course, they could have moved faster if they'd sent down Borgs instead of guards. They had done this when Cowl first pulled Bas out of the Compound, so it wasn't outside the realm of possibilities. Stupid realm.

Hissing through his teeth at the foolishness of their situation, Cowl turned on his smartwatch and typed in the appropriate commands.

"Ummmm..." Cowl glanced up at the tiers stretched out over the room of the Pit. "This says they are right on top of us."

They were probably using night vision. And if they

moved that fast, they were definitely using Borgs. That made everything a bit harder. Shooting Borgs wasn't quite fair . Not that they had anything high-powered enough to get through their body armor at anything but point blank range.

"There," Bas said. "I think I see them." He pointed out over the distance. "This way. Menrva, can you run?"

Menrva's hand brushed Cowl's shoulder but she instantly pulled back. "Run? We can hardly see!"

"Stick close to Bas. He'll lead us around any major obstacles. Just move as fast as you can." Cowl grabbed the rope and tugged in the slack.

"Stop!" A note of panic filled Menrva's voice.

"Shut up! If they don't know we're here yet, yelling is going to make it pretty obvious," Cowl hissed.

"Just..." She snatched the rope back, her voice lower now. "...Let me."

Why she was so freaked out was beyond him. She'd been the one to break their trust, not vice versa.

Bas began jogging, glancing back at them often. It was easy enough to keep pace with him Bas was probably even going too slow, but the ground was a menace.

Menrva dragged behind him, jerking the tether. He should just cut her loose.

No, that wasn't fair. She was shot, after all, and not following Bas. Stupid ass. If she was going to be so stubborn, she was going to get her leg broken and then she would be slower than ever.

A crack in the ground caught Cowl's foot, tearing the thoughts out of his head as he struggled to regain his footing. Bas slowed, grabbing his arm and hoisting him into the air before placing him back on his feet.

The ground shook. For a second it was as if Bas had put him down wrong, or that his legs were weak. But that was a definite shudder, running right through the Earth.

When Cowl lived in the Hub, he'd never noticed any sort of disturbance in the ground around Bunker. Since moving down to the Pit, though, there seemed to be more every month. This was worse than last time.

Something like a gunshot ripped through the air and the whole cavern moaned. The shaking increased and something slammed into the ground just a few feet from them. Bas's arm connected with Cowl's chest, shoving him back and right into Menrva. A moment later a distant crash grew into a powerful roar. Cowl ducked, covering his head with his arms, as rocks and dirt showered down from above.

"What the hell?" he whispered, rubbing his wrist over the dust settling on his goggles. "That was pretty bad!"

"Landslide," Bas said, by way of explanation.

"What?" Menrva coughed violently. "How do you know?"

"I saw it," Bas said. "We have bigger problems, though. I think they just spotted us."

"You think they did, or they did?" Cowl asked, brushing the dust from his shoulders.

"Hard to tell, with the dust in the air. We should keep moving." Bas tugged on the rope.

The ground couldn't have been shaking still, so it must have been Cowl's legs. He forced himself into a slow jog behind Bas, second-guessing each footstep. A lot of shit just fell from above, which meant more garbage to slow them down. They were lucky if something else didn't just drop down on them now and smash them. It's not like it'd never happened before. Whoever came up with the idea of living in a hole in the ground? How was getting squashed in a rockslide or falling into a bottomless pit any safer than getting eaten by a Wrecker? Of course, two hundred years ago the aquifer had been full of water and Bunker was just a side project for a bunch of world governments who needed something to spend money on. History class in Basics didn't seem to have a very good opinion of the pre-Wrecker world.

Bas sped up, his back nearly disappearing into the dim shadows. Menrva was like an anchor on the end of the rope, pulling Cowl to an abrupt halt as the rope dug into his hips. He gave a good tug.

"Brother, relax!" Cowl said. "Wait for us."

"They saw us," Bas said, barely slowing.

Cowl picked up the pace, relieved when Menrva kept up. Her breath was sharp and jagged. Obviously the bullet hole was giving her trouble, but they couldn't stop to coddle her now.

The bang of a gun echoed behind him and Cowl ducked, swearing under his breath. So, they were close enough they could shoot now.

The pressure of the shotgun against the small of Cowl's back was suddenly very obvious. A solid slug had a good chance at cutting through the reinforced uniforms of the guards, but only if he was desperate and at close range. If he was looking at getting through a Borg's armor- which given the situation he probably was - they needed a high-powered EM assault rifle. The solid metal bullet propelled with the power of an electric pulse was enough to shear through even the graphene-coated, nanocellulose-and-titanium-blend plates. If he was going to get at one of those gorgeous hunks of engineering genius, he'd have to pry it out of a dead Borg's grip because those were Wrecker-only weapons.

At least, that was the idea. If these guys were carrying EM rifles, even the lower caliber model was enough to take them out from a couple miles away. Oh joy. It had to be Borgs.

Another shot echoed and something whizzed by Cowl as he pivoted on his heel to duck away. Zig-zagging was hard when you couldn't trust your footing. A dart sunk into the dust a few feet away from Cowl's foot. Non-lethal? Not just non-lethal — downright *humane*. A Taser bullet on a low setting could have done the same thing.

"Cowl!" Menrva said.

"What now?" Cowl stiffened as his eyes fell on Bas pulling the knot of his tether free and turning sharply right. "Hey. What are you doing?"

Bas glanced back at them. "If we split up, they will follow me," he explained, slowing to a walk.

Cowl shook his head and put on a burst of speed to catch up with him. "We agreed, none of this stupid, self-sacrifice shit. We do it together or not at all. Don't think that changes just because some girl showed up."

"We don't have time to argue," Menrva said between

jagged breaths. Her track suit was a shade darker beside her hip where the fabric drank in the blood from her bullet wound. She must have pulled some stitches.

"I'm not arguing, and it's not self-sacrifice. I'm faster than you, and I've got a better chance when I don't have to worry about you," Bas said.

"You aren't faster than *them*." Cowl jutted his thumb behind him.

Bas shook his head, meeting his glower with one of his own.

He began to pull away again but Cowl skidded to a halt, pulling his gun out as he did and lowering the muzzle directly at Bas's eye.

"Cowl!" Menrva shouted.

Clenching his jaw, Bas faced the barrel. Cowl didn't waver. "I will scatter your brains all over this cursed dust bowl before I let you go back. You got that?" he said.

Three years ago, when Bas first got out, he'd tried to put a gun to his head. The nightmares were too bad, he said. He couldn't' get the memories out of his head and the thought of going back was worse than the torment.

Bas had finally calmed down when Cowl promised to make sure the City never took him alive. It was a hard promise to make, but after that, Bas had *really* slept for the first time. It was a stupid promise, but it was one he intended on keeping.

Maybe Bas could get away by himself. More likely, he would get himself caught or killed to make sure the City didn't get them. That wasn't happening. If it took a gun to remind him of that, that's what Cowl would use.

Finally, Bas nodded. "Fine." He pushed the gun away. "Keep running. If we can get to town we might be able to hide in the crowds."

Cowl stuffed his gun back into his belt and looked at Menrva, who had stopped not far head. She glowered at Cowl and turned her back on them, starting forward again.

Cowl risked a glance behind, catching nothing but the murky darkness and the specter of Bunker hovering overhead.

Menrva's scream caught his attention. He turned just in time to see her slide forward into the dark. The tether jerked tight, pulling him from his feet and yanking him after her. Bas grabbed his arm just as his feet slid over what looked very much like the edge of the world.

Chapter Twelve: Collision Course

Bas grabbed for the rope as it snaked into the darkness. Through the clouds of dust and darkness, the edge of a great crack became immediately obvious. Menrva's face, pale with fear, was just visible where she clung to the rope around her waist.

"I've gotcha," Cowl called, climbing back up the edge and motioning to Bas to tug the rope.

A dart ricocheted off a rock beside Bas's hand as he jerked the rope back. Menrva scrambled out of the hole, maybe a bit faster than was comfortable, with both men reaching for her.

"Thanks." Her voice shook as she brushed her hands uselessly over her pants.

Bas plucked the dart off the ground and glanced back. The Borgs were gaining fast. A tranq dart like this was far from accurate at this distance but they would be within range in a matter of minutes. If they were using Taser bullets, they'd have hit their targets already. Why were they holding back?

There was no way to go back. But if Bas didn't do something soon, they would be surrounded. He rolled his shoulders. If only he could get a good look at how far the chasm was across, maybe he could jump.

Squinting, he searched the far side for signs of his target. About twenty feet ahead, amorphous shapes rose out of the cloud of dust. He could make the jump, but could the rope stretch?

Far in the distance, a few silhouettes flashed against the glare of a low floodlight, casting monstrous shadows across the ground. More Borgs were to the right, probably trying to cut them off. If they veered any more to the left they would get pinned to the wall. For now, the only way out was still straight ahead.

"Give me the rope," Bas said. "We got another group aiming to cut us off, gotta pick up the pace."

Cowl didn't hesitate, tugging the end of rope from his waist. He reached to help Menrva, who slapped his hands away.

"I've got it," she said, dragging the rope off and stuffing it into their hands.

Bas's hands fumbled as he reattached one end around his waist. A dart hit his tech, glancing off the metal and skidding into the dirt. Swearing, he backed up a few steps. "Hold this end. I'll jump."

"You can hold us both?" Menrva asked.

He jutted his chin toward the far side. "I'll anchor it."

"I don't know, that's pretty far." Menrva squinted at the canyon but he ignored her. Dust spat out under his feet as he sprinted forward and leaped off the crumbling edge. He hit the ground with enough force to send him tumbling. Rocks rolled under him, tearing into his flesh.

There was no time for hesitation. The pressure made by the shifting earth had pushed up shards of rock all around, creating a jumble of boulders at the edge of the rift. Finding a secure anchor, he attached the rope and waved back. Hopefully, they could see him. Cowl's eyesight wasn't as good as his.

"Now!" he yelled.

He gripped the rope with both hands to prepare for the extra weight. If they were hit, he was on the wrong side of the canyon to be of any help. The rope jerked, snapping against the stone and a second later the sound of flesh meeting earth preceded a pained grunt.

Menrva groaned as Bas pulled her over the edge. Her face contorted against the pain of her gunshot wound.

"I hate your ideas," Cowl said, crawling over the lip of the canyon. "I lost a gun in there."

Bas shook his head. The more stressed Cowl got, the more he treated everything as a joke — until he snapped. Now was a good time to funnel some of that tension into escape. "Come on," Bas said. "We can't wait. The canyon won't slow them down. But look." He pointed into the distance.

Ahead of them, dim lights reflected out of countless windows. Most of the homes spread across the floor of the Pit, but a few curved upwards along the walls and columns, arching with the ground. It was a surreal sight, as if a giant had emptied a shotgun into the cave floor, letting the glow of hell shine through.

"We are close."

Menrva limped behind them, barely able to move at a jog. Her wounded body wasn't handling the trip across the cavern very well. Bas slowed enough to fall just behind her.

Cowl copied his position, rifle nestled in his hands.

"You gonna make it?" Cowl asked her.

Sweat gleamed on the golden arch of her cheeks. "No choice," she said, fixing her eyes on the city.

She was tough, but tough didn't mean much with danger so close behind.

"Cowl." Bas paused, pulling his rifle against his shoulder. The haze had swallowed the Borgs, but they would be moving fast. "They'll be gaining. Let's alternate cover."

Gamers were almost as good as trained soldiers. Almost. If he had a Borg by his side right now, the field would be different, but Cowl wasn't quite a burden.

"Oh, goody. Shooting." Cowl grinned through the earth coating his face. "Flood lights, tranq darts...for some reason these guys want us alive. At least one of us. And they are pretty determined, so watch your back."

Bas chuckled despite the gravity of their situation before turning in one fluid motion and planting his knee in the dirt. Looking through the night-vision equipped sights, he counted their pursuers. Ten, eleven. He swore at himself. They were Borgs, just as he'd suspected. Even with their armor on, a few were immediately recognizable. People he knew from his youth, as much as he knew anyone. An arch-backed woman with a wide gait: Generation Three Serial Thirty-two. A man with an obviously bent leg: G3S15. They were from the generation before his, as good as brothers and sisters... some actually were. One lifted his gun to check the range. Bas fired. A plume of dust marked the place where the bullet hit the ground uselessly. He would take the kill shot if he needed to, but for now a distraction would be as good as anything.

A hail of darts answered. He held his position, but tactically it was a poor choice. There was enough of a haze that he had some cover, even with their night vision, but they didn't seem too interested in Cowl and Menrva. As they drew closer, he shifted his position in an attempt to confuse them. Despite his efforts, the darts hit far too close for comfort. The infrared filter on their helmets would give them a clear target, despite the poor visibility.

"Set." Cowl's voice carried through the black.

Bas dropped his stance and swore as a dart hit the dirt right beside his knee. It was answered with one of Cowl's bullets. He sprinted. The stale air turned into a whistling breeze as he passed Cowl and caught up with Menrva.

"How you doing?" he asked through stifled gasps. "We're close."

"Quit asking," Menrva said. "You don't want to know the answer."

Bas glanced behind him to see if Cowl was still alive. He couldn't find him. A few more feet and he would take another turn so he could check through the scope.

The settlement loomed out of the darkness, looking more like a collection of crypts than homes. Without any electricity, they were only lit by occasional flickering red light. Fuel was a rare commodity and the oxygen-starved environment made an open flame a dangerous luxury. As a result, the red stain imprinted into the emptiness was almost more intimidating than the surrounding wastelands, especially if you understood the horrors that took place inside. Despite all that, it was the only safety they could count on now.

"Keep going," Bas urged Menrva. He was barely able to make out her answering nod in the smoky gleam of the spotlight. He watched her jogging toward the threatening buildings until need pressed on him to act. She should be safe enough now. There was some cover. Bas dropped onto his stomach and trained the gun on his previous targets. They had gained a lot of ground, more than he expected. Even with the help of the scope, he couldn't find the other detachment. They might have already made it to Dust Town. They might have to get their hands dirty after all. Cowl would make sure they didn't walk into anything unprepared.

"Set," he called out, aiming at the closest Borg. He couldn't play nice anymore. They were too close. His gun wasn't of a high enough caliber to do much damage anyway, not this far out. The shot rang out, and the man reeled back and spun until he slammed into the ground. He'd be back up. Bas rolled to a new vantage point and lined up the next shot.

Footsteps approached, and Cowl flashed by as he rocketed toward the city, head lowered against the dust. He almost stepped on Bas as he ran by.

"I got you from the dust town!" he yelled. "Just don't let them get a shot in. I like my asshole where it is."

Bas hit another target but couldn't feel the regular thrill of battle. As he stood to change position, something drove into his chest like a missile. He flew into the dirt, his gun thrown aside.

A Borg stood at the ready, directly above him, paused

with his gun aimed. Probably speaking into his comm. He wasn't alone.

The other Borg stumbled back to his feet from where he'd fallen after Bas slammed into him. Bas acted before the other Borg could fully recover. He kicked and caught the first man at the knees, snapping them out from under him. As he fell, he fired an accidental shot, the sound ricocheting against the distant cave walls.

Bas rolled to avoid the second soldier's charge and sprang to his feet. He grabbed Bas's hand before a punch to the throat sent him sprawling back. Turning to find a gun trained onto his face, Bas froze but the man hesitated to pull the trigger.

Bas grabbed the gun with both hands, twisting it to smash the butt into the man's helmet. The man's head flew back, but he brushed off the blow. By then the first Borg had climbed back up. He grabbed Bas from behind, first one arm then the other.

The Borg's fists cut the air right out of Bas's lungs. Two hits...three. They couldn't feel pain, but he was weakened by it. He couldn't let them land too many blows.

As Bas's vision began to blur, his enemy got too close and Bas headbutted him, gaining himself a second. He threw himself to the side, dragging his captor to the ground with him. Another twist and agony ripped through his shoulder as it dislocated in the struggle. It was just enough for him to slip free.

Ignoring the pain, he grabbed the man's head. One jerk and he could break his spine, but he couldn't take the kill. It wasn't this man who was trying to capture him, it was the guard controlling him who was the enemy, and he was well out of reach. Swearing, Bas debilitated him with a punch to the weak area in the armor's flexible neck. The man melted into the dust.

Bas looked up to the dark point of a gun muzzle, hovering just inches from his chest. The other Borg had been quick.

"I'll shoot," the Borg said.

"Set." The call came from behind Bas. A moment later a warning shot whizzed past the Borg. His stance was weak. Bas narrowed his eyes. The Borg's finger hung carefully on the outside of the trigger guard. So it was him they wanted alive. He'd been holding on to hope that the tranqs were for Menrva. These guys were packing lethal rounds, or at least Taser bullets, which were just as deadly at this range. They were probably for Cowl and Menrva.

"Shoot me then," Bas said before he turned and sprinted toward the city.

The report of Cowl's gun echoed through the empty space, but Bas didn't slow to see if the aim was true. Something pricked his elbow, just sharp enough to be noticeable: a tranq dart. He knew the feeling well enough. The numbness was fast acting, spreading through his bad arm and radiating through his aching shoulder. With shaking fingers he pulled the dart out of his flesh and flung it underfoot. He couldn't drop now. He was so close to the Dust Town.

As the drugs began to take effect, Bas's legs grew heavier. He stumbled to his knees, hitting the dirt before he jolted back to his feet and struggled to keep running.

Another tranq dart hit Bas's boot with a *thunk*, but it

couldn't do any harm there. He nearly fell as he passed the first buildings, clipping his leg on a low dirt wall as he swerved from his course.

"Bas. You hit?" Cowl urged him to the side from his cover behind a crumbling wall.

"Tranq," Bas said, his words slurred. "Give me a minute. I got it out before it could do any real damage."

"You don't have a minute," Cowl said, glancing out into the waste. "Come on, this is ridiculous. How am I the only one who hasn't been shot yet?"

A dart sank into the wall of the building a couple feet away.

"They are shooting blind," Bas said. "I think they've lost us. Let's keep it like that."

"Don't tell me you have more ideas. No more ideas. I don't think we can survive any more of your ideas."

"I was just going to suggest we hide," he said, struggling to keep his eyes open.

"I could go for that idea," Menrva agreed.

Nodding curtly, Cowl scooped his body under Bas's arm to support him on his feet. It was all Bas could do to hold back a scream as the dislocated shoulder wrenched against the offered help.

A dust town was a web of mud-daub houses cobbled together with whatever people could scrounge from the unclaimed garbage. The alleyways were close and claustrophobic, the ground alive with rodents.

Spots of light like foreboding ghosts rebounded off the brittle structures. The Borgs slipped in, silent in their heavy armor apart from the occasional thud as the plates struck one another.

Bas's legs were failing as they found a small space under a beaten piece of recycled metal siding that hung awkwardly from a nearby shack. Cowl helped him slide in, and Bas barely managed to swallow a groan as he rolled over his dislocated arm.

Menrva crawled in beside him, her skin damp from sweat and blood where it rested against him. She pressed close to Bas in the cramped space, her breath echoing in short, shaky bursts. Though it was probably an odd thing to notice in the situation, he couldn't help but marvel at how good she smelled. He relaxed against her warmth, leaning his head on the rock below. Releasing a sigh, he allowed his eyes to close as he gave in to the pull of the drugs.

Chapter Thirteen: City of Dust

Bas's pulse beat firmly against Cowl's thumb. A bit fast, as was typical for him. His heart had to work extra hard to fuel such a big body. If it was just a common sedative in the tranq, it wouldn't have much effect on him. A few minutes and he'd be back in action.

Didn't mean Cowl couldn't worry a bit.

"So, now what?" Menrva whispered.

Cowl scooted to a lying position and tried to get a glimpse at the world around them. "I've got a few contacts in this dust town. Of course, I didn't think we'd have the Borgs hot on our asses, but I've got a lot of guys down here who owe me." It wouldn't be as comfortable as the cave, but a few places even had generators. They'd lay low, wait for things to settle down, which would give him a chance to work on Bas's Live Metal some more. Then they could find their way out with the right smugglers.

Menrva's elbow bumped against his ribs as she shifted her weight. Her face was set into a questioning look as she studied Bas, almost nervous. He was a bit intimidating. After three years, Cowl had lost any reasonable fear. It was hard to be scared of a guy like Bas. He was the stereotypical gentle giant. More than that, he was fragile, in his own way.

If Menrva could see the stuff Bas had to deal with on a daily basis, the way he struggled at first to even talk or smile, she wouldn't have been so scared. He could kick ass when he wanted too, sure, but most of the time he was a barely functioning shell of a human. Sad, when he thought about it. That's why he didn't like to think about it.

Stupid Nerve, coming into his life and reminding him what normal used to look like. Then again, he'd asked for it. So not stupid Nerve, stupid him. No. Still stupid Nerve. She'd been the one who got them in this situation now.

That could possibly be his fault too, but he wasn't going to try to figure out how. There was enough to worry about right now.

"He sure spends a lot of time unconscious," Menrva said, crossing her arms over her chest.

Cowl chuckled. Since she'd known Bas, he had been out of it, sure. But so had she. "Isn't there some saying about a pot calling the kettle black?

Menrva shrugged and turned to look outside.

Bas cleared his throat and Menrva jumped like a shot had been fired.

Cowl chuckled. "Hey, brother. How you doin'? Did you enjoy your nap?"

Bas grunted and carefully shifted his weight. Poor guy, never could seem to get comfortable.

"I don't understand why we came here," Menrva said, ignoring Bas. "Because right now it looks like we just locked ourselves into a really bad place."

"Why don't you leave the thinking to those of us who actually do so before acting, hey?" Cowl snapped.

Menrva's face seemed to freeze over as she turned to look at him. Shit, how did women do that? He had to learn that trick; he could save on bullets.

"That's interesting, coming from you. Impulsivity is a central cog to your tiny, inhuman heart.You are still alive today because you don't give a shit about anyone else's life. So no, I'm not going to leave the thinking up to you." Her voice raised a few decibels. "If you think I'm trusting you with my life, you'd better put that so-called intelligence of yours to better use. The only reason I'm still here is because I'm already dead, thanks to you."

Bas laughed awkwardly.

"I wasn't being funny," Menrva snapped. "And the fact that you can laugh at that makes you as much of a jerk as him."

"Hey." Cowl twisted to look at her. It was one thing being an ingrate, but there was no need for name-calling. Bas just didn't know how to read people.

"Now might not be the best time for an argument," Bas said. He carefully climbed to his knees, body pulled in tight to fit the small space. "I don't see the City."

He unclipped the scope from his rifle and scanned the horizon. The dust town looked haunted in the green cast of the night vision. Rats skittered back and forth intermittently, disappearing into the lumps of garbage that marked the outskirts of the dust town. A few child-sized people skulked around in the darkness, deformed and shrunken from a lifetime of dietary deficiencies.

A couple feet away a man lay at the edge of the settlement, waving away rats as they snuck ever closer. His legs were long since rotted away and skin hung from his arms like a tattered robe. This world was full of the living dead.

That was all normal. The only reason to freak out was if they caught sight of a Borg, and the coast looked pretty clear.

Cowl shimmied up through the tiny space afforded by their hiding spot and twisted around for a double check. Yup. Clear.

He kicked Bas's arm and waited until he'd pulled himself out and settled in the dirt.

"So...back and around, or through?" Cowl asked

Menrva shoved her way out of the hiding spot and pushed away the hand Bas offered in help.

"What kind of help are we going to find here?" she asked, rubbing her injured hip.

Dust towns weren't much more than collections of Bunker's criminals and unwanted. Some had been thrown out of Bunker for their crimes, forced to work in the mines. A rare few had been born down here. Others had escaped execution to find a place in the wasteland below. Here they could die a lot more slowly. Resources were always getting lower and the tunnels had become increasingly barren and fragile.

The City found a use for the Pit's population, which was why they never really exerted any effort to do anything about them. Scavengers weren't a danger to them, and the only blight moving from the Pit up to Bunker itself was the illegal shit that kept Cowl in business.

Occasionally the City sent down a few trucks of food and

water to keep their workers alive, but for the most part everyone here lived on the brink. Guards came through daily, indiscriminately herding people into the mines without regard to age, health, or gender, often shooting anyone who tried to escape. There were probably worse things. Mom had always said that someone, somewhere has it worse than you.

People said stuff like that because they liked to feel better about their shitty lives. For Mom, it hadn't worked. Cowl didn't like to play around with those kinds of lies. Someone might have it worse than you, but it didn't mean your life sucked any less.

A pale blue flicker caught Cowl's eye. When something was out of place in the Pit, it was always immediately obvious. That light was one Cowl knew well. Technology.

Clusters of people walked toward it, dull and zombie-like as they trailed along after each other. Well, that was probably not a good sign. If they followed, they'd be like a couple of zits on a teenager's face: obvious as hell.

Going around the edge of the dust town to the pot farm where his contact lived was a really good way to get caught. No doubt the Borgs were already watching the exits.

"What do you say?" Cowl motioned toward the glow. "Shall we join the party?"

Menrva scowled, shaking her head. "So, run toward the death. I thought you were supposed to be the smart one."

"Okay, look. Peace." Cowl held up his hands. "I was a bit harsh. Can't have you shooting me in the back."

Menrva muttered under her breath, just low enough that

Cowl couldn't quite catch what she was saying. It was strange, thinking that at one time this woman had been as close as family, if not closer. She was a mystery now.

"Are you okay?" he asked. Maybe if he made an effort she'd meet him halfway. She seemed willing when he'd asked her for help for Bas.

"I'll be okay for as long as I need to be," she said, a distinct note of bitterness in her tone.

Shaking off the frustration, Cowl tucked his gun close to his body and slipped into the stream of passing people. Most didn't even seem to notice. Those who did focused on Bas.

Because they were missing several, important dietary needs and vitamin D, most Pit dwellers were tiny and fragile. Bas, as much as he tried to make himself smaller, could barely pass as the same species as the malnourished humans rushing around them. In fact, some might say he wasn't. Those 'some' were idiots, of course, but idiots existed.

"Maybe we should get out of the flow," Bas suggested as they drew closer to the center of the dust town. The dust cleared as they got deeper in, and oil lanterns burned, making it easier to see their surroundings. Mud was built up around repurposed slabs of siding that had been salvaged and put to use. Between them alleys opened up, meandering in skinny, intricate webs until they disappeared into the darkness. Typically, if you had to go into the center of the dust town, you wouldn't want to find yourself in those small spaces. In the open, you could move fast and pull your guns...or get your ass out of there if need be. In the alleyways, gangs of starving children and desperate loners took advantage of the tight spaces to tear apart anyone foolish enough to get close. Hunger was one of those things that turned people into Wreckers. People were bad enough as it was.

Cowl slid his body through the tight space, hoping Bas could make it through. Menrva's breath reverberated off the walls, tight and panicked and so close to his ear that it might very well have been his own breathing. Either way, it was too loud.

"Keep a look out," he whispered loudly as he kicked aside a rib cage laying exposed in the dirt. "We aren't going to hang out in here longer than we have to."

Bas looked like a bug pinched between two fingers, wedged like he was between the walls. If he had to, he could probably just break down the houses on either side. But that would get them some unwanted attention.

Clamoring, violent noise forced its way through the alley, filling it like a physical force. Cowl paused at a cross-section between buildings and considered the widening space in front of them.

"Stay here," he whispered, pushing toward the blue light and the low roar of human voices. Tech meant City, and Bas needed to stay clear of the City.

"Like hell," Bas answered. He couldn't do much about it, though. He could barely fit as it was, much less slide around Menrva.

Menrva shoved right along after Cowl, though, her face set in determined anger. Of course, stubborn woman. Maybe it was better they stay together anyway.

The alley came to an abrupt halt into a sort of city center. The raw, beaten earth hid beneath hundreds of people surrounding what could only be described as a tank. It was far bigger than the typical four wheelers and Rovers that guards usually brought out from the city. A man stood on the highest point, silhouetted against a massive screen that had folded out of the vehicle. People pushed up against the side of the tank, reaching out with bony hands even though there was nothing being given.

"These are incredibly dangerous criminals." The voice of the man on the tank echoed out over the crowd.

A group of pictures floated across the screen. Menrva, sullen and blue-haired. The picture of Bas was ancient, barely recognizable with his shaved head and sunken eyes. How crappy of a situation did you have to be in to actually thrive in the Pit? Cowl's own picture made him chuckle. He was a good-looking kid, but he was still a kid. The only thing missing from the photo was a binky and a worn blanket.

"Because of this, the City is willing to offer a full pardon for any crime and free living quarters in the Hub for information leading to the capture of the criminals. Nothing will be given if they are dead," the man continued.

"I think I shot the gears on this one," Cowl whispered.

"That is our cue to get out of here," Menrva suggested. "I have a feeling these people would kill for a scrap of bread. A pod in the Hub? No chance we get mercy."

That wasn't a completely wrong assessment. As much as Cowl wanted to hear about just how dangerous and capable he was as the bad guy in the City's little fairy tale, they couldn't trust good luck anymore. Especially since none of them seemed to have much of it to begin with. The man continued his announcement amid cries for food and water as Cowl turned to the others.

"Shit, that kills my plan. Anyone we could have gone to is gonna want to turn us in now. That's too good an offer," he said.

"The Borgs will have surrounded the dust town by now," Bas said tonelessly. "It's suicide to head back into the Waste."

Cowl cringed. Bas's voice held none of his classic fumbled attempts at emotion. When he dropped pretenses like that, he was really getting worried. It was probably because he knew there was really only one option from here.

"Capricorn's place?" Cowl asked.

"Wait." Menrva held out a hand, her voice almost loud enough to alert the edges of the crowd outside. "Capricorn? I know that name. Capricorn Pierce? Like the mass murderer?" Capricorn was a name that came up often in Basics as Bunker's most recent example of a deranged terrorist, but everyone thought he was dead. About twenty years ago Capricorn had blown the support off a housing unit in the Industrial Tier, dropping the entire structure and over five hundred people — families — sleeping inside, to the ground. Menrva knew coworkers who'd lost family in that disaster. It was a fresh wound in Bunker's scarred history.

"He's not a mass murderer," Cowl said, pushing her back the way they came. She jerked away like he'd burned her. No touching. He could catch the hint, but she had to do the same and go back the way they came so he could move. "He was framed. He is, however, a genuine jerk."

"He won't turn us in?" she asked.

"No, they won't give him a pardon," Bas said, sliding back through the alley, gun first. "He knows too much."

Chapter Fourteen: Unexpected Places

Menrva turned the phrase over in her mind a few times. Knows too much. Too much about what? About the City? About Bas?

That didn't sound like a positive thing. She didn't want to place her life in the hands of Capricorn. He sounded dangerous.

Cowl and Bas seemed confident. It probably shouldn't have comforted her as much as it did. They had, after all, caused quite a bit of hell for her already.

She stumbled on something underfoot, and the pain dragged her thoughts back to the present. Her hip couldn't take much more of this.

Surviving had to be the main focus. At least she had a gun and two men, both armed to the teeth, with her.

Cowl grabbed her from behind as she approached the end of the alley. She shrugged off his hand quickly, but froze in her tracks. Just outside of the small alcove, bodies pushed around in a mass. They stopped, as if time itself had been paused, and parted. A great hulking figure, even bigger than Bas, strode through. Red light refracted off sliding plates of armor, each shifting in perfect rhythm with the movement of its host like a living creature.

Menrva didn't need to be told it was a Borg, not with the

familiar armor in place. She'd seen the same thing in every Tournament Sim she'd played. Every tactical shooter Sim. Somehow, it seemed more real in the virtual world, but the very presence of the Borg pressed in on her consciousness. She couldn't even breath until it passed by the alley, eyes set ahead.

It wasn't until the crowd began to move again, shoving and clamoring, that she trusted herself to take in a gasp of musty air. It didn't help much with the lightheadedness.

"Here."

Bas's deep voice made Menrva jump. Thank God he wasn't in that armor. He was intimidating enough as it was.

Bas waved Cowl down a side alley to the right and motioned for Menrva to follow. He had pulled his handgun, but even that looked too big for him to easily maneuver in the alley. Menrva pulled her own gun before slipping into the passageway. Cowl was in front of her, so hopefully he would intercept a threat before she had to pull the trigger, But she wasn't going to depend on it. If she was the one who could get into position the fastest, she couldn't just ignore that because she didn't want to shoot anyone.

A soft grinding noise emanated from Bas as he slid into the alley behind her. He had angled himself sideways and now his tech ground against the dried mud that formed the walls.

"I have no clue where I'm going," Cowl hissed. "It's like a maze in these alleys"

"Let's just get clear of this mob," Bas said, keeping his voice low.

From the sound of it, that was a good description of what

the crowd was turning into. Cries for food and water morphed into screams and angry yells. A few gunshots went off in the center of the town and the groan of the vehicle driving away echoed through the walls, as if the whole Earth was growling. As that settled, and a cloud of dust blotted out the soft light from Bunker overhead, the yells reached a new fever pitch.

If those people got ahold of them now, they would tear them to pieces long before anyone could turn them over to the government.

"We need to pick up the pace," Bas said, his voice like the roar of an engine so close to Menrva's ear.

"Why? They are gone," Menrva said. Despite that, she followed Cowl as he veered down another alley and sprinted across an open 'street,' gritting her teeth to keep from yelling in pain from the bullet wound. A few people drifted around aimlessly. They must have avoided the mob. One of them let out a yell as Cowl slipped into another alley and frantically waved for Menrva to follow.

Cowl twisted to climb under a sagging wall. Menrva slipped through and checked to make sure Bas could follow. He shoved through with impressive dexterity for his size and urged her on.

The roar of the frenzied crowd grew all around them until it filled the air. Bas turned his back to her, working to pull his gun around.

"They're in the street," he said, shoving Menrva forward with one hand. She stumbled, swearing at the stabbing ache traveling up her ribcage and down her leg with each step.

Bas fired off a few shots, the boom echoed through the alley until Menrva's ears rang. Cowl scrambled to a stop, shoving her back as they reached an intersection. The alley ahead was choked with boney human forms, shoving and pushing, scrambling over each other in their eagerness. The wall behind them gave way, collapsing on them to a chorus of squeals and yammering.

To her left a pile of reeking garbage, more living rats than refuse, blocked the opening of an alley. Menrva grabbed Bas's shirt, tugging him toward the pile as he shot off a few more rounds.

"Cowl, here!" She climbed through the heap as much as over it, scattering sticky bones underfoot and shoving aside the scrawny bodies of what could have been hundreds of rats. One ran up her arm, biting her on the shoulder before she snatched it off and threw it against the wall. The alley on the far side was mostly clear, though the walls on either side seemed precarious at best. Holes and cracks running along the walls gave the alley the appearance of a mouth grinning around missing teeth.

Ahead of them, the soft reddish glow of the open street beckoned. Her hip was starting to go numb from the pain and she almost had to drag it forward.

Her heart slammed into her stomach as she got a clearer view of the street just in front of them. Pit dwellers filled the space, pushing and clawing at each other in an attempt to reach the alley they had just climbed into. They were going to have to shoot their way out of this.

"What do we do?" she asked, slowing down to look behind her.

A hand, thin and fragile, shot from a shadowy alcove in the wall and grabbed Menrva's leg, pulling her to a complete halt. She barely managed to swallow a yell, more from the pain in her hip than surprise. She pulled away and aimed her gun into the hole, forcing her hand to hold still. A slim, dark-eyed face appeared from the darkness. It was a woman, most likely. Hard to tell. She raised a thin finger to her lips, hushing them without fear as Cowl and Bas lowered their guns at her.

With a glance into the busy street, she waved her skinny fingers, beckoning them closer.

Swallowing hard, Menrva leaned in, careful to keep her gun aimed. The alcove was actually a tunnel. It had been dug out, probably by hand or with a small piece of metal, based on the lumpy, round shape. It was impossible to see where it went, but as soon as the woman saw Menrva notice, she slipped inside.

Menrva looked down the alley and back at the mob tumbling over each other in the street. There was no other way out. Maybe this woman was leading them into a trap, but they had guns. It couldn't be any worse than the situation they were in now.

Sliding her feet in front of her, Menrva scooted forward.

"Nerve. What are you thinking?" Cowl said, grabbing her arm. "It's a trap."

"What trap is going to be worse than this?" Menrva shoved past him and slid down the hole.

It wasn't deep, maybe four or five feet at the most. It opened into a slight drop in a dark, hot space. Blindly, Menrva lifted her hand, stumbling until she found the wall.

It was a good-sized cave, though she couldn't quite stand without hitting her head.

Bas slid down behind her, his presence obvious by his struggle to fit into the cramped space. Cowl followed with a string of swear words, and flicked his flashlight on the second his feet hit the ground.

Menrva ducked her head under her arm to avoid the sting of the light in her eyes.

It took a half-second for her vision to adjust. The woman who'd caught their attention sat pressed against the wall. She was so skinny it was hard to pick out any defining features on her but bones. Thick wads of hair clung in patches to her skull and hung over her sunken eyes. She was on her knees, but a quick appraisal showed her legs were severed not far below. With eyes flitting between the three of them, the woman wrung her hands and chewed her thin lips.

The room they were in looked like some sort of fissure but with a ceiling of hardened mud, making a sort of cavern. At the far end, where the ground wound steeply downward, two tiny children sat huddled. They looked like baby dolls that had been lost in the dark a long time ago. Glassy, squinted eyes watched them with intense interest.

As soon as the woman was able to quit blinking in the light, she waved her hands at Cowl. "Off. See. They see."

Her words seemed less inhibited by lack of knowledge and more by sheer weakness. As if it hurt to shove them out.

Cowl hesitated a moment, scanning the room before turning off the light. There was no real threat from the inhabitants.

Menrva slid down the side of the cave, letting her aching leg lay flat.

Who was this woman? She had been hiding here, with her children, and taken the risk of pulling three armed strangers into her home. Why? She obviously couldn't defend herself or her family. There was no reason for her to reach out to them, except pure altruism.

It made her chest burn to think about it. This woman was in the worst of situations — poor, hungry, half dead —and she had more than Menrva had in the Hub: family and kindness.

For a long time the only sounds in the space were the breathing of the others and the yells of the mob drifting down from above. It was hot and oppressive, and the stench of sweat and human waste filled the air. At some point Menrva must have drifted off, despite the smell and the ache of her wound.

She woke to the sound of the woman scrambling back down the hole, knocking dirt and rocks with her. "Gone. It is clear," she said, her voice still low.

Cowl turned on the light again, this time keeping the glare muted under his shirt. "Thank you," he said, his eyes scanning the people in the room with more compassion than Menrva had ever seen.

He pulled a bag out of his packet and opened it to reveal a couple handfuls of silver-clad rations inside.

"It's food." He lay the bag on the floor of the little cave. Tentatively, the woman picked it up and looked inside, her eyes shining with tears.

"Don't eat it all at once. They will make you sick. One can last a grown man three days," Cowl said.

He watched the woman for another second before turning and climbing back through the tunnel.

Sure enough, the alley was empty, as was the street at the end.

"I probably just killed that poor family," Cowl said as Bas climbed out and they set off down the street. "Someone will find out what they have and take it."

"You did a good thing," Menrva assured him, trying to ignore the renewed ache in her side.

As they worked their way through the alley and to the edge of the city, Menrva trailed farther and farther behind. With the crowds in the center of the dust town, it didn't take them long to reach Capricorn's small but distinct home. It might not have been a castle, but it had a different feel from the rest of the dust town. Settled, civilized.

Rays of iron stabilized the mud walls, though they leaned and sagged noticeably. A short wall wound along the edge of his property, more as a warning than any real impediment.

"Think we'll have time before the Borgs look here?" Bas asked, hanging back.

"Cap has a good system of bribes with the guards to keep them out of his business," Cowl said. "I'm hoping that applies here too, but we want to stay on guard. We might have to shoot our way out."

Menrva's stomach ached at the thought. They had just gotten here and it looked more civilized than anything yet.

Cowl knocked and, before he even stepped back, Bas had

his gun trained on the door.

The door swung open and Menrva had to squint to let her eyes adjust to the reddish glow. The man inside was a short, broad-shouldered man with a stern face. His skull had been crushed by something long ago, leaving a calcified lump consuming most of the left side of his face. His arms were long and powerful, ending in wide hands.

"Trouble?" he asked, his voice oddly clear and soft. Still, his distaste at seeing them was more than evident.

"Think we can get a place to duck and cover for a while?" Bas asked.

"It isn't like I have much of a choice." Capricorn waved a hand to urge them inside.

The hut looked more like a home than even the apartments in the Hub. It felt lived in and well-loved, and yet oddly empty. A lively fire glowed in a hand-crafted fireplace beneath a chimney of rocks and mud mortar. The furnishings were mostly built of the same, with old cloth draped over them or folded as bedding. He had managed to find something to use for paint and had created a variety of truly beautiful art pieces in sepia tones applied directly to the walls. The entire space had the solemn and thoughtful feeling of an old-fashioned study, though it was all cast in a media of soil and collected garbage.

"You must be new down here." Capricorn held out a hand to Menrva. "From the Hub?"

"I'm Menrva," she said. "How did you know?"

Cowl dropped the extra weapons on the floor before returning to hover over Menrva's shoulder, as if he was waiting for Capricorn to strike.

"You are far too healthy-looking to be part of the lot down here. Once your eyes start growing accustomed, it's easy to pick out newcomers," Capricorn said to Menrva.

He was contradiction incarnate. He looked worn and broken but moved as if he were a king, head held high and gait haughty as he led them into his home. "I don't know how you fell in with this lot, but if you want something a bit better, I can get you a well-to-do husband. You are pretty enough under that ungodly hair."

"I'm married," Menrva said. It wasn't entirely a lie. The divorce hadn't gone through yet. There was never a moment when she thought she would be grateful for that fact.

"Well, of course, you *were*. Can't waste perfectly good genes. But if he's not down here he's not your husband anymore." Capricorn pulled a large, yellowed bottle of water from his cupboard and blew dust from the lid. He dropped the bottle and a stack of cups on the table and turned his eyes to Bas.

"I told you there would be trouble if they found out you were alive. Didn't I, 459?"

Chapter Fifteen: Don't Name It

Menrva swallowed the fear climbing up her throat like vomit. Cowl and Bas didn't seem scared, but they weren't comfortable, either.

Bas rolled his good shoulder, his face twitching as he clenched his jaw. Life in Bunker was dehumanizing enough as it was without being labeled with a number like livestock. Capricorn's use of it was more than just disrespectful, it was almost an assault.

"You weren't saying anything new then and you sure as hell aren't saying anything new now," Bas said.

He sounded venomous. He hadn't so much as raised his voice yet but the change in tone made him sound dangerous.

Cowl brushed the dust from his hair, sending a cloud slowly drifting to the floor. "We could use some medical supplies. Do you have some antiseptic and clean cloth?"

"For the girl, sure. But you best get 459's shoulder back in its place first. It'd be a pity if that Live Metal got tweaked."

"I can take care of myself," Menrva said quickly. If that man came near her, she would shoot him, no questions. "Do you know how to fix a dislocated shoulder, Cowl?" She had a basic understanding of the procedure, but probably not the strength to pull Bas's arm back where it belonged.

Capricorn shoved a bottle of rubbing alcohol and a roll of bandages at her. "Let me. You're gonna make things worse."

Ignoring her morbid desire to watch, Menrva focused on cleaning her popped stitches. The wound looked worse than it was, thanks to the dried blood adhering her clothes to her hip. Bas had done a good job with the aftercare.

"How is it looking?" Cowl ambled over, crouching beside her. Maybe he was trying to distract himself from the scene behind them, too. He had always been a brick wall when it came to himself but sensitive about the few people he cared for.

Her fingers shook despite her best efforts, as she dabbed the crusted blood from her skin. She looked up at the worst time. Capricorn twisted Bas's arm slowly upward. Bas held his ribs in his good hand, his face contorted. With a sick pop the shoulder slid back into place.

"Man up," Capricorn said. "You were trained for this shit."

Menrva looked quickly back at her own wound. She'd just started to tape the bandage in place when Bas pulled her fingers away. His hands were so big it seemed he could have wrapped one of them around her entire waist. But she barely felt them, he was so gentle. His finger trailed along her skin as he pulled his hand away to reach for a bandage, and a shiver followed it. Menrva swallowed the knot rising in her throat.

"Just checking," Bas said.

"Were you trained in medicine?" Menrva asked as he ran

his fingers over the stitches.

"Field trained, but I've been on the receiving end of a fair share." He grinned as if he were part of an inside joke. "I'm pretty impressed by you; all that running after getting shot?"

"Menrva's a badass," Cowl said. "I should know, everyone was terrified of her in Basics."

"*You* weren't," Menrva said. He was being nice again...as nice as he ever was.

"Sergio bet you wouldn't hold still for that knife-between-the-fingers trick," Cowl continued, his eyes alight with the memory.

"I remember. It was a horrible trick, I still have a scar." It was not the only scar she had.

"Badass," Cowl repeated, smacking Bas's arm. "She punched him *with* the hand he stabbed. He was covered in blood, his and hers."

Bas grinned as he smoothed the bandage in place. Menrva stuffed down the warmth traveling from the palm of his hand into her entire body. Foolishness.

The story reminded Menrva of home, and the muffled fear at the thought that she could never go back to the Hub. Would she become one of the pale, bony creatures filling the darkness outside?

"You still got the guards eating out of your hands? How long you think we've got?" Cowl asked, turning to Capricorn.

"Guards? Boy, it's been three weeks since we've seen anyone down here. No work on the mines, no new people, no food or water. If you'd come around like you were supposed to, you'd know that already."

"No mining? Really? No food?" Cowl rubbed his hand violently through his hair, a sign of his agitation.

"Did I stutter?"

Cowl lifted his lip in a sneer and kicked a bag of supplies he'd dropped on the floor.

No wonder the citizens had been so desperate. If it had been even a few weeks ago, maybe they would have been safer in the dust town. Maybe that's why Cowl brought them there in the first place. People did crazy things when death was near.

Why would the City even do that? She'd heard rumors, conspiracy theories, about violent population control in some of the tiers. The idea the City might kill off the people they didn't feel were necessary to survival wasn't too far-fetched, especially not after everything that had happened. But the Pit *was* necessary. Even recycling everything, they needed new resources every day.

"Has the City ever done anything like this before?" she asked, interrupting Cowl's miniature tantrum.

"How the hell should I know? Hasn't happened in the twenty-something years I've been here," Capricorn said.

Menrva studied Cowl's face carefully. Was he not at all worried by that? Was he so focused on his crusade for Bas that he was unfazed by something potentially life-altering? Survival was a precarious thing. She'd always been taught that if the City didn't play its role, ensuring everything happened exactly as it was supposed to, everything would fail. Now it was the City who was deliberately changing. Why? There had to be a reason.

Cap rubbed the scruff on his jaw and looked over their pile of supplies. "You can't be parking your asses here. They'll be by sooner or later."

"What's the plan, then?" Menrva asked.

"Forget a plan," Capricorn interrupted. "Turn yourselves in."

What did he mean by that? Was he planning on betraying them?

"You've been so arrogant, thinking you've outsmarted them with lead bracelets and some fancy coding. The only reason why you are still alive right now is because the City thought 459 was dead." Capricorn sat heavily into a makeshift armchair. "You have in your hands the most important piece of technology in the world. Period. You think they are going to stop with a man-hunt?"

Menrva glanced over at Bas, trying to gauge his reaction. *Technology.* Did Capricorn not even care what Bas heard him say? The muscle twitching in Bas's clenched jaw was the only acknowledgment he gave to the statement.

"You seem to know a lot," Menrva said. Cowl had pointed out Capricorn's familiarity with the City. Maybe if he could give them some of his insight, they'd have a chance at coming at this whole deal a bit more tactfully.

"Too much," Capricorn replied, looking around the small hut. "If we are having this conversation I need my moonshine."

"Then let's not have the conversation," Bas said, his low voice tumbling out like a growl.

What conversation was he intending on having? They needed to plan, not to waste time on stories. Menrva opened her mouth to interrupt, but the look Capricorn shot her stuffed the words right back in. Clearly, he felt she needed to hear this. She would just have to glean the information she needed.

"The lady asked." Capricorn retrieved a well-used, blue glass bottle and pulled off the lid. He sighed as he situated himself across from them. "I may not look it anymore, but I am one of the top scientific minds of Bunker."

"I don't think you ever looked like it," Cowl said. "Bashing that skull in was an improvement. It could use more, in fact."

"Shut up, boy, unless you want to fare out there with the scavengers," Capricorn said. "It's good she knows this. You didn't fill her in on all the details, I'm sure."

Menrva studied the two now-silent men beside her. Bas stared into space, his eyes unfocused in a blank and unfeeling visage.

"I started out same as most." Capricorn began. "I was assigned to a project by the City, aiding in the genetic engineering of, well...him." He motioned toward Bas. "Him and three hundred ninety-nine other children. Generation Four. It was a failure. An utter and complete disaster. Something went wrong on the genetic level and got replicated across every single subject."

Capricorn paused for a deep drag of moonshine. The alcohol was strong, by the scent of it on his breath, though he didn't show any of the effects.

"We pulled the product from the incubators, literally a year worth of resources. The boss took one look at them and said to cull them. All of them."

Rage threaded its way through Menrva's body. "*Cull*?" she asked. "You mean kill." Four hundred babies. One baby was a loss. How could anyone willingly harm a child, much less throw away four hundred? Capricorn was so cavalier about it.

"There is no use for a mutated baby." He took another chug of alcohol, his lip curling with obvious disdain. Maybe he wasn't as callous as he was sounding…maybe it was the alcohol that numbed him.

"We didn't have to be happy about it. I was a father, Menrva. Don't think for a minute I didn't care about those kids." Capricorn must have sensed her disgust. "We don't have sufficient resources for our own progeny. I doubt most of them would have made it past a year, anyway. Lung mutations, breathing issues. One had bone growing outside its body like a second skin. Nasty." He paused his list of excuses and stared up at the ceiling before continuing.

"We usually cull infants in the Topside airlock. We just throw them in and open up the hatch. It's quick and effective, doesn't use any resources."

"After we closed the hatch and started pulling out the dead we noticed a few of the infants had survived. Five, to be exact. Five out of four hundred."

"We did some tests and found that each of these infants had a specific mutation that created another chamber in both lungs, allowing them to recycle the CO_2 they breathed in and survive without oxygen."

"Like a Wrecker," Menrva interrupted.

"Close. It's really a whole new evolution of that

adaptation, superior in most aspects. Not only does it essentially recycle breathable air, it will filter out toxins and bacteria in the environment. Most Skins have modifications allowing them to survive in extreme conditions. They have to be able to make it on the surface even if their armor is punctured. This lung mutation is something else altogether. As far as I know, 459 is the only survivor from that generation. The other four died of complications over the years." Capricorn looked over at Bas expectantly.

He nodded in answer. "G4S147 died during a test the year before I got out."

"Because *that's* intelligent," Cowl said, "Create super soldiers, then kill them all while you try to figure out what they can do."

Menrva shifted on the couch's hard surface and clenched her fist. How was Bas able to hold back from tearing this man apart? Resisting the urge to grab the bottle of moonshine and take a swipe with it was hard enough for her. "I don't get it. How can you bear to take up oxygen? They told me you weren't a mass-murderer, that you were framed. You are exactly what I heard you were even if you didn't drop that housing unit." The hot words rolled off Menrva's tongue, even as her mind screamed for her to think again and shut up. "If I were you, I wouldn't be able to even look Bas in the eye, and here you are acting like *he's* the one who's not human."

"He's not," Capricorn said, his face darkening. Menrva shuddered as his eyes glinted. "Not human enough. Not that it matters. The single most dangerous idea in all of history is the notion that we are equal. Class distinctions may seem arbitrary to you, but lines like these are what keep this species alive. Someone always has to be on the bottom of the pile or the whole thing falls. Socialism. The Protestant Reformation. The American Civil War...read your history."

He drew himself up until he blocked the firelight. Bas raised his arm like an iron railing between her and Capricorn.

"Don't presume you can lecture me on collateral damage. By protecting him," he motioned at Bas with one hand, "you are denying humanity the weapon that might finally exterminate the Wreckers. It means more soldiers like him will get ripped to pieces, more breaches will claim more lives, and more civilians will be culled to prevent overcrowding, just because you idiots got attached." He focused on Bas with a sneer. "You never should have named him."

Reckless anger rose in Menrva and she struggled to choke it back. Nothing good could come from it. The rage subsided when a heavy hand landed on her shoulder.

"Thank you, but it's okay." Bas's voice was low and calm in her ear, holding not even a hint of bitterness. How was that possible? It wasn't okay. Menrva had experienced what it felt like to be dehumanized before, to be treated like a tool to be used up and thrown away, and her heart hurt for Bas. Not just for him; for humanity. When had it become okay to treat people like this in the name of survival?

"You see, Menrva," Cowl said, his voice sickly sweet with

false nonchalance, "Capricorn here is what we call an asshole, but he's a necessary asshole. Cap hates everyone but he hates us least."

"I wouldn't even say that," Capricorn said. He dropped back into his seat. "But any enemy of Pope is a friend of mine."

"Pope?" Menrva asked.

"Jonathan Pope. He runs things," Bas explained.

"He's in charge of the Compound and the Borgs?"

"Borgs?" Capricorn laughed. "You are calling them cyborgs? I suppose I've heard just about everything by now. But Pope isn't just controlling this project, he is controlling the City."

Menrva had never even met anyone who knew the leader of Bunker. She wouldn't even know what to call him. President? Commander in Chief? King? According to history class the original government was carefully built to avoid becoming an autocracy. She didn't know any details on it, but one thing was made clear in Basics: the City functioned the way it did because of necessity. Somewhere between then and now, the government had largely shrunk away from the eyes of its citizens. They exercised their complete control of the populace but there were very few people who knew how it functioned or even the names of any officials.

Capricorn's face remained bitter as he stood and strode over to the cupboards. He pulled a handful of silver-packaged rations from a pot.

"Tomorrow I will be out until late. I expect to come back to an empty house. If it's not, I'll have two slaves to sell and a Skin to turn in. You understand?" he said as he tossed the rations to the three of them.

The packet was light in Menrva's hands. They contained anything she could need, in theory, but they were a far cry from the fresh grown produce and juicy meats she was used to.

"We're working on a way to get out of here," Cowl said. "Or we would be if you hadn't sat us all down for story time."

Capricorn shook his head in exasperation and stalked over to his dirty bed. Loud snores erupted the moment he fell into it.

Menrva ate her ration in silence, and no one initiated conversation. Even Cowl was quiet, for once. Bas glanced her way a few times, out of the corner of his eye. Why was he so worried about her? He was the one who should be upset, and despite it all, he was as placid as ever. If anything Capricorn said bothered him, it wasn't enough to break his facade.

No one removed their guns before they lay down, though. She wasn't the only one worried about what waited outside those doors.

Chapter Sixteen: Proof of Strength

Bas flexed his gloved hands, watching the ice fall off in sheer flakes.

This wasn't right, how did he get here?

The armor he wore didn't do much good against the coldness of the surface. His feet were frozen to the ground. A white fog obscured his vision. He dragged his arm over the face shield of his helmet, hoping to clear it away, but the stubborn milkiness remained.

Coughing against the cold, Bas carefully began to pick his way down the black, crumbling hillside.

If he was topside, why wasn't he Connected?

Because this wasn't real. Of course. He was dreaming, or maybe he was hallucinating. As soon as the thought took root in his mind, the fog retreated into the starless black sky. All around him bodies blanketed the frozen earth as far as he could see.

Bas slowed his pace as he approached the carnage, and his eyes fell on a single, massive Wrecker, standing in the center of the massacre. Its eyes met with his and something seemed to grow in the back of his mind.

"He sees...he hears..." The words pressed in on him, as if they were coming from inside and flowing out all around him. The Wrecker didn't move forward, but the whole world collapsed under its feet, sucking Bas toward it.

"Kill. Kill. Kill." The voice filled the void around him until everything was alive with them, hot and vibrant and oppressive. "Kill. Kill. Kill."

He dragged himself backward, trying to fight the force drawing him in. He clawed desperately at the moving ground, and he began to fall.

A second later he collided with something hard.

Bas blinked, rolling stiffly off the floor into a sitting position. Was he awake? This wasn't his bed. The dirt under his fingers was wrong. Too hard.

What if he had dreamed all of it? Was he in the Compound?

The thought cut the breath right out of his lungs. Struggling to stem the rising tide of terror in his veins, Bas forced open his eyes and scanned the room. Dirt walls, flickering fire, plastic bins stacked against the walls. This wasn't the cave. Where was he?

"Bas?"

It was Cowl.

Bas sighed deeply, rubbing his neck with one, shaky hand. Whatever was happening, Cowl was there. It couldn't be too bad.

"Hey, Brother. You have a bad dream?" Cowl dropped to the floor beside him, his voice low.

Across from them, Menrva lay on a thin blanket, curls wrapped around her cheeks. She slept like nothing had happened, one hand raised to cradle her face.

Snores echoed around the small room. Capricorn. That's where they were. The memory slowly drifted back to Bas, muscling out the soft voice still chanting its refrain in the back of his mind. "Kill. Kill. Kill."

There was no more meaning to those words than there was to the slam of his heart against his chest, or the way his body trembled violently no matter how much he tried to calm it. He was losing his mind.

"You okay?" Cowl asked, tilting his head so Bas had to look him in the eye. "Bad one?"

Bas tried to shake away the fog still hovering around the edges of his mind. His body felt lethargic still, numb, as if it didn't quite belong to him.

"Uhhh..." He pressed his palms against his eyelids. "No. No. Not bad, just different."

Cowl nodded slowly, concern painted across his features. Was it concern? Or was he just tired of this? "Bas," Cowl said, again moving his face into Bas's drifting eye line. "Hey. Stay with me, man. It was just a dream. You're just stressed out."

Was he? Could he blame it on something like stress? Just like he'd never been the master of his own body, his mind was often somewhere outside of his control. It had been okay for a long time. Maybe he hadn't escaped the insanity.

Sighing, Bas stretched out his legs, letting his body ease. Ignoring the pinch of the tech on his spine, he leaned back and dropped his head on the couch where he'd been sleeping.

"I know what you are thinking," Cowl said, joining him.

"Do you?"

Cowl pulled a gun out from behind his back, twisting

around for a moment in an attempt to get comfortable. "You are hating yourself for having another attack."

Was he? Close enough. He didn't hate himself, but he didn't trust himself, either. Nothing was safe from the Live Metal creeping through his body more and more each day. Not him, not anything or anyone around him.

"You realize that the same thing you think is weakness, is what proves they couldn't turn you into a machine."

"I don't understand," Bas said.

"Machines don't have bad dreams. Machines don't have rough nights." Cowl grabbed the bottle of moonshine Capricorn had half-finished from the table and looked down the neck. "You think he backwashed in here? He's gotta have something dangerous or gross, right?"

"So you think the fact that I'm weak --"

"Proves you were strong enough to stay human, when they tried so hard to turn you into Cap's version of things," Cowl interrupted, wiping the lip of the bottle against his shirt before taking a swig. He frowned and spit.

"My shirt was probably worse than Cap's lips." He looked down at his chest. "I feel like I just made out with a toilet."

He passed the bottle to Bas. "Want some?" he asked.

"You just said it was gross." Bas quickly put the bottle on the table.

"Oh, dear, sweet, naive baby Bas. That's the whole allure of alcohol." Cowl lay a hand on his shoulder before climbing onto the couch. "That's why I love you."

Bas shook his head and took a deep breath. He caught sight of Menrva, still in the exact same position, as her eyes flashed open. It was just a second before she closed them again and went back to her passivity.

"Get some sleep, Cowl," Bas said, pushing himself to his feet. He had to get away from Menrva, get out of her eyesight. The idea that she'd seen his panic attack made his skin itch. Cowl needed the sleep, anyway. It had been over thirty hours since they'd left the cave. "I'll take guard for a few hours."

Chapter Seventeen: Empty Arms

The Pit was always quiet. It was hard to believe there was anything but empty houses and ghosts around them. The numbers on Cowl's watch blinked 10:00 a.m., but somehow the five hours Bas had spent on watch felt like minutes. The lights hadn't gone out for the night, as they usually did, and thus hadn't blinked back on to signify the start of the workday.

Bas twisted the end of his scarf around his finger until it cut off the blood flow and the skin turned white. He released it and studied the rings left behind in the aching flesh.

Capricorn was right: he'd been trained to endure pain. In the end, that was what mattered the most. He didn't need to know how to patch up wounds; people didn't survive Wreckers. Combat training was more for muscle memory, if not just for distraction. When all was said and done, all he had to do was not pass out from the agony so that his body was the best tool it could be. But pain. You don't get used to pain.

Bas was jolted from his thoughts by soft footfalls approaching from behind, and turned as Menrva stepped up beside him. The light from the fire made her look almost unearthly, framing her in a warm glow. A crown rose from her forehead and wings of gold stretched out behind her.

Bas blinked, shaking away the image. That was just a trick of the shadows. Or of his failing sanity.

Her face creased with concern as she studied him, her large, dark eyes fixed on his face as heat climbed up his neck and cheeks.

"How are you feeling?" Bas asked.

She pulled her pale blue curls through thin fingers. "I've been shot. I feel like I've been shot." Absentmindedly, she twisted a few strands into a braid.

Bas tried to smile as she came to lean against the wall. She was a bit distant...not scared, just wary. He wouldn't describe her as cold or angry, but talking with her was like slamming yourself repeatedly into invisible walls.

"You probably shouldn't be standing by the door. You wouldn't want someone to see you," Menrva said.

Bas looked out. There was one thing he missed about his life before: seeing the surface. There was something about the sun that made life apart from it lonely, even if it was shining down on a dead world. The Pit was massive but he could never quite shake the feeling of claustrophobia. He had spent most of his life locked in a tiny, featureless room. It was probably a bit strange he felt so constrained in a hole as massive as the Pit.

"I just needed a break. I figured a few minutes couldn't hurt." Bas pulled back from the door and let it swing shut.

"Capricorn get to you?"

"He sure got to *you*." It was almost funny how frustrated she had gotten. He wasn't stupid, though. This wasn't only about him. There was something personal behind her anger.

Menrva crossed her arms sullenly over her chest. "People are jerks."

Sliding down the wall, Bas sat cross-legged on the earth and bare stone. She joined him, staring at the floor and trailing her finger through the dust.

Balancing awkwardly, she slid her legs out. "I guess it didn't hit me before now just how differently they treated you. I mean, my childhood sucked too..."

"I'm sorry."

A shocked look crossed her face. Did he say something wrong?

"See, that's why it's so weird to me: you're just so...sweet. And normal. I mean, besides the creepy hunk of metal fused on your back," she said.

Bas's stomach clenched. More often than not it felt as if the bionic spine defined him completely. So was it him she was so afraid of, or just the tech? And where did one end and another start?

"I wasn't always like this," he explained, heat rising to his cheeks. "When people treat you like... Well, I was kinda feral. I guess Cowl evened me out." He glanced over to where his friend was draped over the couch.

The memories of his first days away from the Compound were both his worst and best. He had never understood just how bad life was until he had a taste of better things. If you don't know what it feels like to have someone care about you then abuse wasn't quite as bad. Cowl was the first person to show him what it felt like to be human. At least, for as far back as he could really remember.

"Yeah, he's a pretty awesome guy. He got me through some shit, too." Menrva rolled a braid between her thumb and finger and studied the ground, oddly sullen despite the words.

Bas studied the young woman in front of him. Everyone was hurt. It was a normal part of life. It seemed so out of place in Menrva, though. If there was going to be one perfectly happy life in this desolation it should have been hers. He couldn't even put his finger on why it mattered. He hardly knew her. Maybe it was the fact that she had put herself in danger to help him, or maybe it was the innocence still drifting just under the surface, like a puddle under an oil slick. Maybe it was because there was just so much pain there. It filled her up and stole her away from herself.

"Do you have any good memories?"

His head snapped up and he studied her. Menrva wasn't looking at him anymore, making it even harder to decipher where she was coming from.

"Yeah. I do. I had a nurse when I was really young. She used to sing to me; rock me. I know it was her job: to make sure I developed correctly in those first years...you know. I used to sing those songs to myself every night to help me forget so I could sleep." Bas chuckled, the warmth of a blush spreading across his cheeks. Why did it feel so raw, so embarrassing? He hadn't felt so vulnerable when he first told Cowl stuff like that. "What about you? Any good memories?"

Menrva hesitated, her hands trembling as they slipped down to cradle her stomach. "I had a baby. A daughter." A whisper of a smile slipped over her face "I know a lot of women complain, but I liked being pregnant."

The words hit him like a physical blow. That's why she had been so angry when she heard Capricorn's story. Bas might not have had a good understanding of the traditional family unit, but there was some sort of deep relationship there.

"She was perfect. Her name was Angel. She didn't make it," she said, the smile melting away into anger.

Bas reached over slowly, acting on impulse, and wrapped her tiny hand in his. Empty hands. Hands that should have been cradling a child. There were things she wasn't telling him. The way her hand trembled told a story that words failed, but she didn't pull away.

Chapter Eighteen: Savage

A noise in the corner caught Bas's attention and he looked up to see Cowl watching with an expression of deep pain. He must have not known about the baby, either. At least his emotions were easy to read. He offered Bas a half-smile and climbed off the couch.

"Well, looks like none of us are sleeping." He dropped down in front of them. Menrva slipped her hand out of Bas's. His palm felt cold in its absence.

Bas tried to resist another glance at Menrva. Why did he need to keep checking? Even if she wanted his comfort, what could he do to help? How do you understand pain as deep as the loss of a child? He didn't even know what family felt like, much less parenthood.

Cowl didn't seem to have the same reservations. He handled the situation the same way he handled every situation.

"What I wouldn't give for some shaving cream right now." Cowl indicated Capricorn's sleeping form.

"Why?" Bas said. Capricorn was actually clean-shaven, more than either of them at the moment.

"It's...nothing. I'm just being dumb," Cowl grinned and punched Bas's shoulder.

"How are the guns looking? I didn't clean mine before we

laid down," Bas said, trying to ignore the small voice in the back of his head reminding him just how much of an outsider he was, even with Cowl.

"You know, I didn't even think about that," Cowl said, pushing himself to his feet. "I swear, Cap makes me crazy. Such a douche."

Bas cracked his knuckles and followed him. Cleaning the weapons with Cowl, checking the ammo and smoothing away the dust, was one of his favorite tasks. When he had first started settling into life outside of the Compound, the moments of meticulous labor helped to soothe his mind. He and Cowl had gotten to really know each other over the deadly puzzle-pieces. Every time he set his cloth to the detailed machinery, he was transported. Things just made sense.

"What about Capricorn? He said he wants us out." Menrva asked.

Cowl shrugged as he pulled his handgun from its shoulder holster and dropped it to the floor along with the already-impressive pile of weaponry. A few hollow points spilled from one of their knapsacks, rolling across the floor. Bas stooped to snatch them up but froze, his hand hovering over the loose bullets as someone knocked heavily on the door. His heart hammered in his chest in rhythm.

"Shit," he said, keeping his voice low. "Take cover." Where could they even find a place to hide? He shoved Cowl toward the shadows behind one of the couches and leaped over the clay monstrosity as another heavy-handed blow to the door stirred Capricorn from his sleep.

"Here," Capricorn whispered, holding out one of the

tattered blankets. Bas lay against the base of the shelf serving as Capricorn's bed and pulled the musty cloth over him, hoping its thin weave would be enough to keep him hidden. Across the room, Cowl hunched over Menrva, who was tucked into a ball in the corner. If not for the glint of Cowl's pale hair in the dying fire, he would have been invisible.

The door slammed open as Capricorn tugged the end of the blanket over Bas's face. "What the hell!" Capricorn yelled.

The blanket fluttered with each breath Bas took, sending bits of dust in whirlwinds over the floor, though he tried to control the gusts. Red light glinted through a large hole over his eye, just high enough that all he could see through it was the tail-end of one of Capricorn's murals. Carefully, he tilted his head back to angle the tear for a better view.

"You missed your drop yesterday," a grainy, voluminous voice replied. A man stepped into view, his body dissected by the threads crisscrossing the hole Bas looked through. Short, thin and bald except for a few gray hairs hanging over his forehead, the man looked like he had been pulled from the dirt like a potato.

"And what, you thought you could actually threaten me into getting you your stuff? Adorable." Capricorn's shadow shifted through the blanket, a ghost in the corner of Bas's eye. "If you would have just been patient, Sal, you would have gotten your load. Now...well...I figure I'll just skin you and add you to the rations."

A shadow crossed in front of Sal. A hunched, bony man stepped into the light. Bulbous eyeballs hung out of his sunken sockets, pearlescent like badly scratched glass. He skittered across the floor, barely keeping the tattered pair of underwear serving as his only clothing around his waist. A moment later he was joined by a second, equally piteous man. Their shadows undulated through the room, followed by crashes and clatters wherever they went.

"Hey, control your men!" Capricorn yelled.

"They're hungry. They didn't get their dinner yesterday because I didn't get what I paid for," Sal said, the threat obvious in his false concern.

"I'll get your shitty order, but you'd better call them off before I do something you will regret. Don't forget who's holding the rations."

One of Sal's sidekicks loomed in Bas's vision. Slobber coated his face from constantly wiping his hands over his cracked lips. A rancid smell preceded him, as if he were already rotting. The darkness hid his features as he approached, turning him into a wraith. Much closer, and he would see Cowl and Menrva huddled behind the couch... that is, if his eyes still worked.

"That is an impressive pile of weaponry. Which one of your runners got you that mess?" Sal asked. Bas cursed himself. Weapons were valuable, and there was no telling what someone would do to get their hands on an arsenal like they had accumulated.

"They are defunct," Capricorn said. "Scrap metal."

"Sure."

The man came closer, his flat feet slapping the floor as he neared the bed. Cowl and Menrva didn't move as the man scuffled around the beaten earth in his search for scraps. He obviously didn't care about guns, only his need for food. His desperate eyes glinted with muted firelight as they flashed in front of Bas. How had he not been discovered yet?

He held his breath, counting down each moment of safety. This couldn't last, not unless Capricorn did something. The muted conversation was either completely distracting him, or he didn't care what the scavengers turned up.

The shuffling paused, and a low humming sound emanated from the desperate man. Bas tugged the blanket, carefully exposing just enough of his face so he could see. The man stood only a few feet away, his face hunched low as he stared directly at Cowl and Menrva. He weaved, his claw-like hands scratching at his legs before he leaped back.

"Someone else is here!" His voice rasped and cut in and out, like a siren.

Without hesitation Bas reached up, grabbing the back of his head. He twisted, pulling the man backwards and shattering the weak neck bones.

"Hell!" Sal yelled as Bas tossed aside the limp remains. The second man looked up from his exploration of the kitchen with a yelp and ran toward the door. Cowl reached him first, skirting the couch and pulling his knife in one fluid movement.

Sal reached for a shiv at his belt, backing cautiously toward the door as he did. "Don't even think about it! I swear I'll spread your guts across the floor."

"Crap," Capricorn said, turning to glare at Bas. "He was

one of my best customers, too. You just had to bring your shit here, didn't you?"

"Don't think I won't do it!" Sal said, his bravado melting slightly as his back hit the wall. Bas reached him in a few broad steps and slapped the blade from his hand, sending it flying across the room. He yelped, clutching his arm to his chest.

"I'm sorry, I won't tell. I swear to it, no one will know you are here."

An undertow of pity slipped through Bas's guard, cutting through his cold determination. He let the taste of humanity battle his killing instinct, wishing he could take advantage of the rare emotion. The pleasure of the hunt still beat in the back of his skull like a threat, easily overpowering the moment of sensitivity. Still, it would have been nice to allow himself to actually feel the regret instead of forcing it aside. This wasn't just to protect his own life.

There was no choice to make, so maybe it was better Sal's begging bounced off his emotional armor. He could at least make it quick.

Sal's neck crumbled like a piece of paper under Bas's fist, the constant lack of nutrients having made his bones brittle. He slid down the wall, his eyes wide and mouth still open in protest as his head lolled on the crushed remnants of his spinal column.

"Shit. I hate the close contact stuff," Cowl muttered behind him. Bas glanced at him, raising an eyebrow as Cowl cleaned the knife blade on his pant leg. A pool of blood spread under his feet, still flowing from the cut that had all but disemboweled the scavenger. He frowned over at Menrva, stepping awkwardly away from the corpse before drifting toward Bas with a shrug.

"Well, the place needed a little color." He grinned, pulling out his characteristic humor, an obvious cover for his distaste. It was one thing shooting someone at a distance, but Cowl had never much liked using a knife.

"Nothing but trouble, you two. You are going to single-handedly cost me my business."

"I built your business," Cowl argued. "I'm your best runner."

"Starke was my best runner, and if you went the way your brother did, I wouldn't complain. Shit."

Behind the couch, Menrva stood slowly, surveying the damage with an unreadable expression. Maybe she was relieved for the rescue. More likely, she was realizing just how dangerous her new traveling companions were. Life was different in the Pit. Bas couldn't compare anything with the social structure of Bunker, not past what Cowl had told him. But even in the Compound, death wasn't as rampant or as gruesome.

Cowl looked like he was about to say something to her, reaching out for a moment before letting his hand drop limply to his side. It was easy, with just the two of them. They knew what needed to be done, but for once Cowl seemed just as confused about how to deal with a situation on an emotional level as Bas was. Cowl always knew what to do.

Bas edged in front of the fallen body. What did she think of him? That he was a monster? She was probably right.

"So, what am I supposed to do with these bodies now?" Capricorn asked, standing over the first scavenger. Menrva put a hand over her mouth and turned away.

"Just dump them," Bas said, looking down at the crumpled remains of Sal. What else was there to do? They could risk a run to the burial ground, the abyss where people dropped the bodies they didn't want ravaged.

"Or throw them in the pantry," Cowl said grimly as he pushed his knife into its sheath. "Anywhere you toss them, someone is bound to pick them clean anyway."

"I'm a high-quality dealer, I don't sell human flesh. But that's not even the issue here."

"Cut them thin and label it bacon."

"That's disgusting even for you, Cowl," Menrva said, skirting the body and edging toward Capricorn. "They are human beings!" He was probably looking a bit safer than the other options. If only she knew what he was capable of.

Cowl shrugged. "I'm too jaded to be sensitive about that shit."

"You know, Sal's wives are going to come looking when he doesn't bring home the rations he paid for," Capricorn interrupted.

"By then, he will be a skeleton," Bas pointed out.

"Wait, do bodies seriously get eaten down here?" Menrva interrupted.

Bas rolled his shoulders, shifting away from the dead man at his feet. Desperation made people do insane things, and there was nothing but desperate people down here, especially now. That was without factoring in the rats. This was as close to hell as you could get. It was inconvenient for moments like this, when three shattered corpses could draw more attention than was wanted.

"Salamander isn't a nameless nobody. People are going to miss him when they can't get their girls." Capricorn headed into the kitchen and began rummaging through one of the still-open cupboards.

"I don't regret killing him so much, now," Bas said.

"Why do you think they call him Salamander? He's a slimeball. My point is, someone might just recognize him and I'll get a good amount of angry customers at my door. Since you three are trying to keep a low profile, what's bad for me is bad for you."

Cowl kicked the floor and swore. "Just throw them in a corner. It'll be a few days before they start to stink any more than they do already."

"What would you normally do? I'm assuming this isn't the first body you've had in your house." Menrva crossed her arms over her stomach, her face twisted with disgust.

"What do I normally do?" Capricorn laughed. "Just depends what I'm getting paid to do. Some people want their loved ones buried, and we take them out of town. You can toss the little ones out the door, let the urchins have them. It's just Sal we need to worry about." He pulled a plastic jug from the cupboard.

"You just need to hide his identity?" Menrva asked.

"Here, out of the way," Capricorn demanded. He grabbed Sal by the arm and pulled him to the ground. "Good thing I've kept this on hand. I have use for it every once in a while."

"Is that hydrofluoric acid?" Menrva asked.

"Yes." Capricorn dragged the corpse through the door.

"I think I'm going to be sick," Menrva said, her voice muffled behind her hand.

Cowl grabbed one arm from the scavenger at his feet and pulled it across the floor. "You got a garbage pile?" he called from the door. When no answer came he shrugged and continued on his way.

Bas risked a glance at Menrva. She was uncharacteristically pale, her eyes focused on the floor. They hadn't even gotten the chance to really get to know each other, and she had already seen him kill multiple people. That had to leave a bad impression. He wasn't going to say he didn't enjoy it, as much as he hated that fact, but he had only done what was necessary. She might not understand it, but it was something he couldn't change. He kept her safe, kept Cowl safe, and that would have to be enough.

Distracting himself from the tangle of unpleasant emotions, he retrieved the remaining corpse and shoved his way out the door. A few weeks in the Pit would change her outlook a bit. The thought wasn't as satisfying as it should be.

Capricorn looked up from his task as Bas carried the body out the door and into the hazy light still blazing down from Bunker. "After that, you can drag your own sorry asses out of here. I'm just about finished cleaning up after you." He stood over Sal's body, unscrewing the plastic bottle with ginger fingers. With a furtive glance over his shoulder at the looming shanties surrounding them, he poured the contents onto the corpse.

There wasn't much to look at in the shadows of the Pit, but Bas could just make out the pale shape of Sal's face, bent on the disjoined neck. The clear liquid crawled over his skin, dripping into the dirt. At first, nothing happened, but after a few moments the flesh began to peel away in ragged chunks. Acid pooled into the grooves like tears, gradually dissolving the skin until bone glinted through the oozing red meat.

Why couldn't he look away? The destruction held some sort of chaotic beauty, a hypnotizing charm that went far beyond morbid interest. He tore his attention away from the unfolding drama, a shiver running through his whole body as a ghost of a smile tugged at his lips. He was a monster...maybe he should be in a cage.

Shaking himself free of his self-disgust, he walked to the edge of the walled-in area, squinting into the hazy atmosphere for any sight of watching eyes. Was there even a chance someone hadn't seen them? All he could hope was that he wasn't recognized. Nobody cared about a dead body. It was as common a sight as the crumbling hovels littering the broken earth, or the rats scattering with every step. He was the one thing that was out of place...and valuable, if they could connect the dots.

With that in mind, he dropped the body over the fence into the waiting tide of rodents and jogged back to the house. The claustrophobic space was far from safe but Bas let a sigh of relief slip through his lips as he ducked through the door.

Menrva hovered by the couch, a damp cloth clamped

between her white knuckles. "Here," she said, shoving the threadbare material toward him. "It's not a lot, but I thought you would want to clean up a bit."

He accepted the offer, cradling it in his hands. There was barely enough precious water on it to qualify it as a wet cloth, but he scrubbed the streaks of blood from his skin thankfully. Menrva watched, a parade of enigmatic emotions running across her features. Eventually she backed away, finding a seat on the couch.

Cowl sat on the couch, dismantling a gun and glancing anxiously between the door and Capricorn.

If Capricorn decided to follow through with his threats, they wouldn't make it far. What could he really do, though? They had the guns, they had the numbers, and even apart from that, Bas himself was enough of a threat to keep him from trying anything. He couldn't physically shove them out the door. So they had the upper hand, at least for now. Killing a stranger was one thing, but he couldn't stomach hurting Capricorn, as much as he disliked the man.

"So?" Menrva asked as Bas scooped up a rifle and extracted the bullets. "What do we do now?"

Cowl shrugged, stubbornly avoiding her eyes. "I don't think we can afford to waste any more time here. I'm not going to make any gambles that someone didn't see that."

"The sooner the better," Capricorn said, crossing the floor to shove the acid back into the closet. "What do I have to do to get you out of here?"

"Ready to beg?" Cowl asked.

"We need a way past the blockade," Bas said.

Capricorn narrowed his eyes, studying him with the same contempt with which one might regard dog vomit. "Just let me know what I can do to make your stay more uncomfortable."

The City wasn't the only reason Bas was motivated to move on. He could only handle so much of Capricorn's very particular brand of verbal abuse.

Chapter Nineteen: Trojan Horse

Bas rubbed his head, trying to massage away a growing headache. Capricorn's house was always a temporary fix, but getting pushed out too soon could only mean bad things. The Borgs would still be running sweeps, and the danger in the dust town would probably never clear.

"It's time we start putting together a plan," Bas said, dismantling the weapon in his hands and carefully pulling the cleaning kit from the bag.

"We could wait until the guards drive the daily quota down into the mines. That will give us some room around the citizens," Cowl suggested.

"You'll be waiting a long time," Cap said. "I already told you. No guards, no mining."

"Shit. That's right." Cowl kneaded the bridge of his nose and sighed. "That's just strange. And inconvenient."

"I've noticed a lot of strange stuff going on lately," Menrva agreed. "Food shortages, more arrests than normal. Back in the Hub, they've been cutting salaries and sending a lot of families into the tiers. It's not just in the Pit that things are different."

"Yes, but no one is starving to death up there," Cap muttered.

"That's not my point. What I'm saying is that something

is going on. If we believe what we've been taught, not much really changed for, what, a hundred and fifty years? Nothing on the civilian level at least." Menrva looked at each of them in turn, as if waiting for them to come to the same conclusion as her. "Something is changing. Something in the City. If we can figure out what, maybe we can take advantage of it."

Cowl shook his head. "That doesn't help us at the moment," he said.

"Why not? Sun Tzu: if you know your enemy and know yourself, you need not fear the result of a hundred battles."

"Don't quote Sun Tzu at me. We aren't trying to win stupid ass battles here. If we get in a battle, we are doing something wrong," Cowl sighed.

"Sun Tzu?" Bas asked. He'd never learned the names of most of the guards, but this person seemed well-known.

"Historical figure," Cowl explained briefly, waving his hand as if to brush away Bas's questions. "Look, Nerve, we are just surviving here. I don't give a shit why the City is changing their policies. If I did, I could probably figure it out. Everything is on a computer somewhere. They have their reasons. Maybe they want to lower the population. Maybe they've tapped out this mine shaft or compromised the stability on this side of the Pit. That won't help us at all. We know what they want. They want Bas." He shrugged. "That's all I need to know."

"But that's just it. They want Bas but they aren't trying to kill him. They used darts," Menrva pointed out.

Bas dropped the cloth he was using to clean the rifle.

"They have good reason to keep me alive," he said.

Menrva's brow raised. "That being?"

"Genetic material," Bas said, hoping she wouldn't need much more detail. It wasn't complicated, but with him having such a valuable mutation, they would want to continue the bloodline directly. If they hadn't gotten what they needed from the others in Generation Four before they died, it would explain why they would be trying to take him in alive.

"The other option: they want to see my mutation in action. They ran a few tests before I left. If they just get my DNA, they will have to wait until they got another Borg like me."

Cowl winced and cleared his throat. "Doesn't matter, they aren't getting you."

Menrva brushed aside the topic with a flick of her slim fingers. "Stop being so hard-headed. Just think about what this could mean. Maybe the Wreckers are dead, and they are switching their effort to colonizing and terraforming. Or, maybe they are running out of resources. There has to be a reason they are being so persistent." Her frown deepened.

It was odd, thinking of the City as having motivation. When Bas was young, they were all that life held. Cruel in many ways, sure, but also the only thing he could understand as normal. They were inextricable from either. As he grew older they'd become an ever-present horror. Evil and fear incarnate. He never knew their reasons for doing what they did. They didn't offer it and nothing would have been justification enough for what he was living through.

Menrva's argument made sense, though. When facing the Wreckers, they knew how to act because they knew what the Wreckers wanted. They were easy to predict.

Thinking of the City as a collection of human beings, with motivations like his own, made it seem like there was a way out of this. It also made Capricorn's arguments feel more real. What if they did need him, his lungs, his DNA? Was he putting everyone at risk just so he could die on his own terms? He wouldn't even live much longer.

"Whatever is going on out there doesn't matter to us. It's all bad news. The City doesn't give a shit about us," Cap said, his voice making Bas jump. "Only thing they care about is getting Bas back. Rest of us can go to hell, if they have their way. That's what the dust town is: Hell's waiting room."

Capricorn sighed heavily and pulled his moonshine from the cupboard. "You've effectively ruined what's left my life," he said.

"Yeah, you know what they say about payback," Cowl said.

Capricorn showed his middle finger in response and took a long swig from the bottle.

Bas laid a hand Cowl's shoulder. "Come on, we have to focus on how we are getting out of here."

"Please do," Capricorn said as he tilted the bottle back again. "I am about ready to deal out some hits of my own; you've all earned yourselves a bullet to the brain."

"I had an idea." Cowl leaned forward. "You know how the City framed Capricorn for that housing unit they dropped?

It's been a few years, but it was pretty far out. Maybe it's still intact. We can't go home, at least not yet. Maybe we can check it out. It will keep us out of the open."

"You want to live in a crushed tin can?" Menrva asked incredulously.

"It wasn't that far of a drop. It could be in pretty good shape still."

"I wouldn't want to be anywhere near it, but he's right. Most of the inhabitants were killed after the fact," Capricorn said, swirling the bottle. He met Bas's eyes with barely concealed rage, a sneer contorting his already twisted features. The wreck was personal for him, though Bas didn't know all the details. At the very least, it had been the source of his disfigurement.

Menrva opened her mouth as if to ask a question, but Cowl shook his head softly and she pressed her lips together and turned her eyes to the pieces of their arsenal.

"We aren't even looking at the obvious. How are we supposed to get out of the dust town?" Bas turned away from Capricorn's anger. With a bounty like what had been offered, there was a near guarantee most of the Pit dwellers would be hunting them down. That was, if there wasn't already eyes on them from the whole deal with Sal.

Cowl looked him up and down. "Yeah, I guess you are kind of hard to miss."

Bas sighed. "We all are."

"Even if we manage to get out of the city how are we supposed to get past the Borgs?" Menrva asked.

"We could split up? One of us might get through without getting caught," Bas suggested.

"By that you mean you think that we stand a better chance of getting through without you," Cowl said, glaring at him.

Bas shrugged. "It's not like I'm exactly subtle. You two might blend in better."

"Why do you keep trying to pull this crap? No self-sacrifice. None."

"Maybe we can sneak by without getting caught?" Menrva said.

Bas and Cowl both turned to stare at her. She obviously wasn't entirely sure what they were up against. Hopefully this wouldn't be too harsh a lesson. The City wasn't going to take it easy on them.

Bas cleared his throat.

"No," Cowl said. He pointed an accusatory finger at Bas. "No ideas. I hate your ideas."

"I haven't killed you yet."

"He's kinda right," Menrva said, turning to Bas. "You are a little reckless."

Reckless? He'd done his best to protect them, take care of them. Maybe he was still not careful enough. "What do you suggest we do?" he asked.

Both of them stared at him with blank eyes. After a few minutes, Cowl dropped his head into his hands. "Whatever. Just tell me your stupid idea."

Bas hid a grin. "We can do what Capricorn suggested: turn ourselves in."

"Finally, someone making some damn sense," Capricorn slurred.

"Yeah, next?" Cowl said impatiently.

"Seriously. They are using Borgs. That means they are all on a set signal. Cowl, you can jam it."

"I should be flattered that you have so much confidence in me, shouldn't I?"

"They will take us back to the Hub. If you hit the jammer at the right time, the Borgs will malfunction."

"Sure, if they don't just shoot us."

Bas shook his head. "They never execute anyone without collecting their genetic material first." He choked on the idea of being back in the compound. They had never had a breakout before, but insubordination was a death sentence. If he wasn't a Gen Four, that would be the end of it. Because he was, there was no telling what they would actually do with him. He couldn't think about that, though. If he did, he wouldn't be able to move. "None of that will happen because they won't get us there."

"You and your tricks. Sounds like a good way to get killed," Capricorn said.

Bas shrugged. "Dead is better than..." He frowned, the very words burning his tongue, and turned to look at Menrva and Cowl. It wasn't a good option, but it was all they had right now.

"Can you do it?" Menrva asked.

"No." Cowl was a bit loud with his denial. "You can't just guess what they will do. We might never get the chance to pull our trick. Then what? We all die, and you get tortured probably, and then die. I—"

"You hate my ideas," Bas finished for him. "But we either get caught and turned in without any plan, or we can go in prepared."

"I'm up for it," Menrva stated. "I know one thing about the City: they are powerful. They have so much control, they stopped looking for the 'dark horse.' They won't kill us right away, because they think we are the ones who should be afraid of them. They won't be looking for a counterattack. We just have to sell it."

Bas grinned. She wasn't a fool. Maybe even smarter than Cowl, and at least more practical. More than that, she was a good deal tougher than she looked.

"Fine. But I'm going on the record to let you know this is a shitty idea." Cowl pulled his tablet from his bag and crossed his legs. "Could take me awhile to get this programmed to do what you want. I wouldn't be opposed to a better idea if one surfaced in that time."

"You three deserve whatever you get," Capricorn said, his words turning into a string of incomprehensible curses as he stumbled over his own drunkenness. He dropped on the couch and lay as still as death, moonshine in hand.

"What about the civilians?" Menrva asked. "They are sure to be out there looking for us still."

"I had an idea about that," Cowl said. "I've got a few tear gas grenades..."

"Needlessly cruel. All we need is a window. Capricorn seems to have a large collection of used food wrappers. If we put a few of our full rations in there and throw it out into the street, it would send out the alarm."

"Just as many people would get killed in the stampede to get that food," Cowl said, snorting out a sarcastic laugh.

"But we aren't going to have to run through the tear gas," Bas said. "And I don't mind avoiding that."

"Fair enough," Cowl said, raising one eyebrow and grinning comically. "We should get going. I want to get out of here before he gets up." He jerked his thumb at Capricorn.

Bas tucked his hands into his pockets in an attempt to hide the shaking. He cursed his cowardliness. If something went wrong he would be heading back to the Compound, and no matter how hard he tried to reassure himself, the thought branded terror into his core. He struggled to shove the flashes of memory back into their glass bottles, and drew in a tortured breath.

Chapter Twenty: Catch and Release

A few feet ahead of Cowl, Bas carefully stepped into the empty street, keeping close to the flimsy building closest to Capricorn's wall. Menrva's little distraction had worked better than Cowl had thought. It was a bit fun too: like playing one of his old tricks. It was a clear shot out of the dust town but the hum of passing vehicles echoed through the buildings. The City wasn't taking any chances of them getting out.

2, 3, 5, 7, 11, 13... No. Not now. He had enough to think about. His brain had a stupid habit of feeding a list of numbers through the back of his mind. If he had something to distract him, it was easy enough to ignore the way he automatically measured every angle and calculated random equations. He definitely had enough to worry about. Running from the City was better than black market runs in that regard.

There was another problem. Cowl couldn't be sure, and there were probably bigger things to worry about, but there seemed to be something happening with Bas. Not the regular shit. There was the panic attack, and he kept rubbing his head and neck like he did when he had a headache. The Live Metal wasn't going anywhere. That wasn't it, though. The problem was that he seemed to be quite taken with Menrva.

Not that Cowl could blame him. She was intimidating, and it was hard not to immediately respect her. Sometimes it was easy to confuse awe and affection. He'd done as much when he and Menrva were teens.

Maybe he was being a bit too mothering. Bas might not have ever experienced this kind of shit before, but he was so not ready for it. Especially not with someone like Menrva. She wasn't going to exactly go easy on him.

Whatever she'd been through had really messed her up. The longer Cowl spent time around her, the more obvious it was. She didn't trust anyone and there was no telling what that might do to Bas.

Maybe he'd talk to him later, see where he was at. Tell him Menrva was trouble.

Maybe if he poked her just the right way, she would crack and tell him what happened. He had a few guesses. If she lost a kid, maybe it was a forced abortion: something was wrong with the baby. It wasn't super common but it happened on occasion. Or maybe they didn't decide until after she was born and...he gagged at the thought.

"Hold on," Bas whispered as he paused behind a sagging wall only a couple feet from the edge of the city. A few Pit dwellers wandered in the broken remnants of houses, picking through shallow garbage heaps and stumbling around cracks and pits. The citizens who were closest to death and had no one to take care of them were usually shoved out to the edges. There seemed more than ever before. It was an oddly frightening thought. Now that he couldn't just slip back into the Hub whenever he wanted...or at least, now that it would be harder to...how was he any different from any of them? It was easier to distance himself before. Sure, he lived in the Pit, but he didn't belong there.

They would figure something out. He'd set it all right somehow. Right now, they just needed to stay alive.

"Get low," Bas ordered, immediately shoving Cowl behind the wall and stepping in front.

Frowning, Cowl searched the collection of weapons around his torso for the distinctive worn handle of his shotgun. He'd stupidly agreed not to shoot anyone. Something he was regretting now. After all he'd done to keep Bas safe, and now they were just playing into the trap. If Bas wasn't right about them not killing people immediately, he wasn't going out without blowing a few brains. At close range, a slug could make a good dent in a helmet, maybe break through.

"I'm starting the clock," he said, pulling out his tablet. He hid it between his chest and the wall. The program was well hidden, good enough that no one would find it without a detailed search. He didn't expect that, though. With all the guns they were carrying, no one would be worried about a tablet.

Once the timer ran out, the program, appropriately dubbed 'Trojan,' would send a signal for the AI planted in City Net to cut the Connection. He was risking exposure with the AI, but if it worked, it would be well worth it.

A glaring light jutted over the horizon followed by a hideous beast of a machine. The Rover crawled over the earth like a gigantic cockroach, easily climbing over the landscape on its treaded wheels.

Menrva took off running, and Cowl bolted into action. Sure, they weren't getting far, but they had to make it look like they were trying.

Cowl risked a glance back, checking on Bas. He paced himself a few feet away, his shoulders bunched up the way they got when he was really scared. Getting murdered or captured might not even be their biggest concern. A stressed-out Bas was a scary Bas.

The sound of a gun spitting behind them slowed Cowl's steps. If playing at running scared was going to get them shot, then maybe it was time to put up their hands and get on with the whole charade.

"Bas..." he said, his throat tight.

Menrva paused and Cowl pushed her behind his back. No use in all of them dying. She couldn't handle a gun like he could. Didn't have the guts to kill someone.

The Rover bore down on them in a matter of seconds, dust billowing around it like a cape. Cowl bent his knees and took aim. Sure, it was an aggressive stance, but he was an aggressive guy. Mom had always taught him to be himself.

The light turned the floating pillar of dust into a yellow-brown mist. A shape moved inside and Cowl followed it with his gun. One of the lights pierced right through the dust, blinding Cowl with its intensity. He hadn't quite recovered before something massive slammed into his chest, driving him to the ground.

His first inclination was to pull the trigger. Well, first catch the breath that had just been ripped out of him, *then* start shooting. Even if his brain hadn't quite had the time to convince his body of how bad an idea that was, he wouldn't have needed it. The man who'd pinned him down clamped his arms to his sides as easily as if he were a paper doll and pressed a thick set of buzz cuffs in place.

Rough hands stripped away his weapons. They might as well have taken his clothes with it. He couldn't have felt more naked. If they so much as scratched his guns, he'd be taking names.

"G4S59 in custody, Sir," a voice called, slightly tinny as it reverberated through the helmet.

The Borg holding Cowl dragged him to his feet, jerking his arms. Why be rough? It was cliché.

"Fugitives in company. Cowl Coven and Menrva Penniweight, Sir."

Who was the 'Sir' they were talking to? It wouldn't be Pope. It could be a high-ranking guard, but there was a good chance whoever it was would have some sort of meaning to Bas.

"Bring them all on board," a female voice answered. Of course, he was using a Borg. He just picked a female.

Ahead of Cowl, a group of Borgs hoisted Bas onto the platform with a bit more aggression than was entirely necessary. If they weren't Connected, Cowl would have killed them all as soon as he got his hands on his guns again. He couldn't blame them for their User's stupidity, though.

A Borg threw Cowl up on the platform like a sack of grain and he managed to catch a glimpse of Menrva from the corner of his eye. She looked scared. A dirty scrape ran down her cheek. Her eyes were hard, though. Determined.

The sharp grate of the Rover's platform tugged at Cowl's legs as they dragged him to a corner and forced him to his knees. "Well, this looks like a party! So glad we weren't late!" he said.

The closest Borg slammed the butt of his rifle into Cowl's chest, sending a shockwave of pain through his body. It was so worth it. Besides, better they keep their attention on him rather than Menrva.

Choking on the forced laugh, he grinned up at the mirrored visor of the helmet. "No humor at this party. Note taken."

A long-legged female Borg turned her attention on him. She didn't have on her helmet, but her clear skin looked spotless despite the dust in the air. Her auburn hair was shaved close around her head, accentuating her heart-shaped face. She was far too pretty for the serious look turning down the corner of her full lips but it didn't do much to reduce the intimidation factor. Why were some women so scary?

She turned to look at Bas and set her feet firmly apart, as if she were about to salute him. "Examine the tech. I need to be sure there is no damage before we risk a Connection."

Cowl bit down hard on his tongue as one of the Borgs pressed Bas's head forward and ripped the back of his well-worn tank top to expose the bionic spine.

"A bit dirty, but overall it's in good repair," he said after studying it for a while.

Of course it was in good repair. None of those idiots had half the skill he did. The only way Cowl would have let it get damaged was if he was pulling it out altogether. The last thing they needed was *more* problems with Bas's tech.

"Plug him into the computer so we can run a diagnostic."

Cowl's stomach tightened. All of Bas's programing was still in place. If they Connected, it was going to make this whole thing a lot harder. The Trojan could cut off Bas's Connection as surely as it could any other Borg, but by the time they overcame the freeze protocol, they might be too late to actually make a getaway.

Cowl leaned around the Borgs in front of him, trying to catch Bas's eye as he was led past. His head was bowed, avoiding the whole world around him. He'd better not be breaking down right now. It was shitty timing.

Shifting his weight to one knee, Cowl kicked the metal platform with as much strength as he could, almost knocking himself off balance. It didn't make much of a noise, but Bas's eyes flashed up.

Cowl shook his head desperately, not even caring who saw him. They wouldn't figure it out until it was too late. A spark of understanding flitted across Bas's face and he violently threw himself backward, colliding with the Borg behind him. The yells of the Borgs reacting obscured the sound of him hitting the floor. He landed hard, already tensed from what had to be the taser in the buzz cuffs.

Bas's training was occasionally helpful. He ignored the cuffs, lashing out at the hands reaching for him. The Borgs reacted like classic villains, kicking and hitting him. Someone would pay for that.

Cowl scanned the dimly lit Rover. There had to be some way to steal a couple extra moments. At this pace, they would reach the Hub too quickly.

He caught sight of a thick black tube, probably packed full of wires, running through a hole in the grating and up into the control panel. It was close to him, but they were laying into Bas hard.

"Nerve," he whispered, leaning as close to her as he could get without falling over. "I'm going to do something stupid. When I do, I need to you to get to that tubing over there," he motioned toward the console, "and yank it out."

Bas was in a fetal position now, dripping blood from scrapes and cuts on his arms and face. Menrva only took her eyes off him for a moment, narrowing them as she glanced up front, but she nodded.

"Hey!" Cowl yelled, struggling to his feet. "How come he gets all the attention? Aren't I pretty too?"

Barely keeping his balance, Cowl aimed a kick at the nearest thing he could reach: the ass of a Borg bending over Bas.

"Come on, don't you want a piece of this?"

Good thing these guys weren't professional or anything. The closest Borg turned and slammed his fist into Cowl's face. "Get the hell down, you little—" His words cut off when Cowl shook off the blow and ducked his incoming hands. Nothing worked better on these guys than a little bit of shit talk.

"That was beautiful, a real ten. I can hear my teeth rattling around in the back of my head. Really, I can!"

The Borg growled and one of his friends joined him, pulling more Borgs off Bas. Not enough. He wasn't looking good.

The second Borg aimed a half-hearted grab in his direction and he easily stepped out of reach, nearly falling over Menrva as she scooted across the floor behind him. Cowl moved to the side to keep their attention away from her. "You know, it's the thought that counts."

That worked.

A few more Borgs joined in the fun, throwing Cowl to the floor like he was made of paper and slamming their fists into him. They weren't holding back much either. Douches.

Struggling to catch a breath, Cowl curled his head into his knees. Hopefully Menrva didn't leave him hanging because he wasn't going to last long. The pain was already making him dizzy.

Shit. They were gonna lay into her the same way, weren't they?

Too late now. From the corner of his eye Cowl caught the jerk of Menrva pulling the cords free from the console. The Rover shuddered like a wounded animal, and the grumble of the engines died. The vehicle jerked to a halt so quickly it sent several Borgs toppling.

Cowl's face hit the platform, his chin connecting solidly with metal. Spitting out a mouthful of blood, he rolled to his side to check on Bas, who grinned at him through similarly crimson-stained teeth. Menrva gasped, her face only inches from Cowl's ear so he could hear the sound right through him.

One of the Borgs turned to climb to his feet until suddenly his body went rigid and he tumbled back again.

Cowl let out a loud whoop. Not a moment too soon, the program kicked in. Prying himself loose from the stiff grip of a Borg, Cowl scanned the group, looking for the most likely candidate for who had cuffed him. The cuffs would only release when the right fingerprint was pressed to the sensors between the wrists.

Cowl found the perpetrator and carefully angled his arms to get a digit onto the sensitive pad. The cuffs snapped open after what felt like an eternity and Cowl took advantage to shove both middle fingers at the downed Borg.

"Think you can get the Rover fixed and off the grid?" Bas asked as Cowl helped him out of his cuffs.

"Hi, I'm Cowl Coven. Nice to meet you," Cowl said. He slid over to the console, shoving aside the frozen Borg at the controls.

From the looks of it, the main power was dead. Easy enough to fix. Cowl pulled his knife and hurriedly spliced the broken wires back into place, careful to slide them into the right positions.

"Why are they all like that?" Menrva asked as Bas began dumping frozen bodies over the side. "I thought you were just disconnecting them. Shouldn't they get their bodies back, like you?"

The Rover's computers beeped and Cowl focused his attention on rebooting the computers. The Rover could be the thing that saved their asses, as long as he could kill the trackers.

"It's a program," Bas said stiffly.

"Freeze protocol," Cowl added. Bas obviously didn't want to talk about it. Best to keep him busy and distracted. "The Black Box in Bas's arm holds a few codes. One will make a Borg's body freeze up, like so, if they disconnect the wrong way or if they seem like they might be dangerous."

Emergency shutdown. One step above emergency self-destruct. Thinking about it too much pissed him off. Computers had emergency shutdown buttons. People should get better than that. Especially the good ones, like Bas.

The computer screen filled with an array of colorful letters and blinking icons. It was one of the newer models, meant to be interfaced with VR tech. No way he was plugging in, though. Like he was going to let the City mess around in his head after all he'd been through. He overrode the program and started an all too familiar download. Once his AI was inundated into the Rover's simple computers, he could execute a full override. It would just take a minute to rewrite the operations.

"What's wrong with her?" Menrva asked.

Cowl turned away from the computer screen to see Menrva standing in front of the redhead who had been giving the orders. The Borg's face clenched in the program's grip but a slight tremor traveled down her arm, as if it were fighting against physical bonds. Blood dribbled from her nose, down over her lip.

"She's fighting it," Bas said.

Cowl swore. Bas was gonna try to play hero. Sure, Cowl didn't want to toss her and leave her to rot any more than Bas did. Not just because she was hot, either. Taking her and the others with them was a sure way to get killed, though. There was no way he could pull all those Borgs out of City Net before the Trojan failed and the Users had free access again. It would be nice, but maybe another day when they didn't need rescuing so much themselves.

"Guys, we're golden. Toss her!" he yelled. More than half lying. He scowled at the slow progress of the AI, looking for any way he could speed it up.

Bas stood in front of the frozen Borg, holding her arm. What was he doing?

He pressed his thumb deep into the inside of her elbow, denting the pale skin. Whatever he did seemed to give her a bit of a foothold. Her mouth wobbled momentarily.

"Go...top..." she gasped through a stubborn mouth. "Up."

"Go topside?" Bas asked.

Her head jerked down just enough to indicate her agreement.

"Thank you. You need to rest now. Just relax."

The Borg eased back and let her eyes close. Her muscles were still stiff as death, but when Bas released her arm she looked as if she could have been sleeping.

Menrva watched with concerned eyes. "Isn't there anything we can do to help her?"

"Not right now," Cowl said, frowning as Bas carefully picked up the Borg and cradled her against his chest. It sucked there were so many Borgs just lost in that hell hole. More people just like Bas. He was just one screwed-up kid. He couldn't save them all.

Bas carefully laid the redhead in the dirt with the others before climbing on the Rover. "Come on," he said, his eyes meeting with Cowl's. "Let's go."

That was not a good look. For once, it wasn't quite clear what Bas's expression meant, but somehow it was not good. Swallowing the ache in his throat, Cowl turned to the console and nodded as the download finished its work.

"What do you think she meant?" Menrva asked as the Rover pulled away. "Why would she want us to go topside?"

"I don't know," Bas said, "but I intend to find out."

Chapter Twenty-One:
Connecting the Dots

The constant hum of the Rover grated on Menrva's mind. She'd slept for at least an hour, paced the platform for another. Most of the supplies were locked in compartments under her feet, guarded with electronic locks that outlasted her best efforts. They wouldn't be able to search through those valuables until Cowl took a moment to divert his attention from driving.

Bas hadn't moved from his vigil from the back of the Rover, ignoring Cowl's attempts to catch his attention and making no effort to clean the dried blood crusted on his naked torso.

Was he thinking about the same thing Bas was? The Borgs? Specifically, the redhead who had warned them about something happening topside?

The warning was jarring enough. She'd been talking to Bas, not to them, that was for sure. But why would she look for help from anyone but a Borg? Unmodified humans were the cause of all her pain.

It was hard to think of the Borgs as the victims. They were nothing if not terrifying with the armor in place and evil Users controlling them. That was the hard part to conceive, though. When the Borgs were beating Bas and Cowl, or throwing Menrva around roughly, it wasn't a User she was seeing. They seemed like the aggressors, and changing that viewpoint after running from them was easier said than done. For the redhead at least, she couldn't escape the realization. She looked so helpless. Scared. Even if her face was as blank as Bas's ever had been. The fear seemed to roll right off her. She needed help and they had left her in the dirt, unable to move, just waiting for her abusers to come pick her up again. How was it fair that they would go so far to save Bas, and just leave the others to their suffering? The only difference between him and them was that they knew him. They cared about him.

Did she care about him? Really, after such a short time? Or was it just fascination?

The thought of Bas, frozen in agony as he lay on the ground with the others, made her stomach ache, giving her the answer. She did care. Bas was unlike anyone she'd ever met. Kind but dangerous, sometimes intensely focused, sometimes lost as if in another world. There was so much pain in him, but it didn't seem to change him. He seemed almost happy most of the time. At the very least, he seemed unworried. There were glimpses she'd caught on his face of something else happening in there. A whole world she couldn't understand if she wanted to.

Like now. He was upset, but she couldn't see signs of it other than the careful contemplation in his gaze. His back was rigid, as always, his shoulders straight, his face blank.

Cowl seemed to know what he was thinking, but to Menrva he might as well be an empty screen. She wanted to know, though.

"Are you okay?" she asked, walking over to him.

From the front of the vehicle, Cowl cast a glare back at her. He was too overprotective.

"Just worrying," Bas said, moving slightly to allow her to take a seat beside him.

Worrying? There was a lot to worry about.

"Would it help to talk?" Menrva asked awkwardly.

Bas tilted his head to look down at her. "To you?"

"Well, if the thought offends you so much..." Menrva pushed a braid out of her face and followed his eyeline into the distance.

"I'm sorry. I'm confused."

Maybe he just wasn't used to people other than Cowl trying to comfort him. It made sense, seeing where he'd come from.

"Are you still thinking about the Borgs?" she asked.

He turned his eyes on her but didn't answer. The answer was obvious enough.

"I wish we could have done more. I feel like we *should* have done more." She kicked her legs out over the back of the Rover and watched the tire tracks chase them.

"There's no easy way to do that. Sometimes I wonder if any of us can ever leave."

"You did," she pointed out.

He frowned and his lips moved for a moment, as if he were not able to force the words out. He shook himself slightly and turned back to the receding ground behind them. "I forget sometimes."

"I can't even imagine how different this all must be for

you," Menrva said.

No one had shared much about Bas's past yet. Capricorn had given her some indications, and it was clear whatever had happened was horrific. If only she could understand, maybe she could start to get an idea of why Bas was the paradox that he was. More importantly, maybe she could figure out how to take it all apart. Make sure this didn't have to happen to any more children.

"For you, too," Bas said, interrupting her musing. "This is nothing like what Cowl described when he talked about growing up."

"I'm curious," she admitted. "Especially about your childhood. How they raised you as a baby, what the training is like, how personalized the care was..." She stopped as a cloud passed over Bas's features. Had she touched a nerve or was he just confused again?

Maybe she should slow down.

"I'm curious, too. I want to know more about you," Bas said. "Tell me what you were like as a kid. Cowl's told me a bit about the Hub but...it's hard to imagine."

Menrva laughed. "I was a tomboy," she said. "And I got teased relentlessly for it. My mom was so embarrassed."

"Tomboy." He rolled the word around in his deep voice as if testing it. "What about your father?"

"He was a guard. He died a few years ago in a riot. We were really close when I was younger." She twisted the corner of her tank top around her finger. "We weren't speaking when it happened, though. I wonder if you ever saw him?"

Bas shrugged. "A few guards stood out, but I didn't pay

attention to most of them. They just kinda blended, I guess." He cleared his throat suddenly. "How did you meet Cowl?"

"We met in Basics. Cowl made fun of me when I cut all my hair off with a pair of the teacher's scissors and then tried to glue it back. I knew my mom would be mad. He bullied me until I cried and then gave me his hat so I could hide my hair."

"Sounds like Cowl." Bas laughed softly, though the smile barely seemed to touch his cheeks.

"After that, he followed me around everywhere. Neither of us were the kind of kids people wanted around, so we just kinda stuck together. Tagged around after his brother and bothered his mom for treats."

For a moment, something like real emotion slipped onto his face. What had she said to make him so serious?

"What about you? What were you like as a kid?" she asked. Maybe the answer was hidden in his past.

Bas's brow furrowed. "I was never a kid, just a machine with a few missing parts."

That was oddly dark for him. She didn't know him too well, though. Maybe he was more cynical than he appeared. He was entitled to it. As rough as the last few days had been for her, they must have been hell for him. He didn't seem to be angry about her questions, though. Just distracted. Couldn't blame him, with the threat of the City still so close.

"Did they always call you by a number, or did you have a name?" she asked, taking advantage of the moment. The more she understood, the better choices she could make.

"Just my number," he said.

Menrva's whole body ached at the hurt laying, suddenly very real, on his face. He continued, wiping his hands on his pants as if to brush aside the feelings.

"For the first five years, they are attentive enough. Those are formative years and there can be issues if there aren't...people around, I guess."

"Yeah." Menrva was starting to notice more than a few signs of those types of 'issues' with him.

"After I left the nursery things were very different."

"How?"

"I was alone in a plain room most of the time. No bed, no blanket. Nothing soft or unique. Every day we trained for hours. Martial arts, mostly. I can still remember when I got hit for the first time and no one came to comfort me. It seems like a strange thing to remember."

"No. It's not strange. I can remember the first time my mom called me stupid. I think people remember the bad things more than the nice things."

Bas turned to look at her, eyebrows furrowed and lips pursed. He seemed more hurt by her memory than his own. "You aren't stupid."

"I know. I'm a scientist, silly." Menrva couldn't take her mind from his story. "Did they hit you a lot?"

"No. Never. The other kids did, during sparring. I was pretty slow learning hand-to-hand. But if the guards wanted to hurt us they use their gauntlets."

"You're going to have to explain that."

The expression slid off Bas's face, leaving only a cold emptiness behind. "They have complete control of my nervous system. They can make my body feel pain, even if it's not real. Each guard has a remote they wear on their wrist that controls it." He said it mechanically, as if he were quoting a book, not speaking of his own life.

"So, they can make you do what they want without ever getting close." Menrva didn't look at Bas to see his answering nod. "And knowing you, you would have been happy for the human contact, even if it hurt."

The more she heard, the more Menrva was able to put together the puzzle pieces that were Bastille. His childhood was soaked in emotional abuse...more accurately: torture. Without the early bonding, it was a wonder Bas could even function around her and Cowl. The human mind was complicated and it had to learn things like social interaction. Isolation could have horrible effects on both the mind and body.

Bas always seemed to read her emotions as negative. Solitary confinement, especially in the way Bas was describing, would have made human expression a foreign language to him. PTSD would have made matters worse by setting his body on constant high alert. Every expression he couldn't place would have been translated as aggression by his affection-starved mind.

All things considered, Menrva should have been experiencing something more like what Cowl described from when they first met. Bas's brain just wasn't equipped for human interaction.

"I did miss human touch...a lot," Bas said, breaking her thoughts.

"I don't understand how you are functioning."

Bas shrugged. "I didn't have anything else to compare it to." He smiled at her. "Now I know." The expression kindled again in his face; the humanity.

"Okay, enough with the sappy heart-to-heart. You guys are sickening." Cowl slowed the Rover and stepped away from the controls. "Why don't I unlock those compartments for you, so I'm not the only one working? Maybe there's something in there that can even our odds."

Menrva gave Bas another moment of consideration. There was a lot hidden under that hard exterior. No wonder Cowl had become such good friends with him.

Chapter Twenty-Two: Mr. Perfect

"I found more suits."

Menrva pulled a helmet from a compartment. They were impressive pieces of technology. In this state, they were sleek, black, and static, but Cowl had been quick to explain how the computers inside allowed the plates to shift to fit every movement of the body, reducing the coverage that would need to be sacrificed for full mobility. The same computers allowed the colors to morph to fit the environment. There were other features as well, some Menrva was familiar with from playing the Sims.

"Food and water," Bas called from the other side of the Rover as he dug through another locker. "It's not a lot but it will last us a month, if we are careful."

Menrva had seen these type of Rovers used in Tournament Sims. It was still mind-boggling to see so many things she thought only existed in computer codes materializing. None of them seemed to be pleasant things, though. No flowers or beaches or beautiful old homes. Only the nightmares seemed able to climb out of the make-believe world and into the waking world. Maybe the beautiful things were too afraid; she couldn't blame them.

Menrva sat back and cradled the helmet in her hands. "Do you think the Borgs will be all right?"

"They'll live," Cowl answered. "You might have to define what you mean by 'all right,' though."

Menrva dropped the helmet into its compartment. The more this world unfolded before her, the more she wanted to crawl back to the safety of her mundane, lonely life.

Cowl had kept the lights of the Rover low. They couldn't risk being seen. It had been a long while since they had left the Borgs behind. There was no sign of life out here. They might as well have been rolling across the moon. The air was distinctly thinner this far from the vents and her lungs were starting to ache from it.

In place of the flood lights, Cowl drove mostly using radar translating their surroundings onto a screen in front of him. The rough landscape appeared in a tangle of green lines against the black screen. It allowed him to get a lay of the land past the limited visibility.

Menrva found a seat on the floor beside Cowl and watched as Bas searched through the compartments. How had she missed all the scars? Probably because the tech was so distracting. Menrva had her scars too; everyone had scars, even in the shelter of the Hub.

"How are you doing?" Menrva asked Cowl.

"I can't blink without hurting. You?"

"I'm okay," Menrva said.

"Oh, you're a tough chick, huh? Trying to make me feel like a wimp? Well, it won't work. I was freaking beat to a pulp."

Menrva laughed, wincing at the pain in her ribs. "Okay, it's pretty bad," she admitted.

"But hey, it worked," Cowl pointed out.

"Bas's ideas always seem to work."

"They always seem to hurt," Cowl said. "I can't say I'm a big fan of the gambling factor, either."

"It wasn't a gamble. He trusts you."

"Yeah." Cowl's voice was hushed, almost awed. Cowl had never really cared what people thought about him. He had always been antagonistic and completely apathetic to any opinion that wasn't hers or Starke's. It was strange seeing him so invested in Bastille. They had formed a brotherhood that made her jealous. "I get why Bas is so attached to you, but why are you so close with him? You literally gave up everything to help him." She didn't want to say it out loud but the words seemed to hang in the air anyway: she was part of that 'everything'.

"Love at first sight," Cowl suggested. "Bas is my forever." He grinned devilishly as Bas approached, pulling a foraged, white tank top over his head.

"Seriously," Menrva said.

"I don't know. I guess at first it was just instinct. Maybe a little bit of guilt. When I realized what I was really doing when I played those Tournaments or what I did to Bas, I couldn't walk away. I mean, who does that?" Cowl paused to maneuver the Rover around a particularly deep hole. "It's a bit more than that, though. I guess I kinda needed a friend."

His words stung more than Menrva had expected. She'd forgotten how much it had hurt when he disappeared. "I wasn't good enough?"

Cowl frowned. "Come on, really? You're gonna pull that on me?" His eyes strayed from the controls to look at her for the first time. "You were the best friend I ever had. You had just gotten married to Mr. Perfect, though. I never got to see you. That and I kinda had a crush on you. Hey, apparently I have abandonment issues, too."

Menrva tucked her legs under her arms. "Sure, Mr. Perfect." She shouldn't have been so confident her words wouldn't carry over the roar of the engine.

"Okay, seriously, Nerve. You gotta tell, it's only fair. You know all about Bas and you just heard my heart-wrenching drama bit."

"Cowl," Bas said. His voice held a hint of warning.

"What? I'm not subtle. No one ever accused me of being subtle. I'm curious." He shrugged. "I mean, I've got a pretty good guess."

"Of course, you do. It's not like it's a secret that Case Nolan is a jerk. If he wasn't so high-ranking in the City guard then I suspect someone would have put him in his place by now."

"You're married to Case Nolan?" Bas asked in surprise.

"You know him?" Cowl asked.

"Nolan is known as Lucifer around the Compound," Bas explained. "He's one of the reserve users."

"I didn't think people were born evil until I got assigned to Case," Menrva agreed. She hadn't talked about it in years, and as she spoke, a dam broke somewhere in her mind. This was the first time she had been given even a hint of empathy.

"The first time he hit me I thought it was just a bad temper. People get assigned to abusers all the time." She studied her nails, rubbing her thumb along the split corner of one where blood had started to pool. Could she backtrack now? She didn't want to share this. When she glanced up at Cowl, he was watching her with expectant eyes, but he didn't press her. Taking a deep breath, she plunged deeper.

"It didn't take long for me to realize Case was much more than just a hothead. He enjoys other people's pain. He relishes it like chocolate. I started carrying a knife with me everywhere I went because I was more afraid of my husband than I was of Bunker law. Most nights I would sleep in the lab or anywhere else I could find where he wasn't."

"I remember seeing you at the lab, working late," Cowl said, his forehead puckered. "Why didn't you come over to my place?"

"You have to ask that? Case would have found a way to kill you, even if the City didn't get involved." Menrva rubbed a spot of dried blood from her hand, trying to avoid the eyes now locked on her. "No one would listen to me. They thought I was just complaining. No one likes their spouse. My mom told me I was being a spoiled child. We had a duty to the human race and the City, and I was just being over dramatic. At least he was handsome."

Menrva pressed her palms into her eye sockets to suppress the tears that threatened to break her. "I tried leaving, I did. My dad told me to go home and make things right with my husband." She laughed bitterly. "Like he didn't know the truth. He worked with Case."

"Shit. What a douche," Cowl mumbled.

She shrugged off his comment. Sure he was, but Dad had

never been one to stand up to anyone. "One night Case came home and, after his usual attacks, locked me in the fridge. I managed to claw my way out with the knife but I don't doubt he would have left me in there to die." One glance revealed Cowl's face wore a mask of rage. "I went to find you. I thought maybe you could hide me, or help me...somehow. You were gone. That must have been the night you met Bas."

Cowl's face softened. "I'm so sorry. I wish I would have known."

"It doesn't matter now." It did. It mattered a lot. It mattered because if he had been there Angel would be alive right now.

"A few days later I realized I was pregnant. Case was really happy at first; he even stopped with the abuse. I felt safe enough to sleep in my own bed again, even if I always kept the door locked. When we went in for a checkup at twenty-six weeks, they found something. They weren't sure enough to abort my daughter, but they were concerned she might have some genetic deficiencies. They wouldn't even tell me what they were." She shuddered at the memories. It had been the worst day of her life. "Case was furious. He claimed I had cheated on him. He said there was no way he could have produced a genetically inferior baby. When he was through..." Menrva couldn't complete the thought. Her voice cracked and her breath threatened to choke her as tears raged behind her eyes. She managed to pull herself back together and continue.

"I tried to protect her. I did everything I could." Despite her best efforts, a few tears brushed past her eyelashes.

The events played in the back of her mind: curling up on the floor, wrapped around her womb in an attempt to form some sort of shield. She strangled the unwanted memory and tried to push to the end of her retelling.

"I went into labor early. I gave birth to Angel right there on the living room floor. The medics came, but her body was too damaged. She died before I could even hold her." Menrva fought the sob clawing at her throat. Now was not the time to break down. They couldn't see her hurting like this. It was too late. Tears melted through her defenses and dripped down her cheek in a hot torrent. She hugged her arms around her empty womb and again felt the ripping pain as her baby left the safety of her body. The blood had pooled under her fingers in a torrent of agony, weakening her with each drop. The prayers echoed in her mind again: prayers for her baby to live or for them both to die. She couldn't stop the memories now, and she couldn't stop the words.

"He did so much damage they say I probably won't be able to conceive again. Case petitioned for a divorce. He said his superior genes deserved much more than me. After that, nobody wanted to come near me. They believed Case when he told them I was such a slut that I got pregnant with someone else's baby. He said all the nights I spent hiding from him were spent with other men. The City wouldn't put the divorce through, so I never knew when he might walk back in." The sob ripping out of her seemed to tear her in half.

Warmth enveloped Menrva, sudden and sweet as Bas wrapped his arms around her. Menrva's face pressed against his chest and she breathed in his musky, masculine scent. Bas should have been the last man to make her feel safe, but as soon as he touched her, everything seemed to right itself again.

Bas held her only for an instant and when he released her, she wanted to climb back into his warmth and sob in his lap like an infant. Instead, she cleared her throat and rubbed the treacherous tears from her cheeks.

"So. I'm not a violent kind of person..." Cowl began.

"You are a very violent person," Bas said.

"Okay, I'm a little bit of a violent person. My point is: I kinda want to tear this guy apart now."

"You wanted to know," Menrva said. She pushed back a few loose curls clinging to her wet skin.

"No, I'm glad you told me," Cowl said. "Now I have a name to start my kill list with. I've always wanted a kill list."

Something else caught her attention. On the screen Cowl was now hardly watching, a few red lights had bloomed from the maze of green.

"Cowl, what is that?" Menrva asked.

Cowl's eyes darted onto the screen and he swore. "We have some warm bodies, people. Since we are so far from the search radius, I'm guessing these are scavengers."

Chapter Twenty-Three: The Hunted

Bas pulled an automatic rifle from the pile of guns stashed in the Rover. "I hope you can shoot while you're crying," he said as he tossed Menrva a gun.

Thanks to the Sims, the weapon wasn't as foreign as it could have been, but it still bore a weight of fear. Menrva was aiming for real people now, not just computer programs; a fact she would rather forget.

"Who's crying?" Menrva checked the ammo with shaking hands.

"How many?" Bas asked as he handed Cowl an automatic handgun.

"Fifteen? Seventeen? I dunno. They keep popping up."

Bas motioned for Menrva to station herself on the opposite end of the Rover. She knelt down, her stance automatic from Sim-play. She was good in virtual reality, but this was a whole different animal. She'd worked hard to turn those experiences into something more tangible after Nolan. Training every night, hitting the gym when everyone else was gone. It wouldn't help her when it came to shooting, but maybe the blend of reality and virtual reality was enough preparation.

"Hold onto your asses, guys, 'cause I'm not stopping," Cowl warned.

Menrva sucked in a deep breath and braced the rifle against her shoulder. The Rover's floodlights powered on, overwhelming the haze until she couldn't even see Bunker's tiers, twisting in a series of dusky cobwebs over her head. On the ground, soft dust wrinkled around aggressive boulders and sudden pits.

Movement behind a boulder alerted her to a man running for cover, so shrouded in dirt he looked like a golem. She swung the barrel of her gun to follow him.

"Stop," a voice called from well ahead of them. "We have you outgunned and outmanned."

"Yeah," Cowl replied, "but we've got you out-badassed."

A bullet ricocheted from the metal over Menrva's head, making her jump. Not everyone appreciated Cowl's sense of humor.

"If you don't play hero, you can walk away from here with your lives," the speaker continued.

"I'm not playing hero, idiot," Cowl said under his breath. "I'm just playing."

The Rover roared to a higher gear, shuddering and moaning as Cowl pushed it to the edge of its limited speed. Menrva had to scramble to keep herself in place as Cowl turned the machine directly toward the boulder hiding the source of the voice.

A rainstorm of bullets pelted the vehicle. She ducked behind the edge of the Rover, gulping in deep breaths.

"Don't get shot...again," she told herself.

A ragged man ran from his cover toward them. He pulled alongside the Rover, close enough that the details of his face were clearly visible through his second skin of dirt.

Menrva squeezed the trigger, wincing as the bullet sank uselessly into the dirt beside him. The kick of the rifle was familiar from the Sims, but she hadn't expected the pain that shot through her arm and chest.

"Come on, Nerve. Don't be a tease," Cowl said. Despite the joke, his voice was tense as he fumbled to split his attention between driving and shooting.

"You concentrate on driving." Menrva fired again and the scavenger fell under the lead. Her heart dropped with him. She had just killed a man, for real. There was no way to unplug from this. She didn't get much time to adjust to her new identity as a murderer. More men swooped into the light, shooting as they ran.

Menrva planted the gun against her shoulder and inhaled to steady her aim. Her next three shots each found targets.

"Good." Bas's voice filled Menrva with an odd sort of pride. Maybe she should have felt more remorse for taking their lives, but somehow it was already becoming commonplace. Either the Sims had desensitized her, or she was just growing accustomed to what reality looked like in the Pit.

The light above her exploded, showering her with hot glass. She ducked, protecting her eyes. Shards tinkled as she shook them from her bare arms and raised her gun again. It was a worthless effort. Without the spotlight, there was nothing to see. Squinting, she searched for her target. The muzzle flashed, but the bullet she fired found no mark.

"Cover the rear, I've got you," Bas called to her.

Menrva turned just in time. A scavenger ran behind the Rover, propelling forward with surprising speed. She dropped to her stomach, naturally cradling the rifle in place. Her bullet wheeled the man around before he dropped to the earth.

Bas stood over her, one foot planted on either side. Was he was stabilizing her against the tilt of the Rover, or using her to stabilize himself? Strangely enough, his presence was calming.

More scavengers appeared. Menrva shot one and swore as a bullet slipped by between Bas's leg and her head. She risked a quick look to make sure Cowl hadn't gotten in its way.

The shooter fell as ammunition from both guns slammed into his chest, but they were not quick enough to stop the influx. A scavenger pulled himself over the right side of the Rover, dropping to the floor just as another caught hold of the ladder in the back.

"Why are you going so slow?" Bas yelled at Cowl before he abandoned his empty gun and leaped onto the scavenger.

"What do you expect, this isn't a rocket. It tops out at twenty-five! And that's without all this shit in the way."

Menrva aimed for the man who was scaling the back but never got a chance to shoot. A woman vaulted over the side and kicked Menrva's hand, knocking her gun away. She aimed another kick at Menrva's head.

Menrva slipped away just in time to avoid the boot and rolled against the woman's other foot. Swinging her arm hard, she managed to land a strike on the scavenger's knee and force it backward. The attacker cursed and fell to the side. Menrva had just enough time to get free but she didn't go far. Large hands grabbed the back of her shirt and dragged her to her feet.

Menrva kicked wildly in an attempt to reach the floor as she was lifted higher.

"Shoot my boys will you, little girl?" a gravelly voice said from behind her.

The owner of the voice propelled Menrva into the floor. Pain shot back through her skull as her forehead split open on the metal. She turned to look at a beast of a man through the blood seeping into her eyes.

As he reached for her again, Menrva punched upward, her fist connecting with his Adam's apple. He fell away, struggling for breath.

The woman climbed back to her feet and raised a knife, her hand trembling as she wiped away a stream of blood dripping from her lips. Menrva ducked the first swipe and barely managed to grab onto the woman's arm as she came back around. She landed two solid punches into the woman's torso. Without waiting for a reaction, she grabbed the woman's arm and twisted her body, slamming the elbow against her shoulder until it bent grotesquely outward and the bone snapped. The scavenger screamed and dropped the knife.

Victory was short lived. Menrva cast a glance back to find Bas raining down blows on the pack of scavengers surrounding him. The big man approached him and a few of the scavengers backed away, cheering as he squared off with Bas.

How they thought he was an opponent worth cheering was a mystery. His head barely reached Bas's chin and his broad chest and muscles seemed to drag him down.

Menrva took the momentary distraction to search for her gun. The scavenger woman had scrambled to the back of the Rover, holding her broken arm against her chest. In her other hand she held Menrva's rifle, weakly pointed at her.

Zigzagging on the approach, Menrva dived at her. She couldn't get a good aim with only one arm. Menrva grabbed her by a scrap of cloth on her shirt as she stumbled backwards, off the Rover. Just before she fell into the dust cloud raised by the Rover, Menrva snatched the rifle from her hand.

The woman screamed before she was gone.

The cheers behind Menrva reached a new high. She turned to see the big man rush toward Bas. Cowl tried to aim his gun at the ground without leaving the controls but gave up. He shouldn't have worried.

Bas paused his fight just long enough to grab the fist the scavenger threw. Menrva didn't breathe for a second, mesmerized by his movement. He dragged the man forward, twisting to catch his head in a choke hold with his other arm.

One of the smaller scavengers in front of him started forward. Menrva swung her rifle as hard as she could, connecting with his head so solidly she had to take a step back. Another jumped toward her but she twisted just in time to shoot him point blank in the chest. A look of pure horror froze on his face as he stumbled and fell with a fleshy thud to the floor. Menrva deliberately averted her eyes, avoiding the bloody mess now laying at her feet. She couldn't stomach the fact that it was her who had caused that.

Bas yelled, grabbing Menrva's attention again. The big man was dead at Bas's feet, face mottled purple and neck bent unnaturally. Another scavenger hung from Bas's arm like a rat, but as he turned, the man slid down Bas's arm, dragging the lead cuff off its place. The scavanger took a few steps back and Cowl shot him through the head.

"Shit!" Cowl cursed as the scavenger fell to the deck.

"Keep driving." Bas dove toward the corpse.

He didn't get far before his entire body stiffened.

"Bas!" Cowl yelled. He twisted around, loosening his grip on the controls and sending the Rover careening back and forth. A few bullets flew overhead from the scavengers that were rapidly falling behind, but Cowl seemed more scared than before.

Bas dropped to the ground on his hands and knees, his body contorted, his head bent down until it almost touched the floor.

Menrva tightened her grip on her gun. What was happening? What should she do?

As if to answer her question, Bas looked up at her, his face contorted in very real pain.

"Menrva, shoot me," he said, his words squeezed through his teeth so she could hardly understand. She pulled her rifle to her shoulder without thinking but couldn't move as Bas collapsed to the floor.

Bas went still and his shoulders flexed awkwardly, as if

he were trying out his body for the first time.

"Menrva!" Cowl said from the front. "He's Connected. Get out of here. I'll handle it."

He whipped the Rover around, nearly knocking Menrva off her feet despite the compensation of the platform. One look at his face confirmed her fears. Cowl wasn't trying to protect her. He expected to die, but he wasn't leaving his friend. She wasn't going anywhere, either.

Bas stood, scanning the area until his eyes met with Menrva. He slipped his hands down his body, searching for his gun. When he couldn't find it, he stepped over the dead body on the floor and came right for her.

"You don't have to die right now, Penniweight," he said.

Menrva's breath caught in her lungs. Whoever had taken over Bas's body knew her.

"It's over. The only way this ends now is with everyone dead, or everyone back in Bunker. We don't need to make it complicated." Bas walked forward with his hands raised, as if he were trying to calm her.

Cowl pulled the Rover over and killed the engine before turning to aim his shotgun at Bas. Was he going to shoot him? He'd said he would, that he would kill him before he let him go back. Was there really nothing they could do?

Menrva backed up slowly, gripping her rifle tight. What if she shot his legs out from under him? The User wouldn't be able to feel it, but a serious injury was better than Bas dead.

"Menrva," Cowl said, voice firm and eyes planted on Bas, who barely even glanced at him. "Get out of here."

He was going to kill him.

Menrva skirted around Bas, backing away from the rear of the Rover. She wasn't leaving. If anyone was going to shoot Bas, it would be her. She wasn't going to let Cowl do that to himself, or follow it up with what she knew would be his next move.

There was another option, though. If the Connection happened when the cuff came off, all she had to do was jam it back in place.

"Cowl, don't let him go anywhere," Menrva said as Bas edged closer to the back of the Rover.

"No one has to get hurt here. We just need the Mod back," Bas said.

"And you aren't getting him without killing me first," Cowl replied. He charged forward to tackle Bas around the knees.

Menrva jumped, colliding with the dead body. Blood slid under her fingers, soaking through the scavengers scant clothing. She rolled him to the side, prying the lead hoop from his fingers. She just barely got her fingers around it when hands closed around her knee, yanking her violently backwards. The grating grabbed at her skin, ripping holes in her knees and palms as she tried to slow herself. The bracelet flew out of her hands, bouncing off the platform and into the far corner.

"I don't want to kill you, but I will," Bas said.

Menrva kicked off the ground, turning herself around just in time to see a fist coming toward her. She rolled aside and threw her rifle. She wasn't going to use it on Bas, but she didn't want him using it on her, either.

The expression on his face was eerie. They were his

features, but she had never seen so much emotion there. It wasn't his.

She kicked, trying to break away from his grip, but he didn't even seem to register it. He grabbed her neck, his thumbs pressing into her throat. Her pulse fluttered against her skin as he cut off her breath. His fingers were hot, hard as stone.

"Stop fighting. You don't even know what you are doing," Bas said, knocking aside her arms as if they were flies.

Cowl slammed into Bas's shoulder. He let up on Menrva's neck just long enough to let her suck in a deep breath, but Cowl might as well have been a child. Bas threw him aside and turned his focus back on Menrva.

She would have to hit something that could create a physical weakness, not just pain. If she could hit a nerve cluster on his arm, she could maybe get a bit of leverage.

Bas's grip tightened. The User must have decided her death was the best option.

The only way this ended well was if she could get that cuff on. From her periphery, she could just make out Cowl, clambering to his feet.

She motioned weakly toward the cuff. Clasping her fist together to form a pyramid, she slammed them up into Bas's elbows, forcing them inward. For a precious moment she managed a few sharp breaths. She needed more power, though. She wrapped her arms around Bas's, gripping his iron forearms until her nails bit into his skin. With the leverage, she slipped her knees through Bas's arms and planted her feet in his armpits.

He scrambled to get his hold again as she arched her

back. As she got more air her thinking cleared. There were nerve clusters in the armpit. If she could numb his arm for just a second, maybe they could slip the cuff on. Bas was too strong for her. Given another moment, she would collapse and he would crush her larynx.

She caught a flash of movement to her right and kicked hard, slamming the heel of her boot into the flesh with all the strength she could muster. With a sickening crack, the shoulder slid out of the socket and Bas's arm went dead. Bas swore and backed up just as Cowl grabbed for his arm.

Taking advantage of the moment, Menrva struck, fingers pointed like a spear head, into his inner arm.

"Put it on!" she yelled, hoping Cowl had actually managed to grab the cuff. She twisted her body into Bas's chest to block his left hand.

Bas wrapped her tight to him, trying to grab for Cowl. Cowl's knee dug into Menrva's back as he wrenched Bas's temporarily dead arm around. Then Bas went limp.

"Got it!" Cowl crowed, dropping to his knees.

Menrva squirmed from under Bas and turned to see the lump of metal that had just saved their lives. The skin around the cuff was bunched and scratched, but it was firmly in place just below his elbow.

Bas was still breathing, his back shuddering slightly.

"You'd better get the Rover moving again," Menrva gasped, lying back to catch her breath.

"Gotta make sure he's okay first. Bas?" Cowl squeezed Bas's shoulder. "Ah, Shit. Freeze protocol. We broke the signal."

He scrambled to the edge of the Rover. "I think I can get

it from here," he said, plugging the tablet into the back of Bas's neck. Menrva shuddered, trying to ignore the blood pulsing just under the panes in the tech. No matter how many times she saw it, it was no less unnatural.

Bas groaned, his body twitching and curling as if he were shaking off something living. The concept made Menrva sick. He was being electrified from the inside out, even as they watched. How must it even feel?

Cowl leaned over him like a mother hen, carefully checking the tech and kneading the scar tissue on his neck. "Come on, brother. Say something. Let me know you are alive." His voice shook, thick with what sounded like tears. Menrva has seen Cowl cry twice in her life. Once when Starke was taken away, and again at his mom's funeral. This must have hit him hard. He didn't look like he was crying, but Menrva wouldn't have had to know him well to see how shaken he was.

Finally, Bas pushed himself onto his side and blinked hard. "You guys okay?" he asked, his voice raspy.

Cowl sat back, sighing in relief. "Now I am. Just about gave me a heart attack, there."

Tears pricked the back of Menrva's eyes and she nodded her head, surprised by the sensation. She pressed her fingers briefly to her lids. This was just shock. A lot had just happened; she couldn't read it as...as what? Affection? Friendship? What was wrong with actually caring for someone? Was she so broken she couldn't let herself trust someone as obviously kind and thoughtful as Bas?

Clearing the thoughts from her head, Menrva turned to Cowl. "We should go."

Cowl glared at her as if she had just suggested he pluck his own eye out.

"I'll stay with Bas," she said. If anything, his frown deepened, but he nodded and headed up front.

"I'm sorry." Bas rubbed his forehead and avoiding her eyes. "I wouldn't have hurt you if..."

"I understand," Menrva said quickly. "Everyone is fine. Just rest."

He crossed his arms and placed his forehead on them, sighing. He looked so much like a child. Like a small, broken boy who just needed to be rescued. Cowl was right to want to protect him. If he ever had to endure that again, it was too much.

Carefully, timidly, Menrva lay a hand on his shoulder.

Chapter Twenty-Four: Arrival

It had been a couple of hours and Bas had still barely moved. He wasn't sleeping, but he had hardly done more than breathe and occasionally shift his weight. Cowl did his best to keep driving, to keep his eyes on the ground ahead.

It had been at least three years since the last time Bas had been Connected. It was the first time Cowl had to ever watch it, though.

He hadn't expected it to be so terrifying. The thought of Bas being controlled by someone else was always a bit abstract. Yes, he understood that it happened. He'd talked over the effects with Bas. He knew what it did to him, knew how it made him feel. It was a whole different thing having to actually see it.

Finally, after what felt like a very uncomfortable eternity, Bas pushed himself up and walked over to Cowl. There was no indication of what he'd just been through, other than bloodshot eyes and the way he cradled his injured arm. His face was fixed in that stupid, blank look.

"Robo face," Cowl said, before he had a chance to think about it. "Ah...sorry. I guess I'll let it slide for now."

Bas didn't respond, watching the lines slip by on the screen.

Patience. He needed patience. Choking some sort of

response out of Bas right now might seem like a good outlet, but it was probably not something many psychologists would recommend.

"Thank you," Bas said finally, rubbing his neck. "But next time, shoot me." A soft grin played across his face.

"Good thing you didn't come over here trying to apologize and that kind of shit," Cowl said.

Bas leaned over, pulling a slim med kit from under the console. "I know you well enough to know you wouldn't like that," he said. He glanced back at Menrva, who sat cross-legged on the platform.

She hadn't moved from Bas's side the whole time he'd been down. Why couldn't she have driven?

"You okay?" Bas asked. "Menrva's a bit cut up."

A flash of heat rushed through Cowl's chest. It was stupid. If she was hurt, she needed to be tended to. Bas had just been through hell, though. Didn't he get a moment to rest?

The look on Bas's face said it all. He didn't want to be relaxing, he wanted to be with her. "What about your shoulder?" he asked, scowling as Bas carefully lowered himself by Menrva's side. She looked so tiny next to him. It was hard to imagine she'd actually done that much damage.

It wasn't fair to get angry at her for popping his shoulder out. It was probably going to keep being an issue, now that it'd been dislocated for a second time.

"I'll take care of it when we get there," Bas said. "It'll be okay for a while."

"I can take care of it," Menrva responded.

Cowl almost laughed but kept it stuffed inside. She had busted it, after all, so he shouldn't be so dismissive of her strength just because she was tiny. He was no Borg himself. Still, that was *his* job. He'd always been the one to patch up Bas. She could damage his Live Metal. Maybe he should stop the Rover and go take things into his own hands.

He thumbed the raw spot on his chin where a patch of skin had been shaved off on the grated platform. That needed to be cleaned and bandaged too, but no...hot girl came first.

It's not like she was the first girl Bas had ever met. Borg girls were better looking, too, with the long legs and those dark eyes that seemed to be in the predominant bloodline.

Swearing, Cowl reached for the switch to turn off the Rover.

"You did really good," Bas said from behind him.

Cowl jerked his hand back. She did good? What the hell, how many times had the two of them completely kicked ass and Bas had acted like it was nothing?

"We lost them," Cowl said, interrupting their...whatever that shit was. Flirting wasn't the right word because flirting was a foreign language to both of them.

"Not for long." Bas indicated the tread marks left behind.

"No helping that. We will just have to keep a guard." Cowl grinned. "I'd like them to try that shit again. It takes a brave soul to see you and not run screaming."

Yeah. So no one here thought he was funny. Maybe he should take a hint and just shut up.

He looked back to see Menrva yank Bas's arm back into his socket, and winced. She shouldn't be jerking like that!

Cowl scowled and focused on the computers as Menrva wrapped Bas's shoulder, talking in a low voice obviously meant to exclude him. He and Bas had been best friends for three years; closer than brothers. Throw in Menrva, and all that went to hell. Why? He was less of a jerk than she was, at least when it came to Bas. He wasn't making any claims about how he related to the rest of humanity.

He risked another glance back to see Bas wrapping Menrva's ribs. She must have broken one in the scuffle. The scars on her stomach were easily visible.

Cowl released a tight breath. The action had knocked Menrva's story right out of his thoughts, but now it came rushing back. When she'd been assigned to Nolan, he should have guessed what would happen. He didn't know Nolan well. Seen him around a few times, sure. It was hard to actively avoid anyone in the Hub. Even as big as it was, it was still small enough that he knew most people by name.

Nolan never seemed that vicious. Maybe a bit alpha male, usually with a following of boisterous guards and a few adoring teens. The very fact Nolan hadn't been assigned a wife until the age of thirty was good enough reason to have extrapolated. Well, hindsight...

The Hub wasn't trying to actively kill their citizens. At least, not the ones they liked. Abusive situations happened. People were stressed, thrown into marriages with people they didn't like, antagonized by a government they couldn't protest. But if someone was a real dirt bag they usually ended up alone. The environment was perfect for psychopaths, so it shouldn't have been too surprising that the trait popped up in the high class.

Whatever the reason, Cowl had missed it. He'd missed it and he did the same thing to Menrva that so many people had done to him: he abandoned her. No wonder she hated his guts.

As soon as things calmed down and got back to normal, he'd take a trip back to the Hub and pay Nolan a visit. The dust town needed some supplies, so he'd have a good excuse. Before pulling the trigger, he'd look Nolan dead in the eye and tell him what a piece of shit he was. It would be a beautiful moment. He could even record it and bring it back to Menrva.

Maybe she'd be able to forgive him then.

He couldn't do anything about the rest of the Hub's disgusting excuse for humanity. She needed help, and instead they dragged her name through the mud and made life hell for her. That deserved something. If not a hole in the head, at least a bit of public name-calling.

It made a bit more sense, though, why they would react that way. For most people, having a kid that wasn't from your carefully selected genetic match was a good way to get yourself killed, or at least thrown out of the Hub. The City was anal about keeping everyone as genetically fit as possible. When Menrva walked away from Nolan's allegations with nothing to show for it, it must have made her look privileged.

Bunch of shallow robots they had in the Hub. Just taking whatever was given to them without questions. People sucked.

"Where are we?" Bas asked, pulling Cowl from his

thoughts.

Poor kid, he was love-struck. It was written all over him. Maybe Cowl should talk to Menrva, tell her to just tell Bas that nothing was going to happen and end it before it turned into an issue.

Unless she liked him too, then that would be a *real* issue.

"Should be coming up on it soon," Cowl answered, hoping his errant thought was wrong. What did he know about relationships? He couldn't hold onto a single one, romantic or otherwise. Not even Bas, apparently.

"Is this thing equipped to Connect?" Bas asked.

"I don't know, it depends. What do you want to do with it?" He didn't need to ask that. He already knew. Stupid idiot wanted to do just what the redheaded Borg said and go topside.

"We have armor?"

"Yes, we do. Very astute. I'm not sure a verbal inventory of the Rover is in order, though," Cowl said through gritted teeth.

Bas stood, carefully pulling his tank top back on. The white bandages peaked out of the stained cloth like something from another world.

"It's that redhead chick, isn't it? You are planning a trip topside."

"Just keeping our options open," Bas lied, keeping his eyes down.

Menrva walked up behind them, arms crossed protectively over her stomach. "What could she possibly want you to go to the surface for? I thought everything up there was gone."

Bas rubbed his shoulder, frowning as Cowl set his jaw and stared straight ahead. "Not everything. But she wouldn't have pushed herself so hard if it wasn't important."

"Why, you know her?" Cowl asked sarcastically. He regretted it as soon as he said it. Bas would care, either way. One shouldn't make verbal jabs while tired, and it had probably been a good two days since he'd gotten any sleep. At least a week since he'd gotten enough to be worthwhile.

"Her name is 306. I've never talked to her, but we've gone up a few times together. We both had the same handler," Bas said.

"Launay?" Another guy he should kill just for the heck of it.

"Yes. That was her User back there," Bas said, rubbing his temple like he did when his head hurt. Connection or Live Metal? Maybe if they had some time at the housing unit, he'd be able to work on his programing.

"Look." Cowl rubbed his hand over his hair and sighed. Whatever was going on topside, it was none of their business. They were just trying to survive. "We can't go chasing long shots right now. We have to figure out our next steps, stay ahead of the City. I'm sorry."

"What is that?" Menrva asked, interrupting Cowl's attempt at reason.

The dim light ahead just barely revealed a huge shape growing up from the earth. With each foot, the view before them became clearer. It was a sobering sight. The City hadn't just screwed Bas and the Borgs. This collapsed giant had once been home for entire families.

The fallen housing unit was obscenely huge, surrounded by a barren landscape. The lights struggled to illuminate even a portion on the crumpled hull. Dust caked on the metal, forming a thick hide. Pieces of torn metal stuck up from the dirt like teeth.

A ragged hole opened up in the side of the unit. Cowl maneuvered the Rover inside and turned off the engine. Darkness and silence crowded in the dead space. Comfy.

Cowl turned on one of the floodlights and let it expose the ghostly scene. The hole that offered them a hiding place had torn out several pods. What remained was caked-in dirt. A door hung tilted on broken hinges, just open enough to show the seemingly endless hallway reaching past it. Only a few feet in front of the Rover a crib lay on its side, half buried in dust.

"This will be safe?" Bas asked, his voice tense.

"How the hell am I supposed to know? It's a start, though."

Chapter Twenty-Five: Mixed Messages

Bas rolled a bullet between his fingers. The glint of the thin light off the tip burned his eyes. The floor of the housing unit tilted under his feet, just enough to keep the collecting dust tucked against the edges of the room. White paint peeled off the walls, sliding down like rotting skin. Bullet holes dented the surface here and there, testament to the real horror that had taken place. Images from the past few days kept playing through Bas's mind. 306 in particular drifted in, her face smeared in blood as she fought the freeze protocol. It only added to the pounding in his head.

The unit felt like a crypt. No, it felt like his cell in the Compound. The distinct echo of footsteps off the metal walls made his stomach turn. There was a bizarre sense in which the atmosphere adhered to his skin, pressing in on him like a palpable weight.

"It goes on forever," Menrva said as she appeared from the cavernous hallway. The layout was simple. One hallway shot straight through the unit without any obvious deviation. On either side, rows of rooms, not unlike the one they were in now, opened up. The room they had occupied was torn nearly in half, the hole providing an easy view of the Rover and the cavern. Cowl had already stocked the pod across from them with some foraged emergency blankets and a lantern. Each pod contained beds welded to the wall and floor, sturdy cabinets, and a cramped bathroom. Most of the rooms Bas looked into had been raided, stripped long ago. Everything is useful when you have nothing.

Menrva ducked under a broken air duct and came to sit across from Bas. Her face was a maze of cuts and scratches. His fault. Even the ones that hadn't been done by his own hand were there because of his stupid idea. If she had never come to help him in the first place, she could be safe and comfortable in the Hub.

Menrva twisted the stem of a battery-powered lantern. The light sent tendrils of agony dancing around Bas's head, but he pushed it aside and refocused. His gaze rested automatically on Menrva's full lips; deep red, inviting. He couldn't entertain those thoughts; he'd done more than enough damage in her life. "How are you feeling?" he asked.

"Stop asking. I'm fine." She smiled and gently pulled the bullet from his fingers. "Figure you are going to need this?"

Bas dropped his gaze to his hands to avoid her eyes. "You never know."

The silence was oddly uncomfortable. Something had changed, but he couldn't quite put his finger on what. "You think they could find us here?" she asked.

"They can find us anywhere."

The stumbling silence was broken when Cowl walked back through the door, bringing a cloud of dirt with him. The sound of his feet on the metal floors echoed in Bas's head like gunshots, making the ache flare. Cowl pulled off his scarf and shook it. Their last adventure hadn't done him any favors, either. Sure, Bas had seen him looking worse. The two of them had been in their fair share of adventures, but he had never been the cause of the bruises before.

"The good news is, we have everything we need on the Rover." Cowl opened a water bottle and drank long and deep. "The not so good news: eventually it will run out and one of us will have to find our way to some supplies."

He found a seat around the flickering lamp and gave Bas a suspicious glance.

"You okay, brother? You look a bit tense."

Bas shrugged, wincing at the pain in his shoulder and neck. "Not a big deal." Cowl shot him an accusatory look. Of course that wouldn't be good enough for him. "This place reminds me of the Compound."

"You haven't stayed in a real *building* since before I pulled your ass from the Compound," Cowl agreed.

He was right. The three years after Bas's escape had been mostly spent in the cobbled-together cave. It was odd, the difference a few sharp angles could make on his fragile mind.

"We need to talk about what happened on the Rover," Bas said. Cowl wouldn't react well, but it had been long enough. "About what 306 said."

"There is no way we are going topside. Are you kidding me?" Cowl's eyes narrowed. "We are just barely staying alive as it is."

"It's hard to break freeze protocol. Nearly impossible," Bas said. "For 306 to risk—" A sudden sharp burst of pain in his skull cut off the words. He took a deep breath, shoving it back into its place. "Don't you think what she had to say would be important?"

Cowl raised an eyebrow and scanned him up and down before letting out a frustrated huff. "It could be a trap."

"She was disconnected." Bas didn't even try to hide the frustration in his voice.

"What could be up there that's so important? It's practically a death sentence to poke your head out of the rabbit hole." Cowl's face creased into a deeper frown. He was dead serious; never an encouraging sign.

"That's what we have to find out."

"Something is going on in the Hub," Menrva cut in. "I'm willing to at least check this out if it could give us some answers. Wrecker numbers are really low right now."

Why would she be supporting him? She offered him an encouraging grin and his resolve solidified.

"No. We have to keep our heads down if we want to survive," Cowl said.

"Everyone thinks that way. That reasoning is why the Compound exists in the first place," Bas argued.

Cowl's gaze battled with Bas's before he sighed heavily. "What will sating our curiosity even accomplish if we are dead?"

"So, because there is a chance we won't make it, you won't even try? Meanwhile we've almost been killed multiple times just for existing outside of the City's norms," Menrva pointed out.

"I guess it's two to one," Cowl said, glaring at her. "I thought after everything, my opinion might have a bit more weight, but that's what happens when you assume."

"Why don't you guys get some sleep," Bas offered, doing his best to shrug off the jab. Cowl was used to getting his way, but this was too important. "I'll take the first guard. We can talk about it more when we are settled in." He wouldn't be sleeping for a while. Headaches like this could last for hours or days, depending on how long the Connection was and how hard he fought it. He'd done pretty well this time.

Menrva shook her head. "I can't sleep."

"I'll take you up on it. I'm beat," Cowl said. He scooped a lamp off the ground. "You kids have fun. Call me if there is any shooting…" His words cut off with a yawn.

Bas kept his eyes on Cowl's back as he disappeared into a pod, his footsteps echoing as they scuffed over the years of dirt built up on the floor. Bas didn't want to be alone with Menrva and the subtle disgust in her endless eyes.

He turned until he could see the Rover through the open door. If trouble was coming, that was the quickest route away, and it was better than locking eyes with Menrva again.

"Is it always that bad… the Connection?" Menrva asked.

Bas's stomach tightened. Why did she have to bring this up now?

"Yeah…" He shifted to get a good look at her. What was that emotion written across her face? Pity? Worry? If only he could understand what she was really feeling. She was so closed off.

"The whole time?" she pressed.

"Yeah."

"That sucks."

Bas nodded, wincing as his head punished him. "I guess so." His eyes drifted recklessly down the curve of her neck. Yeah. It wasn't a good idea for them to be alone. She was terrified of him and he wanted nothing more than... Why did she have to be so inviting?

"I've played in Tournaments before," she said. "I was doing that to people, wasn't I?"

Bas's eyes snapped to her face and the sorrow dragging her lips into a pout, full lips over a determined chin. Could he lie to her? Wipe the guilt away? Instead, he nodded, unable to speak the words.

"How do you forgive yourself for something like that?" she said.

"You didn't know?"

Her eyes darkened "I know now."

Bas shook his head. "You can't hold yourself accountable."

"Can't I?" she asked, leaning forward. "Who gets to decide that? I might not have known what I was doing, but I did it. I did it, and now I can't do anything to change it." She pulled the tip of a braid and stared into the shadows for a long time. "Someone should be held accountable, right? Maybe the City, maybe me. But isn't that part of justice? That someone be held accountable?"

"It's all too complicated for me," Bas admitted. He rubbed his forehead, trying to filter through her words. He'd never felt much about the City other than fear and the desire to escape. Maybe he'd just been so well convinced it was natural. It was still hard now to understand why Cowl treated him like he did.

Concepts like justice just never applied to him. Punishment, sure, if you could even call it that.

Maybe there was a way in which it made sense. When someone hurt Cowl, it made him angry. One day they'd been out on a run when a scavenger caught Cowl with his knife. The rage that had filled Bas was still something he couldn't quite grasp. Was it justice, or just revenge? Whatever it was or wasn't, he didn't feel it toward Menrva.

"Do you really think this thing — topside — could actually matter to Bunker? The City hides a lot, but we are still all alive." Menrva twisted the hair around her thumb slowly. "What if it's good? What if the Wreckers are gone?"

"I'd be surprised," Bas said, clearing his throat. "They were still everywhere last time I went up. But...maybe something changed. I don't know."

"But what if we could go topside again? All of us. What if there were no Wreckers, no radiation, and the earth had been terraformed to make everything right again," Menrva said. "I don't think that's what's happened already, but theoretically. What do you think the City would do with the Borgs?"

Bas shuddered. He'd never felt like they were working toward a goal; just holding back the tide. But the world Menrva talked about didn't have room for him.

"We were made for a purpose," he said. "We aren't good for anything else. I think the City knows it better than anyone."

"So you think they would kill all of them?"

"I don't know." He had been made to follow orders

without question. The idea that he could make his own choices, or be expected to understand the choices of others, was a bit jarring at times. He was getting used to it, slowly. Getting into the City's headspace though... it felt like trying to understand a god.

"I think there is a place for them," Menrva said after a long pause. She carefully slipped around until she sat beside Bas. "I think the world would be a better place for it. If they are anything like you."

Bas's breath froze in his chest. A better place? She hated him, though. She was terrified of him, and with good reason. She couldn't actually mean that?

Her dark eyes didn't blink, though, as she focused on him.

Chapter Twenty-Six: The Bad Choice

Menrva struggled to stuff a thrill of fear back into her chest. How had the conversation taken this turn? She was trying to be encouraging, kind. Bas's brows were furrowed so low she couldn't even see his dark eyes.

"I'm confused," he said.

"About what?"

"I thought you...you act like you don't like me." He struggled with the words, his gaze wandering over the ceiling. Why wouldn't he look at her?

If she was going to be honest, this conversation was bound to happen eventually. Ever since the ride to the housing unit, she hadn't quite been able to oust the distinctly *physical* thoughts of Bas from her mind. His broad shoulders, his dark, piercing eyes, the intense weight of his presence. She was an adult woman. Scientifically, her interest was to be expected. Bas was, after all, everything that nature had programed a female to look for in a male counterpart. But that wasn't it. Talking about Nolan, about what happened to Angel, had triggered some sort of emotional change and somehow it ended with her attaching to Bas. Psychology wasn't a skill of hers, so she wasn't going to guess why. It was such a weak science, anyway.

Whatever the reason, she was going to have to address it eventually. It obviously wasn't going away. It was a bit harder now that she realized Bas didn't have a clue. Here she was, thinking she had been a bit too obvious.

"Look, I know you and Cowl have a 'no lies' type of agreement between you," Menrva said, tugging the ends of her hair. "So I want to be honest with you too. I have...a hard time. With men."

His expression didn't change, but he sat back slightly, as if trying to put more distance between them. She just had to push through and get it out. The more honest they were with each other, the better they would work together. "Because of that, I've found it hard to admit to myself that I'm starting to have feelings for you."

"Feelings?" Bas repeated, his eyes narrowed ever so slightly, his head cocked to the side. He didn't understand. She had to be very clear. He might have never even seen a romantic relationship before.

Menrva chewed on her lip, trying to formulate the best way to convey her thoughts. "What I'm trying to say is that I have romantic feelings for you."

He stared at her. Maybe she had to show him. He didn't know what affection was. Careful not to move too fast, Menrva slipped her fingers over his and squeezed. It wasn't the first time they'd held hands, but the jolt of electricity racing along her skin was new.

"Is this okay?" she asked.

Shaking, she shifted closer until the heat of his body radiated against her skin. Bas just stared at their hands.

"You aren't afraid of me?" he asked.

She couldn't say she wasn't, and it was hard to say if it was because Bas was who he was, or if it was because she just wasn't comfortable around men. But the fact that she was intimidated by him didn't mean anything. He wouldn't hurt her. Despite the fact that he made her nervous, that knowledge sat in the back of her mind constantly. "You are terrifying," she said. "But I trust you. I think."

Bas leaned forward and pressed his lips against hers. He moved so fast, she wanted to turn and run. Despite his haste, his touch was surprisingly gentle. She pushed away the fear and focused on the small ember of desire burning in her chest, letting the heat grow and fill her.

Her breath deepened as she let herself melt into the affection. It had been so long since she'd felt real love, since anyone had been willing to fight for her or beside her. Now here she was, feeling it in every inch of her flesh. Bas cared about her. Genuinely, truly.

Bas slid his arm around her, his body as solid as steel and yet warm and deep, like curling into bed after a long day. The hair on his forearms prickled against her shoulder as he steadied her and constricted his grip.

"Be gentle," she whispered as he pressed up against her aching ribs.

Bas started to pull away and terror shot through Menrva's chest as his arms fell away. No, not yet. She had only just gotten a taste. It wasn't enough, not after so long alone.

Without allowing herself to fully think about it, she pushed herself back into his arms, blocking his escape. After a half a second of limbo, Bas sank into the kiss and let his hands rest on her hips.

Menrva lay her hands on his neck, her fingers molding into his skin. Her breath came like sobs, and she leaned further into him. She kissed him now like she was trying to draw him into her, and he responded. Her pulse pounded in her ears like a drumbeat as he let his hands wander gently up her ribs and back.

One of her hands slipped behind his neck and collided with his bionic spine. He jumped, pushing her away.

"No," she said. "It's okay. It's okay." She grabbed his forearm, trying to keep him from going too far. She had scars, too. There were things on her body she was ashamed of. The spine didn't scare her anymore. It was there, present, but it didn't matter in any real way. All that mattered was him.

Bas reached for her, and she dove back into his arms. He twisted his hands into her thick curls, tilting her head into his own, his other arm wrapped around her waist. A shaft of pain ripped through her side as he pressed against her ribs. Nolan's face flashed through her head and before she could push it out, fear followed.

Her body locked up, chest tightening, blood pounding in her ears. Tears tore at the back of her eyelids. No. She couldn't do this.

Menrva pulled back, placing her hands on Bas's chest to keep him away. He looked down at her, his eyebrows knit as he scanned her body. Was he going to kiss her again?

"I'm sorry," she whispered.

"Don't be," he said quickly, letting his hands drop to his side. "I understand."

Relief flooded her, soothing the ache of unwanted memories

Had he really reminded her that much of Nolan? They were nothing alike, not in how they looked or acted. Bas's very presence was different than Nolan's.

If nothing else, there was the fact he'd listened to her now, he'd seen her fear and didn't make her feel foolish for it. Like he said, he understood. His body had belonged to other people, just like hers had. He couldn't have stopped the pain any more than she could have. Maybe that was why they were drawn to each other: they saw their own reflections in the other's eyes.

"Come here." Bas held his arms wide. "We don't need to do anything, just sit with me."

Despite the anxiety still tingling just under her skin, all she wanted was to return there. She curled up against him, her head cradled against his torso. His stomach rose and fell softly under her head, his heartbeat echoing in her ear.

Chapter Twenty-Seven: Preventative Measures

Bas's heart raced, his throat constricting in a moment of pure terror when he opened his eyes to see the angles of the room around him. He jolted to his feet, groaning as his battered body retaliated. The debilitating ache was enough to yank him back to reality. Shit. He'd fallen asleep.

He scanned the dark room, letting his heart crawl back to its appropriate place. Staying here was going to suck. Warmth seeped back in as he remembered last night, holding Menrva as she slept. She'd woken up enough to stumble to bed, and he'd kept watch alone. He didn't remember going to the pod.

Cowl was just visible through the door, bent over a pile of loose wires and other components. He didn't look up as Bas joined him.

"What are you doing?" Bas leaned over the table.

Cowl pushed a pair of goggles to his forehead. "I'm upgrading my smartwatch, trying to link it to a homemade security system," He held up his smartwatch, half torn apart. It looked remarkably professional for having been half- cannibalized from Rover pieces. "And, I wasted time I could have used to work on your Live Metal problem.

Instead, I had to fix the stupid Rover so you can Connect to go Topside."

Bas didn't answer. Why was he willing to help out now, after everything he'd said before? Maybe he was trying to scare Bas off with the Connection. It was foolish to go topside without a User, and he wasn't going to cheer over the possibility of it. He wasn't going to run away from it, either.

Cowl held up a cord. "I figure we can use your tether as our Connection." The tether he referred to was the input port in the tech. Cowl wouldn't be able to Connect to Bas; he would have to be alert in the Pit to run the program. The only remaining option was Menrva. It wasn't a horrible thought.

"You still need a network. The tether is just enough to get us in," Bas said.

"No biggie," Cowl said. "If we plug right into your tech, we can initiate the Connection and the Ether should carry it from there. We'll run the signal through the AI to make sure they can't find it for a while. Maybe run some sort of constantly changing password so they can't get in."

"It will reach topside?" Bas asked. Cowl knew what he was doing, so Bas would just have to trust that he had figured it out. Even if none of the details made sense.

"I don't see why not. It's just as strong as City Net."

Bas shrugged. "You are the tech guy."

"Yes. I am the tech guy." Cowl shifted, suddenly uneasy. "And... that's why I'm gonna have to get to your black box."

Bas frowned. "Really?"

"I don't want you freezing up in Wrecker town if the

Connection fails. If we lose you, we can't get you back without City Net. It may take another day or so before I can get it all figured out. We probably should have reprogrammed the box a while ago, anyway."

"Yeah, but we didn't because we don't want to kill me."

Messing with the black box was an intimidating obstacle. The embedded device contained all Bas's software, including the kill switch. If they started playing with the programming it could set off a miniature explosion in his chest, tearing his heart apart. To make matters worse, the only way to reach the box was to cut into his arm. They couldn't risk removing the lead brace to connect remotely. The City would take advantage of that immediately.

"Well, what do you prefer? You can get frozen in place on a Wrecker's dinner plate, or your heart could just explode...or, novel idea here, you could just *not* go topside." Cowl's tone was more irritated than sarcastic.

"Okay, we'll do it." Probably not the answer Cowl wanted to hear.

"Yeah, because we prefer unmedicated surgery to staying put. Screw logic. Let's just climb up to the most inhospitable environment known to man on three words from a random Borg." He was throwing a fit. Childish, sure, but he had a hard time letting go. Most times, Bas would have just given him his way. Why not? This wasn't something he could just walk away from, though.

"You are going to shoot me up with that tranq gun, first," he said.

Cowl sneered at him. "Fine, I'll be nice." He held up a rifle "You and your stupid ideas."

"What now?" Menrva asked from behind Bas, her feet scuffing the floor as she shuffled from her pod.

Bas rolled his shoulders and carefully avoided Menrva's eyes. What if her feelings had changed since last night? He should have been more careful. She couldn't have really meant everything she'd said.

"I get to cut open Bas's arm," Cowl said cheerily.

"Seriously?"

"We've gotta get to the black box," Bas said, doing his best to ignore the sound of his pulse in his ears.

"Yeah, I'm gonna be the one doing the cutting." Menrva crossed her arms across her stomach and frowned at Cowl.

Cowl shrugged. "Fine with me." He dug through a med kit, pulling out a prepackaged sterile blade. "Just remember, this is what happens when you get stupid ideas."

Bas plucked the knife from Cowl's hands. "You must be loving this."

"I should. It's almost poetic justice... but..." He paused. "No, not really. I actually like having you around. Call me crazy."

Bas's fingers brushed against Menrva's as he handed her the knife. She pulled away immediately, but a slight blush colored her cheeks. "I have a favor to ask you." He ignored her reaction.

She twisted the knife in her fingers. "Other performing surgery?"

"Maybe worse."

She raised an eyebrow. "Okay."

"Would you be the User, when I go up? Cowl would do

it, but he needs to monitor the tech."

"I wouldn't do it either way," Cowl said, frustration playing on every inch of his face.

Menrva blinked. She looked sick. "You want me to control you?"

"If you are okay with it," Bas said quickly. Even if she wasn't, there wasn't anyone else. Even just asking was almost cruel, but it was the only way.

"Why can't we all go up? I was planning on going with you," Menrva said.

Was she serious?

Bas shook his head. "Not with Wreckers. It's not safe for you. Or for me. If I run into one up there I have a much better chance under a Connection. That's why they built me this way."

Menrva brushed her hair off her face with shaking hands. Her eyes searched his. What was she looking for?

"I trust you," Bas assured her.

Menrva nodded. "Okay."

Bas was interrupted by a sharp pain in his stomach. He looked down to see a dart lodged between the folds of his shirt.

"That felt good. I never knew how much I wanted to shoot you," Cowl said with a sardonic smile as he set the dart gun aside.

The effects were quick. Bas eased down to the floor as his limbs began to grow heavy and his heartbeat slowed.

Cowl was definitely still angry.

Chapter Twenty-Eight:
Freeze Protocol

Menrva looked from Bas's prone body then back to Cowl.

"Really. No warning?"

Cowl shrugged. "Best get in there," he said. "We have maybe forty-five minutes. But he's a big guy, so it might not even be that long."

"What am I even doing?"

Cowl reached down and held up Bas's muscular arm. He pointed at the metal band fused in place. "Under this, there is a black hard drive about the size of a matchbox. I can't take off the cuff. Can't risk it. You will have to go in from the side and cut under. Just, whatever you do, don't cut any wiring."

Menrva pulled the wrapping from the scalpel, trying not to shake. "What happens if I cut a wire?"

"If it's within an inch of the box you'll flip the kill switch and his chest will explode."

"Oh really, is that all?" Menrva struggled against the bile rising in her throat.

"It's so they don't try to tear them out." Cowl scowled and shrugged, as if to brush aside an offensive image. "Still better than getting eaten."

Ignoring the fear attempting to take her hands, Menrva knelt beside him. She had killed people, broken a woman's arm with her bare hands, and saved Bas from a Connection. This should be easy. Despite the reassuring thoughts, she struggled to touch the blade to Bas's golden skin. It was one thing cutting him open the first time, when he was a dangerous stranger. But now, he was so real and so fragile. She pressed her finger around the edge of the lead cuff until she found the rigid shape of the tech underneath. It was barely noticeable.

Now that she was about to make the incision, the grime covering everything was suddenly overwhelming. The housing unit was far from a clean working environment. She pulled a sterilizing cloth from the kit and scrubbed Bas's arm.

"You got this, Menrva. He'll be fine." Cowl's voice was firm and confident. Did anything scare him? She was about to cut into his best friend's arm and possibly blow out his chest.

It was not a good idea to think about exploding his chest. It was a very nice chest... She blushed at the thought and pulled her focus back to the task at hand.

Menrva pressed the knife to the flesh, swallowing the fear planting itself in her throat. Her head ached, alerting her to the fact that her teeth were clenched tightly. She tried to imagine she was cutting into a tissue sample in the lab. No different, just a bit more volatile.

Red tears burst from Bas's skin as the knife slid into the flesh. The box wasn't shallow. It nestled almost against his bone. Maybe the people who installed it had been concerned about a situation just like this. The flesh parted and was obscured immediately by a wave of blood. Menrva wiped it away and pressed the skin apart with her fingers. Everything looked the same: solid, raw, and red. Through the gore, a hint of something unnatural poked through, and Menrva carefully worked toward it. A web of metallic black thread wove through the flesh, more than she could have guessed. It hadn't quite registered before how much the technology was a part of him. This couldn't be reversed and it couldn't be removed, the damage was permanent. How did Borgs adjust to these changes? Could they even live normal lives? Did they have perverse health issues, die early? Did the City even care or did they just keep pumping out new children, without thought to how it would all end? Maybe they just expected that all of them would meet their end at the jaws of a Wrecker.

The deeper she delved into his arm, the more the false nervous system showed itself, as did the effects of its unchecked growth. In many places it wrapped around the muscle or balled up into ugly, metallic tumors. This was her mother's doing. Would Leslie have been proud of her work right now, looking down at this? It was sadistic, like chains running through his body. If she could have reached Leslie, she would have eagerly strangled her. It did, at least, explain why the woman was so distant. You couldn't do this kind of thing to living humans before going home and tucking your daughter into bed and kissing her goodnight. No, Leslie had killed her humanity a long time ago.

"That's it, good. Just a bit closer," Cowl said.

"How do you know? Have you done this before?"

Menrva snapped.

Holding her breath, she slid the blade down his arm. She risked a glance at Bas's face and was comforted by his peaceful visage.

Finding her mark was like running blindly to the edge of a cliff. The Live Metal veins were everywhere, and there was no way to tell where one would pop up. What would happen if she cut a vein further from the box? Maybe it wouldn't heal right. What if she permanently damaged his arm?

The knife hit something solid. Menrva froze. After a few tense seconds there was still no explosion. She lay a hand on Bas's chest and waited for the steady rise of his lungs. They would hear or see an explosion, right? Even a small one. Maybe that was a misconception. It wouldn't take a lot to mangle his heart.

Cowl wiped the swelling tide of blood away with a clean cloth. "I think that's it," he said, squinting into the wound. "Now you just have to find the base of the wires."

"The wires I'm not supposed to cut?"

"Yeah, those ones."

Menrva shook her head, releasing a pent up breath through her teeth. A droplet of sweat slid down her cheek. Slowly she dragged the tip of the knife along the hard edge of the box. The box dead-ended into a mass of wires, a jumble without any clear order. It was all grown into the meat, making an impossible maze of the natural and the mechanical.

"Perfect. I got it from here," Cowl said. "Just be very careful when you pull the knife out."

"Should I be relieved yet? He's still alive," she said, as much for her own benefit as it was for Cowl's.

"You did great, Nerve," Cowl said. "This is going really quick. You sure you aren't a serial killer? You are very good at dissecting people."

Menrva shot him the nastiest face she could through her anxiety. She withdrew the knife so slowly it was as if she wasn't even moving. Putting the instrument aside, she replaced Cowl's hands with her own and pulled the wound open so the light illuminated the gore inside. Cowl wiped the blood away again. He inserted a few wires and connected them gingerly to the base of the black box.

"You seem to know what you are doing," Menrva said.

"Are you kidding? I'm pissing my pants here."

Laughing was a bad idea. The situation was too tense for her to be chuckling and she didn't want to jostle the wound, but she grinned despite herself. Cowl wiped the blood from his fingers and leaned over the screen now connected to Bas's arm like an otherworldly parasite.

"What are you doing now?" Menrva asked.

"I'm trying to turn off the programming. Kill switch, gauntlet, freeze protocol. That way if we get disconnected he will get full control of his body."

"The freeze protocol is what made those other Borgs all stop working when we jammed the signal, right?" The memory of the eerie scene on the Rover drifted back into Menrva's mind. They were like corpses with rigor mortis. No wonder they were going so far to rid Bas of the program.

"Yup," Cowl answered, distracted by the task at hand.

Trying to push out the image of Bas frozen in front of a pack of Wreckers, Menrva turned her attention away from the incision. She caught a glimpse of Bas's face just in time to see his eyelids flutter. His head turned just slightly toward her and her breath caught in a knot in her throat.

"Cowl. He's waking up."

Bas's face creased into a cringe. He felt it. He felt them digging in his arm. A moment of panic nearly debilitated Menrva.

"Don't let him move," Cowl said. He fumbled to push the computer off his chest. "I have no idea how fragile those wires are or what will set off the kill switch."

Chapter Twenty-Nine: In His Bones

Menrva scanned the room desperately, not entirely sure what she was looking for.

"Get that tranq gun - make sure you have the right one please - and shoot him," Cowl said, replacing her hands with his own.

It had been less than twenty minutes, but Bas was just too big for the tranquilizers to be fully effective. The gun slipped in Menrva's hands as she checked the cartridge. The thumbnail-sized darts sat in orderly rows, waiting for their deployment.

"Cut him, now shoot him?" Menrva aimed the gun at Bas's chest.

"Well, you have to start your relationship out on the right foot," Cowl said, his words coming out like a growl.

Menrva's face burned. She shook off the embarrassment and pressed the trigger. Bas jolted as the dart sank into his chest. He lifted his head, and she sucked in a sharp breath as his features tensed. She knelt by his side and ran a hand over his face. Touch soothed him, maybe it would help. Her fingers left streaks of blood on his face as she smoothed the hair away from his forehead.

"Just lay back. It's okay," she said gently. "We've got you. Relax."

Bas's expression eased. He lay back on the floor, and a moment later he went still again.

Menrva returned to her post at his arm.

"Good job," Cowl said, offering her a nervous smile as he retrieved the tablet. "I think I've almost got it."

Menrva shuddered. She wanted to grip Bas's hand or, better yet, run. Instead, she focused on watching the blood seeping into the wound, swelling until it spilled out between her fingers.

Finally, Cowl put the computer down with a heavy sigh. "I think we are good."

"You think?" Menrva asked.

"We are," Cowl clarified, a bit more confidently this time. He gently dislodged the wires from the box. Menrva pulled her fingers away from Bas's arm, wincing as the skin relaxed together. The wound was sickening. Deep and raw.

Menrva frowned at the uneven lines of the cut as she applied the liquid bandage, praying he wouldn't get an infection. Wrecker genes might help with that aspect; they seemed to be able to fight off just about anything. That was why bio warfare had been such an epic failure.

Bas's fingers began to twitch as Menrva cleaned the blood from the sealed wound. He had barely been out fifteen minutes from the last dart. His muscles flexed and tightened until the skin puckered around the liquid bandage. He was going to pop the wound open again before the glue could dry. Menrva grabbed his clenched fist in her hands, pushing his arm down as gently yet firmly as she could. Bas jerked away, but when his eyes found her he relaxed again.

"How'd it go?" he mumbled.

Menrva shook her head and threw the bloodied wipe to the rest of the garbage. "You're a light sleeper," she said.

Bas chuckled, his eyes still half closed. The smile brushing his lips was shaky and brief. He looked oddly peaceful: features smooth under the scruff obscuring his etched jawline. Maybe he hadn't felt the pain yet? It was sure to catch up with him.

"So, I can add surgeon to my resume," Cowl said from where he was cleaning his hands. "If I wasn't buried in the center of the post-apocalyptic earth right now, I could make a killing."

Menrva cleaned up the last of their tools. "Well, we may have fixed your black box but that arm is going to give you trouble."

Bas stretched his fingers, testing his arm. "But it won't give *you* any trouble," he said, looking her in the eyes pointedly. He stood up. "Let's try it."

Menrva froze. "You just got out of surgery. No way am I going to play puppet master right now. You need to rest."

"A few minutes is all." He smiled, though it seemed more for her sake. "We can test it and see if it works to break the Connection."

"Come on, Bas. I think you are taking this too fast. Take a breath. You can't do anything if you are dead," Cowl advised.

"It will only be a couple minutes. It's better we know now," Bas said.

As much as she hated to admit it, he was right. If they have made a mistake, it would be a pretty easy fix right now, while the wound was still fresh. She could easily cut through the bandage and reach the black box again. Once it started to heal, which would be quickly thanks to the liquid bandage, it would be a whole new surgery. "Let's do it," Menrva agreed.

"What? No. Wait. You were on my side!" Cowl said.

Bas smiled his thanks and reached to grab her hand. Menrva marveled at the warmth that flowed up her arm. She had never felt sunshine before, but she imagined it was a lot like this. The affectionate gesture didn't last, and left her longing for more.

"It won't take long, and it will be good to know if it worked or not," she explained. If Bas went into freeze protocol topside after all this...she didn't want to think about that possibility.

"*I* did it; of course it worked." Cowl threw his hands in the air, pacing a few steps away.

"Cowl." Bas looked him in the eye. "Come on."

"You could say please."

"Please," Menrva said.

"Fine." Cowl waved them toward the Rover, his anger still hovering like a barely contained thunderstorm. "What would you guys do without me?"

"Die," Bas said in all seriousness.

"Speak for yourself," Menrva said, raising an eyebrow.

Cowl grumbled under his breath as he climbed into the Rover. He rummaged under the console a minute and pulled out a clunky cord with an attached scanner. It was considerably more threatening, now that Menrva understood exactly the reason for its existence.

She was used to seeing the object attached to the back of a chair. This option looked a bit less stable, but it didn't matter. Her receiver would cut off most of her nervous system's communication to her brain, paralyzing all but the necessary functions. She wouldn't move an inch once she went into the Sim. It was no different than dreaming, except the outcome would be more permanent.

"We have to Connect you directly," Cowl explained, pulling out a second cord. "You can't unplug because I don't have the stuff with the Ether all figured out yet."

"How likely is it the City will see the connection?" Menrva asked.

"We are using the Ether," Cowl said. "Totally different network; it will look just like a Sim to them, with a little help from my AI to camouflage the signal. That's why we have to use the tether. The Ether wasn't built for this kind of shit."

"It's a lucky thing we got this Rover," Bas said, climbing stiffly on the vehicle bed. "We would have been screwed without it."

"You mean we wouldn't be able to send you up to the surface. Oh, the horror," Cowl said, twisting his face into a melodramatic gasp.

Bas dropped a hand on Cowl's shoulder. "Trust us, will you?"

"I'm doing it, aren't I?" He held up the scanner pointedly.

Menrva settled onto the floor. The click of the scanner onto the back of her neck was all too familiar. Heat rushed through her veins, making her heart beat faster. Ever since she was a child, she had loved the escape of the Sims, lies or not. In there, the world suddenly had purpose. The trees, the sun, the grass might have just been computer code, but it still felt like humanity was meant for those things. The feeling was hard to shake.

"Okay, when you are ready," Cowl said, backing away from Bas like he'd just set a bomb.

Menrva looked to see Bas smiling his reassurance. As if she should be the one who was nervous.

She took a deep breath and closed her eyes. The buzz of the initial Connection was much more noticeable, now that she had been so long without it. Her body went numb for a moment and then she opened her eyes. Had the Connection been made? Everything looked the same.

"Nerve, you in there?" Cowl asked.

Menrva looked up at him and was surprised to see him leaning over her own limp body.

"Weird," she said. Her voice made her jump. No, not her voice. Bas's.

She stood slowly, vertigo following her all the way up. Bas was so tall. What had she expected, though? This was no different than the tournaments. She had experienced this very thing countless times. Bas's body could have been her own, only a bit more awkward. She had almost expected to feel Bas beating against her from inside his head. She had expected to feel him *somehow*... or maybe she just wanted to.

She crouched over her own prone form. Her face looked horrible, scabbed up and tattered. The roots of her hair were growing black and thick, trailing into the pale blue ends that made her look almost ethereal.

She had to remember it was all an illusion. She wasn't really pressed into Bas's body. It was just her brain reacting to outside stimulation. Bas wasn't really with her, he was trapped in his own mind, watching her direct his movements through a haze of pain.

"Are you sure you are okay with this?" Menrva asked instinctively.

"He can't answer you," Cowl said.

Menrva blushed, or more accurately, Bas blushed. "I know, I just wasn't thinking." Of course he couldn't answer. She was using his voice.

"You ready to pull the plug?"

Menrva nodded. She didn't like the feeling of Bas's body, of knowing he was trapped without the ability to even give consent. She was like a jailer. Clenching her fist, she sucked in a deep breath. If this didn't work, they were back to square one. Putting Bas through more of this was unthinkable.

Cowl rolled Menrva's head forward. It was surreal. Shouldn't she be feeling his fingers on her neck? He paused for a half a second, clenching and unclenching his hand briefly as if to chase away tremors. Part of her wanted to scream "Not yet!" but before the thought could even take root everything went dark for a second. She looked up to see Cowl's gleaming blue eyes above her. She hadn't even felt the Connection break.

"Bas?" Menrva asked, jerking up. She half expected him to be gone, disappeared like he'd never existed.

He stood a few feet away, his head in his hands the way he always did when fighting one of his headaches. He turned to look at her, squinting through obvious pain. "Good," he said. His voice was tight, almost a whisper. "We're almost ready."

>><<

Menrva shifted on the hard slab that had once held mattresses and sleeping families. Dead families. Her ribs ached with each wrong move. It had been a long time since she lay down to sleep without some kind of pain. This was different, though. Memories of Bas's body kept dragging her back from the brink of sleep. Did she really want to be the one to torture him like that?

A sound reverberated from the pod beside her where Bas slept. Was he a snorer? That was almost cute. But no, he moaned. He was dreaming. Menrva climbed to her feet. Should she go check on him? Was that awkward?

He said her name. He didn't just say her name, though, he called to her. His voice was tormented.

Menrva trailed one hand along the wall to find the door as she followed the sound. A beam of light from the lantern in the front made its way through the darkness of Bas's room, illuminating his sleeping form. Dust fairies drifted around him. He was positioned on his side, as usual. The tech must be uncomfortable to lay on.

Menrva sat cross-legged in front of him. The tank top he wore, just a bit too small, tightened across his chest with each breath. She could have sworn his heart beat visibly against the front of it. Dust framed the worry lines around his eyes and on his forehead, making him look old and tired. Instinctively, she reached out and smoothed her hand over his face.

Bas's eyes shot open and he caught Menrva's hand. His grip was firm, but his fingers shook. He must have recognized her because he relaxed again and smiled. With a soft tug, he drew her into his arms. She lay against his body, her head cradled on his bicep and her face tucked under his chin. She should have been terrified, but after being in his body, it was hard to still feel afraid of it. It was familiar.

His breath ruffled her hair as he tangled his legs into hers. With one massive hand he held her own hand up to his heart, the flutter of his life pressing against her fingers. It beat fast, maybe still racing from whatever dreams he had been fighting.

How could anyone cause him pain? There was a special cruelty in the process that brought him here. It wasn't just that they were turning people's bodies into death traps or torturing them the entire time. People had always endured pain; it was part of what it meant to be alive. No, the cruelty was in what they were denied. Bas had never known a family. His father was a human invention, his mother was machinery. He'd never had anyone to hold him like this. To the City, he was nothing more than a loaded gun.

The thoughts sent hot anger rushing through Menrva. This was a sadistic punishment for anyone, but for him, it was so much more. Bas was gentle, almost fragile in his own way. He was a man who held her like a baby with a teddy bear because he had bad dreams. He was a man who gave tender hugs when tears flowed. He was a man who had gently cradled a suffering Borg and trusted the words she struggled to speak.

"I won't let you go back," Menrva said. She pulled herself away so she could look into his placid face. "I will protect you with every breath. I promise."

It sounded foolish in her own ears. She was a scientist, not a bodyguard. If anyone needed protection it should have been her. But Bas didn't even chuckle.

"Don't promise," he whispered. "I don't want you to live with that."

She opened her mouth to answer but Bas hushed her with a kiss. His lips were sweet, despite the layer of dirt clinging to his face. She let herself disappear into it, breathing in the scent of earth and gun-cleaning solvent that clung to him.

"Just promise me more of this, even if it's just for tonight," he said. His fingers barely skimmed over her, soft as a whisper. He must have been worried about scaring her again, but she was a million miles away from fear. Bas was a bomb shelter, his powerful arms shielding her from any dark thoughts. Life flowed between them, beating through their locked lips and spreading through every inch of her. She could have sworn electricity coursed through her veins and over her skin, vitalizing her in a way she had never experienced before.

"I promise," Menrva said. Did he know how much that promise meant? Did he know how hard it had been to trust his hands at first, how hard it would continue to be? Maybe she would always be afraid. Except for now. Right now was perfect.

Bas tightened his arms around her and turned on his back, dragging Menrva onto his chest. She gazed down at his face, drinking in every part of him: his skin of burnt gold, his eyes like black holes drawing her in. As he breathed out she drew in, and when his heart beat hers answered. She lay her head on Bas's chest, cradled in the curve of his neck, listening to his pulse under his skin and the gentle buzz of his tech. Why hadn't she noticed that before?

Chapter Thirty: What's to Come

Maybe he should just leave. Cowl kicked a pile of dirt left by the Rover and swore into the darkness. Three years he'd been the one keeping Bas together. Menrva walks in, and just cause she was good looking, she was now point man...woman.

Now she was playing along with Bas's stupid risk-taking. Could she not see how much he was struggling? Of course she couldn't, she didn't know him. She had no clue what it did to him to go through a Connection, or how insanely dangerous it was for him to go topside. She had her bleeding heart to soothe, so why not use him? If she was going to play hero, why couldn't she do it with her own ass?

If she wasn't there, pushing Bas to climb topside, Cowl could talk him out of it. Well, if Bas had Menrva, maybe it was time for him to get out of there. If he took the Rover and just left, not only could Bas not go topside, but the scavengers and maybe even the City would follow the tracks and leave Bas alone.

It was a good plan, but the thought of leaving after all they'd been through made his stomach ache. Or maybe that was hunger. Rations were the worst.

The security system Cowl had set up was far from state of the art, but he only had a limited amount of junk to work with. He'd repurposed the two cams on the Rover, both on the far side of the housing unit. Because the building was basically just a giant rectangle, he was pretty confident they could catch anything on the front half if they just stayed vigilant. The back end was problematic because it was quite a long walk to get all the way around.

Thank the technology gods for night vision.

He would have to dismantle the security out front to get the Rover running again. Another excuse not to leave quite yet. He'd pulled cords out of the engines to power the laser sensors. A few modified tablets and laser-sights from the guns made the ugliest security system under the earth, but they worked. The hope was they weren't actually going to be seen, anyway.

Cowl glanced at the entrance of the housing unit. What were Bas and Menrva doing right now? Sleeping? Sleeping together? Should it matter?

The last thing Bas needed was a mess like *that* to sort through. Things had been so simple. Straightforward. The City didn't bother them. The scavengers kept their distance. Capricorn got what he needed every week and there was always plenty of resources. Cowl was so close to fixing that issue with the Live Metal, too. Now it might be too late, if he ever got back to it. No, not a good way to think. That was all before Menrva had to go make a mess.

Now she was taking away the only thing Cowl had left. Why couldn't she stay in her nice, plush, white-washed life and leave him alone?

There was one thing he could fix. Why did he always have to be the one to save their asses? Bas was the superhuman.

All he needed was a connection to City Net and a couple hours to shift through footage. No use wasting Bas's life when he could check out the surface with a simple hack. It might not turn anything up, but it never hurt to try. That, and it would give him something to think about other than what might be happening on the other side of the wall. Gross.

It was worse than imagining his parents doing it.

Cowl found an especially large boulder and tried to find a comfortable spot. Who was he kidding? He hadn't been comfortable since he came down to the Pit, and it hadn't made that much of a difference in his life. Being comfortable was overrated. Comfortable people were lazy and stupid.

2, 3, 5, 7, 11...

He turned on his tablet and flicked through the initial screens.

13, 17, 19... Shut up.

Focus.

His AI was planted securely in the City Net and filtering past new firewalls every day. There were a few it needed help with, but for the most part it was easy access. He'd gotten access to the cams a long time ago. That was part of how he found Bas in the first place.

The memory made his stomach ache. Bas had come such a long way. Where they really going to throw it all away for the sake of something that may or may not be hiding above the surface? The Connection would drive Bas crazy. How could he endure hours of that kind of torture and not come out of it in shreds? He was already having nightmares and dissociative attacks just from the whole situation with the Borgs.

"Dumb, self-sacrificing moron," he muttered.

Bas had been raised to believe he was a tool. Even when he was making his own choices, it was based on the lie that his life was somehow less important than everyone else's. That he was a pawn of sorts, and it was his purpose to go out and get himself killed.

The surveillance program opened on the screen and Cowl scrolled through. Most of the cams were distorted by ice. It only took a second for the gears to warm up and the picture to clear.

The sight of the surface never failed to make his stomach turn. It was hard to believe there had ever been anything up there but the bleak, frozen desert there was now. It was impossible to tell if it was day or night. The same weak light seemed to shine no matter the time of day, but that might have just been the night vision on the camera. The Sims portrayed a very different world, one that seemed more fantasy than anything else. Grass, flowers, trees, living animals. If he hadn't seen those things for himself in the farming tier, he would have doubted they were ever real to begin with.

Sometimes it was easier to think that way. That history was a lie and life had always been this way. That the Wreckers had always belonged above them in the nightmare realm and the underworld was always theirs. He'd had theories before, that the City just told these lies to keep everyone working hard and in their place. It was a popular conspiracy, especially in the working class.

Everyone was easier to control if they believed it was for survival's sake.

Cowl wasn't sure how he felt about that one. The City seemed pretty desperate, especially lately. The poor idiots who believed the surface was actually livable and that the elite were keeping it for themselves were the ones he thought were complete idiots. Of course, if you'd never seen a Wrecker before, or caught a glimpse of the surface even with the cams, there was probably room for that kind of stupidity.

Using the AI, Cowl connected to the helmet cam of one of the Borgs. According to the tag in the corner of the screen, it was a Gen Five. Gen fives were twenty, only a year younger than him. Poor kid.

The backs of two other Borgs bobbed in the distance, spread out to cover ground. The camera bounced slightly with the Borg's long step as he followed the curve of a hill. There wasn't any sound. He'd have to work on that, but he could pretty well fill in the silence with his own imagination.

Nothing looked particularly interesting. Cowl could only guess at what exactly he was supposed to be seeing. The Borg's warning had been pretty vague. There was nothing obvious. That was some sort of answer, wasn't it? If the world was suddenly all right and the mythical heaven of centuries ago was in full bloom, there would have been some sort of sign.

The Borg stopped suddenly and checked his gun before turning to scan the landscape carefully. Something was wrong. He had settled into some sort of fighting stance.

The barrel of the gun dipped in and out of the camera lens as the Borg broke into a run, doubling back toward the others.

Something flashed to the right of the cam, and Cowl's heart jumped into his throat.

The Wreckers were still there. Nausea kicked at the wall of Cowl's stomach as he watched the unfolding events on the screen. He didn't have to be a genius to know what was going to happen next. He was, and he did...

In a blur of frozen earth and black fur, the Borg collapsed and was jerked over the ground. For an instant, all that filled the camera feed was the dirt and broken bits of coral rushing by beneath the helmet. The shield cracked, splintering into a thousand pieces to let in a massive claw. Blood splattered across the screen and Cowl dropped the tablet.

His heart battered his chest, and his hands shook as he tried to shove the images from his head.

How was he supposed to be okay with Bas going up? Some twenty-year-old kid had just been skewered on a Wrecker's claws, and Bas wanted to rush up there alone and try his hand? And he was supposed to, what, hold the door open and wave his only friend through like it was nothing?

No. He wasn't going to do it. This was one instance where he had no qualms being an asshole and putting his foot down. Realistically, he never had any issue with being an asshole, but still...

Cowl scooped up the tablet, now with a blank screen, and shoved it into his pocket.

He would just have to go in there and tell Bas his plan was stupid and if he wanted to do it, Menrva better come up with the Connection, cause he wasn't doing it. Then he would burn the Rover.

Muttering curses, Cowl stalked toward the housing unit.

He brushed the dust from his shoulders as he ducked into the entrance and tugged off the goggles. The front of the Unit was still empty except for the piles of guns and supplies. Bas and Menrva were probably still sleeping. They'd better be sleeping, or he'd be interrupting whatever they were doing to give them a piece of his mind.

The tablet in his pocket buzzed, a soft chime filling the enclosed space. Cowl brought it back out, frowning as he flicked on the screen.

Breach. The word flashed on the screen.

Breach? Breach of what and by who? No one even knew he was in the system.

A loud crash from Bas's room interrupted Cowl's thoughts. He put the tablet on the closest surface and jogged toward the door. Maybe he shouldn't go in. A strangled yell forced the decision for him. Bas was having another nightmare. A bad one.

Chapter Thirty-One: The Stars Fall

Bas knew from the moment the nightmare started that it was a dream. It was the kind where you are desperate to get out, but there is no door. The kind that makes you feel like you are going insane.

He stood on a frozen peak, his boots digging into the broken earth. The black sky stretched endlessly above him, spotted haphazardly with a few bright stars like bullet holes. Something was off, but he couldn't quite grasp it. It was as if the world was toppling and rolling around him but he couldn't perceive it zipping past.

His hands were hot. He looked down to stare at the red dripping from them, running down his fingers and pooling at his feet until it melted the ice. Blood, so much it seemed his hands were dissolving.

A trail of gore wound down the cliffside, leading his eye to the scene below. Bodies covered the cracked earth below. Men, women, children...the ground choked on their remains. They lay contorted and ripped apart in mounds. Frost already coated their skin, and their eyes were bleached white. Despite that, the blood still flowed, mingling together and sinking into the broken ground.

Bas took a shaky step forward, shuddering as flesh and bone squelched under his heel. The layers of dead were so thick he couldn't find solid ground to stand on. He tripped on one of the corpses and fell forward, choking as the smell of blood wrapped itself around his throat. Cold hands seemed to drag him further down.

He staggered back to his feet. Another step; more death. Something grabbed his leg and he looked to see Menrva's face, empty. Her own blood splattered over her lips and cheek. Ice crystals crept across her forehead as her hair blew about her like a blue flame. Haunted eyes turned and locked on his, and the breath froze in his lungs.

"No. No. *No!*" He screamed the words, which hung in the air and echoed into the reaches of space.

"It's not a dream," Menrva said. Her voice was as cold as the dead hand wrapping around his ankle.

"It's not a dream," another voice said. It too was female, but darker, blacker, and penetrating hot like fire.

Bas looked up to see a Wrecker standing only feet from him. Its eyes burned like shards of the sun deep in its skull as it regarded him. It didn't move. Blood dripped from its claws and ran from its maw. Bas took an involuntary step back, and so did the Wrecker.

Bas couldn't swallow past the knot blocking his airway. He reached up and touched his mouth, feeling blood running from his lips. The Wrecker did the same. He rolled his shoulders. Again, the Wrecker mirrored his movements. Even its breath matched his own.

"It's not a dream." Its voice echoed in Bas's his mind, but its lips never moved. "Save me. Kill them. Kill...kill...kill." With each repetition the words grew heavier. Bas clasped his hands over his ears as the words warped into screams, but it did no good. The sound came from inside his head.

The black sky collapsed on them. Bas screamed, but his voice was lost in space as burning stars pummeled the earth and filled everything with white-hot light.

When he opened his eyes, he stood in the Compound. It was not a hall he recognized. Before him was a door, set with a thick glass window opening to an empty room. He shuddered at the memory of the hard floor and the bland, featureless walls. Those rooms were worse than any nightmare. He jumped back when a face slammed into the window.

It was thin, skull-like. It belonged to a girl a bit older than himself. Her skin was so pale the veins of Live Metal were visible under it, braided into blood vessels. The girl's eyes were sunken until they turned shadowy black. Below them her lips were thin and pulled back to show pointed teeth. Her shaved hair was white, like frost.

"Help me." The voice didn't come from her lips, but it radiated out of her. "Save me. Kill them. Kill...kill...kill."

A hand fell on Bas's arm.

"Come, boy. Let's get you home. I need to put you where you can't hurt anyone else."

Bas turned to see Pope standing behind him. His slim, boyish face pulled down in a sorrowful look, as if he were deeply hurt by the fact that Bas was out of his pod. The crushing weight of his disappointment settled on Bas like a blanket, and for a moment Bas wanted to disappear. A door behind him gaped open to a white room that seemed to be caving in on itself. The floor crumbled, sucking him toward the open door and the claustrophobic space inside.

"You're dangerous." Pope's words fought for a place around the Wrecker in Bas's mind

"Kill...kill...kill." The voice chanted in his head like a drumbeat.

"You will devour..."

 "Kill...kill...kill..."

Pain poured throughout Bas's body. Someone's hands gripped him and began dragging him into a shrinking cell. He twisted, writhing in an effort to escape. The hand fell on his face.

"Kill...kill...kill." It changed from a chant to a scream. "It's not a dream. Kill them."

Bas reached out and touched the warmth of a human body. Soft, weak. He gripped it tight in both hands. The world folded in on itself and he threw himself forward with a roar.

Dust choked him, coating his lungs with each breath he took. He slammed the body in his hands against the wall. It was small... fragile. Bas's attack ripped a gasp from his victim, sending a buzz of adrenaline shooting through his arms and chest. He was about to make a kill. He would feel the heat of blood on his hands and watch the life slip away into the dark.

"Stop! Please. Stop!"

Bas stumbled back at the sound. Realization tore through him like a bullet. That was Menrva's voice.

Chapter Thirty-Two: It's Not a Dream

As soon as Bas released Menrva she crumbled onto the floor, shaking in the shallow light from the door. Light glinted like needle points from her wide, terrified eyes as her hands wrapped around her stomach.

Cowl appeared in Bas's peripherals, silhouetted against the lamplight.

"What? What happened?" he asked.

Reality hit Bas like a bullet. He'd hurt Menrva. He had tried to kill her...and he had loved the feeling of it. He spun around, slamming himself into the wall, unable to arrest the scream cutting its way out of his lips. The metal trembled beneath his wrath.

"Bas?" Menrva's voice was soft, frightened.

He had done that. The fear was his fault. What was wrong with him? Why had he let her stay? Why did he stay? He had to get himself away from both of them. The temperature in the tiny room climbed, blazing until his skin felt like it was blistering. Vibrations filled the air, the pressure growing around him as the walls pressed in. The shadows ran out of their borders, swelling like ocean waves breaking against the light and drowning it out. A low growl bounced off the walls and wrapped around him. He had to go, he had to get out.

Bas sprinted out the door. Cowl grabbed his arm but he didn't slow, tearing free with little effort. The darkness of the housing unit was like the empty black sky above, and Bas lost his place, tumbling through empty space. He couldn't see where he was going, but he didn't hesitate, even as he ricocheted off the walls and stumbled over scattered furniture.

Finally, he hit a wall that he couldn't go around. There was a way out of the room. He had just entered, but the knowledge was a silent passenger behind his raging mind. Bunk beds cluttered the space. He tangled himself in them before he hit another wall.

It was a bad habit. He was regressing. He was being dragged back into dark memories. It wasn't real. What wasn't real, though? Maybe this was the delusion, maybe what he thought were dreams were actually reality. What if he had been devoured and this was hell? Worse, what if he opened his eyes right now to harsh light and white walls? The thoughts strangled him, pushing his breath down his throat like a fireball. No, no, no, no. His knees hit the floor and he doubled over his aching stomach, trying to fend off the fear eating away at his abdomen. Where could he escape? He jolted to his feet, shaking his head to dislodge the growls still hanging in his ears.

"It's not a dream." The dark voice echoed around him, weighing down the air itself.

Bas paced the room. With each turn, he slammed himself against the walls like pendulum. Slam, slam, slam. With each hit he jolted back into his skin, fully alive and present for only a moment before the madness cocooned him again.

His breath was ragged and torn.

Slam, slam, slam.

He couldn't clear away the screaming in his head, the memories twisting like Live Metal. The only thing relieving it was the pain as his body met metal.

Slam, slam, slam.

Hot blood tickled the side of Bas's face as it made its way over his cheek, the warmth sinking through the abstract numbness. A light shone through the room, and he reeled away from its violent arrival, colliding one last time into the wall with a sound like a muted gunshot. Dirt rolled under his fingertips as the wall melted, rolling under him until his head spun. No, the room spun... The world was too weak to hold the weight in him.

"Hey, brother. What's with the drama?" Despite the sarcasm, Cowl's voice was low and calming.

Bas struggled to control the tremors rolling through him, mentally swearing for his inability to speak or move. His body seemed to have pushed him aside and was reacting on its own. It was like a Connection, except the Users were ghosts and memories. He labored to drag in a breath. Where was he?

Every muscle in his body tensed.

Bas slid down the wall until he sat on his heels. He kept his head pressed into the wall.

"Bas?" Menrva's voice sent shivers of shame down his spine. What was he more ashamed of, the hurt he had done her or the dissolving mess of a man he had become in only a moment?

"I'm on your right, Bas. You are going to feel my hand on your shoulder." Cowl's voice was reassuring as he drew closer, steady. Despite the warning, the touch hit him like a whip. He jerked away, stopped mid act by the now all-too-solid wall. All he wanted was quiet. He wasn't supposed to be touched. No one was supposed to touch him.

Cowl's tone never changed. "Don't be a baby. I couldn't hurt you any more than you are hurting yourself. Even if I was going to try," he said, lowering his voice as he sank down.

"Wha... what do I do?" Menrva asked.

Her voice was like ice water. She was here? Why was she in the room with him? He was dangerous. She needed to run. He needed to run. Where could he go to escape this?

"Just relax. He'll be fine. We've had bad dreams before. Right, brother?"

Cowl's hands weighed heavy on Bas's shoulders. He managed to stay under them, despite the waves of terror rushing over him.

"I'm going to put your head down now. Okay. Don't freak out."

Cowl's whole weight pressed onto Bas's head and shoulders, pushing him toward the floor. The feeling of restriction passed. Cowl was holding him down to earth, an anchor in the emptiness, a lifeline.

"Breathe with me." Cowl's voice was against his ear. Bas followed his lead, matching the swell of his friend's chest against his back. "Good job. See, it's not that bad. We got this, just like always." Cowl never stopped talking and the words slowly began to take more form. The murmur of his voice drove out the ringing madness.

A tiny hand brushed against Bas's back like a butterfly. Menrva? He didn't want to pull away from her. He let himself relax as her fingers fluttered in small circles around his back, skipping lightly over his spine. The warmth of them radiated through his shirt like fallen stars.

The world began to find its rest. Bas lay his hands on the floor, relieved it had quit rolling under him. He let out a deep sigh and his body released itself. His tensed muscles cramped and shuddered, angry at being held hostage.

"We okay?" Cowl asked.

"Yeah."

Cowl released him and Bas sat up slowly. Immediately Menrva moved a few steps back. He missed the sensation of her fingertips over his skin.

"It's been a bit since we had one of those," Cowl said, leaving one hand firmly planted at the base of Bas's neck. Thankfulness welled up in Bas at the sight of his best friend hunkered down before him. Cowl never made him feel awkward about his baggage. He said "we" as if he were right there freaking out with Bas. It wasn't condescending. In many ways Cowl had felt it just as potently as he himself did. They had worked through this too many times for him not to.

"That's happened before?" Menrva asked. She, on the other hand, still looked scared. With good reason.

Bas hung his head. "Menrva. I'm sorry. I'm so sorry."

Menrva waved a hand in the air. "You didn't mean too, right?" She didn't look like she was convinced by her own words. The distance between them belied her fear.

Bas rubbed a hand over his face and it slipped over wet blood. He shuddered, pushing back the images flooding his head.

Menrva moved toward him and Bas immediately held up a hand. "Not yet, please."

The words still chanted in his head. "Kill, kill, kill." Like a song. Menrva seemed relieved to be able to keep her distance. She was looking at him like she might look at a monster...like she might look at a man like Nolan. He couldn't blame her. It was probably better she kept her distance, but logic didn't make the hurt any less potent. He wanted her to look at him like she had before...to touch him and soothe him.

"Hey, why don't we go back where there is some light, get you cleaned up?" Cowl suggested lightly. Bas's face turned cold under the warm layers of blood. Now he did feel childish, like a toddler who had just spread a mess across the floor.

Bas pushed himself to his feet, his legs trembling. Dutifully, Cowl shoved his shoulder under Bas's arm in an attempt to keep him steady. He must have run back into the housing unit. The light from the lantern shone down the length of the hall, reflecting from the broken furniture, spilling out of open pods and jagged bits of metal that had fallen or been pried off the walls. Bas steadied himself against the wall with one hand and carefully weaved around the obstacles.

"What was that? Dream?" Cowl asked as they neared the front room.

Bas nodded. His throat was raw. Why? Had he been screaming? Cowl helped him ease to a spot on the floor beside the lantern. Bas accepted the water he handed him.

A gun lay leaned against one of the benches, haphazardly tossed aside in the confusion. Bas glanced out the opening where the Rover sat still. If there was anyone out there, this would have been the perfect opportunity for an attack. They couldn't let their guard down like this. He couldn't do this right now. His ridiculous weakness was going to get them all killed.

"Right here, brother. Let's try to keep your focus right here." Cowl's face snapped into his view, hovering right in front of him.

Cowl lay a medkit down at his feet and pulled a few disinfecting wipes from it. Bas accepted one and scrubbed a scrape that was turning purple along his upper arm. The dull ache of the wound reminded him to center himself, a hint of pain to prove this was real.

Across from him, Menrva sat with her arms still wrapped around her torso, gripping the corners of her tank top until her knuckles turned white. She watched his hands, an array of emotions sprinting across her face.

"Are you hurt?" he asked.

"Just shaken up."

Bas nodded to acknowledge her answer but quickly refocused on his task to avoid her eyes.

"Wreckers?" Cowl asked. He always asked about the dreams. They had agreed on it, part of the 'whole truth' policy they had. The things Bas kept quiet always came back sooner...came back worse. He only wished Menrva wasn't there to hear.

Bas winced as Cowl brushed the blood from his cheek. "Yeah, and then some."

"The Compound?" Cowl pressed. He had been through enough of these episodes that he understood pretty well how Bas reacted to different memories. "Black room?"

Bas shivered at the words. "No. Just the cells."

"Is that what you were dreaming about?" Menrva asked.

Bas nodded and pushed away Cowl's hand. "Thanks, I'm okay." He offered him a half-faked smile.

"What was it like?" Menrva asked.

Bas shook his head. "I'm sorry. I can't talk about that right now. Maybe later."

Menrva pursed her lips and nodded, shifting awkwardly in her seat.

Cowl stood abruptly. "Hey, Nerve. Why don't we give Bas a couple minutes? I need to run a sweep around the housing unit anyway."

Menrva nodded and grabbed the gun he tossed to her. She looked back at Bas, as if she were afraid he was going to climb to his feet in pursuit of her.

"You gonna be okay?" Cowl asked.

"I'm good," Bas reassured him. He didn't look convinced, but getting Menrva out was more important.

"Should we find another place to stay?"

Bas shuddered. The housing unit was too much like the Compound. He couldn't deny that. But there was much more to this attack than just the location. There was something about it that was different, more invasive. He shook his head.

Cowl pulled Bas's head up against his own, firmly gripping his bicep with his other hand. Until that moment, Bas hadn't even realized he was still shaking. Cowl's grip steadied him, chasing away what was left of the nightmares. "You sure you're okay? I can stay." He kept his voice low. "I just figured you'd want a minute without her watching."

Bas returned the embrace, his fingers tangling in Cowl's mussed hair. "I'm good, I promise."

Cowl nodded, pulling away with an awkward shrug. "I'm always here. Okay? Whenever you need me"

Cowl tucked his arm around Menrva, ignoring her obvious distaste for his closeness, and steered her toward the door. She cast one last concerned glance Bas's way before she surrendered herself to Cowl's leading.

The emptiness that settled as they stepped through the door was only a small comfort.

"It's not a dream." The words echoed in the silence.

Chapter Thirty-Three: Safe is a Dangerous Place

Menrva scuffed her foot in the dust and the soft grains billowed up against her ankle.

"You okay?" Cowl asked. Her eyes followed the light from his flashlight but he didn't seem entirely worried by what was possibly hidden in the darkness.

"Do you care?" Menrva flipped the gun in her hand. "Someone just tried to kill me. It seems to be a trend in my life."

"Shut up, you know it's not like that." Cowl cleared his throat and sighed. "He wouldn't have really hurt you."

Menrva glanced at the looming housing unit and shuddered at the memories flashing in her mind. Of Nolan, of her old life. This situation wasn't the same, but she couldn't shake the terror tightening every muscle in her body.

She hadn't expected such a violent reaction when she tried to wake him up. She hadn't even thought it was possible. Despite his initial intimidating appearance and his military training, Bas was stable, safe. She hadn't thought he was even capable of hurting her.

"What happened?" she asked.

"Bas has been through hell. He doesn't let it control him, but sometimes shit breaks through."

"I guess I can understand that." Menrva wiped a bead of sweat from her brow.

Cowl shifted the rifle he carried on his back. "Look. I get why this is freaking you out so much." He turned to look at her, the light illuminating his concern. "When I first met Bas, that was him all the time. He could barely function. He didn't sleep for the first week, didn't eat. Every time I went near him he would react like I was a Wrecker." He frowned at the words. "But this is part of the deal with Bas. If you can't handle it, don't get close."

Menrva brushed what she thought was a piece of dust from her cheek and realized she was crying. Stupid idiot. "What is with you? You think I can shrug off what happened? Sure I'm freaked out, I think anyone would be. It doesn't mean I don't care about him." She crossed her arms, meeting Cowl's eyes with every bit of the vitriol that he gave to her. "You know, he's not *yours*. Stop being so possessive."

"I'm not possessive, I'm protective!" Cowl yelled. "He's been through hell; neither of us needed you here messing shit up."

"Why are we still on this?"

"Because I was happy! Because we were safe and now..." Cowl's voice shook. "Tell me why I shouldn't blame you."

Something else lurked in Cowl's eyes. The same kind of look Menrva has seen there when Starke didn't come back after the City grabbed him. Starke meant the world to Cowl, and in many ways the moment he was taken was the moment Cowl's life started to fall apart. Maybe Bas was his way of trying to put it back together again? He wasn't angry, he was terrified. "Cowl," Menrva said, doing her best to make her voice calm. "He isn't Starke."

Cowl's reeled back a few steps. "I know!" he hissed. "But he could still die like Starke did."

Menrva shook her head. "He won't. You won't let him."

Silence stretched between them for a long time before Cowl ducked his head and cleared his throat violently. "Yeah. Yeah, okay." He turned toward the housing unit.

"I'd better go check on him."

"Let me talk to him," she said, "Let me help." Here was the real test. If Cowl was going to forgive her and let her in, he would have to learn to trust her around Bas.

Cowl chewed on his lip before nodding. "Okay. But I'm going to be right behind you."

>><<

Bas was sitting curled into himself when Menrva jogged into the housing unit. His hands were cupped over his head and he shook almost imperceptibly. Menrva watched him for a moment. He looked so small. His fingers tapped on his skull as if he were counting as his shoulders shook with each breath.

"Bas?"

Bas jumped at the sound of her voice, straightening up so quickly he almost fell off his seat. Menrva's heart jumped with him. She had to separate herself from that foolish fear. Bas slipped, but he wasn't cruel. He wasn't evil like Nolan. He was hurting, just like she was.

"Can I sit?" Menrva asked.

Bas waved his hand to invite her down. He leaned away from her when she settled awkwardly on the space beside him. She had to force her hand away from her side so she could offer it to him. He needed her touch. Maybe she needed his, too.

Bas's gripped it loosely. Reluctant.

"I'm fine," Menrva insisted, "but we both had a bit of a scuffle with our demons today."

Bas rolled his shoulders. "Your demon looks a lot like me."

"It wasn't your fault," Menrva said. She gripped Bas's hand tighter. "You just had a bad dream."

"I could have really hurt you."

"You won't hurt me," Menrva said, grinning. "Though I think I might not sleep in your bed tonight."

Bas didn't look up.

Menrva squeezed his hand "I just wish I knew better how to help you. I'm not-"

"You're perfect," Bas said, meeting her eyes. He leaned in to kiss her gently on the forehead. "I just hate that you are scared of me."

"I'm not scared of you. I'm scared of bad memories and you just happened to bring a few up."

Bas's shoulders fell forward, shame etched in every line of his huddled form. She slipped her hand over his shoulder and his muscles tightened under her fingers. He was scared, too. Menrva moved toward him, slowly so that he wouldn't pull away. Or maybe it was to calm her own fear.

His head remained bowed, his shoulders stooped as if he were trying to form a cage around himself.

Menrva edged forward until her cheek rested against his soft curls, allowing his smell to wash over her.

"See? If I was scared, I wouldn't do this."

Bas wrapped his arms around her waist and squeezed her. "You are amazing."

"Gross. You're absorbing her like an amoeba," Cowl's voice said from behind.

Menrva jumped back and Bas dropped his arms. Cowl stood beside the Rover, arms crossed. He didn't actually look angry, though. That was a positive step. Maybe he didn't hate her so much anymore.

"How are you?" he asked, brushing dust from the front of his tank top.

"Fine," Bas answered, trying a small, very unbelievable smile.

Menrva took her seat again. She didn't grab Bas's hand, but she wasn't going to move from her place beside him, either. Cowl was just going to have to get over it.

He didn't seem too upset as he sat across from them, placing the gun on the bench. "Checked the perimeter. Still no sign of anyone, but we should think about moving on."

Bas shook his head and immediately winced. "Not until we go topside."

"I hacked into a cam," Cowl said. "Checked topside."

Menrva leaned forward. "Did you see anything?"

The look he gave her was not encouraging. "I saw a Wrecker kill a kid," he said, eyes narrowing. He turned to look at Bas. "I don't think you should go up, brother.

Especially now. Especially after this."

"It was a dream. It's not going to cause any problems," Bas said.

"The City Connected, then you had the worst panic attack you've had in at least a year. You think that's coincidence?" Real concern saturated Cowl's words. He glanced at Menrva, his eyes pleading. She didn't want Bas to go up any more than he did. But if they wanted any chance to get free of the City, they would have to get some information.

Bas rubbed his forehead. "We have to go up. I know you can't understand right now, but this isn't about me. That Borg was trying to help us, Cowl. If we don't act on this, we will regret it. I know it."

Cowl frowned. "Agree to disagree."

Chapter Thirty-Four:
The Definition of Insanity

Bas rubbed a sore spot on his arm. His shoulder still ached. He seemed to be collecting wounds faster than they were healing. A thick scab caught his fingers as he brushed his hand down his arm and he frowned. Another scar...what did it matter now?

"Your hair is almost as long as Nerve's," Cowl said, joining him at the Rover. He didn't look quite rested. Stress didn't get to Cowl like it would most people, so he wasn't losing sleep from that. He must have been up listening for him for the third night in a row.

"I should probably take a knife to it," Bas agreed.

"And you need to shave."

Bas rubbed his chin and nodded in agreement.

"How are you doing?"

"No more nightmares," Bas said. That was mostly because he hadn't really slept. He didn't explain to Cowl that he could still hear the haunting voice in his head. Cowl would understand, but Bas didn't want to acknowledge whatever it was. He wanted it to go back to the dream, where it belonged.

"This isn't a dream..."

"What?" Bas jumped.

"I didn't say anything." Cowl raised an eyebrow.

"Oh." Bas rolled his shoulders and lowered his eyes so Cowl couldn't pin him with that disapproving glare. What did he want?

"Come on, man. If you are dealing with stuff, let's work through it. Just tell me what's going on."

Bas shook his head. "You've dealt with enough."

Cowl turned away, sighing heavily as he ran his hands over his head. "Look, I know I've been a bit of a jerk lately."

"What?" A jerk? Bas rubbed his neck, watching Cowl struggle with the words. He'd not been any different from normal, had he? Stressed, sure. They were all tired. Maybe a bit more angry than usual, but it was understandable. He didn't want Bas going topside.

"Just let me say this. I'm jealous. Like a little girl. Like a really handsome, incredibly gifted and awesome little girl. I was freaking out because of you and Menrva..."

"Me and Menrva?"

"Cause you guys are all romantic and shit. I guess I just figured you didn't need me anymore." He shrugged and kicked a rock. "See, it's stupid."

Had he really been feeling all that? And why? Menrva was amazing. She brought up all kinds of emotions and thoughts he'd never understood before and opened a whole world of new freedoms. But she was never going to be able to replace Cowl. Cowl had saved him. Pulled him out of hell and showed him what it meant to be a human being. Even now, he was still pulling him from the dark. That was more than friendship, and more than anything he had with Menrva.

"Anyway, we all know that I'm a gooey mess of dysfunction, probably why you and I get along so well. So, let's just pretend this never happened."

"You don't still think that, right?" Bas asked.

Cowl sighed and rolled his eyes. "No. Obviously you still need me. And I'm not going anywhere so...I'm over it."

"Okay," Bas said.

"Okay," Cowl repeated, a hint of a grin stealing across his lips. "And I will help you go topside. I don't like it and I think we are shooting the gears, but I trust you. So...yeah."

Should he be relieved by that announcement? Bas nodded, slowly. It would be different this time. He had Menrva and Cowl behind him, and freedom ahead of him. If this was something as important as he hoped, maybe he could bring the City to its knees.

Bas looked up just in time to see something flash from his peripherals.

"Did you see that?"

"What?" Cowl's eyes didn't leave him.

Bas flicked on the light attached to his gun's barrel and angled it into the darkness. "I just saw something run by."

Cowl reached for his own gun and leaned into the dark, swearing as he studied the emptiness. "Scavengers?"

Bas rolled his shoulders. "I don't know. It was quick."

Cowl shoved his body against the wall and scanned the landscape outside the unit, gun readied for action. There was no sign of anything, not even settling dust. Bas frowned and pulled his handgun, intent on the place where he'd seen the movement.

"My alarms haven't been set off," Cowl said, glancing at his smartwatch. "Let's go have a look."

Bas shuddered slightly as he and Cowl left the housing unit. Something in the shape and movement of what he saw was far too familiar. He couldn't shake the dread settling on his shoulders. The gun weighed heavy in his hands but he didn't feel the thrill of the chase this time, only the vague unease of a hunted man.

Menrva was still asleep. Was it safe to leave her?

Bas and Cowl fell into a practiced formation as they scanned the horizon. Bas didn't have to turn to know that Cowl lagged behind, watching their back. His footfall was the only sound in the vastness.

Despite a lifetime of training, Bas struggled to keep his head clear as he approached the place where he had seen the movement. The dust was smooth, marred only by a few ripples. If something had come by, it would have undoubtedly left prints.

"There's nothing here," Bas said. He waited without an answer from Cowl.

A chill ran down his spine. Something *was* there; its presence was as real to him as the thoughts in his own mind. He looked up and his breath dropped out of his lungs as he saw a massive Wrecker before him. Its black hide blended into the darkness around it, making its skull appear as if it were hovering in the air. Ribbons of acid trailed down it's fangs and dripped to the ground.

Bas snapped his gun up and fired two bullets, stumbling backward as he did. A familiar pinch climbed the back of his neck, and he swore. His cuff was on. There was no way anyone could Connect.

The Wrecker didn't react to the assault. The bullets passed through him like smoke. It only stood, watching with obsidian eyes as Bas continued his retreat. Bas lowered his gun. Still, it only observed.

The pain in Bas's neck and head intensified until his vision blurred. Waves of nausea grappled with his fear.

"Bas?"

Cowl's voice barely pierced through the swirl of confusion. Bas fell to his knees, unable to call out the warning on his lips.

The Wrecker continued to stare down at him silently. It grew with the pain that tore into Bas like fangs, looming over him until it filled his view.

"What's going on?" Cowl asked as he took a knee beside Bas. His voice held a note of panic.

"Please tell me you see that, too." Bas barely managed to force the words from between his clenched teeth.

Cowl followed Bas's gaze before shaking his head.

Somehow, that realization was more terrifying than an actual Wrecker could ever have been. Borgs regularly lost their minds back in the Compound. It was nothing if not expected. As long as they were still serviceable, it didn't matter. Bas had considered himself to be one of those crazies, at one point, but that was a lifetime away from this moment. It seemed completely illogical he would lose his own mind now, when he was happy.

"What do you see, Bas?" Cowl asked. Bas had to shake himself from his stupor. The pain in his head began to fade.

"I see a Wrecker. Right there." He glanced up and the

alien shrank away, fading with his headache. The two were connected. What did it mean?

Cowl walked over to the place where the creature stood. Despite knowing it wasn't real, Bas had to fight to keep from dragging his friend back from the waiting jaws. Cowl paced the ground before returning with a frown.

"There are footprints," Cowl said "but they are human. Just one set, but they got past my wanna-be security, so I feel like they knew what they were doing. That, or the system is malfunctioning. It's weird. It's like your brain was warning you about it."

Human? Why would his mind have translated that into a living, breathing Wrecker? Where would the prints have come from? It could have been one of them, but it was too far from the housing unit to be part of their normal rounds. The worst explanations were probably more realistic.

Bas rubbed his forehead, expelling the last of the headache. "So I've just finally snapped."

"Don't flatter yourself. You've been crazy for a long time," Cowl said. It was one of those distant, unfeeling jokes he used to distract from a deeper emotion. The nastier the wisecrack, the more he was trying to hide. He offered Bas a hand. "Don't worry. There could be a hundred different explanations. You did pretty much bash your own head in three days ago."

Bas frowned at the empty place. Yes, there could be a hundred explanations, but none of them were encouraging. When was it ever a good sign to start seeing things that weren't actually there?

"Who do you think left those tracks? I only saw one set.

Wanderer or scout for the scavengers or the City?" Cowl asked, tugging his scarf up over his nose. There were instances of loners that just drifted through the endless black of the pit. It wasn't likely one of them would run into the housing unit by happenstance alone, not when there were so many people deliberately looking. Maybe it was someone who came to scavenge, collect scrap metal to take back to a Dust Town. It was all just assuming these tracks weren't from one of the three of them.

"Expect the worst," Bas said, almost as much to himself as to Cowl. The Wrecker felt so real, and its presence still cast a shadow in his mind. He had experienced hallucinations before. It was one thing about being locked in a featureless room for most of your life. After a while of having nothing to focus on, the brain began to invent its own entertainment. Those images were nonsense: teeth growing out of the walls and ceilings, mazes built of broken glass, seas of loose bullets... not living creatures. Not something so convincing.

Bas could still feel the eyes of the imagined Wrecker following them as they trudged back to the housing unit. He didn't pause at the door, continuing right on until he stood over Menrva's sleeping form. She was alive, safe and in one piece, despite the nagging in the back of his mind trying to convince him otherwise. Even if the threat wasn't real, the danger still felt just as tangible. Menrva didn't even stir as the light drifted over her face. Her lips pursed and her brows furrowed in some distant dream. He hoped it was a good one. One where he didn't exist.

"Could it be a tech malfunction?" Cowl asked as Bas

joined him at the guard post again. "Maybe you are spying on someone else: some sort of hive-mind thing."

Bas shrugged. "I've never heard of it."

"You aren't exactly the norm," Cowl said.

Bas frowned. Wasn't he, though? Other than a few special genes he was no different than any of the other soldiers. Why would an extra set of lungs affect his mind?

"I could just be losing it," he said.

"Nope. That's not happening."

"Because you say so?"

"Of course. I'll let you know when you are crazy." Cowl propped his feet on a broken section of wall and grinned up at Bas.

Bas shook his head, "'Cause you would know."

"I know everything." Cowl laid his gun down. "Seriously. This isn't the first time this kinda shit has happened. We just take it in stride, just like always."

Bas nodded and looked out into the darkness. He wanted to agree with Cowl but this time *was* different. This wasn't just a bad dream or a flash of PTSD. Nothing had followed him out of his nightmares before. He couldn't put his finger on why this situation was so distinct, but when he closed his eyes the problem was there, staring back at him with the eyes of a Wrecker.

Chapter Thirty-Five: The Way Up

Menrva woke up stiff and achy from the broken rib and slow-healing gunshot wound. Her mouth was cottony, but worse than that: she was alone.

She moved her hand around on the hard floor, not entirely sure at first what she was seeking. Slowly she became aware of masculine voices speaking in low tones outside the door. It was just a hum at first, but she soon understood what they were talking about and it made her sick.

"It's been over three years." Cowl's voice echoed off the walls. "I wouldn't go up there with any expectations. With shit as unstable as it is, everything could look different."

"I can't waste time. That helmet will only protect me from the side effects of the Connection for so long." The concern in Bas's voice carried through the walls. The side effects? What would those be?

"Give it a few miles radius. If you don't find anything, come back. We can try again if we have to," Cowl replied.

Menrva tugged on her pants and stumbled from the room. Cowl and Bas sat with heads bent close as they looked at a tablet.

"Serious business?" Menrva asked. She walked to the desk and scooped up a nearly empty bottle of water.

"Worrying," Bas explained.

Worrying. It was funny how he used that word as a junk drawer term for all his struggles. He was never dishonest about what he was feeling, but he always minimized it. Was it a leftover habit from being raised to be emotionless?

Bas held out a hand to Menrva. Heat climbed up her neck and face as she slipped her palm into Bas's, ignoring the whisper of doubt she had to silence every time. The affection was so familiar already, and yet a thrill of fear and excitement still climbed her arms and tightened its grip around her heart.

Bas tilted his head, though he didn't need to reach far, and brushed his lips against hers. Menrva tried to hide the bashful smile tugging at the corners of her mouth.

"You ready?" Bas asked. He didn't release her hand.

"No," she said truthfully. "But we need this, right?"

"It could answer some questions," Bas agreed.

Cowl raised an eyebrow at the two of them. "What, no one's going to hold my hand?"

Bas held out his other hand and Cowl grabbed it with a slap, swinging them lightly.

"So, what is the plan?" Menrva asked. She leaned over the tablet, chuckling when Cowl still held on to Bas's hand. The tablet displayed a loose blueprint of Bunker and some of the surrounding area. Menrva could only assume the blinking green light symbolized the exits, since that was what was most relevant.

"Nearest exit is here." Bas pointed at the screen.

"You can make it there pretty quick?" Menrva asked.

"Thirty minutes," Bas agreed.

"Don't brag or anything." Cowl dropped Bas's hand and reached for a helmet laying at his feet. "So, this is going to be your lifesaver." He glanced from Menrva to Bas. It felt odd, being involved in a debriefing when it wasn't technically her that would be pulling the mission. Or was it?

"For one, it will keep us in contact. And we all know how much you losers need me."

"You are life itself," Menrva said, rolling her eyes.

"You betcha, gorgeous." Cowl turned the helmet over so they could see inside. "O2 converter, not like you need it. Comm and visual...I can see you, but you will also have this screen so I can send you multimedia." He pointed out the features as he spoke. "Then we have this little jewel back here. This will take some of the load off your system so you won't be at as much of a risk for brain-swelly fun."

"At risk for *what*?" she asked, brushing her fingers over the port.

"Overextension. If he's in too long, or if he fights it, the Connection can do damage to his nervous system and brain. This grounds the electricity so that it's got somewhere to go."

Menrva tried not to show how much the idea scared her. Maybe she hadn't quite understood everything this entailed when she agreed. It was too late for that now. She'd made a promise, and there was too much riding on it.

"And the suit is armored?" Menrva asked.

"Yes, but don't use that as an excuse to give a Wrecker a

hug."

"No worries there," Menrva said.

"We need to keep a heads-up for Borgs, too. They are always running scouting teams topside, even with the drones and surveillance," Bas pointed out.

"Got it. So what exactly am I looking for?" Menrva asked, twisting her hair into loose braids as she spoke.

"I have no clue," Bas said, "but I don't think you will have to go far."

"Okay, so get in, get out?" Menrva said.

"Just surveillance," Bas agreed.

"I know you know some of this already," Cowl said, setting down the helmet and catching Menrva in his cold gaze, "but I have to be sure you understand. You are controlling Bas's body, not a machine. No respawn, no save points. If he gets knocked out you will lose your Connection. If he takes a serious injury you cannot force his body to do something it's too broken to do." Cowl's expression was deadly serious. He might as well have been laying the entire world on Menrva's shoulders. "Nerve, your receiver won't allow pain over a certain level, but Bas is going to be in there, feeling it all. Don't make it hell."

"No," Bas interrupted. He stood and lowered his head, crossing his arms over his broad chest. "You do what you need to do, whatever that is. Don't overthink it. Trust yourself. I'll get over a few cuts and bruises, but if you hesitate even for an instant with those things, I don't get a second chance. The moment you start to second guess yourself is the moment you've killed me."

Menrva's breath left her lungs. Pain or death, were those

the only options? Why were they so eager for this?

"Maybe—"

"I trust you," Bas interrupted her. "You got this. It's just a Sim."

It wasn't a simulation. It was his *life*. But she understood what he was trying to say.

"It's late morning topside," Cowl said, checking his watch. His hand trembled slightly. "We should get a move on. Last thing we need is for you to get stuck topside after the sun is down." He was pouting, and the whine carried in his tone.

"I'm ready," Bas said. There was a hint of fear behind the words, but his face was passive, even empty. Brave face. Menrva was beginning to understand why Cowl hated it so much.

Menrva could swear they held their breath as one as Bas slowly slid the lead cuff down his arm and off the tips of his fingers. Cowl had made sure the tech would only Connect through the Ether, but that didn't make the moment any less terrifying.

He climbed into the armored suit. It was obvious how completely the suits had been tailored for Borgs. It attached into the bionic spine with multiple claw-like connectors, sealing around the tech completely. Maybe it was a way to preserve the signal and minimize interference. The armor fit to his skin in a variation of whirs and clicks, the camouflaged plates sliding into place. Bas cinched all the buckles and clips automatically. How many times had he climbed into this suit and left the safety of Bunker? Menrva could only hope this would be the last.

"Flattering," Cowl said as Bas pulled a pair of fatigue pants over his armored legs, clipping the last of the pieces over the loose fabric. Bas rolled his eyes in answer.

Menrva couldn't shake the dread at the sight of Bas in the armor. He looked different, almost alien. His stance was harder, more violent. Militant — that was the word she was looking for. He looked dangerous. It was a stupid thought. Nothing about Bas was ever safe, but he was a good man and that made all the difference in the world.

"I'm good." He clenched his hands inside their gloves. Menrva tried not to shudder at the raw power barely contained in the curve of his knuckles.

Bas turned to her with a smile and those thoughts drifted away.

"You ready?"

Menrva frowned. "Don't be so happy about this. Just focus on getting back alive."

"I can do that."

"Great," Cowl said as he climbed into the Rover. "This is an encouraging conversation. Let's just get this over with."

Menrva followed him onto the Rover and found her seat by the console. Bas reached over to grab her hand for a final squeeze as he eased himself down beside her and crossed his legs. For a while, the only sound was Cowl hooking the tech in place.

"I'm just going to say one last time. This is a bad idea," Cowl said.

Bas tilted his head slightly in a nod to acknowledge the concern. "Thanks, Cowl. You are a good friend."

Cowl paused, staring down at Bas before ducking in for a

quick hug. After a moment he backed away, clearing his throat. "I would be flattered, but you don't actually have any friends to compare me to."

Bas laughed in response. Menrva gripped his hand tighter. He would come back. There was no other option. She would make sure of it. He had to come back.

"And...we're go," Cowl said, interrupting her thoughts.

Menrva took a deep breath, wishing the angry ache in her chest would ease, and closed her eyes. When she opened them the world felt very different. The suit Bas wore was tight, enclosed, and made each breath uncomfortable. The edges dug into her back. It wasn't painful, just *there*. The odd thing was that she had never noticed it before. She hadn't been aware of anything but the thrill of battle during the Tournament Sims. For her, it was nothing more than entertainment, so of course she hadn't given it much thought.

A soft weight pressed against her hand and she looked down to see her own slim fingers in Bas's...limp.

"We good?" Cowl asked.

"I'm in," Menrva said, frowning as the words pressed against the constricted breastplate. She took the helmet Cowl offered her.

"Your map is on the interface," he said.

Menrva pulled the helmet over her face. The world around her turned bright green as the night vision illuminated every shadow.

"Remember. Don't push it too much. You won't feel tired like Bas will," Cowl said. He slapped a hand on Menrva's shoulder though she barely felt the weight of it through the armor. "Don't worry, bud. We got you up there."

That wasn't meant for her.

Menrva sorted through the array of weapons that had been chosen for her, finding places for them in the many appropriate accommodations the suit provided. Fully automatic handguns, a semi-automatic rifle with a sniper feature. A few of what Cowl would call 'baby guns'. Five firearms in all, along with extra ammo and a dual set of intimidating diamond-edged knives. She was running hot.

Before she stepped out of the door she paused to wrap Cowl in one last hug. Her own fears lashed out against the contact, but Bas would be craving it. If she didn't she could come to regret it, but she couldn't dwell on that possibility.

"Two for one," he laughed, his face pressed against her shoulder. He was so absurdly short all of the sudden.

"Keep us grounded," she said, turning reluctantly to leave. The darkness swallowed her as she began to jog.

>><<

Cowl was right, Menrva didn't feel winded no matter how much she pushed. How far was too far? It was impossible to say without having the full range of sensory input from Bas. She did her best to judge his heartbeat and breathing. Still, she should have been asking permission for each step she took. That would have been right, but she couldn't ask and Bas couldn't answer. She had his voice. Wiping those thoughts out of her head, she replaced them with Bas's earlier words. "Do what you have to do."

The exit, a simple tower shooting up through the ceiling,

loomed ahead of her. It was in poor repair, making an eerie sight. Metal plating had been ripped from its sides, and above her the tiers, long since abandoned, hung in broken pieces from the cavern roof. At one point in time, the City had kept all the exits in good repair and well-guarded. Dad had often been gone days, running watch duty on some of the closer towers. Even if there wasn't hope of ever sending the populace back up, they should have been present to make sure the Wreckers didn't manage to get down.

"I wonder if they are surveilling it?" Menrva said aloud. Bas's heart noticeably quickened its pace. Was his body still responding to his emotions?

The exit was little more than a single tower stretching into the thick darkness above. The door hung open. The room inside was covered in a blanket of dirt, just like everything else in the Pit. Touch screens, keyboards, and overturned chairs littered the room. A few old-fashioned suits hung in the corner. One was torn.

"It's like they just gave up," Menrva said. A single sliding door was staring at her from across the room.

"That's the airlock." Menrva jumped when Cowl's voice echoed in her helmet. She had forgotten she wasn't alone. "There should be a screen beside it. I can get you hacked in."

Blue light followed Menrva's fingertips as she cleaned the dust from the screen. The glow nearly blinded her as her night vision struggled to adjust.

"Access granted," a droll voice hummed. The doors whirred before grinding open. Dust caking the metal fell like bits of egg shell onto the floor. Goosebumps pricked her arms as she stared into the vault-like entrance. This was the last vestige of safety before the purgatory above.

"Cowl, I'm in."

"What? That's weird. No code?"

"No, it wasn't locked or anything." Menrva stepped into a cylindrical decompression chamber just inside the door. Gears spun and air whooshed as the second set of doors opened to a wide, industrial elevator. Despite the danger of her situation, excitement burst in her veins like bubbles as she pulled the lever and the elevator began to rise on squealing, exposed cables.

The metal cables groaned. Would armor be of any use in crumbling infrastructure?

The elevator squealed to a stop in a wide, plain building that looked like some sort of massive waiting room. The skeletons of chairs sat in stiff, stubborn rows, covered in thick black dirt and ice. Empty planters were strewn about the floor and bent into the corners as if thrown with great force. The room bore the marks of war. Black streaks traveled across yellowing walls like lightening and great holes yawned in the ceiling. Blocks of the thick, concrete walls were cradled in beds of bent chairs and broken desks. A degraded statue, now barely recognizable as a human form, bent over Menrva like a valkyrie.

Menrva stared through the holes, unable to look away despite the pain of the light in her sheltered eyes. Even with the sun shield on her helmet it was brilliant. When her eyes finally began to adjust she saw that outside of her incomplete shelter the sky was inky black.

Chapter Thirty-Six: Daedalus's Wax Wings

Menrva hadn't been on the surface for almost six years. She hadn't, of course, known she was actually on the surface then. She was just wasting time and gaining fame on a Tournament Sim. It was an entirely new experience now that she knew what was actually happening.

"Is it weird this earth feels like fiction, and the Sims feel real?" Menrva said into her helmet. She wasn't sure if she was talking to Bas or Cowl, or if she was just talking to herself.

"Hold up, Nerve," Cowl said. "I'm having some issues down here."

Menrva rolled her shoulders... but no. That was Bas's habit. He did that when he was nervous or frustrated. Now that Menrva could feel the constant weight of the tech between her own shoulders and the stiffness of the muscles and scar tissue, she understood exactly why he formed that tic. It wasn't supposed to be possible for Bas to control his movements, though. She was overthinking things.

"What's up, Cowl? Talk to me. I'm not exactly in a good spot here." Menrva lay a hand on her gun, reminding herself even as she spoke the words that the world was out to kill her.

"I'm having an issue hacking into the City Network."

"What does that mean?" Menrva fought a wave of panic. Were they using City Net? The whole point of going through Bas's tether was to avoid using the network. Would the City be able to see them? Would they be able to pull her out and take Bas? Why hadn't they yet?

"It just means I can't see where they are so I can't update you on anything topside. I was hoping to at least be able to tell you where to look, and where to avoid," Cowl replied. "Just understand your ass is out there for Borgs as well as Wreckers. I can't give you a heads-up."

"That's fine." Menrva tightened her grip on the gun. "I don't plan to be up here for long. Just tell me where I should go first."

"If you don't see anything of immediate interest, head toward the Hub. That's where most Borgs would surface on a routine scouting mission, so that's where our girl most likely would have seen something."

Menrva skirted debris to find her way through the gaping hole where she could only assume the door had once been.

As soon as she stepped out of the building she was met with a leering skull and wide jaws. A Wrecker.

Menrva threw herself back, grabbing for her rifle.

"Nerve!"

Her heart thudded against her ribs. Nothing happened. Another glanced proved all that was left of this creature was crushed, broken bones and a bullet-riddled head.

"It's dead," she informed Cowl. "Looks like it's been here

for a while."

It was an odd place to come across a skeleton, if anywhere. Wreckers were thought to devour their dead and wounded, especially now that food sources were gone. Maybe this was what was left over afterwards? It seemed to be more intact than most kills Menrva had seen in records. Wreckers didn't leave much of a corpse after they fed, not with a bite force in excess of eleven thousand pounds per square inch. Pressure like that could break through the typical human femur with ease, and chew it into powder.

The map blinked back onto her screen, distracting Menrva from her rabbit trail. It was easier to think of the monsters in terms of numbers and stats, like she always had, instead of imagining what they could do to Bas. She began to jog in the direction of the Hub. She was thankful for the grip on her boots that kept her from sliding on the thin layer of ice covering the black, cracked earth. Skeletons of long dead reefs cluttered the ground, decomposing in the direct sunlight.

Without the atmosphere, the oceans had boiled, evaporating into empty space. All that was left was a few frozen remnants. The story was often a topic of conversation in the lab. Even now, the source of the collapse was almost entirely speculation.

There wasn't anything immediately catching her attention as something worth this risky mission. She had hoped this would be fast, but it was going to take some detective work.

Menrva hesitated as she noticed thick furrows cutting

through the ice before her. Claw marks? She wasn't a tracker but the flakes of loose ice around them seem to indicate they were relatively fresh.

"Yeah, not good. Best get going," Cowl warned, his voice echoing in her helmet.

Menrva swallowed hard and looked over the barren earth. There were many dark and frightening shapes looming against the empty sky. The withering sunlight glinted off the landscape as if from the edge of a knife.

Her finger cradled the trigger guard of her gun as she started running. She kept her eyes up, scanning the skyline. The very air seemed to be hunting her. That was more or less true. The crust was treacherous, broken by the absence of the oxygen that had once bound it together. The light of the sun, though unbroken by ozone, was barely noticeable without anything to reflect it. It was a hellscape in the truest sense of the word.

Something shimmered in the distance, something obviously man-made. Menrva checked the video screen. She was getting close to the Hub, so it must have been the exposed dome. As she picked up her speed, a loud beep filled her helmet and a red dot flamed to life in the corner of her video feed. She didn't need to ask what it meant. Even if she hadn't played the tournaments she would have understood. She was being hunted.

Menrva spun on her heels, raising her gun as she scanned the vast emptiness. Ridges of cracked earth, crusted with white coral and ice, made it impossible to get the long-view.

When she finally did see the danger, she wasn't ready for

it. The Wrecker was at least twice Bas's size. Short black fur glinted like polished jet around the macabre skull that formed its head. Obsidian eyes caught her in their glint as the creature glowered down on her. She couldn't have been more afraid if death itself had incarnated before her.

It charged.

Each footfall shook the very earth, but it's roars were strangely silent. There was no atmosphere to carry the sound.

Menrva snapped her gun to her shoulder and squared her body. Her finger fumbled on the trigger for half a second and then she squeezed it against the metal. The Wrecker didn't take any more notice of the bullets burying into its chest than it would a raindrop. The third bullet went wild as it grabbed the barrel of the gun in one of four fists.

The Wrecker wrapped two meaty hands around Menrva's waist and her feet left the earth. She scrambled to pull free. Even Bas's powerful arms were worthless against this creature.

Cowl's voice faintly howled over the sound of blood pumping in Menrva's ears like it was trying to flee her body. The Wrecker's tiny black eyes glinted inside hollow sockets. They only spoke of one thing: hunger.

Struggling against the strength of the Wrecker's grip, Menrva pried her knife free and drove it into its fleshy grip. The beast's maw opened in a soundless roar as its hands slipped. She turned to crawl away but was halted when a heavy weight descended on her leg. A terrifying force dragged her backward. Looking back, she found her leg was clutched between the Wrecker's long fangs. Crushing pressure enveloped it as the second set of pincer-like fangs worked independently to tear at her armor in search of flesh, but there was no pain.

The Wrecker grabbed her, picking her up off the ground. A long, toothed claw grew out of its wrist, hanging threateningly over her.

Menrva grabbed one of the Wrecker's arms and used the leverage to propel herself forward, digging the dagger into its eye. It disappeared past the hilt. The creature reared back and Menrva dropped onto the cracked earth. She struggled to draw in air, but she couldn't afford to recover. Drawing a handgun, she began firing. Two in the chest, one in the head.

The Wrecker dropped to the ground, twitching.

Menrva pulled herself back to her feet. Her leg didn't hurt, but it was weak, probably broken. Blazing hatred filled her as she stood over the monster that was still trying to reach her from the ground. Blood seeped through its fur. She hated it for what it had just done to Bas, what it had done to the world around and below her.

She placed the muzzle of the gun to the beast's head and pulled the trigger. It lay still.

"Menrva!" Cowl's voice finally broke through the haze of combat as Menrva dislodged her knife from the creature's eye socket.

"We're alive." The pronoun slipped through her lips without a second thought. Yes, two of them had just survived the attack. Bas must be in so much pain.

Menrva looked at the torn flesh on her leg and realized the suit was redistributing itself to seal the wound. It tightened over her leg as the below-zero temperatures outside began to freeze the blood oozing through the hole. The skin twitched, blistering from some unseen heat-source. The bleeding slowed and smoke rose from the wound.

"What is happening?"

"Bas's leg is broken. The suit is using his Live Metal to cauterize the wound from the inside," Cowl replied.

Menrva swallowed the nausea climbing up her throat. That didn't sound pleasant. Still, it was probably keeping him alive. How had she never noticed these things in the Tournament Sims?

"Come on back. We need to get that taken care of."

Menrva tested her weight against her leg and glanced back at the Hub. She was so close, and from here she could just see something big not far from the dome. The suit was rigid enough that it was acting as a brace. The City had apparently had a lot of time to perfect the design. Trial and error... or in this case, Borg lives. It had to end.

Menrva took a deep breath. "Do what you have to do," she whispered.

"What?" Cowl asked through the comm.

"I'm going to keep going," Menrva said out loud. "I think I see something. It's not far."

"What? Get your skinny ass back here," Cowl yelled. The radio crackled as it tried to convey his passion. "You are walking him around on a broken leg, Menrva. He's in agony. Don't you dare put him through that."

Menrva started jogging toward the Hub. "He asked me to," she said. "You know he wouldn't want me to turn back now."

"You don't know what he would want. He can't tell you."

"I'm already here," Menrva said as she approached the massive dome. It lay like a great black eye staring into space, collecting tears of ice along the edge. A camera stared down at her from one of the multiple posts ringing the giant circle. She shot it out and began to walk around the edge.

"I'm going to pull the plug on you," Cowl threatened. He wouldn't. It would leave Bas up here alone. Menrva ignored him as he shouted expletives and continued to trudge around the curve of the dome. They were close.

It didn't take long to find what she was looking for.

"Cowl, shut up," she said, interrupting an unusually long rant. "Do you see what I'm seeing?"

Menrva wasn't an engineer, but she knew a rocket when she saw one. Right off the edge of the Hub a huge launch pad had been constructed, on which a rocket perched precariously. It must have fallen out of repair only recently. A few broken beams hung from the scaffolding, and loose cables swung in the air like broken arteries. Black burn marks dripped off the edge of the platform where furrows were etched into the earth in testament to multiple launches.

The words *Daedelus 5* were scrawled across the shattered rocket, the letters now obscured by a thin coating of ice and ash.

"They have been leaving Earth," Menrva said.

"Shit." Cowl said. "Yeah. That's...why?"

Menrva scanned the blackened earth. "Well, it's not for

space exploration, that's for sure. I'm going to guess they are looking for alternatives to Earth."

"Even with the atmosphere so weak, that's a hell of a lot of fuel. They wouldn't use those resources unless things were serious."

Menrva stared up at the rocket, suddenly feeling very vulnerable and small. They were evacuating Earth. It was the only thing that made sense. For most of her life there was always one goal: wait out the Wreckers and recolonize. It was what they taught in Basics. It was the excuse they gave when they asked the citizens for a big sacrifice. For that to have changed meant something was really wrong. Something massive.

"Do you think they are running out of resources? Maybe they are trying to retrieve them from another planet. Just a grab and go," Cowl said.

"No way. Too much expenditure for too little gain," Menrva said. "This isn't a run to the cafeteria we are talking about. This is light years of travel with nothing set up on the other side for harvesting the materials."

"So no return trips," Cowl agreed.

Menrva slowly backed away from the spacecraft. This had to be what the redhead warned them about. Now the only focus was getting Bas back.

"Maybe they are just giving up," she said as she began jogging. "Letting the Wreckers have the planet. How many flights would it take to evacuate? I feel like they are going to run out of resources before they run out of people."

"They don't need to bring everyone," Cowl said. "They can grow them from scratch with the artificial wombs they use for the Biobot program."

Menrva's stomach dropped. "You think they would just leave people behind to die? How many would they really..."

"Would you expect anything else from the City?" Cowl pointed out. "Think about this. Colonization. They will want only young, fit, strong people. People who can survive the trip, explore, weather disease and a new environment, and rebuild. That cuts out a lot of people, Nerve. A lot."

Menrva shifted her weight to her good leg and rolled her shoulders. 309's fight to warn them was not a waste. There was no feasible way they could evacuate the entire population. Any way they cut it, people were going to die; a lot of people. What did the City care? Genocide was just a temporary setback for them.

The morbid thoughts screeched to a halt in her mind as a sudden, terrifying realization bobbed to the top. "Cowl," she said, "don't Wreckers usually run in packs?"

Silence. Menrva pulled her gun to her chest and turned around. "Cowl? You there?"

There was no answer. Had they been disconnected? Her hands went numb and her vision blacked out.

Menrva opened her eyes to the familiar darkness of the Pit, and an unfamiliar face.

She had been disconnected. Purposefully.

Menrva struggled to move her limbs but someone had already dragged her to her feet and pulled her hands behind her. Shaking herself free of the haze darkening everything around her, she scanned the room. There were Borgs everywhere; at least ten. They were armed, their faces hard. 309 stood directly in front of Menrva, her cold eyes locked onto her.

"This is them, right?" a young girl beside 309 asked. Menrva narrowed her eyes and studied the woman's face. It was the scavenger whose arm she had broken on the rover, still cradling her obviously untended wound. "So I get the reward."

309 turned to look down on the shorter woman. She moved so fast Menrva almost didn't see the gun appear in her hand before the woman sunk to the floor. The sound of the gunshot echoed through the housing unit. The girl garbled as blood seeped into her mouth, grasping at her stomach before her eyes slid shut.

"Do we have G4S59?" 309 asked.

"Can't make Connection, Sir," one of the Borgs said from the console.

309's lips rolled together until they were a thin white line. "Inform the Hub. Have them try from there."

"You won't get him," Cowl said. Two Borgs held him by the shoulders only a few feet away. His face was a pulpy mess, and he seemed to be having trouble standing. Of course, he had fought. "He's not on City Net. You just killed him, you idiot. You disconnected him topside with no way to reconnect. He's in freeze protocol and bleeding. By the time they get up to him, all that's left of him will be what the Wreckers pick from their teeth."

Menrva took some comfort in his lie. Bas had a chance, especially if the City thought he was dead.

The Borg at Cowl's side dealt him a heavy blow for his boldness. Cowl spat blood across the Borg's face. "Red's your color," he sneered through clenched teeth.

Cowl was a perfect distraction. Menrva dropped to her stomach and rolled away from the Borg. Her hands were still clenched in the buzz cuffs, but she could run. A jolt of electricity ran up her arms as she jumped from the Rover, landing in a heap on the dirt. It was debilitating, but she stubbornly forced herself back to her feet.

She had made it further than she had expected. But they didn't move to chase her. A sharp pain struck her lower back and she dropped to the earth. Nothing in her body would obey her command; she couldn't even blink away the dirt drifting into her eyes.

Menrva could only stare helplessly as two Borgs walked to retrieve her and everything around her began to fade.

Chapter Thirty-Seven:
The Way Down (Icarus)

Bas's freeze protocol must have kicked in. He couldn't move. The sudden disconnection must have knocked him out. He ran a mental checklist, testing each body part, flexing his fingers and twisting his tense muscles. His leg was awash in agony, but functioning.

The black sky seemed to be crushing him, pressing him into the earth. Fighting to draw breath, Bas rolled and slowly climbed to his feet.

"Cowl, Menrva, you okay?"

What was the likelihood the Connection to Menrva had been severed at the same time as the radio communication? Something had happened.

Bas eased pressure onto his shattered leg and swore as the pain radiated up his body. He took a few deep breaths, wringing the gun in his hands. He couldn't afford to give in to the pain. Despite the discomfort of the actual Connection, he missed Menrva's guidance. If she was pulling the strings, he wouldn't have to worry about getting home safe. She would have gotten it done. Was she safe? All evidence pointed to the opposite. If it was bandits, she might already be dead. The City would keep her alive longer but that might not be a good thing. Pope didn't believe in torturing for information but he would be willing to do just about anything when pushed.

Bas checked the screen in his helmet. The closest entrance was the Hub, only a few feet away. He had to resist that temptation. His way down lay a good distance beyond it. As dangerous as the surface was, it was like a private heaven when compared to the Compound. Heaven with a few demonic intruders.

Drawing on his training, Bas began to jog. With each step, fire ignited in his shattered bones. He had to remind himself to take each breath. The soldier in him pushed him on, but all he wanted to do was curl up in the dust and sob like a child. The thought of Menrva and Cowl in danger drove him like a whiplash.

The dome lay silent. Bas half expected it to open like a trap door and suck him in as he sprinted past. Was he delirious? More than likely. Snapping off a Connection like that couldn't have been good for his brain. Not that the Connection was *ever* good for his body. Something seemed to be buzzing in the back of his head, like wires pulled loose in his head. This was more like muffled words, or a bad radio signal.

Bas picked up his pace and found a rhythm beyond the pain. After a few minutes, he approached the Wrecker corpse. It lay in a tattered mound on the ground, its black-bone face ripped open by the bullet. He slowed as he passed it. There was far too much damage to this body. Something had been there. There was only one option as to what.

The radar in his helmet should be going off if there were any Wreckers nearby, but there was no doubting this body had been fed on. Bas pulled the rifle to his shoulder and took a few steps closer to the dead beast. This wasn't paranoia or delusion. There was something here.

He peered through his gun sights, scanning the horizon. But even as he did, the map on his helmet blinked and died. Bas swore. The helmet must have been damaged in the fight. The air was the next thing to fizzle out. He didn't need it. The visibility, however, he did need. Without the computer guiding the visor, the entire thing turned black; no sun shield, no night vision, no clarity.

Bas regretfully tugged the helmet off his head. The negative temperatures drove into his skin like death's scythe. This was one of those instances when the alien genes dictating his life came in useful. There was not much between earth's surface and the rest of the universe; he might as well have been space walking.

Even as the thought crossed his mind, Bas saw what his radar had missed. A Wrecker. Unlike the last time, this wasn't some lone wanderer. Like the dawning of a nightmare, a pack of at least nine crested a nearby cliff. They stood against the sky, dark and massive, like black holes in reality.

They already knew he was there, He couldn't make the situation any worse. Without hesitation Bas lifted his rifle and burned through one magazine without releasing the trigger. Two Wreckers fell under the hail, but it would take more than a few hunks of lead to save him now. Not with this gun.

Spasms climbed Bas's leg and hip as he took off running. The suit tried to counteract the fresh blood, riddling his flesh with renewed heat.

As he ran he dropped the empty magazine and jammed in a replacement, struggling with the tremor in his hands.

He spun on his heels to squeeze off a few more shots. His broken bones made the action clumsy and he struggled to keep his feet under him. The Wreckers bore down with a ferocity that made the ground rumble. Bas had never faced this many head-on, and never without a User.

Pouring the bullets out on their heads with each step, Bas gritted his teeth against the waves of terror washing over him. The fear should have been worse, though. It had always been worse. Another Wrecker fell but they were too close, now. Time to change tactics.

Dropping the rifle on its tether, Bas pulled out two powerful handguns, fighting to keep his pace steady. The moment he turned back to his targets, the ground under his foot crumbled and he slammed into the ground. Immediately, he shoved his body back into motion, but as he did, he caught sight of a section of ground moving and rolling back. It was an entrance to the Compound, one he'd used before. A platform rose up through the hole left behind, and a detachment of ten battle-ready Borgs, were on it.

Bas swore, forcing his stiff leg under him. He was going to have to put on some speed if he was going to make it back to the entrance. If the City wanted him, they would have to pry him from the Wrecker's jaws. He gripped his gun closer, ignoring the shooting pain in every step. A chant began in the back of his head. "Kill. Kill. Kill."

Never in his life had he wanted to pull the trigger more. If he stopped to kill Borgs, he was giving up Cowl and Menrva. He had to keep moving.

His breath came in ragged shreds, tearing into his body like cold spears. He risked a glance behind him. The shattered remnants of the old terminal rushed toward him. He couldn't hope to outrun the Wreckers, though. They had him. This was going to be a fight and there was no way he was winning it.

The moment of distraction cost him. A powerful hand grasped Bas by the shoulder, and he flew upward before slamming back to the ground like a sledgehammer. He writhed in agony, pulling himself into a fetal position. The bulk of the hunting Wreckers filled the void above.

Forcing the unnatural fear from his veins, Bas shot two rounds at the closest Wrecker. The bullets grazed its head, sending a rain of broken bone to the ground. It reeled back, mouth wide in a soundless scream. Wounded, but it wasn't enough.

Another Wrecker rushed into the gap. Its disemboweling talon swiped over Bas's chest, shredding his armor like paper and searing through his flesh. The first cut was shallow, but the second dug deep into his side. The talon caught under a rib, taking Bas with it. For a moment he hovered over the ground before the bone snapped, and he hit the dirt, unable to move. One of the guns flew from his hand, knocked away by the force of the impact. He turned on his stomach to reach for it but was immediately pinned down as the weight of a pouncing Wrecker slammed on his back. He struggled to draw in a breath, fighting against a darkness closing around him. Why couldn't he breathe? Each attempt only brought pain.

Teeth pierced the armor on Bas's leg, and he was violently jerked backward as another Wrecker tried to pull him away from the first. His back exploded in furrows of cold agony as claws tore into his armor, peeling it from him like foil.

The ice crystals on the ground seemed so clear, melting slowly as his blood warmed them. He wasn't going to make it. Everything spun around him, blurring into a black vortex.

"Kill. Kill. Kill." The chant started in the back of Bas's head and swelled until it filled him. Until his body was alive with wrath. His hand connected with the hard handle of his gun.

Reaching back, he grabbed a Wrecker's arm and pulled himself around. He raised the gun. The Wrecker's mouth closed over the weapon, enveloping Bas's arm. The teeth punctured the armor effortlessly but Bas ignored them, squeezing the trigger. Burgundy blood and shards of bone exploded overhead, pelting Bas's face. The Wrecker fell dead, pinning another under its body.

Bas didn't get a chance to climb to his feet before a Borg jumped over him, landing on the alien corpse. He turned his gun to the pinned Wrecker, finishing him off with a single, powerful shot.

Another Borg grabbed Bas's shoulder, hauling him to his feet. "Get up. Move!" Fire radiated out of Bas's very bones, filling every piece of him. The Borg pulled Bas back toward the Hub, half supporting him while he fired off shots at the agitated Wreckers.

Bas twisted around and drove the handle of his gun into the Borg's spine, sliding free of his grip as he did. The Borg convulsed and dropped his gun. That was all it took for a Wrecker to knock him off his feet and descend on him. Bas didn't wait to see the results. He broke into a sprint, leaving the chaos behind him.

Another Wrecker leaped over the first two, charging after Bas. More Borgs converged upon the attacking Wrecker.

He was so close, the opening of Bunker yawning in front of him. Each step propelled him closer to safety.

Claws slammed into him from behind, throwing him forward. He twisted to see the Wrecker, still poised for the kill, torn apart in a hail of bullets as the Borgs turned their attention back on him.

Bas barely managed to roll free of the falling body. He gripped his gun tight, pushing himself to his knees. The tattered face of the Wrecker he'd wounded appeared over the corpse of the other. Bas fired a few loose bullets over his shoulder as he crawled into the leaning doorway. Only a few more feet.

He skidded across the ice, scrambling into the crumbling structure. Behind him the broken edges of the wall exploded into frozen splinters as the enraged Wrecker barreled through. Bas dragged himself backward, firing as he went. Each bullet buried itself into the alien's chest, but it ignored them in the blind passion of the hunt. The beast would tear Bas to shreds before it even realized it was mortally wounded.

The Wrecker struck him hard, and Bas skidded across the

floor, losing his remaining gun as he slammed into the cage around the elevator.

The beast descended, its arms outstretched. Bas grabbed the talon as it swung toward his chest, gripping it with every last drop of life in him. With a vicious twist, he tore it from the flesh.

Unshaken, the Wrecker wrapped its hands around Bas's waist and leaned in with its mouth gaping. Bas drove the broken talon upwards with both hands, plunging it so deep into the Wrecker's neck that his hand followed into the flesh. The crunch of breaking bone reverberated down his arm as the talon found its way into the alien's brain.

The Wrecker fell with so much force dust shook loose from the shattered ceiling. Bas curled into himself, trying to brace against the pain piercing his very core.

He dragged himself free of the remains, every piece of him protesting the movement. His flesh sizzled, a desperate attempt to staunch the profuse bleeding. He was already a dead man; or, he should have been. How long did he realistically have? What had he even been fighting for? The chance to slowly bleed to death just inches from safety?

A few Borgs climbed through the entrance right behind him. If they caught him, they would make sure he didn't die. That was worse than being torn apart by Wreckers.

Bas wrapped one arm around his chest, trying to hold his tattered frame together and dragged himself onto the elevator with the other. The elevator lever was stubborn. He fell onto it, forcing it downward. The elevator began its descent into the darkness.

His suit busily conducted medical patches. Heat radiated from Bas's bones, searing shut the exposed blood vessels and melting his flesh together. He could barely react to the pain; he was too broken. Despite that, he was thankful for the patches. If he was going to make it back to the housing unit he would need whatever blood was left in his body.

With that thought in his mind, Bas dragged himself to his feet. Immediately, the pain slammed him back down. He rolled his shoulders, working up the courage to push through. It would be worth it when he knew if Cowl and Menrva were okay. Cowl would have his skin for this, though. Bas cracked a smile as he imagined Cowl's anger and shock. He would have to make a point to apologize for not taking his advice. His thoughts were interrupted as the elevator jolted to a halt, almost throwing him down.

Bas stumbled into the airlock, leaving a streak of blood across the wall as he dragged his hands across the glass. The door behind him closed with a pneumatic rush of air.

"Decontamination." The words blinked on the screen attached to the door. "Please remove your clothing."

He couldn't do that, since the suit was holding him together. Radiation had long ago settled into harmless amounts. The procedure wasn't necessary, though the Hub still followed it. The screen blinked a few more times before a gush of cold water dropped on him from above.

"Decontamination." The computer blinked. "Please use soap and wash thoroughly."

Bas wiped the water from his face. He was having a hard enough time breathing without being drowned. Behind him, the elevator rose back toward the surface. The Borgs must be coming down after him. Hopefully, the airlock and decontamination would give Bas enough of a head start to avoid getting caught.

The water clicked off and the airlock opened. Rivers of red-dyed water tickled Bas's skin, dripping muddy prints along the floor of the station.

He wouldn't make it far like this. He could barely walk across the floor. Most of these exits had vehicles nearby; he could only hope this one hadn't been raided yet.

Bas hobbled out the door. Instantly his blistered and frozen skin was masked with mud as dust settled on the water and blood. He took a moment to lean against the wall, gasping in breaths. A trickle of water caught in the force of his breath exploded into a hundred tiny, ruby droplets. Bas shook his head, trying to shake the surrealism floating around him. He had to hang on to reality. Once he let his mind drift, he was lost. His fingers tapped on the metal as he counted his surroundings. Count his heartbeat, count his breath, count anything to keep his mind from shutting out the world.

"I've been through worse," he assured himself. Was that an accurate statement, though?

The tower's outer wall guided him until he spotted the rusted shed he was hoping for. An old-fashioned lock hung from the door. Maybe what was inside wasn't worth the effort, but running was about as useful as waiting for the Borgs with hands raised. He had to try.

Bas aimed his gun with a shaky hand. The sound of the gun firing made him jump. The noise was skull-shattering after the dead quiet of the surface. He pushed the door open and breathed a sigh of relief as his eyes fell on the shapes of two canvas-covered quads. Behind them, the back of the shed was torn apart, allowing dust to drift in.

He prayed the vehicle was still in working condition as he dragged the tarp free. Cowl's offhanded lessons were his lifeline as he hacked the simple touchscreen and the quad roared to life. Bas dragged his leg over the seat. He had to stifle his groans into his arm. His hands were clenched into claws from the effort as he focused every bit of concentration to grip the handlebars. The lights of the vehicle flooded the tiny room and glinted off a collection of orbs encrusted onto the wall.

Bas's stomach dropped. Wrecker eggs.

He'd destroyed more than one clutch in his time, but they were always topside. Once they found them they had to act fast. The eggs themselves were tough to destroy, but once they sensed prey they would hatch in a matter of months.

He'd have to leave these to the Borgs behind him. Right now all that mattered was getting back to the housing unit and Cowl and Menrva.

Despite the reassurance he was nearly sick with guilt as he cast the responsibility aside and focused his energy on escape. He leaned into the bike and shot from the shed, leaving a cloud of dust behind him like a storm.

"I'm coming," he whispered to himself as he left the exit behind.

Chapter Thirty-Eight: The Face of Evil

"Way to ruin all the mystery in our relationship," Cowl said as he noticed the fold-out toilet in the otherwise empty cubical room that they found themselves in.

Menrva slid a bare foot over the polished white floor. She had lost count of the days she had been alone before they had brought Cowl in. There was no explanation as to where he had been, or why they chose to put them together now, but she was thankful for it. The emptiness of the room was torture in and of itself. "I don't think they expect us to be here long," she replied.

"We must be in the Compound," Cowl said. He looked like tenderized beef. His face was so swollen Menrva couldn't even make out his ever-present dimples. He held his stomach tight against his cuffs, bent over in pain. The guards hadn't bothered to take them off. They made quite the pair, with Menrva sporting a few new scuffs and bruises herself. City guards didn't seem to care too much for their charges.

"How do you figure?" Menrva asked. The corridors all looked the same, and all of the ones she had been dragged through were unfamiliar and completely devoid of human beings.

"This looks like the room Bas was in when I first

Connected," Cowl said.

They were quiet for a while. More than likely he, as much as she, wanted to talk about Bas, to wonder out loud if he had made it back. If he was alive. What if he walked into a trap? What if he couldn't get help and his leg got infected? What if he tried something rash to get them back? Bas was always one for gambles. She couldn't voice any of her concerns for fear of being overheard, but she didn't have to. The fear furrowing Cowl's forehead was words enough.

"At least we are still alive," he said. "I'm not entirely sure what that means."

Menrva shrugged. "They want to remove our genetic material?"

Cowl grinned. "Man, they hit the jackpot here. They must be excited." Cowl strained his neck to look at the single camera hanging in the middle of the room. "Just think, Nerve. After they kill us, we could have a kid together."

"Poor kid," Menrva said. She didn't want to let on how much the thought terrified her: the possibility that her child could end up like Bas. One baby lost to a nightmare was one baby too many.

"How are you? Anything more serious than that nasty cut on your eyebrow?"

"Nope, nothing new," Menrva said. Her ribs ached, and her back was strained from the long ride back to the Hub and from being jerked around mercilessly. But it could only be healed with time. She was all pain, and all fear. This wasn't fear for herself. She had left Bas in the middle of hostile territory with a busted leg. She was afraid for him. It was hard to think of anything else, to force herself to be present. "You?"

"I think they busted my nose. I'm going to look like I have my face permanently stuck against a glass pane. So much for being a pretty corpse."

Menrva leaned forward. "No, it's not broken, but your cheek bone might be." She shook her head. "I don't understand why they didn't give you medical. They checked me over at least. "

Cowl shrugged it off.

Who would have thought not long ago Menrva would now be in this situation? It was a long way from her comfortable pod and her happy ignorance. She thought of Cowl's tenacious companionship, of Bas's soft lips and gentle, healing touch, and she smiled to herself. It would be worth it if he was alive.

Then again, he might not forgive her for getting his leg half bit off.

"How long you think it's been?" Cowl asked. "A week? A month? Feels like it's been a month."

"Once your circadian rhythm gets thrown off by the light-" Menrva jutted her head at the intense overhead light. "-you lose track of time. It was already messed up with the floodlights in the Pit. Now without even a watch there is no way either of us would have an accurate handle on time. It might feel like it's been a while, but I think, judging by the how far our injuries have healed, maybe two days? I might not be able to evaluate that very well, though. My cognitive functions could be impaired by the isolation." She studied a purple bruise on her forearm. "And everyone heals at different rates, too."

Cowl made a face. "Well, when you put it that way."

"Psychologist believe isolation like this can cause brain damage in less than three days," Menrva said, looking around the empty white room. No stimulation. It was a dangerous place to be for a human mind.

"Now imagine spending your whole life in here," Cowl said softly.

He was talking about Bas. The thought settled like a rock in Menrva's thoughts. No wonder Cowl had fought so hard to make sure Bas never had to come back.

The door swung open, and Menrva jumped. A group of four City guards stood just outside, their faces as cold as masks.

Cowl pushed himself between her and them. Around his shoulders, Menrva caught a glimpse of a man limping through the door toward them. He wasn't much taller than her, made shorter by his dependence on a thin, black cane. His back was bent with severe scoliosis, and his right leg looked as if someone had wrapped it around a table leg, it was so twisted. He had strawberry-blond hair smoothed back from transparent skin, and a childish face dominated by large green eyes. Only the slight wrinkles around his eyes and mouth suggested he was older than her. The expression etched across his features was soft, almost earnest, though it did not steal from the confidence in his bearing.

"I apologize for the accommodations." He spoke with a calm, even tone. Menrva shuddered. He sounded like Bas. Not exactly. More like one family member might have a similar rhythm to another. His voice wasn't as deep, but he had the same musical cadence to his words. "I would have had them remove the cuffs, but I am afraid I don't trust you." He looked Cowl in the eyes as he spoke.

"Trust issues. Probably a good thing. If I wasn't cuffed I could break you over my knee. Hell, Nerve could probably break you over her knee."

One of the guards jolted forward but the man held up a hand to stop him. "Frisco, relax."

The guard scowled but settled obediently back into his stance.

"My name is Jonathan Pope. You can call me Pope. Everyone else does," the man said, smiling as if he had just introduced himself for an evening of relaxed entertainment.

Menrva reevaluated the slight man. Pope. She had expected a more imposing man to be the dictator of humanity. This was who had been responsible for Bas's hell. He didn't seem capable of such evil. His smile was too genuine.

"Menrva. I have a problem that I am hoping you can help me with. In fact, I am hoping this will be of benefit for both of us." Pope leaned into his cane. "Would you be so kind as to walk with me?"

Cowl stiffened.

"Don't fear, Cowl. I will not hurt her. You have my word."

"Yeah, I have trust issues, too," Cowl said.

Menrva pushed herself awkwardly to her feet. "It's okay. I've got this."

Cowl raised a doubtful eyebrow but didn't protest as she walked around him.

Menrva felt small, insignificant, between the guards. They watched her with cool eyes. Menrva had almost forgotten how much those judgmental stares hurt, even coming from people she despised. She hadn't missed them. Was this their reaction to all their prisoners or just for the ones that messed with the status quo? The fact that these men wore the grey uniform that so defined her father made everything much worse.

Should she fight or run, or just go with it? If Cowl were free he would have caused as much damage as he could, logical or not. Was she betraying him and Bas just by walking with Pope without trying to kill him? Acting out just wasn't the logical move to make. If Menrva had something he wanted, it meant she was in a position of power. That was a good position to be in right now.

She would bide her time. This man couldn't be all evil; maybe he had something he could offer. She glanced back at Cowl's stormy face as she followed Pope out the door. He would just have to understand.

Once outside, Pope waved away the guard. "She won't hurt me. Will you, Menrva?" He looked at her as if they had been friends their entire life. Somehow it was unsettling.

She nodded stiffly, not entirely sure if she was being truthful or not.

Pope's eyes didn't leave her face as the guards left down the door-riddled hall. "I have to say, I have been quite impressed by you. At the risk of sounding threatening, I've been watching you."

"I've been a fugitive," Menrva said. "Obviously, you've been trying to figure me out."

"Oh, I was watching far before that." Pope waved a hand for her to follow and began limping down the hall. Menrva studied the doors lining the hall as they passed. Reinforced and labeled with simple numbers on digital interfaces, they never seemed to end. Were there Borgs behind each door? Maybe Cowl was wrong and this was just the prison unit.

"The truth is, I've been keeping an eye on you since you were a young girl. I had a different motivation back then. I suspected you might be a good match for Nolan. I hoped you would be strong enough to withstand his violent tendencies and maybe soften him up a bit."

Hatred overwhelmed Menrva like a wave. She had always assumed she was matched with Case because of their genetics, like most marriages in Bunker. Instead, this man had hand-picked her knowing what Case would do. "That was your fault?" she said. "You really are a heartless monster, aren't you?"

Pope frowned, his shoulders drooping as if he had been heavily affected by the comment. "I am sorry. If it helps at all, I regret that choice. I had thought Nolan might be the man to replace me...a decision I also regret." He paused, turning to address her directly. "Regret is the constant companion of a leader."

"Excuse me if I lack pity," Menrva said. She should grab the man's cane and drive it through his eye. No one would be able to stop her.

Pope chuckled. He was being condescending. The arrogance was infuriating: that he would cause her pain and then mock her for it.

"He doesn't know you are here," Pope said quickly.

"Nolan, I mean. I'm confident I could keep him from injuring you, but I wanted to assure you that you don't need to worry about him right now. I'm keeping him occupied elsewhere."

Menrva shuddered at the thought of Nolan in the Compound. He was close. Closer than she ever wanted him to be again. She knew how to defend herself now, but the thought of him still made her skin prickle.

They pushed through a set of double doors, and Menrva forgot her anger as she entered a massive room filled with hundreds of replicator machines. They were barely waist high, comprised of a complicated stalk holding a glass sphere. A thin red tissue clung to the inner wall of the globe, but as she peered into the nearest one she could see the faint shape of a developing infant inside, attached by a web of black threads to the machine. The baby curled its hands gently, and hot tears clouded Menrva's eyes at the sight. Angel had been about that size when she was born.

"I'm sure you have figured it out by now. This is where Bas spent the first nine months of his life." Pope joined her, peering into the machine. Menrva jerked away as if he had burned her.

"I did as well," he said.

"You are a Borg?"

"A Borg? That's hardly an accurate term. Cyborg would insinuate that the technology is assimilated into their bodies. The truth is far more ghastly. But no, I am not a biobot, nor am I genetically improved at all. My predecessors wouldn't have allowed it. I am a clone."

Menrva stepped further away. A clone? Scientifically, it

was possible, though she'd never heard of a successful human trial. She should have expected it from the City. They wouldn't let bioethics get in the way of something they needed.

"*The* clone, at present. The science is not as advanced as we would like. My genes have been recycled down through the years from the very first Pope, who was one of the scientists responsible for Bunker. Unfortunately, I think this era has come to an end." His eyes grew so sad that Menrva couldn't ignore the rush of pity filling her chest.

"I was raised for a specific purpose, with a certain design. The design is no longer effective." He turned to Menrva. "The last attempt at another clone failed. I am certain now that it was a good thing. Providence almost. Things can't continue the way they are. Don't you agree?"

Pope ran a hand lovingly over the globe and the growing infant within. The red glow of the life within reflected in his eyes.

"In a way, it is a fitting picture. My body is crumbling... and so is earth. We are both dying."

Chapter Thirty-Nine: A Purpose

Menrva fought alternate waves of disgust and hatred as Pope looked into the incubators holding the next batch of victims. How many generations now? If Bas was the fourth, they were sure to have built more waves of soldiers between him and these babies.

Pope leaned heavily on his cane and seemed to be struggling with the words to speak next. Menrva was happy for his momentary silence. She shifted uncomfortably between the glass orbs.

"I was very involved with Generation Four," Pope said "My predecessor was responsible for the previous generations. The special circumstances, as well as my desire to handle my responsibilities with care, made me a regular in these halls."

He cleared his throat. "I remember the man you call Bas well. He was a unique child. He was very attached to his caregivers, and to me, as well. As an infant, he cried inconsolably when he wasn't being held. If you picked him up he would bury his face into your neck and cling with both hands as if you were life itself."

Menrva bit back nausea. She didn't want to hear this. This man was pretending to actually care about Bas, talking about him like a father sharing stories of a son he was proud of. He couldn't have felt any fatherly love. Not with the torture he had so willingly inflicted. After all, according to Capricorn, this was the man who had given the kill order for the entirety of Bas's generation.

"I remember visiting him once when he was about three years of age. He rushed into my arms, like always. When I picked him up he focused those intense eyes on me and placed his hands firmly on my cheeks. With every ounce of conviction in his body, he said 'I love you'." Pope smiled, nostalgia playing across his features.

"When Bas reached his eighth birthday I took it on myself to be the one who talked to him. Typically that is the job of the handler, but I knew Bas would need a gentler hand than what he could offer. I sat with him and we talked for a long time. I explained that things would be different. That he would experience a lot of pain, but in the end, we had to do what we had to do. When we were finished, my men took him to the operating table where he was strapped down. I don't often sit in on the surgeries, but I felt it was important for his."

Pope turned to fix his eyes on Menrva's. He seemed sorrowful, but the words he spoke were anything but. "I watched as they cut into his back and I didn't look away as he cried and begged, or when he reached out for me in his fear. I did not leave the room as they installed the device effectively turning him into a weapon. I took responsibility for that choice."

Menrva was more surprised by the hot tears brimming in her eyes than by the sudden vicious turn the story had taken.

"I don't say this to upset you, though I see that I have. What I hope you understand is that this is not easy for me. It is not something I want to do. I have done what I must to keep us alive. It is a heavy burden, one I do not bear lightly. The device *has* to be inserted that early, to keep the metal from growing too far. The spine is designed to grow with them with minimal interference. And we can't possibly afford to fully sedate such a large number of children, but we do try to manage the pain locally. I do the best I can."

Why was this man so eager for her to agree with his methods? It was insane. There was nothing good in what he was doing.

"You just explained how you tear apart children's bodies to fuel your power trip. Do you expect me to be sorry for you because you feel guilty?" Menrva could barely look at him. Her mind was filled with images of Bas writhing against the blade of a surgical knife.

"You are reacting just as I expected, but this is what I hoped for. At first, I thought I needed a successor like our mutual acquaintance, Mr. Nolan. Someone who doesn't feel any regret for causing pain. A man without conscience. A stone wall between us and extinction." Pope took a few steps toward Menrva, and she backed away.

"Only a few short years ago we became aware that earth was dying. It is breaking apart, wobbling on its axis. It seems that what we once thought was human destruction is instead a tactic of our invaders. The same acid that burns the skin off our soldiers is responsible for the disintegration of our atmosphere. Under the stress, the earth will crumble and break apart, carrying a new generation of alien eggs to another planet."

"The rockets..." Menrva interjected.

"Correct: there is only one hope left for the human race. We must evacuate. We have chosen from some of the planets that were earlier assumed to be uninhabitable. If you remember the planet Timur X1 has been proven to support life. Our initial investigation shows a lot of promise for the human race. With technology salvaged from humanity's glory days, we've managed to shave the time down to a mere year."

Menrva frowned. She'd heard about possibilities of other planets, but space travel wasn't something they taught much about.

"But," Pope continued, "like Moses in the Bible, I will not be setting foot in the promised land. Doctors believe I will be dead before we arrive."

Menrva resisted the urge to express her satisfaction. She couldn't have said she had never wished anyone dead before, despite having many enemies, but Pope was in a league all his own. Was there any terror in the world now that couldn't be traced back to him? Maybe the Wreckers.

"But I cannot rest in peace yet. You see, I have two things I must be assured of before I will gladly step into history, for better or worse. After such damage as we have suffered, after what we have become, humanity needs a unique leader. One who is strong, who is not easily frightened or broken, yet is gentle and kind. You have suffered so much, and yet you have remained motivated, empathetic and un-movingly self-controlled despite a tempest that blows around you. Not many people have this special quality. Furthermore, you are brilliantly talented. In the few short hours you had with Bas's blood sample, you isolated qualities in his DNA that have eluded my own studies, as well as those of my colleagues."

Menrva tried to ignore the pang of guilt shooting through her at the reminder of what she had done. If she had never taken that blood sample, Bas would still be hidden safely away in the cave, far from the Wreckers and from Pope.

"This is where this story truly becomes a miracle," Pope continued. "Of all the biobots you could have reached out to, it was *Bas* who you made a connection with. Bas, whose mutated genes were achieved by pure accident when we needed them most. While Timur is, in most senses, habitable, it has one fatal flaw: it's atmosphere is deadly to any normal human being.

Our calculations predict that a human colony on this planet will last only a matter of one or two generations. We do not have the resources to support that level of sophistication. We can barely outfit the army we have with the necessary breathing apparatus." He paused to take in a deep breath, seemingly waiting to give her a chance to speak. What was there to even say?

"Bas's mutations have given us the answer to that problem," he continued. "Once we find the mutation, we can replicate it. We can essentially force an evolution in mankind that will allow us to start life on a new world." Pope twisted his cane in his hands and smiled gently, as if he were trying to convince her that this was a good thing.

"When we start a new life, we cannot continue with the same cruel cultures. I don't expect we can use the product of these labs as weapons and still accept them as our own children. The only way to save the human race is through fire, and we will have to come together afterwards in ways that have never been seen before." He shook his head, closing his eyes. "My greatest wish is that we can be a whole people again, that we can feel kindness. I believe you can be the one to lead us there."

Menrva wrapped her arms over her stomach. "You seem to think I want to clean up your mess. I'd rather die than be part of your legacy. History will remember you with less pity than the Wreckers," she said.

Pope's eyes shimmered with real hurt. "As long as there are still people to remember."

Menrva spun on her heels and walked quickly past the rows of artificial wombs. "Just put me back in my cell," she said. The words were sharp against her lips, but not as sharp as the sorrow ripping her chest apart.

"We aren't putting you into your cell," Pope said, following her with pained steps. "We are letting you go."

Menrva spun to face him. "You are letting us go? Why?"

"I'm afraid I can't release you both." Pope passed Menrva and held open the door. "We have reason to believe Bas is alive, though I think you and your friend already had hope of that. You managed to get around his freeze protocol, didn't you?" He smiled, almost proudly.

"He appears to be dangerously injured. We were able to track him from the housing unit to a dust town before he left the vehicle at the edge of a canyon."

Menrva squeezed her eyes shut to hide the fear in them. She had let him get injured; this was her fault. What if it was even worse? Had something else happened? He had been left up there alone. She willed Pope not to speak the words, but they were bound to come.

"It seems that Bastille ran into a pack of Wreckers on his return. It's a true testament to our work that he actually survived, but if we cannot find him and treat him, it will not continue to be the case. It looks like he has lost a lot of blood."

Horror hit Menrva. "Bas would prefer death to coming back here."

"No doubt. But I'm not necessarily asking you to bring him back...yet. We both want him to live." As they talked, Pope led her into an adjacent room, easily identifiable as a medical ward. It was at least as state of the art as the civilian ward below, if not more. A woman about Menrva's age lay in a bed near the back of the room, wrapped in thick layers of cloth and breathing mechanically. To her right, a willowy teenage boy watched with dead eyes as a tech stitched a long gash on his leg. He didn't even look up at them.

Menrva couldn't help but stare at the him as she walked by. He looked so empty: a mere shell. A skin.

Remembering how the City would extract genetic material before executions, Menrva dragged her legs like lead across the floor as she followed Pope through the wide room. It was illogical to be afraid. If they wanted to kill her they wouldn't have wasted their time with a personal tour. Still, she couldn't force herself to trust the man before her.

"All we ask of you, Menrva, is to do exactly what you

would want to do: find him and help him. You have my word we will not attempt to follow or track you." He pulled a large silver box from a cupboard. "At least in this matter, you and I have the same goal."

Menrva accepted the box and opened it. It was a well-stocked med kit, complete with bags of artificial blood, antibiotics, and more. Precious resources.

"How exactly do you expect me to trust you?"

Pope leveled his gaze on her and she couldn't help but feel as if he were aiming a gun at her head. "I don't lie. If Bas doesn't survive then neither will we, so you can say that I am motivated. I only ask that you consider all I have told you. We do not have much time left."

Menrva snapped the box shut and tested its weight. "What about Cowl?"

"I'm afraid we cannot allow Cowl to follow you just yet. We will give him all the appropriate care. You have no need to worry about him until I have your answer."

Menrva didn't want to leave Cowl in those empty white rooms but she couldn't help him, even if she was there...except to stave off the insanity degrading the mind in that kind of isolation. That was assuming they would be in the same cell. She knew what Cowl's choice would be. He would have put the gun to his head himself if he knew Menrva was hesitating on his account. "So you are holding Cowl hostage?"

"By withholding Bas from us you are holding the entire human race hostage. You can understand why we are desperate."

"Bas makes his own decisions," Menrva said.

Pope smiled smugly. " I can assure you of one thing: in the end, Bas will do as he is told. It is what he was built for. It's all he knows how to do. You make your decision, and he will follow."

It was what he was built to do, and maybe it used to be what he knew, but Bas wasn't that same crying child that had reached out to Pope from the operation table. He was a man, more human than anyone in the Compound. They would never know that, though. They would never see anything but a tool.

Menrva's hands shook as she rubbed them across the top of the box. If Bas was dying, she had to go to him. Was it worth the risk of them finding him?

Pope's words echoed in her mind. If Bas died then they all died, but they weren't looking for a knight in shining armor. They didn't want a hero. They would tear him apart and build their new world from his bones.

Menrva glanced at the Borg boy who sat behind her. That is what they wanted to do to Bas. Again. Carve him out. Pull out everything that was beautiful about him. Turn him into an empty suit of armor. Yet, the alternative was no better. What they had done was far from noble, but without it, could humanity have survived this long? Would they be able to survive into the future? Could she balance Bas's safety against the human race? Either way, a lot of people were going to die unless she could find another way.

Menrva picked up the medkit, though her fingers didn't want to cooperate. She could do this, at least. She could make sure Bas was all right. While she did, maybe she would find a little more time. Time was precious now.

"I want my gun," Menrva said.

"Naturally."

Menrva took a deep breath. "Okay," she said. "Get me out of here."

Chapter Forty: Belly of the Beast

"37, 41, 43, 47." Cowl tapped the cuffs against the door, letting the clink of the metal against metal drown out his time-worn habit. He'd been looking for possibly hours for some sort of way into the locks. Just like the last pod, there was nothing to be seen. If he had Bas's strength he could just tear the frame down. He'd tried that, though. After swinging on the slight lip for a couple minutes, he gave up. Hopefully they weren't watching the cameras too closely, because he'd never felt less like a man.

Kicking wasn't much good either, though admittedly it was more to give a rhythm for his rebellious chant. That's what he was choosing to call the knockdown, drag-out fit he'd had after the door frame didn't crumble in his hands. Because if your masculinity was in question, the best thing to do was to behave like a child.

He missed his gun. Not the bullets or the ability to actually kill anyone, just the feeling of the weight in his palm and the stubbornness of the trigger just before it gave way.

The memory was comforting, and it was giving him a chance to imagine the look on Pope's face when the bullet burrowed into his chest. It helped drown out the constant stream of numbers forcing their way into his unoccupied thoughts.

He'd had enough time to imagine that, though. Where was Menrva?

It had been long enough; she should be back. Not that he knew how long it had been. If he believed his body clock, which was probably smashed into a million tiny, unfixable pieces by now, it had been a couple of hours. God only knows how long it had actually been. It could have been a couple minutes, it could have been days.

Why had Menrva gone with Pope so easily? Anything could have happened to her. At least if he was with her, no one could have touched her without going through him.

Instead he was left behind...again. What the hell? Wasn't he important? What did she have that he didn't? They wouldn't torture her for information, would they? It seemed excessive. Especially since they thought Bas was dead. Hopefully.

And hopefully they were wrong in that assumption. Cowl chewed his lip and twisted his chafed wrists in the cuffs again.

The door hissed open, and Cowl looked up to see a short, broad-shouldered man standing in the hallway. His reddish brown hair was shot through with the same gray that nearly overtook his well-groomed beard, though he didn't seem to be that old. He nodded at the guard to his left, a young kid who looked a little bit terrified to be beside the man, who helped Cowl to his feet and removed his cuffs.

"Follow me," the first guard said, a hint of a smile playing across his lips before he hid it.

"Where is Menrva?" Cowl asked, jerking his arm free of

the smaller guard and shaking the feeling back into his fingers.

"You don't need to be worried. Miss Penniweight is safe, but you won't be staying with her," the guard said. He raised a thick, dark brow at Cowl and nodded down the hall. "Would you please come with us?"

Cowl studied the closest guard. His arm was covered in a black glove of sorts, what looked more like a wrist brace. A gauntlet. He'd seen it before, though he hadn't recognized it then. The remote that controlled the Borgs. Around his belt, a set of cuffs sat in their holster along with a small handgun, more for show than anything. It was probably carrying soft Taser rounds, charging in their case.

If he grabbed the gun, how many could he kill before they got him? He'd have to get his hands on a few rounds, but each guard probably carried a few clips. If he played his cards right, he might even get near an exit and actually survive. Taking out a few assholes would be worth it, either way.

Cowl flexed his fingers, testing the unfeeling digits. Shooting might not be so easy right now. Maybe in a minute or two.

His hip hurt from sitting on it so awkwardly. Either that, or he injured it when he was trying to break down the door. It was hard to keep track of what had injured him in what way.

One of the guards fell behind Cowl as they walked. Neither looked particularly worried. They had full control in here, after all. How would they be reacting right now if Bas was here? He'd put the fear of God in them, gauntlet or no.

"Where are we going?" Cowl asked, studying the doors he walked by. He'd been here before, back when he'd first pulled Bas out. It was a long time ago, but nothing really looked different.

The first guard turned to look him out of the corner of his eye but didn't answer.

Maybe they were going to execute him. If they thought Bas was dead, they had no reason to keep him alive. What about Menrva? Was she already dead? The thought filled his chest with a sharp ache. More dead family. That's what Menrva was: family. She always had been, he'd just lost sight of it for a while.

If that was true, and she was gone, he'd kill every guard in sight before they ended it. He wasn't going to walk calmly into a gas chamber for them. If they wanted to kill him, they were going to have to fight for it.

At least Bas would still be left. He would leave behind someone he loved.

Cowl tested his hand again. Still tingling, half asleep, but he could make it work. He sped up slightly, closing in on the guard in front of him. He was a skinny kid, easy to overpower. A good old bullet was always preferable to hand-to-hand, but he could do what needed to be done. Hell, if Nerve could throw the punches she did, as small as she was, he could, too.

The memory of her made his stomach ache. He'd never wanted to be wrong so bad.

No more delay. He had to get that gun. He took a step forward and reached for the guard's belt, but before he could grab it the guard stopped so fast he nearly slammed right into him.

Cowl pulled his hand back as the lead guard pulled open a door to another pod. "Here you are."

Stretching out his neck, Cowl strained to see inside. It was a simple pod, small, but well furnished. A few pictures flitted across the screen making up one wall, and a cool breeze flowed out from the air conditioner.

It didn't look like a gas chamber. No, this wasn't where you brought people for execution.

The guard in front of Cowl stepped aside, leaving his passage to the door open.

"Care to explain?" Cowl asked.

The lead guard fixed his eyes on Cowl. "You are determined to make trouble, aren't you?"

Cowl blinked his eyes slowly and clasped his hands together. "What did I do?"

The guard motioned for the others to leave. "I'm an old man; experienced. I may not look like much, but I know when someone is scheming. And I saw you reach for the gun."

The other guard snapped his head around to look at Cowl, his hand hovering protectively over his side arm. Too late to grab it now, anyway.

Stepping cautiously through the door, Cowl turned around in the small space. It was a homey jail cell, but it was still a cell. At least here he could work on getting out. Maybe he could hack the screen and break out that way. Maybe...

Cowl jumped as the door behind him shut with a distinct

click, locking him inside with the lead guard. What was he doing in here still?

The guard held up both hands as Cowl backed away. "Don't worry, I'm on your side."

"I didn't realize I had a side," Cowl said, eying the gun at the guard's hip.

"Well, maybe I can convince you that you should be on our side, then?"

"*Our?*" Cowl asked. "Like, the City? Cause that's not gonna happen. Might as well shoot me now."

"Just...hear me out." The guard made a few vague motions with his hands, his eyes staring at Cowl like they might just burn through him. "My name is Dennis Pool and I'm a ranking officer of a resistance force."

A laugh burst out of Cowl before he could stop it. "Resistance? Like hell."

Dennis pressed his lips together and nodded. "We're young. Newborn, really. I can understand how this sounds foolish, but we mean this in all seriousness." Dennis motioned toward the bed, inviting Cowl to sit. "Would you let me explain?"

Cowl shrugged. What could this guy say that would even make any sense? If he was what he said he was, he'd probably be dead himself before the week was out.

"There have always been a few of us guards who were not comfortable with how things worked here in the Compound..."

"Awww, how horrible for you. I'm so sorry you were uncomfortable, torturing and enslaving other human beings."

Dennis cracked a smile, his upper lip tucked under his mustache. "That's a good response. It should make you angry. I'd expect nothing less, from what I understand of your relationship with 459."

"Bas," Cowl snapped.

"Bas," Dennis agreed carefully. "Cowl, I won't lie, we might have been cowardly before, but a lot of us have families to think about. Even more of us have people here, in the Compound, who wouldn't fare so well if they were under the care of other guards."

Excuses. Decent excuses, but still just excuses. If these guys expected him to have any interest in helping, they were gonna have to get up to his speed. "So, what changed?"

Dennis glanced at the ceiling, probably where the cams were hidden, and stepped a bit closer. They'd better have been smart enough to get someone on that camera feed, or he wouldn't even be lasting the week.

"The City is preparing to evacuate."

"We know," Cowl said.

Dennis chuckled. "Of course you do. Well, even though the City has made a lot of accommodations for those of us who work for them, there are still a lot of people we are being asked to leave behind without argument."

"Assholes," Cowl muttered. "Think it might be a bit late to jump into action, there, genius?"

"Probably," Dennis agreed. "We made a lot of mistakes. But one thing I know for sure: we have some man power, but no one here is going to know how to keep this hunk of metal running when we decide to act."

"What do you mean? Life support and shit?"

Dennis nodded solemnly. "Most of the high-ranking scientists and technicians are loyal to the City. They are insulated from what is really happening. They don't have reason to be concerned. We can't depend on them when the coup happens. We need someone who can keep us all alive until everyone settles down again."

It made sense. Bunker survived because of the computers that ran everything. If there was a hiccup and no one to fix it, all hell would break loose.

"So what are you asking me to do, exactly?" Cowl dropped onto the bed, a hint of adrenaline blooming in his veins at the thought of retribution. Flipping the system. Dropping the City on its oversized head. What he wouldn't give for a gun right now. No way they were gonna just leave him in here while they had all the fun.

"Just be ready when we come for you," Dennis said.

"Why not now? Give me a gun, I'll take care of the problem for you."

Dennis shook his head and looked over his shoulder. "It's not that simple. We have more people to line up. Medical professionals, more soldiers, weapons experts. We need to figure out what it is the City is trying to escape, and how to deal with it ourselves. We have to get the citizens on our side, and they don't even know the Compound exists, or what it does. There is no telling how they will react."

Cowl rolled his eyes. "I get it. Complicated shit. Whatever. I have Bas and Menrva I gotta think about, here. I can't just wait around."

Dennis tapped on the door loudly and it popped open.

"Just worry about yourself," Dennis said, stepping into the hall. "Nothing can happen without you."

Cowl shook his head. "You don't get it. Me and them: we are family. There is no me without them."

Chapter Forty-One: Humpty Dumpty

Bas's blood struggled through his veins like the last drops drained through a straw. He could have sworn his heartbeat echoed against the walls. The cave felt so empty without Cowl. It remained untouched.

He shifted and cut off a scream as his broken ribs squelched under him. There was no comfortable way to lie down. Everything was torn.

How many days had he been lying there? He'd spent each one fighting against a fever as stubborn as any User. The strength he needed to climb back to his feet kept eluding him. Maybe there just wasn't any left.

There was no doubt where Menrva and Cowl were, and he wouldn't be able to reach them. He wouldn't have been able to reach them if they were sitting right across the room. Even if he were able to stand and fight, he wouldn't have a chance. But the options were to stay here and die alone, or see how many of them he could kill before his body gave out. He just needed to leave one bullet for himself...just in case they got him first.

Those were dark thoughts. They were warranted, though he couldn't follow through with them. There wasn't enough of him left to make it back to the Hub.

His thoughts were interrupted by the sound of footsteps

on the loose rocks outside the door. He twisted to aim his gun at the sound, his vision blurring with pain.

"Bas?" Menrva's voice rang out. "Are you here?"

He wilted back, letting the gun fall to the floor. "Menrva."

A light blazed through the cave, and Bas winced at the brilliance.

"Oh, my..." Menrva's voice trailed off as her eyes fell on him. In her gaze he was utterly exposed, but somehow safer. She was beautiful: vibrant and alive.

"You're safe." Emotion choked Bas's words. He tried unsuccessfully to push himself up, scanning the darkness behind her. "Cowl?" Fear blossomed in his chest. Why was she alone?

"He's alive. He's safe. I think." She dragged a huge silver case into the room and kneeled beside him. She *thought* he was safe? That was not at all comforting. "Bas..." she whispered. Her fingers traced down the mud-crusted chest plate that crumpled into his torso like shredded tin foil. "You are barely in one piece."

Bas reached up and grabbed her hand. "It's okay. You're here now." He spread her fingers in his and pressed his lips to her palm. "I'll be okay if you are here to take care of me." There was no greater comfort than just seeing her alive, despite the fact that Cowl was still missing. He would just have to trust her.

Menrva leaned down to brush her own lips against his blistered face. "I am."

"Did you bring water?"

"I brought more than that." She pulled open the case and

pulled out a bottle of water. Clean, pure water. Water that wasn't from anywhere in the pit. A knot of fear lodged itself in his chest but he didn't have the energy to address it. He trusted Menrva. He would ask her about it when he could breathe again.

"Let's get that armor off and see if we can glue you back together."

Menrva's hands trembled against his skin as she began to peel the armor away. It came loose with a fleshy slurp, tearing chunks of entangled flesh and dried blood with it. Bas tried to bite back the screams and only half succeeded. The effort left him breathless as fresh blood ran in thin rivers over his chest. In the pale light, it looked black.

"You don't need to be tough," Menrva said, setting aside the remains of the suit. "I will totally understand if you need to let it out."

"There is time for that," Bas said through gritted teeth as she extracted one leg. She was careful to support him so he didn't have to strain his shredded muscles. Despite that, the effort was almost more than he could handle. He bit his tongue until blood seeped into his mouth.

"I'm so sorry. This is my fault," she said as her hands slid gently across his shattered thigh.

"You did good. Better than..." a scream interrupted the rest of the thought as she pulled the armor free. "I'm sorry," he whispered automatically. If this were the Compound he would have received serious retribution for his outbursts.

Menrva ripped away his shirt and the bloodied threads remaining of his pant legs.

"You're running a fever," she said. Still? It would explain why her hands felt so cold. That wasn't a good sign. His body had an incredible ability to fight infection and illness, but even his superior immune system had its limits. "How are you still alive?"

"I shouldn't be," Bas said simply. She filled a syringe from the medkit. Antibiotics of some sort. Bas barely noticed the prick as she started the IV and attached a blood bag.

"Good news. I've got morphine." She held up the drug like it was a prize.

"Really?" Bas asked. He'd never actually had morphine before; it was a rare commodity and Borgs were not allowed any.

"Though from the look of it, it might not be enough."

"It's good. You are doing good." Bas lay his head back and focused on his breathing as Menrva began to pull his body back together. He had learned methods for dealing with pain, but it pushed him to the edge of his ability to lie still as she cleaned his wounds and pulled the torn flesh back together. Her care wouldn't be enough. His lung had collapsed, and from the tightness, he could assume air was filling his chest cavity with each breath. Eventually, the pressure build up would be too much for the other lung to compensate for, causing a complete failure. There was no way of telling how long the mutated chambers would keep up, or if his body could even compensate. This wasn't something you could solve without medical equipment and know-how. It wasn't even accounting for the infection that was surely setting into his charred flesh, plus the internal injuries he was sure to have accumulated.

It left them with two options. In short: Bunker or death. As smart as she was, Menrva had probably already figured it out. She must have also known which one he would choose, unless his growing suspicions were true.

As Menrva smoothed a reinforced bandage over a particularly deep cut across his chest, an unexpected wave of panic overwhelmed Bas. Despite his best effort to keep himself present, he couldn't escape the fear that he would look up to see the stark white of the Compound hospital. He stopped Menrva's hand with his own.

"Are you okay?" she asked.

Bas pulled in a deep breath through his damaged lungs. "Yeah. Sorry. I just forgot where I was for a moment."

Menrva sat back on her heels, her eyes inescapably tortured. Bas rubbed his hand down her arm. "Don't worry," he whispered, pleaded. She didn't seem to find any comfort in his words. If he had been stronger, he would have held her tight.

"I talked to Pope."

Bas dropped his hand, a knot forming in his stomach. The name *Pope* was attached to far too many bad memories. "Really?"

Menrva busied herself with the last of the bandages before sitting back and rubbing a wet wipe vigorously against her bloodied palms. She avoided his eyes. Bas knew what effect Pope had. He could make you feel guilty about breathing while he committed the worst atrocities with a mask of righteousness and humility. He could make you feel like he was doing the best thing for you even while he was tearing you apart. You left the presence of Pope feeling like the dirt under the rug. Menrva carried too much guilt as it was.

"They took us. Cowl is still there." She threw the wipe aside violently, glaring at the remaining red stain.

"How did you get away?"

"I didn't. They knew you were injured. They need you alive so... I wasn't followed, though. I made sure."

Bas nodded slowly, trying to look more composed than he felt. That explained the medical supplies and the clean water. Cowl was in the Compound, then. The thought of him trapped in the cold cells was like fists to his soul.

"He says Earth is crumbling... that we have to evacuate. He says the only planet we can inhabit has an atmosphere we can't breathe. The only way for us to survive more than a generation or two..."

"Is my genes," Bas finished for her. That is why they hadn't shot him when they had him in their sights before. What they wanted him for was more than just casual study. If he went back, there would be a lot of experimentation, a lot of indignities. He'd endured some testing before, but they never could quite seem to decide if his mutation was something they liked or not. Now... He pushed back the nausea rising in the back of his throat.

Menrva nodded. "Do you believe him?"

"Yes."

Menrva wiped a hand across her cheek to catch a tear, leaving a blood stain in its place. Bas opened his arms. "Come on."

"Right, like you are up for snuggling."

"I could use some."

Menrva laid her head on his chest. She was very gentle, but though she didn't fully relax, her subtle weight still sent agony racing through his limbs. It was the most beautiful pain Bas had ever felt.

"He showed me the artificial wombs. And the hospital." Her voice trembled with the horror of her words.

The incubators must have been especially hard for her. She had lost her own child to violence; she had a softer spot than most for injustice done to infants. He silently cursed himself for dragging her into that horror. If it wasn't for him, she would never have had to experience that.

Menrva didn't shed another tear, but her face pressed into his ruined rib cage as if she were seeking some escape. "Don't go back."

Chapter Forty-Two: Devil's Promise

Bas traced a finger over Menrva's arm around the cuts marring her once smooth skin. They were a testament to the damage he had done.

The world was set against Bas, pressing him back into the cage. He couldn't regret the last three years, the taste of humanity, but he knew he would. The decision was already made. The truth was, it had always been only a matter of time. This had never been anything but a temporary reprieve, though they had all tried to pretend otherwise.

"I wish I could hug you," Menrva whispered.

"I can do more than that." He pulled her closer, wincing as his wounds protested.

"Not right now, you can't. You're held together by tape and prayers."

Bas leaned in to rest his head against hers, and she squeezed her eyes tight.

"What will we do without you?" she whispered.

"You are smart, strong. You'll be okay," Bas said. "I'll make sure of it." Once he was back in the Compound, the clock would start. Pope wouldn't hesitate to kill whomever he felt necessary if he thought he was saving the human race. If Bas went back, he would give Pope what he needed for the last ditch effort at survival — but maybe there was time for better. "Menrva." Bas waited until Menrva met his eyes with her own before he continued. "When I'm gone you and Cowl can't give up."

"We won't," she said quickly. "We will get you out."

"No. Not on me." Bas paused to drag in a tight breath. "Thousands of people will die if Pope evacuates. You have to find another way."

Menrva shook her head. "Pope has teams of scientists; he's had years to plan this. If there was another way, don't you think they would have found it?"

"No. He would have looked for the best chance and bet everything on it. Pope doesn't take long shots. We do."

"Do we?"

"You have to try."

Menrva's fingers reached as if to cling to him. She pressed her head into his chest and Bas let his arms fall around her. She didn't move. Her breath brushed warm against his chest. Her hair tickled his chin and caught in his beard.

"I'll do everything I can. And after it's done, however it ends, we are coming back for you."

"You need to do whatever it takes. If it takes my mutation to fix this, you have to use that, too," Bas said.

Menrva gripped his arm. "How could you ask that?"

"Because if you don't, a lot of people will die," Bas said. The pain in her voice cut to his heart. "If that's what it takes, you have to try."

The silence stretched on for a long time. She wouldn't want to, but Menrva would understand. More than any of them, she would be able to do what he asked. Cowl was strong, but his focus was too narrow. Menrva was just as strong as Cowl, but she would use it to help people. All she needed was to be released from this. From him. Once he was gone, she would do what needed to be done. Maybe. Hopefully.

"Okay. We will," she said finally.

"And if Cowl won't—"

"I'll do it alone," she interrupted. "You are right. We can't just abandon them."

Bas let out a sigh of relief and the silence fell again, deep and satisfying. If anyone could make a difference in the fate of the world, it was Menrva. She was stronger than gravity.

Bas lay his cheek against her head and listened as her breathing shuddered and deepened into slumber.

She looked like something in a dream with her blue hair curled beneath her dark skin. Bas used a finger to brush away a crust of drying blood she had wiped on her cheek earlier. If only he could wipe himself out of her life so easily. He never wanted her memory to fade in his mind, but there was nothing she could do for him anymore. And nothing he could do for her, nothing but cause pain. It would be better if she could forget him.

Bas let her head settle onto the blood-stiffened bedding and pulled the slow-dripping IV from his arm. Artificial blood trailed from the needle onto the dirt floor.

Menrva stirred as he pushed himself up, maybe missing his warmth, or disturbed by the agony escaping his lips in a soft moan. The medical care hadn't been effective; at least, in any lasting way. However, the blood and pain meds had revived him a bit. It was a temporary fix, a last push to the end.

It was foreign to see Cowl's computer monitors so dark. For the last three years, there was always something happening. He'd gotten used to Cowl's silhouette against the blue glow.

Bas leaned heavily on the cluttered walls for support before he could put pressure on his legs. Without the armor, they wanted to simply fold under him. A few old cans clattered as he brushed against them and leaned on the broken table, waiting for his heartbeat to slow. He launched himself across the final few feet and gripped the empty chair, just barely managing to hold down his gasps as he eased himself down.

A click, and the screens flickered on. The light didn't seem so calming now, more ghastly than anything. He squinted as he waited for his eyes to adjust.

Bas typed in a code on the touchscreen, connecting the systems to the Ether. Cowl had taught him enough to get by, but he still struggled to find the right keys as much from a lack of courage as from confusion. The computer pinged softly, the sounds filling the emptiness as it searched for its target. It didn't take long, unfortunately.

"You are calling a restricted address. Please enter your identification to proceed," the computer intoned. Bas pulled the gun from his waistband and laid it on the desk. He might need a bargaining chip, and it seemed his life was important to the City.

Bas hesitated, his fingers drifting over the numbers. They were more than just keys; they were triggers. G4S59. He typed the number into the screen, where it blinked red. A condemnation.

The screen went momentarily black before a serious, shallow face appeared. It was his handler, Jordan Launay. He peered into the screen, his black eyes narrowing at the sight of Bas. He studied him for a moment, thin lips pursed. Bas knew the look well.

Launay had been a permanent fixture in Bas's life since his fifth birthday when he had moved out of the nursery. He was a harsh and unforgiving man who seemed to have no concept of mercy and compassion. Everything about him was almost mechanical, focused on the program he trusted so well and the task at hand...whatever it might be. That look on his face was one he wore regularly: disappointment.

"Hello?" Launay said into the screen. He sat a bit straighter, smoothing the breast of his grey uniform. "You've keyed in a number belonging to a missing asset. Please identify yourself."

"You know who I am, Launay," Bas said.

Launay frowned, obviously irritated at the irreverent address. He valued respect as much as he valued his precious rules. For a few more hours Bas had the freedom to speak to him like a fellow man. "I need to speak to Pope."

"You can speak with me. I have the authority to-"

"Pope, or I blow my brains out right now." Bas lifted the gun off the table for extra effect. "You don't want to be responsible for that, do you?"

Launay gave the screen a long, contemplative gaze before turning to speak to someone off screen. Bas took the opportunity to check on Menrva sleeping peacefully behind him, or at least pretending to be. He didn't want her to be part of this conversation. It was underhanded, leaving her out, but he couldn't be distracted. His resolve was already weak. If she begged him to stay, he wasn't sure he could overcome the selfish urge to curl up and die in her arms.

"Bastille." Bas jumped as he heard the address from the screen. Jonathan Pope peered at him from the other side, his eyes familiar and old. The name sounded so foreign on his tongue; dirty. Bas shivered.

"I assume you know why I'm calling you?" Bas asked, trying to force his voice to remain steady.

"I hadn't expected this format, but yes. You're ready to come home."

Bas rolled his shoulders, uncomfortable under Pope's deliberate gaze. It was strange how Pope was the one who tortured babies and murdered countless civilians but when caught in his sights, Bas was the one who felt guilty.

"I have my terms."

"Naturally," Pope smiled. "Menrva and Cowl, I assume?"

"Free, safe, and back in the Hub. When we evacuate, they need to be the first ones leaving." If he could buy them some time, maybe Menrva and Cowl could find a way around the evacuations. But he wasn't taking the risk. Thousands would die if they didn't, but those thousands wouldn't include them.

"Already done," Pope said "I can only imagine how difficult this must be for you. I want to do whatever I can to assure you that your sacrifice isn't for nothing."

"Don't..." Bas caught his breath as a shot of pain radiated up his side, payment for his anger. He had no interest in Pope's drummed-up pity. Maybe he cared, maybe he didn't, but it wouldn't change what was about to happen. If any of them had ever mattered to Pope, he hadn't allowed it to get in the way yet. "Just do what you have to do," Bas said finally.

"Where can we find you?"

"I'll come in tomorrow. I'm walking in. You don't need to send anyone for me."

With some more blood, he'd make it. If Cowl and Menrva needed to get away from the City again, they would need this place. If they figured out how to stop the evacuation, maybe.

"Understood." Pope stared out of the screen with pitying eyes. Bas reached for the key to cut off the call but pulled back his hand as Pope began to speak again.

"As you can understand, once you reach the Compound I will have to return to my usual distant behavior. For now, allow me to say how very proud of you I am. You have become an exceptional man." Pope leaned forward, the emotion of his speech genuine across every feature. His voice had taken on that fatherly tone it did when he wanted to inspire devotion.

Proud? Pope had no interest in what kind of man Bas was, only what kind of machine he could be turned into.

"I do not fail to understand the depth of the agony you are about to face. Thank you. Truly."

Bas ground his teeth together and met Pope's eyes. "You just take care of your promise."

Pope nodded. "Get some sleep, Bas. I'll see you in the morning."

The screen blinked off and Bas was left staring at his mangled reflection. He ran his hand along the handle of the gun, wishing for the sweet bite of the bullet. It could be over, with one movement. He wouldn't have to face the Compound again, or the torment he knew was waiting. That had always been his plan: enjoy his freedom for as long as he had and end it when the doors started to close. If he took the easy way, then it would be everyone else who was left to pay the bill. It would be Cowl and Menrva. Bas left the gun on the table, pointed at the empty chair.

Menrva barely twitched as he lay beside her. He gathered her in one arm until her body nestled against the empty ache of fear swelling inside him. As she curled against him he let his eyes drift over the walls that had been his home for the last three years; his refuge. This was his last chance for a real goodbye. Tomorrow would mark the end. Bas closed his eyes and tucked his face into Menrva's thick hair. She smelled sweet, soft. Like a good memory. The pain and the soft gusts of her steady breath rocked him to sleep.

Chapter Forty-Three: Brave Face

Bas was awake. Menrva could almost feel his awareness curled up behind her, though she didn't turn to look. His hand curled loosely around hers, his forehead pressed against her neck. Every once in a while his tortured breath escaped in a low moan as he struggled to inflate his pierced lung.

Menrva rubbed her thumb across his broad hand, tracing the blood vessels and tendons. She had seen him kill men with those hands, but this was their natural place.

Menrva shifted until she could see his face. A specter of torment settled on his features despite the smile he flashed at her. She hated that brave face, it reminded her of the empty gaze of the Borg teen in the medical ward. That wasn't Bas. In so many ways she had been robbed of the real him, and now he was slipping through her fingers. Maybe he was building up walls to stand against the horrors he was about to walk into. She couldn't blame him, but she wanted as much time with the real man as she could get before he was turned back into a robot.

"How did you sleep?" Bas whispered.

She didn't tell him about his voice echoing down through her sleep as he planned his return to slavery. "Home," Pope had said. "Are you ready to come home?" But this was Bas's home, *she* was his home.

"How are you feeling?" Menrva asked, deciding instead to change the topic.

"Good," he said, brushing his lips against hers.

"How are you even going to make it to the Hub?" she asked, ignoring his lies.

"Same way I made it here." He pushed himself into a sitting position, visibly shuddering against the pain. "Would you do me a favor? Grab some clothes for me out of that chest." He pointed at a nearby container.

Menrva extracted a black tank top and a pair of grey sweats. "Are you hungry?"

Bas shook his head and struggled to pull the shirt over his head. Menrva knelt down to help him, despite his embarrassed flush.

"Why can't we just call them to come get us?" Menrva asked, careful to avoid bumping the bandage that was more or less keeping his rib cage in his left side. If the cut was only a bit deeper, it could have easily been fatal.

Bas shook his head. "No. If I'm going back, I'm going back as a man." Bas wasn't stubborn about much but he faced a future stripped of humanity and self-agency. It made sense that he wanted to at least walk in on his own two feet. Pain wasn't as much of a factor to him as it might be for someone else.

There was a splint in the med kit that they used to brace his shattered leg. He looked a good deal better after the meds and blood the night before, but his skin was still pale and slightly blue...a sign that his lungs were failing. He didn't have too much longer. His eyes were sunken and he trembled with barely contained pain as he climbed to his feet.

He packed an unnecessary gun into his holster and twisted a scarf over his face. Maybe he would be ok. The City wouldn't risk letting him die, not as long as he had what they needed so desperately. At least now he would get the appropriate medical care.

"Ready?" Bas asked, holding out a hand. Menrva scooped up the medkit, now significantly lighter, and dropped her hand into his. She didn't let go as they trudged through the dirt. Bas didn't try either. His grip was firm, a cage around her hand. No matter how he stumbled and struggled he never let her fingers slip. Menrva tightened her grip as they approached the Hub.

Bas didn't slow and didn't look at her. His expression was entirely fixed, so flat that he might as well have been cut from paper. Still, he rolled his shoulders and his fingers shook. As they reached the struts his struggle to breathe overwhelmed him and he tugged on her arm, halting to lean against the structure. She fiddled with her hair, tugging it into a few loose braids as she tried not to stare too much at Bas. Despite knowing that Bas was terrified of the Compound, and for good reason, she couldn't be as apprehensive. He simply couldn't survive without help. Even if they could somehow get Cowl back another way, there was nowhere Bas could go to hide from his wounds.

Not far away a bright light grew on the horizon, piercing the dusty haze. Menrva blinked and instinctively ducked.

"Bas. There're guards over there," Menrva said.

Bas lay a hand on her arm and pulled his gun, his breath

rattling in her ear. They sat there for what seemed like a millennium and watched the lights multiply. A Rover arrived, and the flood light burst on to reveal a flurry of motion. More vehicles arrived every moment. The sound of them mixed with raspy screams and shouted commands.

"They don't see us," Menrva said. She leaned forward to get a better view of the activity. Multiple guards surrounded what was quickly becoming a small caravan of Rovers. They moved some sort of large, limp objects from the Rovers to the entrance of the Hub.

"Bodies," Bas said.

"They are moving people?" Menrva asked in a hushed voice. She could see clearly now that he had suggested it, they were indeed people. They looked dead, but the logic didn't track. Bodies were discarded in the Pit, not collected. Her question was answered when one of the limp bodies suddenly started to kick and writhe. The guards that were carrying it dropped the body and let it roll for a moment before lifting it up again and continuing.

Bas frowned. "They are getting ready for something."

"The evacuation," Menrva suggested. "Collecting Pit dwellers that they think they need."

"It won't be many," Bas said. "When I'm gone, you and Cowl will have a tough fight ahead of you."

Menrva scowled. He acted as if he were walking to his execution. They could get him back out. After all, the boys had gotten her out. But he was right, they needed to take some sort of action against the evacuation. What they could do was a mystery. Staying on Earth was a death sentence for all humanity while the evacuation would leave hundreds of thousands to die. It was a proverbial "rock and a hard place" scenario and they had no clear timetable with which to work. It could take them years to isolate the genomes responsible for Bas's mutation, and longer to tailor it to fit into a human genetic code in the way they were hoping. And of course, they would want to understand how it worked and measure the benefits and dangers. Preparations might take even longer than that. If they were already collecting passengers, then maybe they had found a way to move up the timeline. Who knows, it could be a matter of weeks or even days.

"Once you are back with Cowl you should go find Capricorn," Bas said. "He has a lot of resources at his disposal."

Menrva turned away from the scene and sneered. Capricorn. She didn't like the idea of going back to him for help, even if it was a situation this dire. This wasn't a good time to be concerned with the thought, they would have time for that afterwards. For now she had to focus on Bas and on retrieving Cowl.

"There is nothing we can do for them," she said, "not right now."

Bas nodded, saving his words and his shortening breaths. He pointed to an open door in one of the nearby struts. Menrva tried to shove down the dread that threatened to choke her. There was only one reason for the door to be open: they were expected.

It was a struggle for Bas to climb the short landing to the maintenance elevator. Menrva closed the gate behind them, wincing as Bas stumbled against the far side.

It rose slowly, creaking on dusty gears until it jolted to a stop at the bottom of another short flight of steps.

The door at the top of the stairs stood open as well. Somehow it seemed even more threatening than the gaping jaws of the Wreckers above.

Bas paused on the last step, his face creased with the pain from his crumbling body. The gun hung loosely in one hand. He smiled sadly at Menrva, his eyes glinting with barely hidden terror. Brave face. "Not far now," he said as he stabbed the gun back into his holster.

Menrva grabbed his hand again. His skin was cold: oxygen deprivation. His body was giving out. They had made it to the Compound but had they made it in time? He was almost dead on his feet, and not in the colloquial way.

"Just a few more steps," Menrva urged. That could be as much a discouragement as not.

Bas joined her on the top step. Menrva tucked his arm over her shoulder. It wasn't any real support, she just wanted to be close. These were their last moments together, at least for now, but she wasn't going to just abandon him to those monsters. She would come back for him.

Chapter Forty-Four:
It Was His Choice

The hallway was suspiciously empty. It was a potent reminder to Menrva of the day that Bas had returned to those halls to pull her out of the City's hands. Maybe she could do the same someday. She could burst through the halls and tear through the guards like paper and carry him away.

Bas stumbled as they reached the end of the hall and stepped into a large, dark room. Rounded walls curved up into the ceiling like a polished glass bowl dropped upside-down on the floor. It was empty except for the elevator doors at the end. The lights were low but reflected eerily off the immaculate black tile. As they stepped into the room, the door behind them slid shut automatically.

A lone, molten tear slipped from Menrva's eye and burned a path down her cheek. Bas was shaking now. Was it from physical weakness or terror? She was afraid that he would drop where he stood, he trembled so violently. Knowing she couldn't really do anything to steady him, she placed her hands on his arms. He was slipping away.

Bas pulled her closer. His hands were cold against her cheeks as his fingers wove into her hair and he stared deep into her eyes. In the pallid light his face was even more ghastly and the dammed-up tears glinted in his eyes like needle-points. Each breath rattled in his chest, as if it had to fight for room. Menrva wanted to breathe for him. Hopelessness picked her bones clean and she couldn't fight it away. She was desperate for help to come, but knew when it did that Bas would be gone.

"I love you," Bas said. The brave face fell away. Shadows of sorrow rushed over him and tears fell, matching her own.

Menrva choked on the sob that tore from her throat. "I love you, too." She wanted stronger words, something to express the screaming pain that carved out her chest. There was an emptiness that opened inside her, an echoing emptiness that rivaled even what she had experienced before she had met Bas. She wished, for a moment, that she had never met him, that she had stayed in the safety of her vacant life before. It was only the ghost of a wish, though. The pain of losing him couldn't match the fullness of her life with him, and the purpose that drove her now. Bas was sacrificing himself for her, for Cowl, for Bunker and everyone below. It was her job to make sure that it was more than just a defeat. She could only hope that she could get him out in time.

Bas lowered his head until his forehead rested on hers and Menrva reached up to twist her hands around his neck. The tech dug into her hands and her fingers itched to tear it away. It was the enemy.

Tears fell from Bas's face onto her own, running down her cheeks and neck. His breath was shallow and she deepened her own, willing him to copy her. If only there was some way she could lessen the weight on him, take some of his pain. He was alone and so vulnerable and all she could do was hold his hand.

A soft buzz announced the end of their goodbye. Menrva turned to look for the opening elevator door on the far side of the room but Bas's hands stayed firm on her face, barring her. His grip was so strong she felt as if he were trying not to be swept away. She curled her fingers around his shoulders, wishing that she could fuse to him, that she could join into him so they couldn't pull him away without cutting them apart.

"Don't look," Bas whispered. "Don't look. Please. I need to see you. I need to see only you or I can't do this." He had never sounded so weak or desperate.

His eyes were wide, terrified, and in them Menrva's own heartbreak reflected back at her. It was taking every ounce of his strength just to stand there. She could never have imagined such panic coming from Bas. He was sensitive and tender but not weak, never weak. It was her turn to be strong, if she could manage it.

"Don't look away. Don't look away." Bas kept repeating the words. Voices echoed through the empty room but she was drowning in her sorrow — in his sorrow.

Bas was so weak, so pale. This was not how she wanted to remember him, but it was all she had. She memorized every feature, trailing her fingers over the subtle curve of his jaw under the thick beard and across his sharp cheekbones, wetted in the tears that fell. She had never seen him cry before.

"I'm right here. I'm here," she said. She was there, but she couldn't stay. It wouldn't last.

"Don't look. I love you," Bas repeated one final time. Menrva obediently squeezed her eyes shut as the shadows of their enemies grew in her peripherals.

Bas was torn out of her hands. Despite his pleading, Menrva couldn't help but open her eyes as he was wrenched away. They might as well have torn her legs out from under her. The room contorted and faded and the cold floor slammed against her hands as she fell to her knees.

The tears that streamed down her face, hot like blood, turned everything foggy gray. She didn't look away, though the people around her were only blurs. The guards almost had to carry Bas into the elevator, but he didn't fight. Cowl was there, proof of Pope's precious honesty, and Menrva was faintly aware of his angry cries as he threw himself against his captors. It wasn't fair, that Cowl's last sight of his best friend would be like this...that he wouldn't even get to say goodbye.

Just before the elevator door closed Menrva's eyes met with Bas's. He pulled himself to his full height, borrowing some deep and dangerous strength from within. Despite his injuries he was menacing between the guards that now looked tiny beside him. His eyes turned cold and hollow, his face drawn into a look that froze Menrva's heart. For the first time, icy fear filled her as she looked on the emptiness that tumbled in to consume him. Then the door closed.

The guards released Cowl from his cuffs and he fell on

the door, pounding with both fists. Menrva couldn't understand the words he screamed in his rage, she was too lost in her own emotion. She watched, oddly detached as Cowl's hands tore against the door until they left vibrant streaks of blood across the chrome.

A ringing sound grew in Menrva's ears, drowning out everything else. A tranq dart sprouted out of Cowl's neck and he fell backward. Menrva was unable to move her numb arms as he hit the floor in front of her. She tilted her head until it matched the angle of his.

"How could you let him..." Cowl's eyes closed.

"Menrva." A voice punctured the safety of her private pain like an arrow. "Menrva, are you ok?"

Menrva looked up to see Pope standing over her, flanked by guards. She took a deep shuddering breath and shoved her palm across her cheek in an attempt to wipe away the tears, only succeeding in making the rest of her face wet.

"He needs medical attention," she said. Her voice sounded oddly calm in her own ears like it was coming out of a speaker. She wanted to scream hysterically. She wanted to leap on Pope and tear his heart out with her fingernails. Instead, she smoothed her hair and cleared her throat. "He's in pretty bad shape."

"We will give only the best of care to him," Pope said, his tone reassuring. Was it really a lie? She recognized the sorrow behind Pope's eyes as if it were her own. It seemed counterintuitive, like looking into the barrel of a gun and seeing a piece of candy in place of a bullet.

The City would take care of Bas, at least physically. They couldn't risk losing something like him. "*Something*," because to them he wasn't a "someone."

The floor beneath Menrva's hands grew warm and began to shake. A sound like a thousand Wrecker roars filled her head. Had she gone mad? Could a human being withstand that kind of fear and pain? But no, Pope looked around the room as well and shifted to compensate for the vibration. The roar grew louder and sounds like metal plates sliding into place joined the cacophony, grinding and squealing.

"What is happening?" Menrva had to scream to make herself heard over the noise.

"We are on our way," Pope said. "We were waiting for you, of course, but the Hub was designed to do more than just contain her people. She can take them away from danger too."

Bile rose in Menrva's stomach. The Hub was the rocket. That is why the rockets topside looked like they were out of repair, they didn't need them. She thought they would have time while the City readied the escape but there was no time. There had never been a chance.

How many people had been left outside? Some would be burnt alive in the force of the rockets. They would be lucky. Those that were left would die from oxygen deprivation or maybe, in the deeper reaches of the tiers, from lack of food and water. Maybe the Wreckers would get them. There was nothing to stop them now. The horror sank in slowly, like the last rays of the sun sinking over the horizon. At this moment, people were dying. Hundreds upon thousands of people. The Hub, and whoever they had dragged aboard, was all that was left, the end of mankind.

"No..." Menrva whispered. "No, no, no, no." She couldn't

scream, as much as she wanted to. She couldn't cry, the loss was too great. Bas had allowed himself to be taken away, believing that they would have time to resolve this. Suddenly his sacrifice felt so empty.

"We have no choice. The process has already begun. Earth is crumbling. If we had stayed even one more week we all would have been torn apart. Some had to be sacrificed, but we will survive. Humanity will flourish because of you, Menrva."

Because of her? Did he still think that she wanted this? She hadn't made this choice. Who would have chosen this? Pope laid a hand on her shoulder and she brushed it off weakly.

"I understand that you are upset. But 459 made arrangements for you. You and Cowl are both free and returned to full citizenship and all its benefits. No retribution will be taken against you. I know it is not much...but it will have to be enough. 459 is humanity's lifeline now."

459. Already his humanity had been torn away. Pope turned and limped toward the elevator. The door behind her hissed as it opened to the empty hall that they had come from. Bas wasn't just some mindless automaton, though. Pope had to know that, had to know that Bas hadn't just followed her decision as he'd thought. This sacrifice was all him.

Menrva dragged in a deep, ragged breath. "Pope," she called.

Pope stopped the closing elevator door with his cane and looked back at her expectantly.

"This was *his* choice," Menrva said. "I didn't tell him what to do. You were wrong about him."

Pope nodded. "I know."

The door closed behind him, leaving Menrva alone as the lights flickered and the room shook as if it too were feeling her anger and grief. She curled into herself, wrapping her hands around her ears to block out the keening of metal as it locked in place. Somewhere below them, the rockets lit with an earth shattering boom that threatened to tear her apart. The sound was only rivaled by the hollow echo of the Earth's crust cracking and falling away as the Hub wrenched free, a zombie rising from a centuries-long grave.

She cursed her weakness, her stupidity, but the words were drowned out by the sound of the sword coming down on humanity's neck. They had failed. She had failed. Out of the chaos of thoughts that tumbled around in her mind, one thought stood out from the others, though it was maybe selfish. Now that they were pulling free of the earth there was nowhere left to run. That meant that there was no way now to free Bas. He was truly lost.

Dear Reader,

It would take more words than are contained in this book for me to express my gratitude to you for picking this up and reading all the way through. Many hours of joy and pain have gone into the creation of the book you just read. Through it all, the first thought I always had was of you. I wanted to introduce you to the characters that had become so real to me. I wanted you to feel and think deeply. I wanted to be part of your life, in some small way, and for you to be part of mine.

If you enjoyed reading this novel, you might want more. If that is the case, you are in luck. The prequel, Revelation, is available for FREE through most ebook retailers. Malfunction is the first of a Science Fiction Trilogy and there is so much more to come. If you want to get your hands on them, be sure to go to my website: www.jillanepurrazzi.com and sign up for my newsletter where you can get monthly updates on my writing and alerts when I'm about to publish a new book. Or you can sign up for the "alerts only" mailing list if you just want to know when a new book hits the stores. I hope to see you there!

One thing that is endlessly important to indie publishers is a good review. Be sure to leave an honest review of Malfunction and help me out. I really appreciate it.

Personally, I love to hear people talk about my books and I am always eager to improve. If you have questions or comments, you can reach me at jepurrazzi@gmail.com

J.E. Purrazzi

The Malfunction Trilogy
www.jillanepurrazzi.com/malfunction

The Raventree Society
www.jillanepurrazzi.com/trs

Other publications and free books
www.jillanepurrazzi.com/other